Liza

Also by Irene Carr

Liza

Irene Carr

Hodder & Stoughton

Copyright © 2003 by Irene Carr

First published in Great Britain in 2003 by Hodder and Stoughton
A division of Hodder Headline

The right of Irene Carr to be identified as the Author
of the Work has been asserted by her in accordance with
the Copyright, Designs and Patents Act 1988.

2 4 6 8 10 9 7 5 3 1

A CIP catalogue record for this title is available from the British Library

ISBN 0 340 82035 7

Typeset in Plantin Light by Palimpsest Book Production Limited,
Polmont, Stirlingshire

Printed and bound in Great Britain by
Mackays of Chatham plc, Chatham, Kent

Hodder and Stoughton
A division of Hodder Headline
338 Euston Road
London NW1 3BH

Liza

Prologue

SUNDAY, 20 JANUARY 1907, NORTH SEA

A bad black winter morning. Liza Thornton clung to the leather and steel solidity of the chair as the ship's soaring and plunging tried to tear her loose. She was stronger than she looked, a slender, dark-eyed, dark-haired slip of a girl, soon to be twenty-one years old. The chair was of polished wood and leather and bolted to the deck, one of a dozen set around the table in the day-cabin set aside for the dozen passengers usually carried. The windows looked out on to a wild sea and Liza could smell the salt tang of it along with the leather. She had not bargained for this weather and feared for her life, but also for her future if she survived this crossing. She was facing humiliation and poverty.

The ship was the SS *Florence Grey*, a tramp steamer out of Hamburg with a general cargo and passengers, making her nine knots and bound for the port of Sunderland at the mouth of the river Wear. Now she heaved up for the thousandth time as a huge wave passed under her, then smashed down into the trough on the other side. She seemed to shudder throughout her length and Liza swallowed nervously. She was no stranger to ships or travelling but had never experienced a storm like this at sea.

The door of the saloon swung open, letting in a blast of cold air, and another girl entered. She was the only other passenger who had come aboard at Hamburg, crossing the gangway at the same time as Liza. The newcomer was also dark but taller by an inch or two and she was dressed in a tailored tweed coat with a fur collar and court shoes of fine leather. Liza, by contrast, wore a plain coat of blue serge reaching to her buttoned boots, which had been repaired several times. A plain felt hat perched on her piled hair while the taller girl sported an expensive-looking straw with an ostrich feather. She had been followed up the gangway by a porter carrying a costly leather suitcase and a voluminous travelling rug. At her order, 'Put them in my cabin, please,' he had dived below.

She had one of the two first-class cabins amidships but below deck. Liza had one in steerage, right aft and close to the thunderous beat of the engines. She had slept poorly, beside a porthole washed by the pounding sea. When the storm blew up on the second night out she abandoned the cabin to doze uneasily in the saloon. From long familiarity Liza recognised this girl's clipped accent and manner: she was used to money and servants. The girl had glanced at Liza, across the social gulf that divided them, had seen she was carrying a cheap cardboard case and ignored her.

She did not ignore Liza now: 'I'll join you, if I may. I find the cabin stuffy and not very comfortable.' She was pale and her full lips twitched. She slid into the chair next to Liza, who moved the cardboard case to make room for her.

Your cabin's a sight better than mine, Liza thought. Tell the truth: you're too scared to stay down there on your own. But she could understand the girl's fear: the cabin, like Liza's, was below the waterline. She answered, 'You're welcome, Miss.' Welcome for her company, a fear shared . . . Liza's accent was almost a copy of the other's now because she had learned it as part of her job.

'I'm Cecily Spencer,' the girl introduced herself.

'Liza Thornton.'

Fragile smiles were exchanged. Cecily had brought with

her a rug and now she shook it out and spread it over their knees. 'This will keep us warm.'

'Thank you, Miss.'

They were both distracted by the storm and sat silent for some seconds, tense, as the ship bucked and soared again. Then the door was flung open and a seaman shouldered in, bulky in oilskins and sou'wester glistening with seawater. He grinned at them: 'All right, ladies?' They nodded, forced smiles, and he tried to reassure them: 'There's no cause to worry. This old gal has been through a lot worse than this.'

They tried to look calm. 'Bring my suitcase up, please. I won't be going below again,' Cecily asked, or rather ordered.

'Aye, ma'am.' He backed out, closing the door, but returned in a few minutes with it. 'There y'are, ma'am.'

'Thank you. That will be all.'

Thus dismissed, he left. Liza thought her case looked cheaper than ever beside the luxurious leather one, which was embossed with the initials CS. Her companion smiled. 'I have some papers in there I would not like to lose, but nothing very valuable. It's really just an overnight bag. My main luggage is following.'

'Oh, yes?' Liza replied. Everything she owned was in her cardboard case and nothing very valuable, either. She had only a few coins left in her thin purse after paying for her passage.

As if to prove the seaman wrong, the ship rolled. She tilted to starboard as if she was going to capsize, and everything loose in the saloon was tossed across the deck. The two cases slid down until halted by the side of the cabin. Cecily squeaked and seized Liza: 'She's turning over!'

'No, she isn't!' Liza's reply was more prayer than denial. She held on to her chair as Cecily's fingers dug into her arm and slowly, terribly slowly, the *Florence Grey* heaved herself back on to an even keel.

'Silly of me. Of course she's all right. I'm sorry.' Cecily spoke quickly, betraying the need to speak, to say something, anything, to blot out the storm. 'Still, I'll be glad to step ashore and set my feet on *terra firma*.' Liza knew that tag, had learned it from an employer. But Cecily was running on: 'I didn't want to come in the first place. I've always kept away from the north, but I'll be twenty-one soon and I have to see the lawyers in Sunderland about my inheritance. I was orphaned when I was sixteen and my father's estate is held in trust for me. I inherit on my birthday, four weeks from today. I had a guardian, my uncle, but he has just died – Edward Spencer, the shipowner. I expect you've heard of him.'

'No,' Liza replied baldly, wishing Cecily would be quiet. She did not want to talk, just to sit braced against this mad sea. So they shared the same birthday? Liza had nothing to celebrate.

'I'm surprised. He's well known in Sunderland.'

'I've never been there in my life.' Liza explained: 'I was born and grew up in Newcastle but I couldn't get a passage to the Tyne. I found this ship could take me to Sunderland and I can catch a train from there.' Besides, the *Florence Grey* was cheap and Liza could not afford to wait in lodgings for a ship that would take her to Newcastle. But now she thought that this young woman might possibly be an answer to some of her problems. She asked respectfully, 'Will you be needing staff, Miss?'

Cecily shook her head abstractedly, her eyes wide as the ship pitched. 'No. I expect there will be staff at my uncle's house.' She added, 'I thought you might be in service.'

'Yes.' Liza was not surprised by the deduction. A young woman who was unescorted and obviously without money was likely to be in service. 'I'm a lady's maid,' she added proudly. That meant she was the cream of household staff. She did not open doors, dust furniture or sweep carpets on her hands and knees. She had done all that, but had graduated by hard work. A lady's maid looked after her mistress, dressing and undressing her, laundering and ironing, doing everything to make smooth her employer's days.

Cecily thought that accounted for her accent, very like Cecily's save for a suggestion of North Country. 'Are you going home for a holiday or seeking a new position?'

'I'm looking for another place. I resigned from my last one to better myself.' That was not true but Liza could not say she had been dismissed – unfairly, but still dismissed – in allegedly shameful circumstances. Her cheeks heated.

Cecily did not notice this, more interested in her own affairs and the storm. 'Do you think the weather is ameliorating?'

The ship did seem to be riding more easily. 'It's blowing over,' Liza agreed.

Cecily sighed and seemed to relax a little. 'I hope I don't have to stay too long in Sunderland. It's an awful place, and I'll be out of it as soon as I can. There's a young man, my fiancé, waiting for me in London.' And that was only partly true: he was her lover, and her late guardian had known nothing of him. 'We're to be married soon.'

'Yes?' Liza was also relaxed now – and tired. She guessed that Cecily had slept in the comfort of her first-class cabin before the storm broke. But she was interested: she had once been close to marriage, and there had been another time when she thought she was, but that sadness and shame was in the past. 'Are all the arrangements made?'

In fact Cecily had not slept well, had found the little cabin cramped and claustrophobic. She yawned, a hand over her mouth. 'It will be at St George's in Hanover Square . . .' She let her imagination run on. She was feeling more at ease and enjoying her storytelling. The servant girl seemed impressed, too. There's no harm in it, Cecily thought, and we'll probably never meet again. From talking of her imagined wedding she harked back to her time at her Swiss finishing school and the discipline imposed there.

She stopped when she saw that Liza's eyes were closed and thought, nettled, The girl is asleep! But then she found herself yawning again. She settled drowsily into the chair and tucked the rug around her. In minutes she, too, was sleeping. Both girls were tired and now lulled by the slow lift and descent of the ship as she rode the long swell.

An hour later they were roused by the sailor shoving the door open. When he saw them waking and blinking he apologised: 'Sorry, ladies, I didn't know you were having a nap. I just looked in to tell you we've reduced speed to dead slow on account of the fog.'

They peered out of the salt-encrusted windows of the saloon and saw the mist writhing greyly. From above them the ship's siren blared a long, mournful note. There was a smell of coal smoke and Cecily said, anxious again, 'Something's burning!'

'Don't you worry, Miss. That's only the smoke from our funnel. Now we're going so slow we're not leaving it astern and it's hanging about us.' The door slammed behind him as he left.

'I was telling you about my finishing school when you fell asleep,' Cecily said.

Liza caught the note of reproof. 'Yes, Miss, I'm sorry.' She could only recall vaguely the details of the planned wedding and did not want to hear about the school, but she was polite because she still hoped she might find work through this girl.

It seemed Cecily had tired of talking about school. 'That's all over now, though. When I'm twenty-one I will be able to do as I like, spend my money as I please. I just have to put up with other people's arranging things for the next four weeks, because my guardian's solicitors made the travel arrangements. Left to myself, I would have spent the time in London and gone north when I was due to inherit . . .' Her voice trailed away and she stared at Liza with one finger to her lips. Then she smiled. 'But you are looking for a position.'

'Yes, Miss,' Liza said, puzzled.

'You could work for me for four weeks.' Liza was bewildered. 'You could *be* me! Nobody knows me in Sunderland. If you take my place I can go to London.'

Liza was vaguely aware of distant sirens wailing as, stunned, she took in this preposterous suggestion. 'I can't,' she said.

'Of course, you can.' Cecily fumbled excitedly in her handbag and found her purse. 'I'll pay you five pounds.'

Five pounds! That was nearly three months' pay! Liza swallowed. 'I – can't. They'd find me out.'

'No, they won't! How can they? I told you, they've never seen me. Uncle Edward hasn't even a photograph, except the one of my class, taken when I first went to school in Switzerland. I was seventeen and among another dozen girls. It could be anyone.' She hurried on: 'Look!' She held out her palm on which lay five golden sovereigns. 'Just for four weeks. Then, when I am due to inherit, I will come north and say, "Here I am!" I'll give you *another* five pounds and off you go to Newcastle.'

Liza was dumb. She stared at temptation in the shape of the sovereigns but common sense told her this was a mad idea. She shook her head regretfully: five pounds – no, ten

– would buy her a breathing space in which to put her life together. The siren moaned again. She averted her gaze from the coins in Cecily's palm and turned to the window.

She saw the black mass materialise out of the grey, formless at first, then swiftly hardening into a ship with her bow pointed at the *Florence Grey*. Liza watched it charge towards her, looming larger with every second. There was a running figure on the deck of the other vessel, his arms waving, and she could make out men on the bridge now. She heard Cecily shriek, 'She's going to hit us!' And seconds later the sharp bow smashed into the *Florence Grey* amidships on the starboard side.

She heeled over from the force of the blow and her engines stopped as her assailant ground along her side with a screeching and clanging of tortured metal. The ships parted then and that lethal bow, crumpled now, was turning away, then slid off into the fog, lost to sight. The siren of the *Florence Grey* blared continuously, the signal for a vessel in distress. It sounded like the wail of an animal mortally wounded.

'Captain says to take to the boats! You ladies come along o' me!' the sailor shouted from the door.

'Take my suitcase, please!' Cecily called. She rolled the rug into a ball and tucked it under her arm. The sailor muttered under his breath but obeyed – and took Liza's as well.

'Thank you,' Liza said.

'That's all right, Miss, but hurry. I don't reckon she's got long.' As he spoke the ship lurched, listing to starboard.

The girls followed him to a boat on the port side. The men there had already undone the lashings and taken off the cover. They helped Liza and Cecily into the boat and tossed in their cases after them. Liza's fell on one corner and burst open. She grabbed it and plumped down beside Cecily as the boat was lowered, with one sailor forward and another aft, manning the falls and ready to cast off. Because of the list it bumped and grated against the ship's side as it descended towards the dark sea. But then the man aft yelled a warning, the ship lurched again and Liza and her case were thrown out into the sea.

She fell between boat and ship, looked up to see the steel wall of the *Florence Grey* and the boat surging in to crush her between the two. The sea closed over her head and she knew she was about to die. Oh, Mother! she thought in despair.

I

Twenty years before the *Florence Grey* sailed from Hamburg,
Kitty Thornton fought for the life of her child.

'This could be the death of her,' said Aggie, sixty and bulky
in a rusty black dress that brushed the floor. 'It was always you
or her folks sent for when there was a confinement or somebody to be laid out. Now it looks like Kitty's turn. She's far
ower auld to hev a bairn, poor lass. And premature!' The whisper carried – just – to the other woman stooping over the bed.

Jinnie was of an age but taller, skinny as a rake. She replied,
low-voiced, 'We cannae dae owt aboot it noo, Aggie.'

Both women were Kitty's neighbours, come in response to
this emergency. Their words did not register with Kitty, who
lay on the wrinkled sheet and cried out shrilly and weakly, in
agony. Outside the wind moaned and rattled the windows,
old, warped and loose in their frames. Rain hammered on the
streaming panes. At one in the morning, the streets outside
were empty, the cobbles glistening wetly in the darkness, each
one a little island.

Aggie whispered again, 'And falling off a chair, Jinnie! What
was she daeing, standing on a chair?'

Jinnie sighed. 'She's been taking in washing since she had
to give up as barmaid. She was standing on the chair to hang
it up in the kitchen.' They were in the small bedroom, the bed
taking up most of the space, its side clapped against one wall,
its head against another. There was a straight-backed chair,

an old chest of drawers and an aspidistra on a spindle-legged table. A print of a sailing ship was the only picture. The grate in the fireplace was black and empty. There had not been a fire in it for years, even in the winter's cold, because of the cost of coal.

'And her man?' Aggie enquired. 'That Andrew should be here, but where is he?'

'The last letter she had off him, he was in America and bound for China.' Jinnie pulled a handkerchief from a pocket of her pinny and mopped the brow of the woman on the bed. 'There now, Kitty, there now, bonny lass.'

'He's all reet, had his fun and buggered off out of it,' Aggie whispered.

'Never mind Andrew, though I saw him just afore he sailed and he'd heard there was a babby on the way. He was in a rare worry. But where's that bloody doctor?'

As she spoke he was climbing down from his trap with its flickering lamps. He left his pony standing in the rain and tramped along the passage, his boots echoing hollowly on the boards. In the kitchen, the other ground-floor room rented by Kitty, he nodded at the other three women, more neighbours, sitting around the fire. A line was stretched across the room, just below the ceiling, festooned with damp washing. Kitty had hung up some of it before she fell and the neighbours had completed the job. The doctor ducked his head to pass under it and went on into the bedroom. Someone whispered, 'He's in a bad temper.'

He was, at being hailed from his bed, with his jacket and trousers pulled on over his nightshirt. He had not expected this call for another month and did not like the sound of it. His only consolation was the knowledge that his fee for the confinement had already been paid. Kitty had scraped it together over months of penny-pinching economies.

The women by the bed moved out of his way as he shed his damp ulster and tossed it aside with his hat. Jinnie said, 'She's having a bad time, Doctor.'

He grunted, washed his hands in the bowl they brought him and examined his patient.

When he stood back Aggie asked, 'Will she be all right, Doctor?'

'We'll see,' he replied guardedly. 'She's not young to be having her first child . . .'

'Ah! Dear, dear!' Aggie sighed.

'Andrew! Oh, *Andrew!*' Kitty cried out.

'Now then,' the doctor said. And braced himself.

The child was born as the light of dawn showed grey through the curtains over the windows. Jinnie handed the scrap to Kitty and asked, 'What are you going to call her?'

Kitty, small in the bed and exhausted now, managed a smile and replied, 'Eliza. Nicer than Kitty.'

'If the poor little bairn lives,' Aggie muttered, under her breath.

2

In the afternoon of that day Millicent Spencer called for her doctor. He came quickly to the comfortable house on the hill that looked down on the town. He brought with him a nurse, and a specialist who came in his own richly appointed carriage and left it in the drive. Millicent had not wanted the pregnancy and was determined to have all the assistance she could obtain for her confinement.

Charles, her husband, backed her in this, but her money would pay the bills anyway. He waited on the landing outside the bedroom, pacing restlessly. At twenty-five he was tall and fair, florid and fleshily handsome. He heard the child's cry from behind the closed door with more relief than joy. 'Thank God, that's over.'

His brother, Edward, a man of forty, smiled. 'Congratulations.' He was shorter, broader, fair but lean.

Charles nodded brusquely. 'Thank you.' Then he reverted to the conversation of a minute or two earlier: 'I think you're wrong. If we sold all the old ships we're running and bought just two or three new, bigger vessels, we could make a fortune.'

Edward demurred. 'As I've already said, I think that too much of a gamble. I prefer to go more slowly.'

Charles flapped a hand impatiently, and the argument went on. They were partners in the shipowning business left to them by their father, but by the terms of his will Edward had the casting vote and he was implacable now.

They broke off when the bedroom door opened and the doctor said, 'Come and see your daughter, Charles.'

They entered and Edward congratulated Millicent, normally willowy, blonde and blue-eyed, now tired and wan: 'You have a beautiful daughter.'

The child was in the arms of her nurse and Millicent declared petulantly, 'I'm exhausted. Take her to the nursery.'

'Have you decided on a name for her?' Edward asked.

'No,' Charles said shortly. He glanced at his wife, his brows raised.

She shrugged her shoulders in an elegant silken bed-jacket. 'Oh, I don't know.'

'My mother – her grandmother – was Margaret,' Edward suggested.

'No.' Millicent wrinkled her nose. 'Much too ordinary. I think . . . Cecily. Yes – Cecily.'

Soon afterwards Edward left. 'I am expecting a young visitor.'

'I think you're making a mistake, taking on something like that,' Charles said, 'but it's your affair. You won't stay to dinner, then?' The invitation was lukewarm.

'Thank you, but I think I should meet him.'

The specialist's carriage had gone but Edward's was waiting for him. He patted the horses' necks and stroked their noses. 'My brother's wife has just given birth to a daughter, Gibson. I'm an uncle.'

'Glad to hear it, sir.' And his young coachman drove him home.

The house was bigger than he needed with its six bedrooms – he lived alone – and another half-dozen for his servants, but it had been his childhood home and had been left to him by his father. He was happy enough there.

The carriage wheeled in through the gates, always open

by his order. He would not bar the way to anyone needing shelter. Mrs Taggart, his housekeeper, met him at the front door. 'Mrs' was a courtesy title; she had never married. Nor had Elspeth Taggart ever disclosed her age and no one dared ask it, but she had been in his and his father's employ, at first as a scullery-maid, for twenty-five years. She was rosy-cheeked, red-haired and straight-backed, with a large bunch of keys dangling from the waist of her black dress. She greeted Edward with a smile. 'The young person has arrived, sir. He's in the parlour.'

'Good.' He walked down the hall, polished floorboards gleaming either side of the carpet, with Elspeth at his heels, and turned into the drawing room at the front of the house – to her it was always the parlour. It was a big room but smaller than the dining room on to which it opened and which stretched the depth of the house.

'It's like a barn,' she would say. 'You could have a dance in there.'

The windows were tall and the furniture was good and plentiful, but it made only little islands in the space. On the walls pictures of ships mingled with portraits of the Spencers, Charles and Edward, their father and grandfather. Two capacious armchairs and a chesterfield ringed the glowing fire but there was also a sprinkling of straight-backed chairs. A nurse in black – shoes, coat and bonnet – sat on one, a small boy perched on her knee. She set him on his feet and stood up when Edward entered. He motioned to her to sit and went to stand before the fire. 'Thank you for bringing the boy,' he said. 'So this is William.'

She nodded. 'Yes, sir, this is Master William.'

The boy was sturdy, but no more than five years old and tired. He rubbed his eyes and yawned, but was silent and attentive. Edward had no children and no experience of them. He was not sure how best to approach this one. 'You've had a long journey, William, all the way from Bristol.'

'Yes, sir.'

'Do you know who I am?'

'You are Mr Edward Spencer, sir, and you are my guardian.' He had that off by heart, as he had been taught. His father had gone down with his ship and all her crew in a typhoon. He had long ago written to Edward asking him to care for his son if he should die. Edward had agreed willingly, thinking it a sensible precaution for his friend to make but never expecting to have to honour his promise.

He thought now that there was something about the boy's face in repose that suggested he might show something of his mother when he laughed. He was not laughing now and looked as if he might never smile again. 'That's right, and you are going to live here with me. Would you like that?'

'Yes, sir.' That was said politely but hesitantly. Then William added, breaking away from his trained replies, 'But I want to go to sea and be a ship's captain like my father.'

'Ssh!' the nurse scolded, shocked, and Elspeth pursed her lips.

Edward put up a hand to silence the nurse. 'My thanks to you for caring for him. I'm grateful.' He glanced at Elspeth. 'Will you find this lady a bed for the night, please, and then come back here?'

When they had gone he turned back to little William. The boy looks like his father, he thought, the dead spit of him. And now he could see in him both parents. Instinctively he went to the child and swept him up in his arms. 'Your father was my best friend.' And he had married the only girl Edward had ever loved. There had never been another like her and she had died giving birth to William.

Edward sat down in an armchair with the boy on his knees and held him close to his chest. When Elspeth returned a few minutes later she found them so, with William sound asleep. She clicked her tongue and said softly, 'Poor little lamb, he's tired out. Let me have him, sir, and I'll tend to him. He'll be the better for being in bed.'

Edward yielded up his ward with barely concealed reluctance. He supposed that would be the best for the boy. Elspeth cradled him in her arms and kissed him. 'And him wanting to be a ship's captain like his father!' She shook her head. 'He'll soon grow out of it.'

Edward was not sure about that.

3

'What are you doing, Dad?' Eliza Thornton, just five years old that day and curious, snuggled closer to the father who came into her life so rarely. He was short, wiry and tough, and she had to learn about him all over again every time he came home. That might be after an absence of weeks, months or a year, but she learned more quickly now. He sat at the kitchen table with the model before him. He had spent weeks making it during his last voyage, starting with a block of wood and using only a knife.

Andrew smiled down at her. 'I'm setting up the rigging.' His thick-fingered hands, the backs tattooed, handled the thin cotton delicately.

'What's rigging?' Eliza asked, brown eyes wide.

'All these lines that hold up the sails.' The model was of a clipper, a full-rigged ship.

'These stringy bits.' Eliza poked a finger at the cat's cradle of cottons.

'That's right.'

'Have you been on a ship like that?'

'A few.' Andrew grinned at her.

'Are you going on another one?' She peered up at him anxiously.

'Not for a bit.' His wife glanced across at him from where she stood by the fire and the open oven door. He saw the sudden droop of her mouth. But then her gaze shifted to Eliza and she smiled again.

'You are clever, Dad,' Eliza said wistfully. 'When I try to sew I get my fingers mixed up, don't I, Mam?'

Kitty crossed to her and kissed her. 'You'll be able to do all those things soon when you're a big lass. You're doing very canny. Now why don't you finish cooking the dinner for your dolly and let your dad get on?'

'Ooh! I'd forgot.' Eliza scrambled down from the chair and hurried to where the rag doll – her birthday present – leaned on the brass fender, polished so it glittered, like the fire-irons of poker, shovel and coal rake inside it. They were for decoration: there was another set made of steel for use. Eliza opened an imaginary oven door and peeped in at an imaginary pie.

Kitty put an arm round her husband's broad shoulders and said softly, 'Isn't she a bonny little lass?'

'Aye.' Andrew squeezed her hand. 'Like her mother.'

She laughed. 'Hadaway wi' ye.' And then, with a sigh, 'It's nearly finished.'

'Just about.' He was talking of the model.

But Kitty had been thinking of his time at home: 'You'll be after another ship afore long.'

'I'll have to,' Andrew said soberly. 'The money from that last voyage won't spin out for much longer.' He was silent a moment, then said, 'I don't like leaving you and the bairn but I'm a sailorman and that's the only trade I know. One of these days I'll have to find a job ashore, but it'll only be labouring. I'll stick to the sea for a few years yet.'

Kitty knew she could not change him, knew also that he followed a dangerous trade. Between 1880 and 1882 more than three hundred British ships had been lost. She said bravely, 'Don't worry about us. Eliza is good company for me now.'

'I can't get over how she's grown,' Andrew said.

*   *   *

In Sunderland Edward Spencer smiled. 'My word, Cecily, how you've grown.' The child stood in front of him, restless in her expensive sailor suit and ankle-strap shoes. She was itching to take the wrapped present Edward had brought her. He could see behind her, through an open door, the twenty or so small boys and girls, dressed in their best suits and frocks, who were the guests at Cecily's birthday party. They waited, with the nursemaids who had accompanied them, for the games to begin. Later there would be tea with thin slices of bread and butter, big cakes, little cakes and scones. Then, to crown it all, a Punch and Judy show.

Edward handed over the parcel. Cecily snatched it and said hastily, 'Thank you, Uncle Edward.' She undid the string and paper to unwrap the doll within, glanced at it, then said proudly, 'I have six now.' She ran off and Edward watched her go, his smile fading. But she was not his child. He thought of William Morgan, ten years old now and growing tall and straight. Maybe Cecily would improve with age. He went to join the provider of the feast.

Charles received him in his study. It was lined with books and furnished with a desk and two leather armchairs. He looked up from his newspaper as Edward entered. 'Ah! There you are.' He rose from his chair. 'What can I offer you?'

Edward did not want anything but said diplomatically, 'A small whisky and water, please.' As Charles poured it and topped up his own, he added, 'I've just congratulated your daughter. I didn't see Millicent.'

'She's out playing whist,' said Charles, without interest. 'Children's parties give her a migraine.' He gestured to the chairs before the fire. 'I'd like to have a chat with you.' They sat down, their backs to the door, and Charles went on, 'We must increase our profitability, make the ships work harder, spend less on them.'

Edward had come prepared for this. 'There are safety factors involved, and we have to think of the men. This is an old argument—'

'I know damn fine it is! Because we never settle the matter!'

'You mean, I don't let you have your way.'

'I'm supposed to be a partner but you rule the roost!'

'Our father—'

'I know what he said, and I don't believe he intended you to run this business as if it was yours alone! He was prepared to take a chance.'

Edward shook his head. 'He always looked before he leaped.'

'You look and look but never leap! You're an old man before your time! If I had my share invested anywhere else I would do far better than being bound by your pinchpenny tactics. Half the time I'm living on my wife's money.'

Old man! Pinchpenny! Edward's temper boiled over: 'If you're using your wife's money it's because you're living beyond your means!'

'To hell with that! And you!' Both men were on their feet now, glaring. 'That is the last straw!' Charles shouted. 'I want my share of the firm – in cash. I'll go through the courts to get it, if I have to, and then I'll be quit of you and this place.'

'As you wish.' Edward's tone was cold but he was sick at heart. He had seen this coming for some time, the constant, niggling arguments, his brother's complaints. 'You'll have no need to go through the courts. I will put the matter into the hands of solicitors tomorrow.'

He stalked out, the study door already ajar. Charles went

with him, flushed with rage. Edward picked his way through the children, who were scurrying about in the game of hide and seek. Charles almost stumbled over them and muttered curses under his breath. He flung open the front door and Edward passed through it. They parted without another word.

Behind them, in the study, Cecily sat hidden by the sideboard. She had crept in there, minutes before, in the game of hide and seek and had listened to the angry words. She crouched with her knees to her chin and tears on her cheeks. She did not understand what had happened, only that it was something terrible that she should not have heard. She would not tell another soul.

A month later Charles Spencer and his family took the train south to London. He had his inheritance and was eager to make his fortune. Millicent looked forward to taking her place in Society in the capital city. On this last day, his carriage sold, Charles took a cab to the quayside. It was the least he could do: a number of officers and men in Spencer ships had contributed to buy him a fine pocket watch engraved: 'For Charles Spencer from Officers and Men of the Spencer Line with Best Wishes'. In truth, few had paid and Edward had made up the difference, but Charles was going down to the river to thank them.

Millicent had never visited the quay or the ships before because neither interested her. Nor had Cecily. As the cab threaded through the narrow, crowded streets, she stared out at ragged children scattering out of the way, then running in its wake. Then there was a shop of some sort and a thin, wild-eyed woman all in black, who ran out to keep pace alongside the cab. She shook her fist and screamed, 'Murderers! Bloody murderers!' The children fled from her and she came closer, yelled, 'I'll see you all burn in hell one day!'

Cecily shrank back, terrified. But now the cabbie whipped up his horse and the mad woman was left behind. 'Good heavens! Was that—' Millicent was interrupted.

'Iris Cruikshank,' Charles finished for her. 'You know the story.' And to his daughter, staring big-eyed with fear, 'Take no notice. The woman is bereft of her senses.' But Cecily was not comforted.

Later that day she sat in the corner of the first-class carriage with tears in her eyes. 'You'll like living in London,' her mother consoled her irritably. 'You'll go to the zoo and see the Changing of the Guard at Buckingham Palace.'

Cecily did not know what she was talking about. 'I just want to get away from this place!' she wailed.

'Well, you *are* getting away from it, so stop crying.' Millicent opened the novel she had brought. Charles was already hidden behind *The Times*. Cecily rubbed her eyes and watched the town recede behind her. There lived Uncle Edward, who had exchanged angry words with her father, and that mad woman with her threats. She hated it and determined she would never return.

4

The storm came on them suddenly as they were rounding the Horn. First there was just a black bar along the horizon but this thickened with every blink of the eye until it loomed as a huge cloud. Young William Morgan stood on the bridge of the SS *Glendower* with the other apprentices, receiving instruction in the noon observation of the sun from the first officer. This was his first voyage and his sextant was brand new. So was his uniform, but that already showed signs of wear: weeks at sea had seen to that. He had a small sum, left him by his father, but that was held in a trust, so Edward Spencer had paid for his kit and the sextant. At thirteen he was the youngest of the four apprentices but not the shortest. Tall for his age, he stood eye to eye with one of his colleagues and topped another by an inch or two.

The first officer finished taking his sight and ordered, 'Belay that! We're in for some dirty weather. See everything is lashed down.' He called the captain to the bridge as the boys scattered to put away their sextants and turn to.

When the gale struck William was returning from working on the forecastle. 'Buck up there, lad!' a voice behind him bawled. 'You don't want to be out in this. I've just been in the fo'c'sle spinning a yarn wi' Billy Danvers, him that has splints on his broken leg. I told him, "Stay where you are in your bunk, you're better off there." Aye. Who'd be a sailor at a time like this? We're in for a blow!' It was the ship's cook,

Archibald Godolphin, short, stout and prematurely bald – he
was only in his early thirties. He was going back to his galley
in the superstructure amidships. As he passed William he
grabbed the lifeline rigged along the deck. 'Come on, lad!'

William followed, used to Archie's patronising him; he got
it from the seamen as well. He knew there was no one more
useless than a raw apprentice. He had to earn their respect.
But one day he would captain his own ship, he was sure of
that. Meanwhile he would not take the patronage tamely.
'Aye, aye, Admiral,' he twitted Archie.

They were down in the waist now and working their way
aft, hand over hand along the line. As the ship rolled they
saw dark sky at one moment, then the sea standing above
them like a cliff. The last wave that broke inboard washed
around their knees and tried to pluck them loose. Archie
swung round on the rope to point a warning finger: 'Don't
give me any o' your lip, lad. I'm the cook aboard this flaming
ship and you're just—'

William yelled a warning as the ship rolled wildly and the
next wave hung over them. Then it fell. It battered William
to the deck, washed over his head and he clung to the
line desperately. When he could see and breathe again, he
struggled to his feet. Archie was no longer with him. The
line looped along the deck but William was the only one
on it. Then he saw that the cook had been snatched from
it and lay in the scuppers ten yards away. He was scrabbling
at the deck as he tried to regain his feet. Now came another
big wave, hovering, falling.

'Look out! Hang on!' William shrieked. Then he realised
there was nothing for Archie to hang on to. The big sea
slammed on to the deck. William braced himself and while
it surged up to his chest he stayed on his feet. It covered the
hatches of the forward holds and took the cook with it in a

tangle of arms, legs and bald head. It carried him inboard then sucked him out again. By God's mercy it took him close to William and he reached out as the man passed, clamped his hand on Archie's fat wrist. The ship rolled, the sea fell away and the cook hung from William's grip as the ship tilted and the deck was nearly vertical rather than horizontal. William hung on grimly – his arm felt as though it would be pulled out of its socket.

Slowly the ship righted herself, and Archie reached up with his free hand to seize the lifeline. Together William and he worked their way along it to the safety of the superstructure. They stepped over the coaming into the passage and slammed the door behind them. Their struggle had been seen from the bridge and now one of the officers and a clutch of seamen came running. They gathered round, relieved to see the pair safe and sound. 'That was well done, young Bill,' the officer said.

William smiled bashfully, but Archie, recovering now, said, 'Thank you, lad. If it hadn't been for you I'd ha' gone to the bottom.'

'No,' William replied. 'The sea took you but then it washed you inboard again.' He paused. 'I don't think it wanted you, Archie.'

The men around them guffawed and Archie grinned sheepishly. 'I asked for that.'

William was glad when talk of his lifesaving prowess faded away with the days, as they entered the Pacific and ploughed north. But the captain entered an account of the incident in the ship's log and wrote a letter of commendation for William's gallantry. And the boy had gained Archie's respect and a friend.

Months later, when the *Glendower* came home and paid off,

Edward Spencer learned of his ward's bravery in a letter from the captain. There was also a report stating that William's conduct had been Very Good throughout the voyage. Edward took it with him when he travelled to London to visit his brother in his big house at Wimbledon. This was at Charles's invitation; he had spoken of it as an olive branch. In fact, the younger man only wanted to display the ostentatious signs of his success: his house, horses, his fashionably dressed wife and their friends.

'I've more than doubled my investment over the past two years,' he told Edward, 'buying and selling on the Exchange, y'know. But you have to know what you're doing. And I'm trying to get into Lloyds, as a Name, insuring ships. There's money to be made there, by Jove! But you have to take a risk, and again, know what you're doing.'

Edward wondered uneasily if Charles did. But he knew he was in no position to argue. And then Charles said, 'It's good to be friends again. We can put all the other business behind us.'

Edward agreed wholeheartedly with that. But when he tried to talk of William he found that Charles preferred to gossip about London and his life in the City, casually dropping a name here and there. Nor was Charles interested in his daughter, except as an exhibit, like his wife. Edward was not impressed by the eight-year-old Cecily: she had listened to him talk of his home and his work but was obviously bored and said so as she walked away. Edward thought her precocious and ill-mannered.

Millicent seemed to live her own life, entertaining or being entertained by other rich wives. Edward saw little of her or Cecily during the week he was there, except when Charles ordered a dinner party, in honour of his brother's visit, on the night before his departure. Then mother and daughter attended, richly gowned and undeniably lovely. Brought out like the best china, Edward thought. He also thought, uneasily, that Millicent was paying too much attention to a young Guards officer, but told himself he was probably imagining things. Charles did not seem to notice.

After the other guests had gone Edward and his brother sat in the library for a nightcap. It was a handsome room, expensively furnished like the rest of the house, and all of the books were new and untouched. Charles had soon finished his whisky, although Edward's glass was still half full. 'I'm going to retire,' he said. 'I have to go to my office tomorrow – some important business – so I'll bid you farewell now.'

'I'll be another ten minutes,' Edward said.

They shook hands and Charles said, 'It's been good to see you, to be together again.'

Edward was sure he meant it. As he sat on alone, though, he felt melancholy. He told himself that it was because he was leaving the next day – but knowing the cause did not make him feel better. He downed the whisky in a gulp and went to bed. As he came to the head of the stairs he heard voices.

Millicent, from her room: 'Edward will hear—'

Charles: 'He's still in the library. Don't make excuses. You were fawning on that chap tonight and we'd agreed we'd both be discreet. Disgraceful!'

Millicent: 'What about you and that Tierney woman just last week?'

Charles: 'You were otherwise engaged yourself that night. I told you I'd be more careful. I'm just telling you to be the same. Now come here.'

Millicent: 'Why?' There was a pause, then she laughed softly. 'Well . . .' A door closed.

Edward walked quietly back down the stairs and into the library. He poured himself another whisky, a stiff one, and sat staring into the embers of the fire. He was shocked. They were man and wife and it was none of his affair but— He consoled himself that at least Cecily had not overheard the conversation.

He did not know she had heard others.

As young William Morgan completed his first voyage, Andrew Thornton came home from his last. He pushed in through the kitchen door with his big sea-bag on his shoulder. It held all his kit, including his 'donkey's breakfast', a straw-filled mattress. He let it fall to the floor with a thump as Kitty and eight-year-old Eliza threw themselves into his arms. He held them both and laughed. 'Aye! I'm home for good! I've been promised a job ashore and I'll plough the seas no more!'

Kitty shed tears of joy and Eliza pleaded, 'Can I stay home from school today, Mam?'

Kitty was firm, though sympathetic: 'I know you haven't seen your dad for three months but he'll be here tonight when you come home. In fact, he'll be here every night from now on so you must go to school.'

Andrew backed her up: 'Aye, you go to school. I might meet you when you come out.'

So Eliza trailed off disconsolately, but soon became more cheerful and finally danced into the teeming playground. She told everyone she knew that 'My dad has come home for good.' She even told the new girl, Betty Wood, who had just come to the school because her father had moved from Stockton to work on the Tyne. Betty was a small blonde girl and Eliza found her in the girls' lavatory. She flinched when Eliza entered and only blinked when she heard the news. Then the bell rang out in the playground and both girls ran to join their class. They formed up two by two under the watchful eye of their teacher.

Amelia Parkin was straight-backed, thin, with a prim mouth and no-nonsense eyes looking bleakly down her nose. A teacher for twenty years, she had established her authority early and maintained it throughout the school lives of her charges. At school they respected her. When they looked back afterwards they added affection to respect.

Eliza put up her hand. 'Please, Miss, my dad came home from sea today. He's not going away again.'

Miss Parkin smiled briefly. 'That's good news. I'm pleased for your sake.' Her voice raised only fractionally, 'Quiet now.' A hush fell over the forty children, whose eyes were on her. 'March in.' They trooped into their classroom to start their day.

Eliza soon settled down, behaved herself and answered quickly when called upon. Some of the others could only produce a blank stare when asked a question. Betty Wood was the worst, seemingly capable of saying only, 'I don't know, Miss.'

Amelia Parkin pursed her lips disapprovingly.

When they stopped for the morning playtime break she called, 'Eliza and Betty! Stay behind!' When the others had streamed out she said, 'I want you two to sit together and, Eliza, you must help Betty to catch up. You understand?'

'Yes, Miss Parkin,' Eliza replied, and followed Betty out to the playground.

'Here she is!' The hissed call came from behind the shed where the caretaker kept his tools. It stood close by the high school wall, but with a yard-wide gap between. Una Gubbins had spoken, a tall, narrow-faced, bony girl, whose parents ran a cheap boarding-house with a dubious reputation. With her was Luke Cooper; his mother kept a drunken husband and a corner shop selling sweets and toffee, and it showed in Luke's bulging belly; he was known as 'Piggy'. Both were bigger than

Eliza and in the class above her, and while usually the children played and made friends with their own sex, these two had formed an unholy alliance. It was Luke who grabbed Betty by the hair and yanked her into the hidey-hole between wall and shed.

Eliza, startled, said, 'Hey! What are you doing?' But she had already guessed.

Luke was holding Betty while Una laughed and punched her. 'You shove off,' he said. He threw out a careless hand to push Eliza away and succeeded in slapping her face.

Fury gripped her. How dare he? She reached in, twined her fingers in his hair and hauled on it as if in a tug o' war. 'How do *you* like it?' He did not and howled, then let go of Betty. Una tried to reach over him to get at Eliza but only for her legs to tangle with his and they both fell. Eliza gave one last yank to help him on his way and he hit the ground nose first. Una tried to seize her leg but Eliza evaded her and stamped on her clutching fingers, then kicked out for good measure. She missed, almost, but grazed Una's thin-lipped mouth. The blood shed mingled with that from Luke's nose. Una saw it and screeched in horror.

Eliza held out a hand to Betty: 'Come on!' She dragged her out into the playground – just as Miss Parkin appeared.

She saw the panting Eliza and the tearful Betty, as Luke and Una spilled from behind the shed, bleeding. 'What is going on here?' Eliza told her, and a weeping Betty admitted that the two had bullied her ever since she started at the school. 'Mind you tell me if anything like this happens again,' said Miss Parkin, tight-lipped. She glanced at Eliza. 'Off you go, the pair of you.' When they had left she snapped, 'Not you two!'

Una had been edging away. 'My mouth's bleeding, Miss,' she whined.

'Serves you right.' Miss Parkin glared from her to Luke. 'It's not the first time you two have been in trouble. It's the headmaster for you, and if you don't improve, one of these days there'll be a policeman coming for you and it will be the reform school. Now, go and tidy yourselves.'

That silenced them. First the head and then— The reformatory was a fearsome place of legend.

They never bothered Eliza and Betty again.

Sitting side by side in the classroom every day, the two girls soon became friends. Early on, Betty said shyly, 'Would you mind if I called you Liza? It sounds more friendly, like.'

'Liza?' She listened to the sound of it and liked it. 'Aye, that's all right.' And she told her mother, 'I'm Liza now.'

'I called you Eliza because I thought your father would like it. That was his mother's name.' She glanced at Andrew, who was sitting on the other side of the fireplace.

He grinned. 'Kitty, Eliza or Liza. I've got what I want now, anyway.'

5

'Now you've got to say, "Yes, Miss Parkin." Go on.' Liza stood in front of the class, pointing at the blackboard with the teacher's cane and looking down her nose as Miss Parkin did, lips pursed.

They all giggled and chorused, 'Yes, Miss Parkin.'

'Do Mr Blackaby again,' Betty said.

Liza gave her imitation of the school caretaker as he came to stoke up the fire at the front of the class, shuffling bent-kneed with an imaginary scuttle full of coal, wiping his nose on the back of his hand. This time the giggles were louder. 'Do Mr Stewart!'

Miss Parkin, who had been watching surreptitiously from outside, decided now that enough was enough and walked in. The giggles were replaced by a shocked silence. Liza straightened as her teacher raised a warning finger. 'I trust you do not dare to mimic the headmaster.' In fact, she knew that Liza did – and so did Mr Stewart. She did not wait for an answer but waved Liza to her seat beside Betty Wood. 'Now, then, dictation and handwriting . . .'

Liza and the class heaved a silent sigh of relief: there was to be no punishment. They did not know why, were just glad.

Amelia Parkin knew that their schooldays were nearly over now and that they would soon be cast out into the world of work, which would probably be back-breaking and certainly poorly paid. She was fond of them and could not chastise them now, could only pray that what she had been able to do for them would help along the way.

The following day Betty sought out Liza in the schoolyard. 'We're moving,' she said miserably. 'My dad's found another job in Hartlepool and we're all going to live there.'

'Oh, I'm sorry,' Liza said. They had been friends for five years now. 'I'll miss you.'

'I won't know anybody there and I'll be going out to work in a strange place.'

Liza put an arm round her. 'Cheer up. I bet it'll be really nice and you'll love it. Now come on, smile.' And, when Betty managed a feeble response, 'That's better. I'll be starting work as well, but I don't know where.' A week later they embraced for the last time and Betty went off to Hartlepool.

Liza's parents were concerned for their daughter's future and discussed it. 'When she leaves school I'd like her to go into service in a big house like I did,' Kitty said. 'It's hard work and long hours but you have some security. She can sew, wash and iron, and she's been out to confinements a dozen times with me and Jinnie. There's not many can say that.'

Security was important. Andrew's work in the shipyards was broken by periods when the yard he worked for ran out of orders. Over the years when he had been ashore he had been out of work for weeks, sometimes months. More than once he had said, 'I'll get a ship.'

But Kitty had answered fiercely: 'No! You'll do nothing of the sort. You're nearly sixty now and that's far ower old for going back to sea.'

He had obeyed reluctantly and until he found work again they had lived on their tiny savings and what Kitty could make from cleaning.

Now he argued, 'She's still only thirteen and I don't want her leaving home yet.'

Kitty sighed. 'Neither do I. And, anyway, all these big houses want older lasses with a bit of experience. But, remember, both of us left home early. It's the way the world is.' She looked out of the window to the backyard where Liza was pegging out some washing. 'But isn't she growing up a bonny lass? And aren't you glad you gave up the sea and you're able to see it?'

Andrew nodded, and agreed fondly, 'Aye, and that's another reason I want to keep her here.'

He was not the first father to feel like that about his daughter, or the first to be disappointed. Eventually after he had another succession of long spells without a job, and their savings had dribbled away until debt and hunger stared them in the face, he agreed to Liza going into service. 'It seems there's nowt else for it,' he said dejectedly. They had just eaten breakfast of bread and dripping and he looked around the cosy little kitchen. 'I just want you to be happy, bonny lass.' He stooped to kiss his daughter, then pulled on his cap. 'I'm away to look for a job.'

Kitty went with him as far as the front door. 'Now don't you fret,' she told him. 'Something will turn up and we'll manage.'

'Aye, you're right. I just wish I was a bit younger. It doesn't help when you're looking for work at getting on for sixty.' He grinned lopsidedly. 'But you always cheer me up.' He kissed her and she watched him go. He turned to wave at the end of the street, then rounded the corner and was gone.

Kitty sighed and returned to the kitchen. Liza was clearing the table. 'I'll be able to help out all day long after this.' It was to be her last day at school and she sang about the house as she worked before she left. That cheered Kitty, but then Liza waved farewell and her mother had the house to herself. Her happiness fell away. She knew it would be almost impossible for Andrew to find work at his age.

Andrew walked the banks of the Tyne for two hours that morning and his spirits were sinking, but then he was taken on at Armstrong, Whitworth's yard. Kitty had given him a packet of sandwiches and these he ate at midday. In the evening he made his way home, hurrying with the joyous news. He had listened to the talk between his foreman and the other men, learned that the yard had just won an order to build a vessel and he had a job for a year or more.

In his haste he took a short-cut through the back lane instead of walking round to the front door. He was humming to himself when he came to the back gate and found it bolted inside. That did not worry him. He was still wiry and active and climbed the wall as he had before. But this time he slipped as he swung his legs over and fell head first. His skull was cracked and he died instantly. The man who had climbed the rigging in howling gales had been killed by a fall from a seven-foot wall.

Liza had to support and comfort her mother through the first days of shock and grief, and then through the funeral. They stood together, with a little knot of neighbours, at the graveside. It was a day of bright sunshine, the cemetery filled with birdsong, a day like many Liza had shared with her father. She could picture him laughing and hear him calling, 'Away, bonny lass!'

The next day Kitty woke her daughter. 'Come on, now, we've got to get on and find you a job.' She had to see her started off in life. 'It's time to look ahead.' She had already done that, and knew she could barely earn enough to feed herself. She foresaw a time when they would have to apply for parish relief or starve. Liza would be better off in a big house where she would have enough to eat and a roof over her head. 'You must try to work your way up to being a lady's maid. It's hard getting there and I never managed it, but a lady's maid is top of the tree. It's clean work, good money, the next best job to housekeeper. And there are even some ladies, widowed or lost their money, glad to be housekeeper in a big house. It's almost like being one of the family.' But, as she had said earlier, big houses wanted girls with experience and strength. Liza was no weakling but not tall and had no experience. Kitty had taught her a lot but a potential employer would not take that on trust. They searched diligently through the newspapers and finally found an advertisement that read: 'Girl required to attend single lady, helping cook and general. Live in. Apply Mrs Fanshaw.' There was an address in Tynemouth.

The house was one in a terrace, with three storeys above ground and a cellar kitchen, which had a window that looked out on to a well at the front of the house and was approached from the street by a flight of stone stairs. There were three steps up to the front door, which, Liza noted, needed cleaning; the brass knocker and letterbox were dull from lack of polish. Kitty bit her lip but said nothing. She had worked in big houses with a score of bedrooms and as many servants. She knew that work in a small house like this was the worst kind. The only girl did everything, and the employer either could not afford to pay her a fair wage or was too mean.

She rapped on the door with the knocker. After a minute it was opened by a breathless, middle-aged woman in a black dress that strained over her ample figure. Her round face was florid and she peered at them owlishly. 'Aye?'

Kitty held up the paper with the advertisement. 'It's about

the position in here. I've brought my daughter to see Mrs Fanshaw, if it's still open.'

'I'm Mrs Fanshaw.' She looked at Liza and sniffed. 'She's a bit small.' Her accent was a high-pitched 'refined'. 'I have no time for idlers and I like my standards kept up.'

'I'm quite strong,' Liza claimed.

'Are ye now?' Mrs Fanshaw did not sound convinced. 'Well, you'd better come in.'

She led them into the parlour, crowded with chairs and armchairs, little tables and an upright piano. Every surface was littered with sepia photographs – and a fine layer of dust. Mrs Fanshaw sat on an upright chair but left Liza and her mother standing. She eyed the girl. 'So what can you do, then?'

Kitty had primed Liza to answer that question and she reeled off: 'I dust and clean, sew and darn, scrub . . .'

Mrs Fanshaw listened to the list, then said, 'Mm. Sounds all right. Whether you can do it . . .' She trailed off, doubtfully. 'Still, I suppose I can give you a trial for a week. But there's some things you have to get into your head: You address me as "Madam", speak when you're spoken to, be quiet about the house, always neat and tidy, and no idling. I'll pay you ten shillings a month, two shillings if you only last the week. You provide your own clothes: black dress, white cap and pinny. If I take you on permanent you'll have one evening off every week and one day a month when I go to visit my sister and can't keep my eye on you. But I want you in here by nine at night. Do you want the job?'

She did not, but knew there was no help for it. 'Aye, I'd like it, please – Madam.'

Liza settled into her little room at the top of the house, with its narrow, hard bed and bare wooden floor. She pretended it was comfortable enough, bearing in mind that she spent little time there except to sleep, but she anticipated that it would be bitterly cold in winter. She was homesick, of course, and cried herself to sleep.

She worked a twelve-hour day – at least. Often it was longer. She would rise at seven to make tea for Mrs Fanshaw and carry it up to her. Then she would clean out the grate in that lady's bedroom, lay and light the fire so the room should be warm when she eventually rose, then take her a jug of hot water for washing when the time came. The downstairs fires had to be lit, the front steps washed and whitened . . . Mrs Garbutt, garrulous and moaning, came in each morning at eight and cooked, but Liza did everything else. She told herself she was gaining experience and everyone had to start at the bottom. She looked forward to the end of the month when she would have her first day off – and she would be able to give her mother seven or eight shillings out of her wages.

Liza learned more about her employer as she worked. While dusting the parlour Mrs Fanshaw lectured her in fluting tones: 'A house in a good neighbourhood like this needs keeping up to scratch and I insist on it. Perseverance and routine, they're the key to success, my husband used to say. Fanshaw was a turf accountant and left me well provided for. Not like my poor sister in Newcastle.' She sighed and her stays creaked. 'Give us them biscuits.' Liza handed her the tin and Mrs Fanshaw munched, shedding crumbs for Liza to sweep up.

Later, in the kitchen, Mrs Garbutt snorted. 'Turf accountant? Ha! I knew Horace Fanshaw and he was a back-lane bookie, with fellers he paid to stand on the corner and watch out for the pollis.'

It was on her second Sunday in her position that Liza answered a knock at the front door. Checking that her white cap was straight, smoothing her pinny, she opened the door and faced a tall, bony girl standing on the top step. Recognition was immediate and mutual.

Una Gubbins gaped. 'Liza Thornton.' In the time since she had left school, a year earlier than Liza, she had put up her hair and adopted a superior expression. She looked Liza up and down, taking in the uniform, and grinned unpleasantly. 'Well I never. So you're the maid here now.'

'Aye,' Liza answered curtly.

'You've got a lot to learn,' Una said. 'You should say, "Yes, Miss."' And when Liza stood tight-lipped, she went on, 'I've come to see my aunt Nelly.' She saw Liza's startled reaction and smirked again. 'That's right. My mother's her sister. One word from me and it'll be the sack for you. I heard your mother had been left on her own. Shame. I expect she needs your money. Now what do you say?'

Liza swallowed her anger and pride because she believed she had to. 'Yes, Miss.' She stood back and held the door wide.

Una entered, shrugged out of her coat and held it out. As Liza went to take it, she let it drop to the floor. 'That was careless of you. Pick it up and brush it off. I'll look it over when I leave to see it's been done properly. I'll announce meself.' She passed through into the parlour.

Liza heard Mrs Fanshaw cry, 'Una, my pet!'

And the reply, 'Hello, Auntie Nelly. That new lass of yours dropped my good coat . . .' The door closed.

Liza served them with morning tea in the parlour, lunch in the dining room at noon and high tea at six. All the time Una ingratiated herself with her aunt, meek and solicitous. And all the time Liza was aware of her mocking gaze. It was a long day and when Una left at the end of it her parting words were: 'I come to see Auntie nearly every Sunday, just missed the last one because I was away. Me and my mam are her only relations, so one of these days you'll take orders from us.' She pulled on her coat and ground her heel on Liza's foot. 'I'll see you next week,' she called. That was ostensibly addressed to Mrs Fanshaw, coming to bid her farewell, but Liza, tears of pain in her eyes, knew it was meant for her.

That threat rode on her back every day and, true to her word, Una returned on the following Sunday. For Liza it was another day of niggling torture and humiliation. Una kicked the dustpan when she came upon Liza sweeping the hall carpet, elbowed her into a spindle-legged table that toppled over to shed its photographs, tripped her as she brought in a loaded tray, which Liza only saved by a miracle of dexterity and luck. And again at the end there was the warning, 'I'll see you next Sunday.'

Liza was due for her first full day off during the following week, but her anticipation was marred because she worried as to what might be in store for her. She was expecting Una to arrive at her usual time of nine, and this was on her mind when she washed the front steps shortly after seven. She whitened them with the stepstone and sat back on her heels to look them over with satisfaction. Then the voice behind her said, 'Now then, lass, make room for your betters.' Liza turned her head and saw Luke Cooper – Piggy – taller and heavy, though not so fat as he had been. He smirked at her, a giggling Una at his shoulder.

Piggy stood in the mud of the gutter, shifting from one foot to the other. 'We came early 'cause we thought we'd make a day of it.' He stepped out of the gutter and shoved past the kneeling Liza to stamp up the steps, down and then up again, shedding mud with every bang of his boots. He stopped at the top. 'You want to get these steps cleaned. They're thick o' clarts.'

Liza choked, eyes filling with tears but this time they were tears of outrage. This was too much to bear. She still held the cloth she had used on the steps and she plunged it into the bucket. Piggy laughed. 'That's right. Get on wi' it. Ye should ha' had it done by—' Then he choked as the cloth was rammed into his face.

Una had been tittering but now she was standing with her mouth open. 'Here—' The contents of the bucket drenched her. She gasped, then screamed. Piggy clawed the cloth from his face but Liza swung the bucket backhanded into his midriff and he doubled over it. She tried to push him aside off the steps but he slipped and fell forward into the mud, so she seized the back of his head and ground his face into it.

Una's screams had brought Mrs Fanshaw to the front door: 'What's going on?'

Una pointed at Liza. 'Look at what she's done to me – and poor Luke.'

He lifted his filthy face to add: 'Aye! See!'

'Disgraceful! I never saw owt like it!' Mrs Fanshaw squeaked.

'I'd just finished the steps when he came and walked all over them, on purpose and laughing at me!' Liza, her blood still hot, defended herself.

And Mrs Garbutt, her head out of the window of the cellar kitchen, confirmed this: 'Aye! I saw him, and heard him!'

Mrs Fanshaw rounded on her, indignant and red-faced – there were neighbours watching now: 'It's none of your business.'

'Don't tell me to shut up!' Mrs Garbutt bawled. 'I'm trying to talk a bit o' sense into you!' And she slammed the window.

Mrs Fanshaw gave a moan of frustration and rage. 'You're dismissed,' she snapped at Liza.

Liza threw down the bucket, and Piggy shied away. She declared, 'I was leaving anyway.' And, with a jerk of her head at Una, she added to Mrs Fanshaw, 'She said when you'd gone I'd be taking orders from her and I couldn't stomach that.' And she ran up to her room.

It only took minutes for her to pack her few belongings into her box and dress for the street. As she came out on to the landing she heard Mrs Fanshaw railing below: '. . . so if it was my money you were after you can have another think! You'll get damn all! I'll leave it to charity!'

Liza looked over the banister just in time to see Una and Piggy leave dejectedly through the front door. Mrs Fanshaw slammed it behind them and stumped into the parlour.

Liza dragged her box down the stairs into the hall. She left it there while she ran down the stairs to the gloomy cavern of the cellar kitchen. 'I'm off, but thank you for sticking up for me,' she told Mrs Garbutt.

'You're welcome, hinny,' said the cook. 'The cheek of her! Telling me off! Any more o' that and I'll be away an' all. Here, I've done you a bite to take with you.' She handed Liza a brown-paper bag. 'A bit o' bread and cheese.'

'Oh, thanks.' Liza accepted it gratefully.

'Now, how are you going to get to the bus wi' that box?'

'I'll have to carry it, a few yards at a time,' Liza said ruefully. It would be a long, hard haul.

Mrs Garbutt winked. 'Harry Sims will be round the back door afore long.' He was the milkman. 'He'll give you a lift.'

Liza hugged her, then went to see her employer. Mrs Fanshaw dug into her purse and counted out ten shillings. She handed them over with a baleful glare. 'More than you deserve after the trouble you've caused. You'll come to a bad end. And don't ask for a reference because you won't get one.'

Liza took the money. 'Thank you.' She tried to look as if she did not care about the lack of a reference. 'Goodbye, Mrs Fanshaw.' The woman turned her back and Liza went on her way.

Harry Sims, round of face and body, took her and her box

on to his float and slapped his horse's rump. As he carried them along he shouted, 'Milk-oh!' He dipped into his churn to fill the jugs as they were brought out to him. Liza shared her bread and cheese with him and he gave her a cup of milk.

The open bus took her into Newcastle and its conductor hauled the box down for her: 'There y'are, bonny lass.'

'Thank you.' Liza looked around her, more cheerful now she was nearer home. She did not relish telling her mother that she had been dismissed but knew that Kitty would not blame her.

Another bus drew in beside her. Its passengers climbed down and one of them was a girl two or three years older than herself. She, too, had a box that the conductor lifted down for her. Liza smiled at her. 'Changing your job, like me?'

The other girl grimaced. 'Oh, aye. The job was all reet and the hoose was all reet but there was nowt for miles! Not a music-hall or owt, nowt! So I walked oot this mornin'. They said, "What aboot working your notice, Bridie?", but Ah said, "Ah cannae stand another day here," and Ah came away.'

Liza hesitated. She was nearly home, but suppose . . . 'They'll be looking for somebody, then.'

'Aye, they will.'

'Where is it?'

'The Grange.' Then Bridie stared at her. 'Are ye thinking o' gannin' up there?'

'Aye.' If they needed a girl urgently they might overlook one or two things.

'You're a bit young and on the small side,' Bridie said doubtfully.

'How do I get there?' Liza said firmly. Five minutes later she and her box were on another bus.

'I'm going to the Grange,' she told the conductor, and repeated the directions Bridie had given her.

'Right y'are, lass,' and he told the driver. Five minutes later the first drops of rain splashed on to the windows. This bus was not open but by the time they set her down at the gates of the house the spots had become a downpour. Liza, heart sinking, climbed down reluctantly. 'Run up and get in where it's dry!' the conductor called.

'Thank you!' Liza realised he thought she had a job at the house. The bus drove on and she and her box were left alone on an empty road under the rain. On one side, beyond a quarter-mile of meadow, lay the North Sea. On the other, distantly vague in the rain, rose the Cheviot Hills. Liza stared at the desolate landscape that was Northumberland on a dismal wet day. She was a town girl. For most of her life the only grass she had seen had been in a churchyard. This was a foreign land to her.

The house and its grounds were surrounded by a stone wall. Wrought-iron gates opened on to a long drive that led up to the Grange, standing grey and grim. There was no gatekeeper's lodge and the gates looked not to have been closed for months, if ever. Grass grew tall around them. Liza quailed, then told herself she had not come all this way to give up now. She wiped water from her eyes to peer at the house. She knew she could not carry her box all that way so she dragged it inside the gate and into some bushes where it could not be seen from the road. She hesitated over leaving it, but did so because she had to. There was nothing of value in it, but it held all she had.

She walked up through the puddles to the Grange. She was wearing her best shoes – in fact, the only ones she had – but they leaked, and an old felt hat that had been her mother's, which sat soddenly on her damp hair. The house was a dozen times the size of Mrs Fanshaw's, but there were still only three steps up to the front door. Liza found that cheering

– not much to wash – but the house itself less so: it looked in need of a coat of paint and the curtains were drab. But if there was a position to be had she would not care about that. She climbed the steps and tapped at the massive oak door. Then she saw the handle set into the stone at one side and pulled it. She heard nothing for a minute or so, then the door opened silently on oiled hinges.

The man who stood there was tall and spare, in black jacket and trousers with a knife-edge crease. His sandy hair was neatly brushed, his long face forbidding. He looked Liza over, from the soggy, shapeless hat to the down-at-heel shoes. 'Aye?'

'I've come about the job, sir, in your house.'

'It is not my house. This is the residence of Mr Gresham. I am Mr Gillespie, the butler. And what job are you talking about?' He spoke with a Scottish accent and did not put Liza at her ease. But her mother had warned her: 'In a big house the butler is next to God Almighty.'

She brushed wet hair from her face with the back of her hand. 'I met this lass in Newcastle and she said—'

'Oh, aye.' Gillespie nodded. 'That would be Bridie.'

'Yes, sir.'

'Well, a lass like you has no business coming to the front door.' He frowned down at her. 'Go round to the back.' And he shut the door.

Liza retraced her steps. As she looked back down the drive she saw a ship far out at sea, a rough sea under the rain. The steamer trailed a long plume of smoke and Liza was reminded of her father. The thought of him and his love for her, then of her mother, put heart into her. She walked determinedly round the house to the rear. There were two doors, one large by a window that looked into a kitchen – Liza glimpsed women moving behind the steamed-up glass. The other was narrow and open, and Gillespie stood just inside. He said grudgingly, 'Ye'd better come in,' and Liza followed him into a small office. There was a table and an upright chair, a shelf with a number of ledgers and a fireplace with a glowing coal fire. This was known as the butler's pantry.

Gillespie sat on the chair and took a notebook, pen and ink from a drawer in the table. He hooked steel spectacles on to his ears and began: 'Name? Age? Nearly fourteen?' He peered over the spectacles. 'You're not very big.'

'I'm strong,' Liza protested.

'Are ye now?' He sniffed and went back to his book. 'What work have you been doing?'

'I want to be a lady's maid.'

'Oh, aye! You and a lot more! You'll have to wait a few years for that.'

'That's what I meant: one day,' Liza said meekly. 'Now I'll do anything.'

'So you say. Previous experience? References?'

Liza tried to evade the latter: 'I worked for Mrs Fanshaw.' She gave the address in Tynemouth.

Gillespie noted it. 'Anyone else?'

'No, sir, but my mother taught me a lot. She worked in big houses.'

'Let me see your reference,' Gillespie said, hand outstretched.

Liza swallowed and said miserably, 'I haven't got one.' She tried to explain, 'Her niece – I'd known her at school and—' How could she put it? 'We didn't get on. She caused trouble for me.'

Gillespie's outstretched hand was up now, signalling silence. 'Are you saying you were dismissed without a reference?'

Liza could only admit it. 'Aye, sir, but—'

The hand was up again. 'How long had you been there?'

'Four weeks, sir.'

Gillespie rubbed his face. He laid down pen and spectacles and shut the notebook. 'So you've had only one position and that was with Mrs Fanshaw. You were dismissed after only four weeks without a reference. Your only knowledge of the work in a house like this is what you've learned from your mother.' He, like many in his position, had seen the results of that before, in girls who thought they knew the work but had to be taught all over again. 'Is that correct?'

'Aye.' Liza could not deny it. 'But that lass tripped me when I was carrying a tray and then Piggy trampled all over my clean step—'

The hand was up again and Gillespie was shaking his head, 'Oh, aye, I expect you have an excuse.'

There was a rap at the door. 'Mr Gillespie? Mr Gresham would like a word, if you please.'

'Oh, aye, I'll be there right away.' He got up from the chair. 'Wait,' he told Liza.

George Gresham was in the library, wrapped in a rug before a roaring fire, a listless, wasted old man. 'Ah, there you are, Gillespie. Pour me a whisky, please, there's a good chap.'

'The doctor said not until after dinner, sir,' the butler remonstrated mildly.

'Never mind the doctor. It's my whisky, not his. And he only wants me alive because he knows he'll get no money from me when I'm dead.'

Gillespie had made his token protest, as he did every day, and now poured the weak whisky and soda. 'Would there be anything else, sir?'

Old Gresham waved a skeletal hand, and Gillespie left with a stiff little bow. As he returned to his pantry he reflected that his difficulty in getting and keeping staff was down to the gloom of the house. There was always a hush about the place, as if its occupants were in the presence of death, which they were. Frederick Gresham was dying.

And this little girl, hardly more than a child, would not do. She was too small, inexperienced, probably undisciplined from the tale she told. If he took her on she would prove another Bridie, here today, gone tomorrow . . .

The ship Liza had seen had come from the Baltic and was bound for the Tyne with a cargo of grain. The smoke she trailed came not from her funnel but her hold where a fire had raged. William Morgan now climbed the ladder up to the deck with an unconscious man on his back. Hands came to take his burden from him as he reached the head of the ladder. Relieved of it, he swung his legs over the hatch coaming to stand on the deck where the canvas hoses snaked, fat with seawater. 'It looks to be out but soak it down,' he told the men who were playing the jets of water into the hold. Then he grinned. 'Although the weather's doing a good job of that anyway.' He wiped off the rain that washed over his face, which was grimy from the fire below.

He had just turned nineteen and this was his first voyage as mate. He was the most junior officer aboard but his captain was impressed with the tall young man, and even more so now when he reported on the bridge: 'Gallagher was overcome by the smoke but I brought him up. I think the fire's out but I'll go down again when the smoke clears and see what damage has been done.'

'Well done,' his captain said.

Gillespie shoved open the door of his pantry and strode in. Liza stood bedraggled where he had left her, a pool of water around her feet. He remembered when he was twelve years old and in his first pair of shoes, leaving home for the first time to work in the big house. 'I'll give you a week's trial,' he said. 'Now I suppose you'll have to go for your box.'

'I hid it down by the gate,' Liza said, in a small voice.

Gillespie sent one of the gardeners, who had been sitting in a potting shed watching the rain, to fetch it on a barrow.

That night Liza wrote a postcard to her mother: 'I have a better position now in a big house. This is my address.'

Before the week was out Gillespie had decided to keep her on. He found her eager to work, hungry to learn and well trained by her mother. Before the month was out old Gresham had died. In the autumn his heir and nephew, Jonathan Gresham, returned from South America with Vanessa, his wife, and their children. The house came to life with a new young regime. The following year Jonathan rented a house in London for the Season and Liza was one of the maids who travelled south to work there through the summer.

Jasper Barbour had reached man's estate and also come to work in London. He had learned his trade in the back-streets of Liverpool and left to seek richer pickings and to avoid a growing reputation. In his first week in the capital he accosted a lone, elderly man in a dark and empty alley. Jasper was not tall but a thick-set, powerful man, brute-faced and fearsome in the gloom. He hefted a club and demanded, 'Give us your purse.' He expected it to be handed over, as it always had been before, his victims fearful for their lives.

But the old man, too, had a weapon, a walking-stick, and defied him: 'You scoundrel! I'll give you nothing!' He lashed out with the stick. Jasper was taken by surprise. He was too late to avoid the blow but deflected it so that it landed on his shoulder. He grunted with pain and rage, and madness gripped him. He beat down the walking-stick with his club and felled the old man, then belaboured him until the body lay still under his blows. He stooped over it, searched for and found the wallet. He took out the money, tossed aside the wallet and walked away.

He went to a squalid tavern near the room he rented. The men in there had already summed him up as dangerous and gave him room. The young woman serving behind the bar was small-waisted and big-busted in a grubby blouse. She wore a beer-stained white apron over her dark skirt, and had a bold eye. 'Give us a pint, Flora,' he ordered. He tossed some coins on to the counter, took a long pull at the beer and wiped his mouth on the back of his hand. This was only the second time he had seen Flora, but he knew what she wanted. He looked her over deliberately and saw her breathe faster.

'Quiet in here tonight,' he said. There were only a dozen in the bar and Flora was listlessly polishing glasses. She moistened her lips and nodded.

'So come out wi' me and see a bit o' life.'

'I'll have to ask him.'

'Ask be buggered. Tell him. I'll make you a better offer than he will.'

She went to the publican, taking off her apron. 'I'm knocking off for the night.'

He scowled at her. 'Wotcha mean? Ye can't walk out whenever you like.'

'Aye, she can,' Jasper said.

The publican glared at him, but shrugged and turned his back. Flora tossed her head and reached for her coat. Outside, her arm in his, she asked Jasper, 'What's this better offer you promised?'

'You'll find out.'

He took her to a music-hall, then to a succession of pubs and bought her supper. At one point they peered in at a tattooist's window. 'Go on!' she challenged him. 'Get a picture done on your chest.' He laughed but had it done: a naked female with the name Flora beneath. She almost blushed.

And at the end he took her to his bed.

Liza did not read the newspaper report of the murder in the alley, did not cross the path of Jasper Barbour, but one day his life would be bound up with hers.

6

Flora panted and moaned with passion. Her discarded clothes lay with Jasper's in a trail from the door to the big bed. A distant clock chimed one in the morning and he sighed and was still. Their coupling done she lay beside him. 'What did you get tonight, then?' she asked.

'A box wi' a lot o' jewellery and a purse full o' sovereigns.'

'Let's have a look.' Flora rolled, naked, off the bed in a flailing of legs as Jasper watched. She padded downstairs to the hall, picked up the leather Gladstone bag and carried it back to the bedroom.

'Come here,' Jasper said.

Flora glanced sideways at him, narrow-eyed. 'You wait a minute.' She up-ended the bag to empty its contents on to the carpet. 'Ooh! Look!' She picked out a gold necklace with a ruby pendant and slipped it over her head. The jewel gleamed in the valley between her breasts. 'There's some good stuff here.' She shook the purse and counted the coins that fell out: 'Twenty!'

Jasper reached for a bottle that stood by the bed, pulled out its cork with his teeth and drank from the neck. Now Flora climbed on to the bed again. 'What can I have?' she wheedled.

'No jewellery, I've told you that afore. If you go waltzing around wi' diamonds hung all over you, people would wonder.'

Flora pouted, and reached out a hand to fondle him. 'Well, can I have a housemaid in here to do some o' the work about this place? Every house in the street has a maid and some o' them has a cook an' all.'

Jasper had made – stolen – a lot of money over the last two years, and a few months before, they had moved into this house, detached and with rooms for servants. It was one in a street of middle-class dwellings, the homes of solicitors, accountants, a doctor or two. Now he said, 'No maid. I won't have one because there's too much to be seen. Gawd knows what she'd find when she was cleaning.' Most of his loot he sold to a fence and banked the proceeds, but some items he kept. There was a handsome clock, an oil painting of a nude, and others.

Flora tried again: 'The neighbours might talk 'cause we haven't got anybody.'

'No, they won't. Not them. They'll keep themselves to themselves like they always do. You just smile nicely and say, "My husband works in the City," in your posh voice, and they'll be happy. Now, come here.' And he dragged her down to him.

'Why, they've not been properly married for years!' Ada's voice was lowered but Cecily, standing in her father's study, could hear the maid clearly. She stood still, dressed in only a thin robe but warmed by the morning sunlight streaming through the windows.

Jane, newly up from the country and being shown the ropes by Ada, said 'Ooh! Really?'

'Well, they've got separate rooms. He's always going off for days at a time. He's been in France for the past week, supposed to be on business. I know what sort o' business *that* is. And she has men come here. They stay in one of the guest rooms so it all looks right and proper, but we've seen them going back to it in the mornings.'

'When the cat's away . . .' Jane sniggered.

'. . . get another Tom,' Ada finished. They both laughed, then she went on, 'That's done.' They had lit the fire in the breakfast room and now returned to the kitchen.

Cecily was no more than irritated. She had overheard that kind of conversation more than once over the years. She knew that whatever her parents did was right, and those who whispered behind their backs were prissy or envious. Now she decided that if *she* ever had the ordering of this household Ada would go. She looked in the bookcase, found the volume she wanted and carried it upstairs to the schoolroom. It had once been the nursery, but the nurse had long since departed and Cecily, now fifteen, was taught by a governess. The latest in a succession of appointments was Miss Estelle Beaumont. She had told her pupil to write an essay on the Norman Conquest but the subject bored Cecily. She had other things to do with her time so she would copy out a chunk of the encyclopedia.

Estelle Beaumont was slender, comely, shy and of good family, but she was without money and had been alone in the world since the death of her father. In the schoolroom that morning she read the hastily written essay and ventured, 'It is – scribbled, rather.'

'Well, you've read it so it's clear enough,' Cecily said carelessly.

'And it seems to be a copy of the entry in the encyclopedia.'

Cecily reddened. 'It'll be right, then, so what does it matter? And don't you dare accuse me of cheating. That's just quoting.'

If Estelle hadn't known before why there had been a

succession of governesses in this house, she did now. She tried another tack: 'Sit up, dear, straight back. It's most important for your posture.' She demonstrated, advancing her shapely bosom. It was at that point that the schoolroom door opened and Charles Spencer entered.

'Daddy!' Cecily shrieked. She jumped up and threw her arms around him. 'When did you get home?'

'Just now.' He held her, but his eyes were looking over her head at Estelle. 'Good day to you, Miss Beaumont.'

She bobbed him a curtsey. 'Good day, sir. I trust you had a comfortable journey.'

'I did.'

'Take me to the park, Daddy,' Cecily said excitedly. 'Or for a drive. I'm bored with this horrid old schoolwork. *Please!*'

But Charles disengaged her arms from round his neck. 'I'm sorry, but I have to go to the Exchange. Business, you know. Now, you be a good girl and go on with your lessons. You're lucky to have a pretty governess like Miss Beaumont.' That made Estelle blush, and Cecily scowled. She returned to her desk as he left, with a last, lingering glance at the governess.

Deprived of the company of her adored father, Cecily took revenge on the nearest and easiest victim. She determined to make Miss Beaumont's life a misery, and did so. She flounced, argued, sneered, and when threatened that she would be reported to her mother, replied confidently, 'Mama won't do anything.'

And Mama didn't. 'My daughter is very sensitive and highly strung. She only needs sympathetic handling.'

Estelle cried herself to sleep, praying that the morrow would bring an improvement. But it did not.

A week had gone by and Cecily was sitting at the window of the schoolroom, idly watching the traffic below. Her governess had gone down to Charles Spencer's study to fetch a volume from his bookcase – Cecily had refused to go. Suddenly the schoolroom door burst open. Miss Beaumont turned a tear-stained face to Cecily, then ran into her bedroom next door. Cecily heard her racking sobs and sat still, taken aback, for a while. Then, cautiously, she approached the bedroom door and peeped in: Miss Beaumont was kneeling by her narrow bed in an attitude of prayer, her handkerchief pressed to her eyes. Her shoulders shook.

Cecily went to stand by her. 'What's wrong?'

'I've been told – to leave. Pack and get out – today.'

'Why?'

Estelle had gone to the study and had found Charles there. She had turned to leave but he insisted she stay. He had paid her compliments, then held her. Estelle had been living on her nerves for the past week, yearned for support, sympathy and affection, and thought she had found them in his arms.

Then his wife had entered. Millicent had summed up the situation at a glance: 'Your light o' love can't live here. I won't have it. You can pay her a week's notice and turn her out. Goodbye, Miss Beaumont.'

'I don't know how I will find a new position,' Estelle wept, 'because I haven't a reference. I've nowhere to go.' She took down her suitcase from the top of the wardrobe and began to pack.

'Can't you go to a hotel?' Cecily asked, with the cruel innocence of youth.

Estelle shook her head. 'I only have a few shillings, and the pay I was given today.' She opened her hand to show a single gold sovereign. 'I'll have to go to the workhouse.'

Cecily had heard frightening tales of the workhouse, but with the comforting knowledge that that fate was for others, not for her and her kind. Now, though, she was talking to someone bound for that institution, with its drab, shabby uniform, its regimentation and gruel. 'Will you really?'

Estelle nodded, white-faced. 'I must pack.'

'I'll help you.' Cecily collected and folded garments, emptied the wardrobe. Now there would be no governess – at least for a while. Then she realised she would miss Estelle, and felt a wave of compassion. She went to the money-box on the schoolroom mantelpiece and opened it – strictly against the rules. She emptied it on to her desk, counted the contents, then held out the coins to Estelle. 'There you are. That's nearly five pounds. It should help.'

'Oh, no. Really, I couldn't,' the governess protested feebly.

But Cecily was firm. 'You must. I want you to have it. Where's your purse?' And she stowed the money in it.

Then she had another idea and ran down to her mother's boudoir. She ignored the bookcase full of novels, which was locked, and went to the writing bureau. There she found some notepaper headed with her mother's name, Mrs Charles Spencer, and their address. Cecily sat down at the bureau, took up a pen and wrote, in her best copperplate, 'Miss Beaumont has been an excellent governess. I cannot speak too highly of her devotion to her duties, her skill and knowledge. I would recommend her to anyone.'

That was quoted word for word from a reference Cecily had seen when her mother had given it to a departing cook a month or so ago. Now she signed it, 'Cecily Spencer', took it upstairs and gave it to Estelle.

Estelle read it. 'But I can't present this. If someone writes—'

'They won't,' said Cecily, confidently. 'And if they do they will write to me and Mother will ask me about it. I'll tell her why I did it and she will write back confirming every word, rather than air a family row in public.' She was quoting Millicent again.

Estelle put away the reference, carried her case downstairs and out of the front door. Cecily went with her, waited with her until she was able to hail a cab, then helped her in. Estelle thanked her. 'You've been so kind.' Then the driver shook the reins and the horse hauled the cab into the stream of traffic.

A few days later Cecily's parents went out to a dinner party. 'Leave out the whisky,' Charles told the butler, 'and I'll make myself a nightcap when we return. There's no need for anyone to wait up.'

His wife waved a hand at the clothes she had tossed aside when she changed, and ordered her maid, 'Clear these things away. I'll undress myself tonight, but see that Miss Cecily goes to bed on time. Then you can retire yourself.' The last duty should have been carried out by the governess, but she had yet to be replaced.

When they had left Cecily went from her bedroom to her mother's. There she found her mother's keys, a small bunch dropped into a drawer of her dressing-table. She ran down to the boudoir with them, and unlocked the bookcase. Inside was Millicent's collection of risqué novels. Cecily selected one and carried it upstairs. It was under her pillow and she was tucked up in bed when the maid came to her.

'It's all right, Mary,' said Cecily, 'I'm in bed, but clear these things away.' She waved a hand at the clothes she had dropped on to the floor. Mary did as she was told. 'Goodnight, Miss.' She turned off the gas-light and left, closing the door behind her. Cecily slipped out of bed to light the gas again, then climbed back into bed, fished out the novel and settled down to read.

Two hours passed, and she heard the clock in the hall

chime midnight when she realised she had dozed. That would never do: the novel had to be returned. She pulled on her dressing-gown and flitted down the stairs to the hall and thence to her mother's boudoir.

Horace, the second footman, was a tall young man who liked a drink now and again, but alcohol was not allowed in the servants' hall. Now he stole down the back stairs in his trousers, shirt and socks. He passed through the green baize door into the front of the house and made for the drawing room, where he knew he would find the whisky decanter. He padded through the gloom of the hall and had started to open the door when he realised there was already a light on in the room. He almost fled, thinking his master or the butler might be there, but then he saw that the light was from one of the new-fangled electric torches; they had only been in the shops for a year. It rested on the table and its beam was trained on the sideboard. A man was silhouetted against it and he was shoving items of silver into a Gladstone bag.

Horace was a simple-minded young man, prepared to drink his employer's whisky but also to defend his possessions. He flung open the door, charged in and grappled with the intruder. He had taken the man by surprise and almost wrestled him to the floor, but then a fist smashed into his face and his grip relaxed. The burglar pulled away and started for the window he had forced and left open. But Horace had not finished. He threw out a hand to seize the thief's clothing and caught the neck of his shirt. He hung on as the man rained blows on him and tried to pull away. Then the shirt ripped apart from the neck, and Horace fell to the floor.

The burglar was free. He glanced back before he scrambled out of the window, and saw a young girl standing in the doorway, staring at him. Leaving the Gladstone bag where

it lay, he yanked aside the curtains and threw himself outside.
He ran, with screams shrilling behind him, tearing apart the
silence of the night.

Cecily stood in the doorway, open-mouthed. She had emerged
from her mother's boudoir just as Horace had tackled the
burglar. She had seen the open door, heard the commotion
and run along the hall. She was just in time to see, by the
light of the torch, the intruder: his chest was bare and on it
was a tattooed portrait of a voluptuous beauty. Now she ran
to the window and peered out but saw no one, only heard the
faint hammering of running feet that faded to nothing as she
listened.

Cecily turned back into the room to attend to Horace.
She had hardly knelt beside him when the butler appeared,
panting, a dressing-gown over his nightshirt and a poker in
his hand. Another footman and two of the maids, one of
them Mary, were at his heels. 'I woke and came down to
see if Mother had returned,' Cecily explained, 'then heard
scuffling in here and looked in. Horace was struggling with
a burglar. He was very brave and hung on but the man
escaped.'

She was lauded by the butler for her efforts, then sent off
to bed: 'You can leave Horace to us, Miss Cecily. Mary will
come with you and see you settled.'

'What were you doing down here at near one in the morning?'
the butler snapped at Horace.

The footman was bruised and bloody, and not a good liar.
The best he could manage was: 'I couldn't sleep. Had an
earache.' He had one now, left by the battering he had taken
from the burglar, and held a hand to his ear. 'I got up and
went for a walk around, then thought I heard a noise in the

drawing room. I dashed in and caught him at it, but he gave me the slip.'

The butler said, 'Aye.' He had a shrewd idea of what Horace had been up to. 'You did well. The master will be pleased.'

Jasper burst into his house and slammed the door with a crash that echoed up the street of decorous and respectable citizens. One or two crept sleepily to their windows to squint out into the night but saw nothing. The neighbourhood sank back into its usual quiet.

Inside the house Jasper was raging. He panted up the stairs to the bedroom and snarled at Flora, 'Fetch me a drink!' She slid out of bed and ran downstairs to do his bidding.

When she returned with a bottle and two glasses he was sitting on the bed, his torn shirt and waistcoat lying at his feet. She said, 'My! What happened to them?'

He cursed, then explained: 'Some bloody fool came in when I was going through the drawers, tried to get hold o' me. He ripped the shirt off me as I come away. Then there was some stupid little cow screaming the place down. I had to get out quick. I lost the bag and got nothing! Here, give us that.' He ignored the glass, set the neck of the bottle to his lips and swallowed. Flora waited until he was calmer, then slid her arms round him. He muttered a final imprecation, then said, 'I wish I'd done for the pair o' them.' He turned to her and thrust her back on to the bed.

The next day Charles called all the servants together and praised Horace, then gave him a gold sovereign. He doubted Cecily's explanation; she had not waited up for him and his wife before. 'You should have been in bed, Miss, not wandering about the house in the dark.'

But Millicent defended her daughter: 'Nonsense! I think she was very brave.'

There Charles agreed with her and handed out another sovereign to Cecily.

It was at the end of the following week that she persuaded her father to take her strolling in Hyde Park. She walked under her parasol, imitating her mother, and watched to see if any heads turned her way. There were guardsmen in red coats, nursemaids by the dozen, pushing prams or accompanying young children, ladies and gentlemen in scores. There were even two policemen patrolling ponderously, side by side. Then, out of the crowd, a tall, hard-faced man appeared. The woman on his arm was expensively dressed, but blowsy.

'Father! Cecily said clearly. 'That is the burglar who tried to steal from us last week!' She pointed a finger.

'Him?' Charles said, startled.

The policemen paused in their pacing. 'What was that, Miss?' one asked.

The man was still walking towards them. Cecily was hidden from him by the taller men. 'I saw that man burgling our house last week,' she repeated.

Charles stepped into the man's path. 'A moment, sir, if you please. I want to talk to you.'

'What the hell d'you want?'

'My daughter saw you stealing from my house a week ago,' Charles charged him.

For a second Jasper did not associate this poised, fashionably dressed fifteen-year-old with the girl in the dressing-gown, her hair down her back. Then he recognised her – and, at the same time, saw the policemen close in on him, cutting off escape. He determined to bluff it out. He laughed. 'That's a lot o' nonsense! When did you say this was?'

'A week ago today, last Wednesday,' Charles answered, sounding uncertain now: perhaps Cecily was mistaken.

'That settles it, then,' Jasper claimed. 'I was at home with my wife all that evening, wasn't I, love?'

'Course he was,' Flora backed him up, stoutly. 'I never heard the like, accusing an honest man on the word o' some empty-headed young lass.' She tossed her head.

'Are you sure, Miss?' one of the policemen asked Cecily.

'O' course she isn't.' Jasper grinned, but his eyes glared at her. 'Little lasses make mistakes so I'll say no more about it.'

Little lass! 'I haven't made a mistake!' Cecily replied hotly. 'He is the burglar and he has a picture of a slut tattooed on his chest. Look and see.'

'Will you come with us to the station so we can confirm what you say, sir,' one of the policemen said. It was not a question.

Jasper knew it and ran, but the crowds hindered him. Charles gave chase, shouting, 'Stop! Thief!' The cry was taken up and a strolling dandy leaped on Jasper, tripping him, and they both crashed to the ground.

Charles was on him at once, and then came the policemen, with handcuffs. 'All right, sir. We've got him.'

On the day of the trial Cecily received a letter from Estelle Beaumont, her erstwhile governess, in which she said she had secured a position with a good family in Hampshire and was happy. She thanked Cecily for all she had done and the girl went with her father to the court in a happy frame of mind. Flora lied determinedly to save Jasper, but the evidence of Horace and Cecily, particularly her knowledge of the tattoo, was damning.

Jasper was sent down for twelve years and was lucky it was not more. When sentence was pronounced he glared at Cecily and bawled, 'You little bitch! I'll see my day with you! I'll swing for you!' His curses came back to her as he was dragged down to the cells.

They were echoed by Flora, but Cecily gave her a cold glance of contempt and turned her back. 'Can we go home now, Father?'

'Of course.' In the cab he said, 'You did very well.' Then, 'Did his threats upset you?'

'He'll feel differently after twelve years. And, anyway, he'll be an old man then.'

She did not lose any sleep over it and soon forgot the affair.

Jasper would not.

7

'Ah! You villain! I shall not surrender myself to you!' Liza, soon to be seventeen and playing the part of Lady Angela, clasped her hands to her bosom in anguish. The audience cheered. The sketch was being performed in the hall at the Grange. The members of staff without parts squatted on the stairs while the Gresham family, parents and three of their four children, sat on chairs in front of them. The stage was the floor of the hall, the ten-foot width of it, flanked by 'wings' of temporarily rigged curtains.

'You have no choice,' the villain sneered. 'You must wed me or take the consequences.' Gillespie, in false beard, pointed his pistol and the audience booed.

'Never!' cried Liza. 'Death before dishonour!'

'Ooh!' wailed family and staff alike.

'You reckoned without me!' Toby, the Greshams' eighteen-year-old eldest son, home from school for Christmas and dressed as a naval officer, burst from the wings to cheers. He was popular with all the staff, tall and good-looking, with a ready smile. Now he stumbled on a trailing curtain but recovered to say, 'Take that!' He fired his pistol but the cap only fizzled. Gillespie clutched at his chest, then fell – carefully but flat.

Liza threw out a hand. 'Saved! My hero!'

And the curtain came down, to rise again so that the cast could acknowledge the applause.

'Author!' Jonathan Gresham bellowed, and Gillespie took a bow on his own. Then Jonathan went on: 'You all did well. First class. But an extra cheer for the leading lady.'

Liza blushed. This was the happiest Christmas she had ever known, but it was the culmination of three happy years, a time when she had worked hard but taken pleasure in it. She had found the Grange was not so isolated as she had thought and she had come to love the countryside. There was a village only ten minutes away, with a church and a shop but no pub. She had guessed that that was why Bridie had left. Liza had learned to dance. In the evenings all the younger members of the servants' hall would practise their steps to Gillespie's fiddle. It was their sole entertainment in the winter.

Soon after Gillespie had taken her on he had announced in the kitchen: 'Mrs Gresham wants an assistant for Madame Jeanne, somebody to do sewing two days a week. Any takers?'

The staff were seated around the table for the evening meal, the butler at the head. He glanced up and down the lines of faces, but they avoided his eye. One said, 'Not me. That Frenchie is ower fussy and bad-tempered.' Vanessa Gresham's French maid was a motherly woman of forty, dumpy and smiling, but with high standards and an acid tongue for those who did not measure up to them. She was not present because she was attending her mistress on a visit to another part of the county. Gillespie sighed. He was reluctant to order one of them to do the job, knowing there would be argument and excuses and probably a blazing row with Madame Jeanne.

Then Liza said, from the foot of the table, 'Can I try, please, Mr Gillespie?' In her excitement and embarrassment at speaking out in front of them all it came out in a squeak. But it eased the tension. There was laughter and a call of, 'You sound like a little mouse, Liza.'

She blushed, but the butler grinned at her. 'You can try. Report to Madame Jeanne when she returns tomorrow.'

'Thank you, sir.'

The others smiled because she had taken the job none of them wanted, but Liza was delighted. She believed this was a step on her way to becoming a lady's maid one day, for which sewing and dressmaking were essential skills. Would her needlework satisfy Madame Jeanne?

The Frenchwoman had the same doubts and pursed her lips. 'We shall see.' After two weeks she told Liza, 'You will do. You have a lot to learn but I think that will come.' To Gillespie she said, 'The little one is ver' good,' and at her urging he asked Vanessa Gresham if Liza might be sent to learn dressmaking one day in each week. Since then she had spent Thursdays in Newcastle, setting out at dawn and returning near to midnight. But she learned, to Madame Jeanne's satisfaction.

Now Liza felt at home, happy in her work and sure she would progress. She smiled as the others gathered round the actors, congratulating them. But there was work to be done. Gillespie pulled off his false beard and called, 'Now then, lads! Let's have this place put to rights!' The family had retired so the footmen turned to, carrying away the chairs. The maids took down the curtains and swept the hall, all save Liza, who went to her room to change out of her costume, one of Vanessa Gresham's old dresses, tailored to fit her.

The green-baize door leading to the servants' quarters lay at the end of a passage that ran past the side of the stairs. There she was out of sight of the hall – and Toby waylaid her. He stepped out of a doorway into her path, one hand behind his back. Liza halted. 'Excuse me, Master Toby.' She tried to step out of his way, as a servant should, but he moved in front of her again and brought out his hand from behind his back. It held a sprig of mistletoe and he flourished it above her head. 'Happy Christmas, Liza.' He kissed her.

Liza was dumbfounded: she had not expected this. She was also momentarily speechless because it had been no peck on the cheek but a passionate kiss on her lips. She stepped back. 'Master Toby!' she gasped.

They were both flushed. 'I had to do that. I've admired you for so long, Liza,' he said.

'Don't be silly, Master Toby,' she whispered. 'You mustn't.'

'I can't help it.' He took her hand. 'I love you.'

The instinct that had made Liza whisper told her now that this was dangerous. 'Please! If your mother or father find out I'll lose my position.' She tried to pull away but he tossed the mistletoe aside and held both her hands.

'Don't turn me away,' he pleaded. 'We can be careful and no one will know. Please. Don't you like me?'

That was the trouble. She did. 'Yes, but—'

'All I ask is that I can see you, now and then. You can trust me.'

She thought she could. And she had known him for three years; they had grown up together. Liza wavered. It would only be for another week and then he would go back to boarding-school until Easter. He would have got over his crush by then. Where was the harm?

'But you will be careful?' she said.

'I promise. Kiss me again.'

She laughed. 'Get away with you.' But she brushed his lips with hers, then skipped past him. She snatched up the mistletoe from the floor, because that was part of her job, then passed through the green-baize door and out of his sight.

Safe in her room, she laughed over the incident. She had been kissed by boys before but they had been members of staff, or she had met them on her day off in Blyth or

Newcastle when out with another girl. Toby was different, the son of her employer. Her fear of dismissal was real. She had heard of plenty of cases where a maid had been found with one of the sons of the house and been turned out immediately.

That was a sobering thought, but she was young and there was a frisson of excitement in thinking about Toby.

He was careful, as he had promised. He never touched her or talked to her when any of the family might see them. It was an affair of quick kisses and embraces in dark, out-of-the-way corners. Until he asked her, 'Will you give me something of yours? I'm going back to school tomorrow. Can I have some small keepsake? Please?' She gave him her clean handkerchief and he tucked it away in his pocket. 'I'll treasure it until I see you again.'

He held her in his arms until she detached herself gently. 'Goodbye, Toby.'

'Until Easter.'

The next day she stood on the front steps, just one of the servants gathered there to see him off, smart in his tailored overcoat. He lingered before her perhaps a heartbeat longer than he had for the others before he moved on, but she avoided his gaze, knowing it would bring on her blushes, and no one noticed. He took his place in the carriage next to his father, the coachman cracked his whip and the twin greys trotted down the drive.

Liza saw him go with relief. She would no longer have to worry that they might be discovered. But there was also a sense of loss and she was miserable all that day. Still, she consoled herself, it was all over now. And she worked harder.

But it was not over. Toby came home at Easter, finished with school for good, and sought her out before he had been in the house an hour. He found her standing on a stepladder, hanging curtains she had made. She squeaked as he gripped her waist and he said softly, 'Ssh!'

'Don't!' Liza whispered frantically.

'Come down, then.' He lifted her off the steps and set her on her feet. 'Aren't you pleased to see me?'

She was, but demurred. 'Not if you misbehave.'

'I won't,' he said, then promptly did.

Liza pulled away from his kisses but stayed in his arms. 'You promised,' she reproached him.

'I promised to be careful and I will be.' He stooped to her again but this time she was ready and put a hand over his mouth.

'No more!' she said firmly. 'Go about your business and let me attend to mine.'

He laughed but obeyed. From then on, however, they met surreptitiously at least once every day. As the summer blossomed they ranged further afield. Toby found an old abandoned summer-house in the woods around the house. When Liza had time off she would meet him there. It was approached by a wide track so they could see anyone coming when they were still a long way off, but Toby had to slip out of the back only once. Then the approaching gardener had stopped short to cut down a dead tree; his horse dragged it away to be chopped into kindling. He did not see Liza, sitting quiet and still in the summer-house.

As the summer drew on, Toby became bolder. 'No!' she told him sharply.

'I'm sorry. I didn't mean to upset you, but . . .' he shook his head helplessly '. . . it's just that I love you. I want you to be mine for ever.'

'No, Toby, please,' Liza said unhappily.

But he would not be halted. 'I mean it. I've been trying for a long time to summon up the courage to ask. I want you to marry me.'

There it was, the question she herself had avoided. Would she wed Toby if he asked? He was handsome, she was flattered by his adoration, fond of him, knew she would live in comfort for the rest of her days. But—

'I'm sorry, Toby,' Liza said. 'I can't. I like you, but marriage—'

'Is there somebody else?'

She could have laughed at the idea that she might have carried on two clandestine affairs. 'No, there isn't.' And then, grasping the nettle, she went on, 'I don't want to see you like this again. It's not fair to you – or me. We must pretend that none of it ever happened.'

Then Liza left him, ran back to the house and up to her room and wept.

The pair tried to put their love behind them. Liza acted the part of the cheerful, smiling girl the rest of them knew, and Toby did not pursue her, but he wandered about with a long face until his father asked him testily, 'What's the matter with you? You're walking about as though you've lost a pound and found a shilling.'

'I'm bored,' Toby lied.

'Ah! Then we'd better find you something to do.' And Gresham told Vanessa, his wife, 'It's time he decided what to do with his life, or at least try a job or two to see what interests him.'

Toby spent a week in a shipping office, another dipping his toe into the deep waters of insurance, a third in a barrister's chambers. Then he went off by train to London. He returned a few days later. His father was pleased with the news he brought, his mother less so, but she told herself she had known he would fly the nest some day.

Later Toby told Liza. He stopped her in the hall. 'Oh, Toby!' she whispered.

'I have to talk to you, but only for a minute and not for much longer.' He paused. 'I just can't stand being in this house, seeing you every day and not being able to speak, look, touch.' He closed his eyes for a second, as if to blot out the sight of her. Then he opened them. 'I've decided to go away. I've been given a commission in the Royal Artillery at Woolwich.'

Liza stared at him, aghast. 'They could send you anywhere in the world! And you could be gone for years!'

'I know.' He shrugged. 'But I can't stay here.'

'I'll miss you.' Liza's eyes filled with tears. 'I can't marry you but I like you, I'm fond of you.'

He managed a grin. 'So there's no hope for me with you?' He read the answer in her shaken head, her tears.

Then the green-baize door flapped open and Gillespie came through from the servants' quarters, to see Toby making for the front door and Liza entering the drawing room. He assumed she had work to do in there and Toby was on his way out. And he was. The door slammed behind him and he strode off down the drive.

Liza, in the empty drawing room, dabbed her eyes. She was losing Toby, probably for good. For a moment she hesitated. Was this love? Should she run after him and tell him 'Yes!'? But when she was calmer she knew that she was not ready to spend the rest of her life with Toby.

The following days flew by and when they chanced to meet Toby would give her a casual smile and nod, as he did the other staff on passing. Then it was time for his departure and the servants lined the steps again, but Liza hid in her room at the top of the house. She did not dare to try to smile and bob a curtsey as he passed, was sure that either Toby or she would give the game away. Her room was at the front of the house on the top floor. She looked down on the open carriage standing on the drive and Toby surrounded by his family. Then he climbed in after his father, the carriage pulled away – and Toby looked up. Liza was too far away to read his expression but knew from the way his head turned that he was searching the windows of the house for her. His gaze lifted and she stepped back a pace, away from the window.

She knew then that he truly loved her.

'Are you telling me we're *broke*?' Millicent Spencer stared at her husband in disbelief. *'Penniless?'*

Charles sighed heavily. 'I am.'

The coachman had cracked his whip over the two bays and was driving the carriage along at a smart clip. The rain was now torrential, lashing against the windows. They were hastening because they were late for a dinner engagement. Charles had come home from his office to find his wife dressed and pacing the hall. He had changed hurriedly.

Now he said, staring out of the window, 'I didn't want to break the news like this but I haven't had a chance to tell you quietly. It's not the sort of thing you discuss in front of the servants.'

Millicent still could not, did not want to, believe it. 'Are you certain? It can't *all* be gone. There must be *something* left!' She clung to the strap by her head to steady herself when the carriage leaned over as it swung round a bend.

The coachman cracked his whip again: they were on the long straight stretch that followed the line of the railway cutting. It was a good road but a slick of rain, puddles and mud covered it.

Charles shook his head, still not meeting her gaze. 'Not what you mean by money. I've suffered some huge losses at Lloyds. The house will have to go, and the servants. We might be able to afford a cook, but that's all.'

Millicent saw now that he was haggard and grey. She realised this husband of hers was looking old, ill – and ashamed. She forgot their rows, his lovers and hers. She reached out to take his hand and said softly, 'I'm sure it wasn't your fault, just bad luck. We'll manage.'

He turned to her at last, grateful, but said, 'I'm so sorry.'

Then a dog ran out into the road. The horses swerved and the carriage smashed through the fence that ran alongside the railway cutting. The coachman and the footman, who had ridden behind on the carriage, were thrown clear as it slithered down the grassy bank but both lay still, dazed or unconscious. The doors burst open and Charles fell out as the wreckage came to a splintering halt, partly on the line, partly alongside it. He was shaken but conscious, and gazed about him blearily. Millicent had cried out once as she and Charles were tossed about inside the carriage but now she was silent.

He looked for her as he climbed to his feet. The horses lay on their sides, trapped by their harness, whinnying and threshing in panic. He called to them reassuringly as he tottered to the carriage, now upturned, wheels still spinning in the air, and the rain beat down on him. In seconds his hair was plastered to his skull but he knelt down heedlessly in the mud and crawled into the carriage.

His wife lay on what had been the roof. She was still and her eyes were closed. 'Millicent!' He could not tell if she was breathing, so he bent his head to her mouth to listen. Water dripped from his hair to splash cold on her face but she did not twitch. Still he could not hear her breathing but there was something else, a distant thrumming. In panic he forced his way out of the wreckage, dragging her with him. He hauled her out and clear of the track just before the train came. It passed within a yard of where he lay with his wife in his arms. The noise beat about him, the thunder of the engine and the squeal of the locked wheels as the driver braked. The smell of steam, coal smoke and oil wrapped around him.

The footman came to him, stumbling, a hand to his head. There was blood on his face, washed down there from the wound on his scalp. 'Run and fetch help,' Charles urged him. 'A doctor and an ambulance. I think your mistress is badly hurt.'

The man ran off and the coachman took his place. 'Anything I can do, or should I see to the horses, sir?'

'Yes, attend to them,' Charles said distractedly. He got out his handkerchief to mop his wife's face and realised she was being drenched. He shrugged out of his jacket and wrapped it round her, held her close. The train had stopped and the passengers had climbed out. Some were helping the coachman to cut the horses free and get them on to their feet while others gathered around the smashed carriage. 'Can you keep this crowd back?' Charles asked two men. They obeyed and he bent his head over Millicent again.

A doctor came, and then a horse-drawn ambulance. They all went to the hospital and Charles waited in a draughty annexe for more than an hour until the doctor, a young man, came out to tell him gently, 'Multiple injuries. I'm very sorry, Mr Spencer.'

He had been expecting the bad news, was not surprised, but it was as if something died in him. He went in to see his wife and then they found a cab to take him home. He was soaked to the skin, but he sent a telegram to Edward before he took a hot bath and crawled into bed.

Edward came post-haste, to find his brother in bed. The

doctor, an elderly man this time, took him aside. 'He's very ill. He spent several hours wringing wet and that, with the shock, has brought on pneumonia. On top of that, I understand he has business worries.'

Edward questioned his brother tactfully about his 'worries' and soon learned that that was an understatement. He tried to cheer him: 'You can come home and join me in partnership again, or I'll advance you enough to get you on your feet.'

Charles did not rally. Instead he said, 'I want to make my will. Everything I have left goes to Cecily, of course, in trust until she's twenty-one. It's little enough, God knows. We'd made plans for her, but now . . .' He told his brother what those plans had been. 'That's all water under the bridge now. Will you be trustee and guardian?'

Edward agreed. 'If you wish, but I'm fifteen years older than you. I could go myself before long. I think there should be another trustee in case of that happening. Is there anyone you want to name?'

'I'll leave that to you. Now fetch the solicitor.' The will was drawn up and signed.

Edward arranged Millicent's funeral and stood beside Cecily at the interment, held her as she wept. Charles had wanted to attend, had even dragged himself from his bed, but then he collapsed and turned his face to the wall. Edward arranged his funeral, too, and held Cecily again while she wept. He thought that it was a bad time for both of them but her more than himself. He waited a few days while he settled Charles's financial affairs, and for Cecily to recover from her first grief. He found that there was little in the estate after his brother's commitments at Lloyds had been met.

He finally talked to Cecily about her future one evening after dinner. 'You can live with me, I'd be glad of your company.' In fact, he was not sure about that. 'And we could find you a good school.'

After her initial heartfelt grief Cecily had recovered with the resilience of youth. She thrust out her lower lip. 'I'm not going to live in the north.' She still remembered the fearsome row she had overheard as a child, the mad woman screaming her hatred and her determination never to go back to that place. 'Never! never!' She recalled now that Edward had been the other man in that argument and regarded him with distrust. She had clung to him at the funerals because she had needed someone. Now he had the right to order her life, but she would scheme and fight him to have her way.

Edward sighed to himself. He had not approved of the way Cecily had been brought up, and it was his bad luck that he had to suffer the consequences. Then he remembered that this child had only recently been bereaved, and there was Charles's expressed wish to take into account. 'Very well. Your parents wanted you to attend a finishing school in Switzerland, so I'll make arrangements for you to go there.'

Cecily pulled a face. 'Isn't there anywhere else?'

'No. If your parents had been alive you would have had to obey them. When you are twenty-one and inherit you may do as you wish, but for now the responsibility is mine.'

Cecily saw that he was determined. 'Well, all right, I'll go to Switzerland.'

So Edward made those arrangements, too. He also persuaded a distant cousin, an elderly childless widow living in Hampshire, to take in Cecily when she was on holiday from school. Cecily also agreed to that, with a grimace, rather than stay with him. 'Will you let me have a photograph of yourself?' he asked her.

She would give him nothing. 'To put on your mantelpiece? I don't like having my photograph taken.'

Edward knew that that was not true because he had seen photographs of her in her parents' effects, but he had packed them away to give to her when she came of age. Now he said nothing, but it was with no regret that he saw her off on the train on the start of her journey to Lausanne. He had thought previously that he could not imagine anyone failing to take pleasure in raising a child because William had been a joy to him. Now he was not so sure.

He returned to Sunderland with relief. He had transferred the deeds and the administration of the trust to a local solicitor, his good friend Ezra Arkenstall. 'I've not told Cecily how little is held in trust,' Edward told him. 'She's suffered enough blows. I will see she is raised as her parents would have wished and foot the bill myself. She can learn the truth when she is twenty-one and not before. After that she will be able to earn her own living.'

On his second night at home he had dinner with William, whose ship had come into port that day. Afterwards they sat in armchairs before the fire and he told his ward about his new responsibility. William was a man of twenty-two now, a ship's captain, tall and wide-shouldered. Edward knew that he said what he meant and meant what he said, so he asked, 'What do you think?'

'I think the lass is going to be trouble,' William told him bluntly.

Edward sighed. It was the answer he had expected.

William did not know how right he was.

Edward received a photograph of Cecily with a group of other girls, taken at the bidding of the headmistress of her Swiss school and sent to him without Cecily's knowledge. It pleased him. That was just as well because she saw to it that there was never another.

It was a year of disasters. Cecily had lost her parents. Meanwhile Liza was helping to serve dinner under Gillespie's watchful eye when the bell jangled in the kitchen, indicating a caller at the front door. The butler frowned. 'Who can that be at this time?' He hurried away.

Liza collected a dish of potatoes from the cook and set out for the dining room. As she began to serve them Gillespie appeared, bearing a silver salver on which lay a buff envelope. He took it to Gresham, announcing, 'A telegram for you, sir. The boy is waiting.'

Gresham took the envelope and tore it open with a twist of his thumb. Vanessa was watching from the other end of the long table, which gleamed with wax. They were dining alone: two of their children were at school now and the youngest was in bed. The telegram fell from his grip and he buried his face in his hands. Vanessa rose to go to him: 'My dear! What is it?'

He lowered his hands and held them out to her. He stared at her, face contorted. 'It's from the War Office. Toby has been killed.'

For a moment all those in the room were frozen in shock. Then Gillespie jerked his head, and herded Liza and the other maid out of the room to give the couple privacy in their grief. Liza, too, needed privacy but could not get it. She had to continue with her duties while she tried to come to terms with the fact that Toby was dead. It did not matter that she wept, however, because several of the girls on the staff did – Toby had been popular. But she was also torn by conscience. Toby had gone into the army because of her.

In the course of the next few days Gresham received

a letter from Toby's commanding officer, expressing his sadness and explaining the freak accident that had killed the boy. It seemed that on a firing practice on Salisbury Plain a shell had exploded prematurely, just as it left the breech, and Toby was caught by the fragments. There was also a box of his belongings. Madame Jeanne helped Vanessa Gresham with these and Liza was called upon as the Frenchwoman's assistant. Along with his uniforms and other clothing there was a woman's handkerchief, a scrap of embroidered cotton he had had in his pocket. It did not bear a name. Vanessa sighed. 'There must have been a girl in London. I wasn't aware of him showing a particular interest in any he met here.' She put the handkerchief away carefully, because her son had treasured it.

All of this bore down on Liza. With the other servants she attended the funeral when the coffin was laid in the little churchyard. Gresham and his wife continued to mourn. They resumed their normal lives, or tried to, but they had aged. Liza saw Vanessa several times each day and frequently she was staring into space, her face drawn. It was too much for the girl who believed she had robbed this poor woman of her son. She could not face Vanessa and her grief every day and concocted a story that her mother was ill and needed her. When she gave notice to Gillespie he shook his head in sorrow. 'I was hoping to keep you for a few years yet. I had my doubts about you when I took you on, a funny little girl all wet from where you'd walked up through the rain, but you've turned out the best I've seen in many a long year.' Madame Jeanne was also complimentary, and Vanessa Gresham gave Liza a glowing reference. In the short interview with her, Liza almost broke down and confessed her affair with Toby but managed to hold back her tears. How would Vanessa Gresham look at her?

★   ★   ★

'What are you doing here?' Kitty Thornton shot up from her chair, alarmed. 'Are you poorly?'

'No.'

Kitty only knew of one other reason for her to come home when it was not her day off, and Liza had dropped her big box on the floor as she came in. 'You've not been sacked?'

'No. I gave notice.' Now Liza clung to her mother. 'Oh, Mam, I couldn't stand it any longer.' And she told her all about it.

Kitty listened, sighed, consoled her and agreed sadly. 'You were right to give up there, though that was a good place. And you can't blame yourself for that lad's death. I think you did right all the way through. You always told him there was no chance. It was just bad luck, that's all.'

Liza was grateful for her mother's support but still felt guilty. Nevertheless she could not sit at home and mope because Kitty needed the money Liza sent her. Besides, she had to make her way in the world. She saw a job advertised in the servants' weekly newspaper, applied for it and was taken on. The place was in Yorkshire, on the outskirts of Leeds, a great red-brick house. A carter brought her and her box from the station to the back of the house. He set the box down for her, close by the kitchen door, said, 'Good luck, lass,' and drove away.

It was October now, the leaves falling. Liza, lonely and heartsore, could just see through the steam covering the kitchen window. There was a small cleared space which someone had wiped to peer out, and people moved inside. Now the door opened and a tall young man stood before her in footman's livery. He was red-haired, fresh-faced, handsome and smiling. 'You must be the new girl.' He spoke with the accent of a southerner. He stooped and hoisted her box on to his shoulder. 'I'll give you a hand with this.'

'Thank you.' Liza had been ready to cry and was flattered by this welcome. She thought it boded well for the job. She could make a new start and she would be happy here.

8

He came upon Liza from behind, slid his arms about her waist
and kissed the back of her neck. She wriggled to free herself
and breathed, 'No, Vince, you mustn't.' She had been dusting
the library and he had entered quietly. Vince Bailey was the
footman who had welcomed Liza to her new position. Right
from that first act of kindness she had taken to him and he to
her. As he had lugged her box up the back stairs to her room
he had said, 'We're both new so we should stick together.'

Now she smiled at him, but urged, 'You get along. We
don't want to be caught and dismissed.'

'I don't mind chancing it.' He grinned recklessly. 'You're
worth it.' But when she gave him a push, he went, warning
her, 'Till the next time.'

Liza's affair with Toby had ended in tragedy, and because
of this she needed someone when she arrived in Leeds. She
clutched at Vince as if he were a lifeline. That had been three
months ago and, while she would never forget Toby, she was
young and, like Cecily, the wound had begun to heal.

Liza finished her task and left the library. Later that day
she was summoned to the drawing room by the wife of her
employer. Henrietta Wakely was sixty years old, puritanical
and strict. She sat erect in an upright chair, held stiffly by her
whalebone corsets, and peered over the top of her *pince-nez*.
'Are you happy here?'

Liza swallowed nervously. Was this the prelude to her

dismissal? Had she and Vince been seen that morning? She replied truthfully, 'Yes, thank you, ma'am.'

Henrietta sniffed. 'Good. Mrs Carey says she is pleased with your work.' That was the housekeeper. She and the butler ran the house for their employers, engaged and dismissed the staff as necessary. 'See that you go on that way.'

'Yes, ma'am, I will.'

'Very well. That will be all.'

'Thank you, ma'am.'

Outside, Liza let out a sigh of relief and smiled. She was happy, as she had said, had regained her joy in life, yet her pay was no better, the work harder, the hours longer, and the whole household attended prayers in the hall, morning and evening. The difference was Vince Bailey. He was always there to help, with his ready smile. He cheered her from the beginning and especially over Christmas, when there was no amateur drama because the Wakelys did not approve of such things, and the staff party was subdued, without dancing. Liza missed her home and her mother, and Vince lightened her life. After a few weeks his kindness had moved on to courting and she had responded, found it easy. She was hungry for comfort and affection.

The house was in the suburbs of Leeds, and Vince had persuaded the butler to allow him to change his half-day off to coincide with Liza's; he said it was more convenient for him to visit the library that day. It worked because the Wakelys were keen for the staff to improve their minds. From Leeds Vince and Liza would take a bus ride out into the country, away from watchful eyes, to where they could go walking together. It was on one of these walks, interspersed with kisses, that Vince told her of his plans. 'I'm saving up to have my own private hotel. I've put away my coppers ever since I started in service.' He flourished a bank book and she saw his name on the cover.

'I've nearly enough. With my experience I'll be able to run it easily. My mother is going to be the cook.'

Liza was impressed. She had never thought of having a bank account. What savings she could garner from her meagre salary she kept at the bottom of her box. She thought Vince's plan sounded fine and she had heard of servants who had gone up in the world in that way, although usually it was a butler well on in years who had amassed the necessary capital.

Vince put his arm about her and said shyly, 'I don't suppose you'd like to come in, as a partner? We'd take on some local girls as maids and you could supervise them. You'd be the housekeeper.'

'Oh, I hadn't thought.' Liza was blushing, caught unprepared. 'I'll have to think about it.' Was this love? Certainly the idea of working in partnership with Vince excited her.

He accepted her answer with a wry smile of disappointment. 'You haven't turned me down yet, anyway.'

Liza had not, and she thought a great deal about him and his proposal. She was in an elated mood as her eighteenth birthday approached.

On that great day the other servants came up to her one by one, each to give her a small gift, like a piece of chocolate or a handkerchief. All except Vince. That evening, when work was done and Liza was about to retire to bed, he whispered to her, 'Don't lock your door. I have something for you.' Then he was gone before she could answer.

Her room was at the top of the house, small and cold without a fire. There was just room for her narrow bed and her box at the foot of it. Liza waited for him, nervous, sitting on the bed in the light of a single candle. If they were discovered together they would be instantly dismissed, put out of the house – she was in no doubt of that. But she had left her door unlocked, would not turn him away as she had Toby.

When the door creaked open, Liza caught her breath. Then he was in the room, closing the door behind him, turning the key and, with his other hand, putting a finger to his lips.

'What is it?' Liza demanded. 'If anyone finds you in here—'

He put the finger over her lips now, smiling, then sat beside her on the bed. He dug into his pocket and brought out a scrap of paper. He unfolded it, and she saw it held a ring. Small jewels winked at her in the candlelight. He offered it to her. 'Happy birthday.'

'Oh, Vince!' Liza took it, slipped it on to her index finger and held out her hand, admiring it. 'It's beautiful, but you shouldn't have. You're saving your money, remember?'

He took her hand. 'That's why I've given it to you. It didn't cost me anything because it was left to me by my gran. But it's to do with the hotel because I want you to come in with my mother and me – as my wife.'

Liza had thought he might propose some time, and she was attracted by his offer to take her into the hotel venture, but marriage was a much bigger step.

'Please say you will,' he begged, his arm around her now. 'I think we were made for each other. Marry me, Liza.'

She was excited. He was close and she remembered what had happened when she had turned Toby down. Vince was offering her a life out of service, a life where they could get on – together. She hid her blushes in his chest and mumbled, 'Yes.'

He lifted up her face and kissed her then, again and again. The candle guttered and he blew it out. 'We don't need that.' There was still a faint light from the window. His hands were on her body, busy and knowing.

'Vince!' She protested uncertainly.

'Don't send me away tonight,' he whispered. 'You're my

wife, except for the churching, and that will be soon. I'll give notice before Easter. When we're both free, we'll be wed. Man and wife.'

Man and wife. She gave herself to him, her slim body silver in the light from the window.

She woke in the dawn to see him pulling on his clothes. He stooped over her to brush her lips with his and whisper, 'My wife, my love.' She smiled as she watched him go.

It was in the afternoon of that day that Liza answered a ring at the front door. She hurried along the hall to open it. A burly man of middle age, dressed in a cheap blue serge suit, was on the step. He wore a cap set squarely on his head. 'I hear you've got a Vince Bailey workin' here, right?'

Vince? 'Yes, sir,' Liza stammered.

'Right. I want to see the master here. You tell him it's Mr Butcher on a personal matter.'

Liza saw now that there was a girl with him, standing at the foot of the steps. She was obviously pregnant, a woollen shawl around her shoulders. Liza made the stock answer: 'I'll see if he's in.'

'Aye, get on wi' it.' He glowered at her. 'And you can tell him I'll come back wi' the pollis if I have to.'

Liza shut the door, ran through to the kitchen and found Vince drinking a mug of tea. 'There's a man at the front door, says his name's Butcher,' she whispered. 'He asked if you were working here and he wants to see the master.'

Vince swallowed and set down the mug, which rattled on the table. The others in the kitchen, the cook and one of the maids, looked at him and Liza curiously. 'What does he want?' Liza asked.

Vince licked his lips. 'I don't know but I'll bet he's come to make trouble. Still, you'd better tell old Wakely and I'll tidy myself up in case I'm called.'

Liza went to Mr Wakely, then ushered Butcher and the girl into his presence. As she shut the door she heard Butcher say, voice blaring, 'I've come a hundred miles lookin' for justice and I'll have it here or in court.'

When she got back to the kitchen, Vince wasn't there. 'He shot up the stairs,' the cook said. Liza ran up to the top of the house and Vince's room. The door stood open but he was not there. A curtain hung on a string stretched across one corner, making a makeshift wardrobe, but it was empty. The livery he had worn was scattered about the floor. Liza looked for a suitcase but could not find one, did not expect to. An old newspaper was lying on the windowsill and underneath it was a letter. It was addressed to Vince but the sender's name, Miss G. Bailey, and a London address were on the back.

Liza made her way slowly down the back stairs again. She harboured an awful fear and fingered the ring he had given her. She had hung it round her neck inside her dress, on a cotton thread. In the kitchen she found them talking about Vince. The scullery-maid, just thirteen, had seen him leave by a side window. 'He had a case and he jumped out and ran!' The child was big-eyed with excitement. 'He didn't go down the drive! Run through the trees and climbed over the wall, he did!'

Then the butler entered. 'Where's Vince? The master wants to see him.' The scullery-maid told her tale again and he pursed his lips, muttered under his breath and set off up the back stairs. He returned a few minutes later. 'He's done a bolt,' he said tersely.

'What for? What's he been up to?' the cook asked pointedly.

'That chap in with the master now – Butcher, he's called – he's got his daughter with him and says Vince has got her into trouble. They both worked in a house down Birmingham way. When she told Vince her condition and said he'd have to marry her, he ran off. Butcher's been trying to find him ever since.'

The cook sniffed. 'Serves her right, if you ask me. She must ha' give him encouragement.' The two maids nodded.

'Aye,' the butler said. 'But I'll have to tell the master.' And he went off to report.

Liza was in a daze, but managed to act normally while she wondered if Vince had made a fool of her or if he would return soon and explain. Surely that had to be the answer, because he loved her, didn't he? But he did not come back, nor did he write, and she faced up to the fact that she had been duped. After a while she had to face another.

Liza asked the housekeeper for two days off: her mother was missing her, she said. 'She's got nobody but me, Mrs Carey.'

'You've only been here six months.' The housekeeper peered down her nose. 'But you've done very well, so, yes, you can have the two days. But you'll lose the pay for them and you can't expect to make a habit of this, mind.'

'No, Mrs Carey. Thank you.'

Liza remembered the address in London and went to it. She caught an early train out of Leeds and was in the capital by noon, then found the long terrace of cramped little houses, many of which had their front doors standing open and barefoot children running in and out. At the one she sought she found a young woman sitting on the step. Her hair was wrapped in a cloth tied beneath her chin and she wore a canvas apron.

'Excuse me, but does Miss Bailey live here, please?' Liza asked.

The girl squinted up at her, eyes narrowed against the watery sunshine. 'I'm Gert Bailey. What d'ye want?'

'I'm looking for your brother, Vince.'

Gert gave a bark of laughter. 'You're not the only one!'

'Do you know where he is?'

'Who's asking?'

'Liza Thornton.' She held out her hand. Gert wiped hers on the canvas apron then shook Liza's.

'I know where he is but it won't do you no good. He come back here a few weeks ago but he only looked in for an hour to say he was off to Australia.' She saw Liza's startled look. 'There's a lass lives round here, she has three brothers and they're looking for him. Gawd help him if they find him. Why are you looking for him? Let you down, did he?'

Liza still hoped, did not want to give up. She related how Vince had wanted her to join him in running the hotel, then added, 'He proposed to me, gave me a ring—'

'That belonged to his gran?' Gert broke in. 'There was a ring. Can I see the one he gave you?' When Liza brought it out on its thread, Gert studied it, then passed it back to her. 'Grandma's ring was supposed to come to me but when she died he made off with it. That isn't it. I expect he's sold it, knowing him. As for my ma cooking for him, she's done that all her life, and now she's old he never gives her a copper.'

Liza knew now that she had been seduced, used. Her dreams and plans were shattered.

Gert stood up, brushing down her canvas apron. 'I've got to go into the factory for the afternoon shift.' She jerked her head in the direction of a grim building at the end of the street. She nibbled her lip, then said, 'Excuse me asking, but has he got you expecting?' Liza nodded, lips pressed tight. Gert said, 'Oh, Christ!' She put her arms round Liza and hugged her. 'I can't tell you any more than I have, can't help. All I can do is say how sorry I am. He's my brother but he makes me ashamed.' She let go of Liza. 'I have to go now.' She hurried away, wiping her tears with the back of her hand. The factory's siren hooted and girls came out of doors all along the street and the flood of them, hurrying to work, swallowed Gert.

Liza stood still, holding the ring in the palm of her hand. She could not think what to do with it, but she would not wear it. She snapped the thread and shoved the ring into her bag. Then she set out on her way back to Leeds, blinking away the tears. She threw the ring out of the window of the speeding train.

Liza handed in her notice before her pregnancy became apparent, left with a good reference and travelled to her home in Newcastle. Dry-eyed now, she told her mother, 'I've been let down by a man.'

'Are you in trouble?' Kitty asked, and when Liza nodded, she sighed. 'Oh, God!' Then: 'Will he marry you?'

'I wouldn't marry him. His sister said he's gone to Australia and he's a bad lot. I never want to see him again.' Liza was definite about that.

'Will you look for a man?' Kitty ventured. 'To give the bairn a name, I mean.'

'The bairn can have my name.' Liza had had time to think, coldly and clearly, after the first bitterness. She did not know if she could entice a man like that but knew she did not want to. She had known of girls who had persuaded a man to wed them, not hiding their pregnancy. She had also heard of one who told her hastily acquired husband that the child she produced so soon was his but premature. That was not for Liza, either.

Kitty never censured her but when she was alone Liza knew she cried. She also knew betrayal, shame, bitterness and misery.

She had some savings, just enough to see her through to her confinement: Kitty could not support her on the meagre wages she earned as a cleaner. Susan was born at dawn on a day of pelting rain and Kitty said, 'Just like you!'

The child was an immediate joy to Liza. Her mother had told her, unhappily, 'You're a lot harder now,' and Liza did not regret this, but Susan brought happiness into her life again, a joy in living. That only made it more difficult to leave her but Liza knew she must. Her savings were almost gone and she had to find work. She applied for two vacancies advertised in the *Newcastle Journal*, local jobs where she would be able to return home once a week, but she wasn't taken on. She began to worry.

One day she was writing a letter, applying for yet another job, when there came a knock at the door. Kitty had taken Susan for a walk in the second-hand pram, so Liza covered her letter and answered the knock herself. The kitchen door opened on to the passage and Gillespie, tall and sandy-haired, the butler from the Grange, was standing there. He smiled at her. 'Hello, Liza. How are you?'

'Mr Gillespie! What a surprise! Come in.'

She sat him down in a chair by the fire and talked as she made him a cup of tea. 'What brings you here?'

The butler grinned. 'You. I kept your address in case.'

'Me? Why?' Liza paused, teapot in one hand, kettle in the other.

'I might have a job for you – or are you suited already?'

A job! Liza poured carefully, put the kettle on the hob, stirred the tea and set the pot to draw for a minute. 'I'm not working at present.'

'Right, then. A couple of weeks back the family paid a visit to some people in Buckinghamshire and Mr Gresham took me along as his valet. I was talking to the butler there, a decent man by the name of Polkington. He told me they were looking for a maid who was good with a needle and at the dressmaking.

They were wanting a woman over twenty-five but I told him I knew somebody younger who would be just the ticket. The job sounds right up your street. You'd be working directly under the lady's maid. I met her, Miss Jarvis, a pleasant lady but one who knows what she wants. You'd get on fine with her. And they're offering twenty pounds a year.'

Twenty pounds a year! Liza had been writing away for jobs paying sixteen. She would be making a real advance. But then she remembered how she had thought she would be happy at the house in Leeds, and hesitated. Buckingham was a long way off. She poured the tea, added milk and sugar, then handed him the cup and saucer. She was tempted. She would love to stay at home with her mother and Susan but she needed the job. They all needed the money.

Gillespie added gently, 'And Polkington tells me Miss Jarvis is a lady of fifty-five and her employers will give her a pension at sixty. Then you'll be lady's maid.' He had remembered Liza's ambition.

Liza was just coming up to her nineteenth birthday. If all went as Gillespie said, she would be a lady's maid at the early age of twenty-four! It was a position always held by women of thirty or older, and it could make an enormous difference to her life – and her daughter's. She had to take this chance for Susan's sake.

'I'll take the job, Mr Gillespie. I'm grateful to you.'

'Good!' He reached into the inside pocket of his jacket, produced two envelopes and a slip of paper, then passed them to her. 'I've written down the name and address of your future employer, Mr Underdown. Write to him and say I'm recommending you and you want to be given a trial for the job. She – his wife, that is – will send you your train ticket and see that you are met at the station. One of those letters is to introduce you to Miss Jarvis, written by Madame Jeanne, who sends you her best regards. The other is from me to Mr Polkington.'

They chatted for a while and then he put down his empty cup and rose from his chair. 'I have to get back.' As she saw him to the door, he said shyly, 'It didn't strike me at the time, but your leaving – tell me to mind my own business if I offend you – had it anything to do with young Toby being killed?'

Liza nodded. 'He said he wanted to get away because I'd told him I couldn't marry him. I felt responsible for his death.'

Gillespie sucked in a breath and put his hand on her shoulder. 'I feared it might be something like that. Don't blame yourself. Things like this happen to people and can't be helped. You did what was right.'

'Thank you.' Liza knew he was correct, but it did not heal the hurt. She still grieved for Toby. He had been part of her youth and she had lost it. She was a lot older now than just by the months since he had been killed.

Gillespie left her with words of encouragement: 'You've got a grand opportunity now. You must look forward.'

Liza watched him stride away. She had not told him about Susan, and that was not because she was ashamed: she felt that if she told him he would deserve an explanation. She did not want to go over it all again.

Gillespie had seen some of Susan's clothes drying on a line, had glimpsed the cot in the bedroom next door to the kitchen where he had drunk his tea. He had wondered if the child was Liza and Toby's. But he told himself steadfastly that it was none of his business. He had already guessed at the story Liza had told him, but had come to help her if he could because she deserved it. Now he was even more glad that he had done so and went on his way, whistling.

9

Cecily emerged from the orchard and strolled slowly, hips swinging, across the yard to the house. Her eyes were narrowed, cat-like, against the spring sunshine. There was real heat in it and she had put on a thin cotton dress that showed off the lines of her young body; she was now a lissom nineteen. Simmie, the coachman and groom, was harnessing the horse to the carriage. He was a stocky young man, no taller than Cecily, and he watched her furtively. She knew it, and what he was thinking, and revelled in it. She greeted him: 'Good morning.'

'Morning, Miss Cecily,' he replied huskily.

She went on slowly towards the house, sure that he was gazing after her and wanting her. Cecily had learned a lot at the Swiss school that had not been on the syllabus, but she had been unable to put it into practice – so far. She had paid visits to the homes of schoolfriends and danced with boys, but always heavily chaperoned. Now she thought she might start with Simmie. She had to spend a vacation of two weeks here; this was only the third day and she was bored already.

Cecily entered the house by the back door and glanced into the kitchen. 'Good morning.'

The cook, Mrs Bagley, was kneading dough. 'Good morning, Miss Cecily.'

Mary Ann, the fifty-year-old, round-faced maid, said reprovingly, 'Mrs Higgins is waiting for you.'

'Thank you.' Let her wait, Cecily thought.

She ran up the stairs to her room but descended again a few minutes later and entered the drawing room where her relative sat, foot tapping. 'Here I am, Aunt Alex.'

Alexandra Higgins, Edward Spencer's cousin, was a widow attempting to keep a carriage, cook and maid on a modest annuity by a thousand small economies. She did not economise on the sherry she drank daily. The money Edward paid her for looking after Cecily in her vacations was a blessing. She let the girl do as she pleased, afraid if she told Edward that she could not control the girl he would end the arrangement.

Now Alexandra stared and shrieked, 'What have you done?'

Cecily had taken part in amateur dramatics at the Swiss school – they were popular at the time. Now she wore a blonde wig, its tresses piled high, and had daubed paint on her face, which was spotted with patches. 'I'm practising my part. I have the role of Marie Antoinette in the village pageant. It's quite an honour.'

'You look . . .' Alexandra was lost for words. Then she wailed, 'What will Edward think?'

'He will be pleased, of course. It will show him I'm making good use of my education.' And then, firmly, 'I'm not taking it off until I feel I'm right into the part. That might take me some days.'

Alexandra accepted defeat and shifted her ground: 'I've been expecting you this past ten minutes and more. You know we have to meet our guests off their train—'

'It doesn't arrive for another twenty minutes.' Cecily pointed at the clock on the mantelpiece.

Alexandra was on her feet. 'One should always be early for an appointment.'

'But not too early,' Cecily corrected her. 'And the carriage isn't ready yet. Simmie is just harnessing the horse.'

'What?' Alexandra scurried to the window to peer out at the empty drive. 'Oh dear! That young man! I told him to be ready at twenty to the hour—'

'You told him you wanted the carriage for fifteen minutes to,' Cecily interrupted again. 'I heard you tell him. And here he comes now, a little early, as you prefer.' The wheels of the carriage crunched on the gravel as it came into view.

'Oh. Well, come along now,' Alexandra said, deflated, and led the way outside. Simmie goggled at Cecily's appearance but held open the door. They climbed in and set out.

The train chugged into the little station on time. Only two passengers stepped out on to the platform where Alexandra and Cecily waited. Edward Spencer was familiar: he had come to see Cecily several times over the years, but it had not brought them any closer. She kept him at arm's length, still remembering the bitter quarrel between him and her father, just as the memory of the mad old woman still haunted her. She had never told him the reason for her antipathy to him: he was her guardian, she had been saddled with him and that was all there was to it. She would put up with him until she inherited and then she would go her own way. It would not be long now.

The man who accompanied him was a stranger. In his early twenties, he was tall and broad, dressed sombrely in a navy blue uniform with brass buttons. Cecily had not met him before but she had known he was coming: Edward had written that he was bringing one of his captains, whose ship was lying in the Pool of London.

'You're looking well, Alex,' Edward said, then paused. 'Cecily, isn't it? What have you done to yourself?'

'It's for the pageant . . .' Alexandra explained timidly.

Cecily smiled innocently. 'They taught me at the school

you sent me to. I assure you, sir, as soon as I have mastered and played my part I will revert to my true self.'

Edward sighed inwardly. He knew he would never understand this girl, and that she was ready to regard him as the cruel guardian if he disciplined her. But she was his brother's daughter and he had given his word to Charles. 'It's certainly a striking performance,' he said drily.

'Thank you, Uncle.' Cecily's reply was cool.

'This is the gentleman I told you about, Alex,' Edward went on, 'Captain William Morgan.'

William carried his cap in his hand and ducked his head in a polite little bow. He was well aware that his uniform was shabby but he had not expected a visit of this sort so had brought no other aboard his ship. It had been good enough for the passage from the Mediterranean. In truth he did not see why Edward had asked for, or ordered, his company on this visit. But it was enough for him that Edward wished it.

'So you only work for Mr Spencer,' Cecily remarked.

William caught the nuance in her tone and thought, As if I swept out the stables. He retorted, 'I captain one of his ships, Miss.'

Now it was Cecily's turn to think. Miss! As if I was a servant girl! She smiled sweetly. 'That is what I meant.'

Edward had not detected her jibe and now spoke up for William: 'He's an important man.'

Cecily noted the pride in his voice, and wondered how she could use it to hurt him.

On the drive back to the house, over lunch and during the stroll through the lanes that followed, she tried to charm William and Edward, and succeeded with the latter. For dinner she wore a dress that buttoned up to the neck but was still bewigged and painted. She played up to the two men again, conversing intelligently and minding her manners.

Edward was delighted and decided to ignore the outrageous disguise. He thought with relief that the girl was growing out of the difficult phase. At last he felt he could grow to like her. 'I've brought you a present,' he told her, 'from Switzerland.'

'Oh?' said Cecily warily. Was this some disapproving report from her school? 'How kind of you.'

Edward took a small box from his pocket and opened it to reveal a tiny gold wristwatch set with jewels. 'For your nineteenth birthday.'

'Thank you.' Cecily was amazed and delighted with the present and almost kissed him – but habit held her back. Still, her feelings showed in her tone and Edward was pleased. William hoped the girl was worth it.

Alexandra retired early: 'I'll leave you gentlemen to your talk.' She took Cecily with her – and a bottle of sherry for a nightcap. She had hidden that in the capacious bag in which she kept her embroidery.

The two men sat in armchairs before the fire and talked of ships and shipping, drank some whisky and went up to bed. Edward led the way and William said, 'I'll just settle this fire for the night.' He checked that the coals would not fall out then put a guard round it to be sure. When he was satisfied, he climbed the stairs. Edward's door was shut and he put out the oil lamp on the landing. Oil lamps were the only illumination here, an economy forced on Alexandra because the house was too remote for gas or electricity to be connected.

When William opened his door he found a lamp burning on the table by the bed. Cecily reclined there, still in her wig, face painted, but her dress was discarded on a chair. Her body was outlined under her thin shift. She gave him a sultry smile and said huskily, 'Close the door, Captain. I've been waiting for you.'

William was taken by surprise, but he had been through this experience before – though not with an English lady. He reached the bed in two long strides and snatched up the dress. He picked up Cecily and carried her out on to the landing. It was her turn to be surprised. She had planned a seduction and had not expected rejection. 'I'll scream!' she hissed.

'Scream away. It'll be your word against mine and I still have my breeches on.' He set her down, shoved the dress into her arms and shut his door on her. She heard the key turn in the lock.

At breakfast she was snappy with a brittle smile and he mostly silent but polite when he spoke. To Edward she was cold, never addressed him and answered his remarks with monosyllables. When the two men said their farewells and climbed up into the carriage she replied only with a flat, 'Goodbye.' She had refused to go to the station and her face was devoid of expression. Edward sighed to himself and accepted that their relationship was back to normal again.

As Cecily watched them go, with the coachman sitting up on the box and driving the carriage, she thought: Well, there's always Simmie.

Days later Alexandra said, 'No one in the village knows anything about a pageant.'

Cecily shrugged carelessly. 'Some girl told me about it and I believed her. Still, no harm done.'

Edward did not discuss the visit until he and William were at home in Sunderland. Then, one evening after dinner, when the maid had cleared the table and he was alone with William, he dropped the first bombshell: 'I would like to make you a partner. I've been told by my doctor that I must ease up a bit and I'd like you to take on some of my work.'

William looked startled, then concerned. 'I didn't know you were ill.'

'I'm not.' Edward gave him a reassuring grin. 'I just have to cut down on my work. Will you take on some of it?'

'I know nothing about it.'

'You'd soon learn in the saddle.' Edward was sure of that. 'Well?'

'Of course. I'll do all I can.'

Elspeth came with the whisky decanter then and set out glasses.

Edward did not wait for her to go because she knew all about his family anyway. He proceeded to drop the second bombshell: 'I took you to see my ward because I want to name you as her guardian if anything should happen to me.' His doctor had told him he might last ten years – or die next winter. 'Will you take that on for me too?'

William's surprise and horror were written on his face. 'To tell the truth I found her ill-mannered and lacking in respect for yourself.' He left it at that, though to his mind Cecily Spencer was a mischief-making slut.

'I know she is a difficult girl. She was not brought up as I would have wished. But she is my brother's daughter and it behoves me to do my best for her.' Edward added hopefully, 'I think she is improving.'

William did not agree but could not hurt this man who had been guardian to himself, could not tell him of his own experience with the Spencer girl. 'I'll act, of course, as that is what you wish.'

'Thank you.' Edward smiled. 'I'm grateful.'

'It's I who am grateful to you, sir. I take it this responsibility will cease when she is twenty-one?'

Edward nodded. 'In just under two years' time.' It was
highly unlikely that William would be called on to act in his
stead for any length of time – if at all.

'It seems to me that the school and her aunt see most of
her. She never comes here,' William said.

'That's true. I sometimes think Alexandra is too easy with
her, but there's no one else and Cecily refuses to come here,
let alone live in this house. She must stay with Alexandra, at
least until next year when she finishes at the Swiss school.'

'What will you do with her then? Send her to train for a
trade or profession?' William asked.

'Alexandra has suggested taking her on a tour of Europe.'
Edward grinned. 'I think she likes the idea herself, and I'll
probably fall in with it. Afterwards – I don't know.' But he
thought the suggestion of a trade was worth remembering.

'I hope she is suitably grateful,' William said, but his tone
showed he doubted it.

Elspeth took in all of this, stored it away and formed an opinion
of Miss Cecily Spencer.

10

NOVEMBER 1906, PARIS

The train ran into the Gare du Nord with a hiss and a sigh, and pulled up with a grinding of brakes and a clatter of couplings. Liza stood in the corridor at an open window. Willi, Albert Koenig's short, tubby valet, squeezed in beside her. They shouted for a porter together and two came hurrying with their barrows. As the train ground to a halt Liza jumped down and Willi followed. Together they hurried along the platform to claim the baggage. Both the barrows were needed: Albert had two massive suitcases, while Beatrice, his wife and Liza's mistress, had four – and three hatboxes. Liza pointed them out to the porters and they hauled them from the luggage car and stacked them on the barrows. She nodded, satisfied. 'That's the lot.'

'*Ja*.' Willi agreed. He was not a good traveller and gladly let Liza take the initiative.

She seemed cool and calm, unflurried. In fact, she was excited, and had been for some months now. She had worked hard for Mr and Mrs Underdown at the house in Buckinghamshire and learned all she could from Freda Jarvis, the lady's maid. Freda was brisk and spry for a woman of fifty-five, always smartly dressed and never a hair out of place. She had nothing but praise for Liza, save when she had caught the girl imitating Mrs Underdown's regal, sweeping walk. The latter was a society beauty in her mid-twenties, and the other servants, who had been watching, applauded. 'That's rather naughty, dear,' Miss Jarvis said.

Nevertheless, when Freda Jarvis broke an ankle as their mistress was about to leave for a long stay in the South of France, she recommended that Liza should take her place and attend Mrs Underdown. Liza, hastily briefed on the duties of a lady's maid when travelling abroad, was a success.

As a consequence, when Beatrice Koenig's maid handed in her resignation in order to marry, Mrs Underdown suggested that Liza could take her place. She explained to her husband as they prepared for bed, 'I would like to keep the girl but this would be a step up for her. If she stays here she will be playing second fiddle to Freda for another four years. Beatrice is an old friend. She is going to Germany to see some of her husband's relatives and stopping in Paris for a while. She hasn't visited his people before, nor been married long.'

Her husband grunted. 'She wed Albert as an act of desperation.' He stripped off his shirt and tossed it aside.

His wife pouted. 'That's a cruel thing to say, though it's true she looked to be left on the shelf. But I'm sure she and Albert will be happy.'

'He should be, with her money.' He put his arms around her.

'*Again?*' she protested, but she was smiling.

So Liza had taken the job and was a lady's maid before she had come of age, with a rise of four pounds a year, giving her an annual salary of twenty-four pounds. She had been able to send more money to support her mother and Susan. She kept the bare minimum for herself, but she knew Kitty was saving for her. Then, to crown it all, there was this trip to France and later to Albert Koenig's family on their estate near Hamburg.

Liza and Willi led the porters, in a little procession, to where

Albert and Beatrice were making a leisurely descent from a *première classe* carriage. Albert Koenig was a portly young man with a thick, upswept moustache, while Beatrice was a plain but pleasant girl, who clung to his arm and simpered at his every word. Albert greeted Liza jovially, 'You have it all? Good! Then follow me.' He took over the lead of the procession.

That night Liza slept in the bedroom of a good hotel, albeit in one of the cheaper rooms. It was a world away from Newcastle and the shipyards of the Tyne, the little house close by the river. She yearned for home, her mother and little Susan, but knew she must be patient.

Cecily Spencer was with a man in another hotel, seedy and little better than a *pension*, a quarter-mile away in Montmartre. When she had left the finishing school on her twentieth birthday she had backed Alexandra Higgins in asking Edward Spencer if she could be sent on a tour of Europe. Alexandra had asked, timidly but with hope, and was as overjoyed as Cecily when he agreed, with the proviso: 'I think Cecily should study painting and also learn something of the languages.' They had spent some time in Italy, then moved to Paris. Later they would go on to Berlin. At this moment Alexandra was sleeping deeply in a much better hotel; she had discovered Cognac.

Cecily had discovered Mark Calvert. She had experienced several brief romances since her near-seduction of Simmie, her aunt's coachman – his nerve had failed him and he had run – but none had touched her heart. Until now. She and Alexandra had sat at a table in a café and she had felt that someone was watching her. She looked around and saw a young man sitting alone at a table across the room. His dark, brooding gaze was fixed on her and did not falter when he met hers. Cecily read the message in those dark eyes and shivered.

She looked away, knowing she was blushing, but when she and Alexandra rose to leave, the young man followed – all the way to their hotel. She peeped out of her room, which overlooked the front of the hotel, but could not see him in the street below. However, when she passed through the foyer later, wondering, heart beating fast, he was there, sprawled in an armchair. He saw her and rose, tall and broad, then stepped into her path. 'I heard you were English when you were talking in that café. I'm Mark Calvert. I know we haven't been introduced, but there is no one to carry out that formality.'

'I quite understand.' She did not care, either. She just wanted to see more of this man. 'I'm Cecily Spencer.' She put out her hand. He bowed and kissed it, held it as if he would never let it go. When he did so she said, 'Shall we sit down?' When they were settled at a small table she explained, 'I'm travelling with my elderly aunt – I think you saw her?' He nodded and she added hopefully, 'We haven't been here long. Would you be a guide by any chance?'

He shook his head. 'I'm a land agent, but resting at the moment.' He said that awkwardly because it was not altogether true and he was an honest man.

'Oh.' But Cecily did not give up. 'Do you speak French?'

'I've learned a little and can call a cab, order a meal, pass the time of day.'

'I have to learn something of the language,' Cecily said, 'and we have not yet engaged a tutor. Could you obtain a reference for yourself from someone?'

Alexandra engaged Mark the next day on the strength of his reference – Henri, one of the croupiers at the casino had provided him with it – and from then on he and Cecily spent many hours together. Sometimes he taught her simple phrases in French from a primer and Alexandra sat nearby, listening or dozing. Otherwise they met when she had retired, believing Cecily to have done the same. Then Mark and she would sit in cafés or bars, but it was not until that night that he had taken her to his hotel room.

They had sat in a bar that was crowded, smoky and noisy. 'I have quite a decent little room,' he had told her, 'but I can't take you there. I have to think of your reputation. You're a respectable girl of good family.' For a moment Cecily thought he was joking. Then she realised he was in earnest, crediting her with a virtue she had tried to discard. She found she was casting her eyes down, modestly, as he went on, 'I would ask you to marry me but there are a few things you should know about me.'

Marriage? Cecily had not thought so far ahead. 'I told you I was a land agent,' he went on. 'In fact that's just a fancy name for a glorified farmer. We – my family – owned an estate of a thousand acres in Yorkshire and I ran it and made a handsome profit. I was the eldest of six children and Father mortgaged the estate to educate us all and to see the others settled in careers or married with a handsome dowry. Then he died, suddenly and unexpectedly. The banks foreclosed and sold the estate to recover the loans. The new owner kept me on to run the place for him but we argued about how it should be done and I told him to do the job himself, though not so politely.' Mark sighed. 'I suppose I'd been running my own show too long. I didn't take kindly to obeying an order from him, especially when I knew he was wrong.'

Cecily laid a hand on his. 'How sad! What did you do?'

'Everything had gone.' There had been a girl but she had departed when he had lost the estate. 'I could have gone to one or other of the family but I wouldn't sponge off them. I got a job as an escort to a young chap who was going to tour Europe. His father had plenty of money, and the son had too much. We came to Paris first. On the boat coming over he insisted on getting into a card game so I joined in. The others won or lost a little, he dropped a great deal and I won a lot. I'd played from childhood and my father was an expert, though only for small stakes. He always said he wouldn't gamble with the estate. It might have been better if he had. But he was a grand man and I loved him.

'Anyway, I offered to give back the young man some of the money he'd lost but he accused me of cheating because I'd won so much. I stayed with him until we got to Paris. Then he wanted me to find girls for him and I told him to go to hell. I got into another card game and I've been living that way ever since, for nearly a year now.' He took a breath. 'So, you see, I'm a gambler.'

'I don't care whether you're a farmer or a gambler.' Cecily looked into his eyes and stroked his hand. 'My guardian would not allow me to marry but soon I will come of age . . . It is so noisy in here. Where can we go to – talk?'

Mark stood up, laid some coins on the table then took her arm.

And so they lay close in the big bed in his room, their passion spent for the moment, and talked of the future. It was by no means their last night in that bed.

A week before Christmas Cecily took the train to Berlin. Mark, as her tutor, attended at the station and was thanked by Alexandra. 'You've been very kind and we've both enjoyed your company, haven't we, dear?' she added.

Cecily nodded demurely. At her insistence Mark had agreed that they would keep their betrothal secret rather than attract unwelcome attention from Alexandra or Edward Spencer.

Soon she would inherit, would be a free agent, and would meet him in London. Behind her aunt's back she stole a kiss from him and whispered, 'At the Jefferson Hotel.' He had suggested it – he would not subject her to a cheap hotel such as he had used in Paris. He had heard his former employer, Randolph Stevenson, speak highly of the Jefferson. Now he watched and waved until the train was out of his sight.

The Koenigs and their staff left Paris that same day, bound for Hamburg and Albert's relatives. Liza was looking forward to Christmas, then a bright New Year and, hopefully, a visit soon to her mother and Susan. It was as well she could not foresee the disasters that lay ahead.

11

'Aye, Liza's getting on very canny now.' Kitty Thornton had paused outside the baker's to talk to an old friend. Jinnie was over eighty now and frail. She had been thin when she assisted at Liza's birth, but now she was skeletal and hobbled along with the aid of a stick. Her skin was like paper stretched over the veins that writhed on her hands like snakes, but she still had a smile for Kitty, who said now, 'She sends a bit home every month.'

Jinnie cocked her head to one side and put a hand to her ear. 'What? You'll have to speak up.'

Kitty did so, smiling: 'I said she was getting on very canny. She sends a few pounds home every month. O' course, I save a lot of it for her, put it away in a tin. She's in Germany now, spent Christmas and New Year there and had a lovely time. She told us all about it in her last letter.'

'Oh, aye. I'm glad. She was always a bonny lass, always had time for people. And this is her bairn?' She nodded at two-year-old Susan, standing at Kitty's side.

'Aye. Takes after Liza, doesn't she?'

'The spit of her,' agreed Jinnie. 'Well, give her my love when you see her.'

'I'll tell her you were asking after her.' Kitty stooped over Susan: 'Say ta-ta now.' Susan obediently waved a fat fist and Jinnie laughed as she limped away. Kitty went on with her shopping and did not notice the girl who had listened to her conversation and who now followed her.

It was Una Gubbins. She had blossomed into a coarsely attractive woman, full-bosomed and sulkily sensual. Now she trailed Kitty back to the house in the terrace where she still rented two rooms. Una made a mental note of its number and that Kitty had the downstairs rooms – she had seen Susan come to the front window and push aside the lace curtains to look out. There was a public house across the road.

Una hurried away to the rooms she shared with her husband Luke. She was now Mrs Cooper, and found him sitting before the fire drinking beer from a bottle and reading the racing form in a newspaper. He was bearded now and harshly handsome, but he carried a long-bladed knife on a belt inside his jacket. The plump youth had become a burly thug in a suit. Neither he nor Una had work but lived on the results of small crime and took a job only when they had to. Una perched on the arm of his chair and took a swig from his bottle. He reached out a hand for her leg but she slapped it away. 'I think I've found our ticket to London.'

'Aye?' Piggy reclaimed the bottle and squinted to see how much beer was left. 'The sooner the better. That bloody bobby is keeping an eye on me. I seem to see him every time I gan oot.'

The following day they avoided the policeman when Una led the way to the public house and they sat in there, ostensibly reading the racing form but in fact watching for Kitty to go out. Eventually Piggy muttered out of the side of his mouth, 'There she goes wi' the bairn.' He folded his newspaper, stood up and together they left the pub. They walked up the street, Una on Piggy's arm, like any couple out for a stroll. Then they crossed the road and walked back. There were other strollers and a few children, but no one stood gossiping at the front doors because of the January cold; nor did anyone pay attention to them. When they came to Kitty's front door they only had to open it and walk in; front doors were not locked or bolted during the day. They hurried along the passage with its worn matting and came to the door to Kitty's rooms. This was locked but Piggy set his shoulder to it and the lock gave way with a splintering of timber. They waited for a few seconds but no one called out from the upstairs rooms and there was no sound of movement inside. They walked in.

There were only the two rooms, and little furniture in them. The search did not take long. Una found the tin at the back of a drawer in the bedroom, hidden under clothing. It had a picture of the king, Edward VII, on the lid and had once held tea. 'Here!' she hissed. Piggy came through from the kitchen, and Una pulled off the lid. He snatched it from her and emptied it on to the kitchen table. There was an insurance policy – to pay for Kitty's funeral – and a double handful of silver coins with a few golden sovereigns. Liza had sent money in postal orders and Kitty had cashed them.

Piggy whistled softly. 'You did bloody well, our lass.' He grinned. 'We're off!' He poured the coins into the pockets of his shabby overcoat, then cautiously opened the door. The passage was empty so they stepped out – and the front door began to open, slowly because little Susan was insisting on pushing it. Una gasped but Piggy seized her arm, dragged her along the passage and out of the back door. He closed it softly behind him. The backyard was empty, with no one in the wash-house or the coal-shed, so he and Una ran across to the gate and out into the cobbled lane.

They hurried back to their rooms and counted up the money they had stolen. Piggy grinned at Una. 'Pack your clothes. It's us for London.'

Una laughed. 'I've put it over that Liza Thornton an' all!
I'd like to see her face!'

Edward Spencer left his office at eleven in the morning. 'Send
the boy out to get me a cab,' he told Featherstone, his chief
clerk. 'I feel a bit under the weather so I'm going home. I
expect I'll be in tomorrow but, if not, please bring anything
needing my attention up to the house.'

'Yes, Mr Spencer.'

Edward shrugged into his overcoat and picked up his top
hat. He thought a breath of fresh air might do him good. As
he got to the street door his office-boy panted up. 'Here's
your cab, Mr Spencer, sir.'

'Thank you, Tommy.'

It was a hansom. Edward climbed in with an effort and
closed the doors across his knees. The driver, seated behind
and above him, opened the flap in the roof and called down to
him, 'Right y'are, sir.' The horse set off at a walk and Edward
sank back against the worn leather cushions. He panted from
the climb into the cab and thought, Fresh air, that's the ticket.
Better in a minute.

His staff stood at the windows and watched the cab move
away. A junior clerk said, 'The ould lad does look bad.'

The chief clerk chewed his lip and sighed, then remembered
his responsibilities. 'Well, we all have work to do.' They
turned back to their desks and he decided that if he had to
attend his employer at his house next day, he would suggest
sending a telegram to Captain William Morgan. He was at sea,
commanding the *Wear Lass*, bound for Bremen in Germany.
The chief clerk would recommend William's early return. He
might be accused of making a fuss over nothing but it would
put his mind at rest.

In the event he had to send a telegram anyway. When the cab reached Edward's house he was dead.

The first telegram came with the doctor. Cecily had sent for him when Alexandra took to her bed with streaming eyes, nose, and a racking cough. The doctor came to their Berlin hotel and diagnosed influenza. Alexandra must keep to her bed for a week, must be nursed, and could not think of travelling for a month. He agreed to her request: a little medicinal Cognac would be in order.

Cecily read the telegram the maid had delivered. It came from Edward Spencer's solicitors. 'I must go home,' she said. She turned to her aunt. 'Mr Spencer died yesterday. The solicitors say I should go back to Sunderland as I am a beneficiary under his will and due to inherit under my father's in February.'

Alexandra wept. 'Poor Edward. So kind, so generous.' Her grief was genuine, and so was Cecily's lack of it.

Cecily, though, was excited by the change in her fortunes, this early release from what she regarded as bondage. She would be free, and Mark Calvert was waiting for her. But she felt a pang of regret that she had not been kinder to Edward.

She comforted her aunt as best she could and arranged for a nurse to stay; Alexandra still had plenty of the money Edward had given her in letters of credit. The telegram had also said her passage would be arranged and further details would follow by letter. Cecily would not wait. She had always sworn not to go to the North Country but this changed everything. She wheedled out of the fragile and mournful Alexandra a sum more than sufficient to cover her passage home and set out the following day. She took only one suitcase and left her other baggage to be packed and sent on.

One of the details in the letter that was still on its way was that William Morgan would take over as her guardian. Cecily did not see it.

When the *Wear Lass* docked in the port of Bremen William found two telegrams awaiting him. The cable and telegraph were his only means of contacting the shore. His ship, like most others of the time, did not have wireless. Both telegrams were from Ezra Arkenstall, Edward Spencer's solicitor. The first advised William of Edward's death, that Arkenstall was arranging the funeral, and suggested his early return. The second informed him that he was now guardian of Miss Cecily Spencer, who had been advised to return to Sunderland in view of her impending inheritance.

William was stricken by the news. Edward had been his father from the age of five, had cared for him, loved him, and that affection had been returned.

He called for the first officer. 'I have to sail for home without delay so I want a quick turn-round.' He had a cargo to discharge and another to load. He did his sums and decided it would be as quick for him to cross the North Sea in the *Wear Lass* as it would be to leave her and go by train and packet, if he had his way. And he did: his ship had the fastest turn-round seen in Bremen for a long time. William worked at the head of his crew from start to finish, clad in a stained seaman's jersey and old navy blue trousers.

For some days Liza had noticed Albert Koenig's eyes following her. It shocked her that a married man in his parents' house could cast his eyes on another woman with carnal intent. But she was a long way from the innocent of five years before and knew what Albert intended. She suffered days of indecision. Should she tell her mistress? She would not be believed. Give notice for what reason? And what kind of reference would she get? She could walk out – but that would still leave her without a reference. Maybe Albert would come to his senses. Maybe she was mistaken. She hesitated.

Liza was shocked, but not surprised, when he seized her and threw her down on the couch. She fought him. 'No! Please!'

'Don't worry. They are all out. I'll give you a present.' He went on trying to undress and fondle her. Liza knew Beatrice Koenig had gone out with her parents-in-law. She had been working in the bedroom on Beatrice's wardrobe when Albert had come seeking her. Now, in fear and despair, she punched and kicked him, her skirts flying above her thighs and her dress shredding. Eventually she escaped, leaving him gasping on the couch. He rose to pursue her and she turned to flee. The door opened.

'I came home because I didn't feel well,' Beatrice said. 'One of the servants told me you might be up here.' She spoke mechanically as she tried to take in the scene before her.

'Thank God you're here,' Albert said quickly. 'This slut is deranged! I came up looking for a book and she started to tear off her clothes and mine, said she loved me. I didn't know what to do, couldn't escape because she had the strength of madness. I tried to reason with her but she just laughed at me.'

Liza pulled her dress together to cover her nakedness and attempted to put her case: 'If you please, ma'am—'

Beatrice could not accept the truth, shied from the evidence of her own eyes. She could see her image in a mirror on the wall and compare it with the fresh beauty of this frightened girl, but she could not accept that her husband had preferred a servant girl to herself. Her mouth tightened and she glared at Liza. 'Go and make yourself decent, then pack your bags and get out. I'll not give you a reference nor pay a penny instead of notice. Think yourself lucky I don't hand you over to the police.'

'It's not true!' Liza protested. 'I'm sorry, ma'am, but he's lying. I was working in here,' she pointed at the dress she was altering, 'and he came in and—'

'No! *No!*' Beatrice clapped her hands over her ears. 'I won't listen to your lies! Stop it! *Stop it!*'

Liza saw that the woman would not listen to her. She stumbled from the room and hid in her own. There she wept from the horror of her experience, for the ruin of her hopes, for fear of what lay ahead.

There was a knock at the door. 'Who is it?' she called tremulously. Had Beatrice sent for the police?

A voice squeaked, 'Heidi!' It was the girl of fourteen who worked as a scullery-maid. She admired Liza.

Liza opened the door to the girl, who smiled and held out an envelope. 'From your mama?' Liza had told her about Kitty and Susan.

She took it. 'Thank you, Heidi.' The girl's smile wavered; she could see Liza had been crying. 'Yes, it's from Mama. I'll see you later.'

Heidi went away and Liza closed the door. It was only then that she wondered at the letter. Kitty wrote regularly, once a week, carefully in copperplate, the back of the sheet covered in Susan's scrawls. But there had been a letter only two days before. Why another now? Was Susan ill? Liza tore it open and read: 'I'm sorry to have to tell you we had a burglar in and he found the money and took it all . . .'

Liza read the rest but the words were only regrets and apologies. The essence of the letter was in those few words. She did not blame her mother, had never had a bank account herself. Like many others she had never had enough money to merit one. When the poor saved a little money there was always some emergency to claim it, like time out of work or shoes for a child.

Liza realised now that she was not only out of work but nearly penniless, and without a reference she would be lucky to obtain anything but the most menial job. She could not carry her box nor afford to ship it because she had to watch every penny. She left it with Heidi and packed an old, cheap suitcase she had bought second-hand some years earlier when she worked in Leeds. Then she set off in despair to go home.

In London, a similar scene was being enacted, though this time a man was the victim. Una Cooper opened the door of her hotel room and called, 'Why, Mr Biggins! You'll help a lady in a difficulty.' She pouted and held a partly full champagne glass.

Henry Biggins smirked at her. He had just turned fifty, and was expensively, if badly, dressed in a check suit he believed gave him a sporty look. He had met Mr and Mrs Armstrong, as he knew them, a few days earlier, when they were all sitting in the foyer of the hotel and the lady had struck up a conversation with him. She had explained that she and her husband were in London in connection with Mr Armstrong's business. She had sighed, 'Business, it's always business.' Mr Armstrong, in reality Piggy Cooper, had remained hidden behind his newspaper, giving only bored grunts when addressed. Henry had told her how he was there to see the sights, a holiday from his own business. He had left his wife at home.

They had met several times since then and he had found Una charming, attentive and interested in whatever he had to say. She had a habit, surely unconscious, of leaning towards him so that he would find himself peering down into her *décolletage.* Now he answered gallantly, 'Of course, my dear. How may I be of assistance?'

Una seized his arm, pulled him into the room and shut the door behind them. 'I'm glad I met you, Henry. You'll understand. It's my birthday. Sit down.' She pushed him on to the edge of the bed. 'I ordered a bottle because Freddie was supposed to come home early. Here, have a glass.' Champagne stood in an ice-bucket on a small table and she splashed some into a glass, more into her own, handed him his and sat beside him. 'Now he's sent a message to say he won't be back till midnight.' She flapped a sheet of paper in front of Henry's eyes and said miserably, 'So I'm all alone. On my birthday.' She sniffed.

'Eh, lass, that's a shame,' Henry commiserated.

Una leaned towards him and laid a hand on his thigh. The room seemed warm and he gulped champagne.

'Business, always business,' Una said, 'and I'm left on my own. He never . . .' She paused, then finished delicately, 'He never demonstrates any affection. That's not natural for a woman like me.' Her fingers dug into Henry's thigh. Then she glanced at the little watch on her wrist. 'But I forgot, I asked for your help.' She stood and turned her back to him. 'I can't get out of this dress on my own. Will you, please?'

Henry began to undo the row of small buttons with fingers all thumbs. As he did so the dress slipped off her shoulders and he saw an expanding area of creamy skin.

Then Piggy Cooper burst in at the door. 'What are you doing with my wife, sir? Adulterer!'

'No! I was only helping her!' Henry squeaked. 'She asked me in.'

Piggy glared at Una. 'I cannot believe it. Is this true?'

Una clutched her dress about her. 'I opened the door to his knock and he attacked me.'

'Liar as well as adulterer!' Piggy bawled. 'I'll drag you through the highest courts in the land but I will have justice – and vengeance!' He whipped out the knife, long and deadly.

Henry saw that Mrs Armstrong had lied to save her own skin. He also knew what justice he would get if the case went to court. A judge might believe him but Henry's wife would not. And there was the knife. 'It's all a mistake, but we don't want to go to court and pay the lawyers,' he wheedled, sweating. 'Can't we agree to settle the matter between ourselves? I'll gladly compensate Mrs Armstrong for any embarrassment she may have felt.'

Piggy grumbled about it being a 'matter of honour', but was persuaded to accept almost the entire contents of Henry's wallet. He stuffed the wad of notes into his pocket, read Henry a lecture on taking advantage of other men's wives when they were only seeking companionship, and sent him off, chastened, to his own room. Then he asked Una, 'Are you ready?'

She turned her back to him. 'Button me up. You took your bloody time. He nearly had me in my bare buff.'

'I was only a minute late,' Piggy replied. They had synchronised their watches so that he could come in at the crucial moment. 'This chap came out into the passage and I had to wait for him to go downstairs. We didn't want anybody near when I charged in.' He fastened the last button. 'Get your coat and come on.' He lifted their suitcases, packed and ready, out of the wardrobe, put in his suit jacket and pulled on a porter's waistcoat. Una led the way to the service stairs, and he followed her, carrying the cases, down and out of the back entrance of the hotel into an alley. At the end he hailed a cab for King's Cross station. From there they took another cab to another hotel. Within the hour they were settled in, with a fresh bottle of champagne half empty and Piggy unbuttoning Una's dress again.

Jasper Barbour sat on one side of the scrubbed wooden table, Flora on the other. The warder kept a wary eye on him. Early in his sentence he had established himself as dangerous when other prisoners had tried to put him down. One he had crippled and now the rest were glad to leave him alone. 'Have you got it all organised?' he muttered to Flora.

'Aye. In a week's time if your man will do it.' Flora copied his murmur but she was frightened.

'He'll do it.' Jasper had waited all through his sentence for this moment. Now there was a warder whose daughter had consumption and needed sanatorium care. Jasper had the money to pay for it. Now: 'I want her found. Her that put me in here,' he muttered.

Flora had stayed true to him through the years, looked after his money, visited him on the rare occasions she was allowed to. This was partly out of fear, but there was also affection and gratitude. He had lifted her out of the gutter and she had never starved, never had to sell herself. Now she protested, 'How can I do that? I told you that her ma and pa had died and she was taken off somewhere. God knows where she is.'

'There's a feller called Galloway. He's an ex-copper with a little office in Finch Street down Wapping way. He'll find her, but don't tell him who wants to know.'

'What do you want to find this Spencer lass for?' Flora asked nervously.

His hands, spread on the tabletop, clenched into fists, the scarred knuckles white. 'She took away my life. I'm going to make her pay.'

The *Wear Lass* sailed from Bremen at four in the morning with

William Morgan looking forward grimly to the responsibility of guardianship awaiting him.

The cargo liner *Florence Grey* left Hamburg four hours later, carrying Cecily, with her thoughts of freedom and her lover, and Liza, fearful of what the future held. She could remember only too well the hardships of poverty she had lived with, could see them looming again. She could never have foreseen that her ill-fortune would plunge her into the cold grey water of the North Sea.

BOOK II

12

SUNDAY, 20 JANUARY 1907, NORTH SEA

A hand hooked into Liza's collar, bruising and strangling but dragging her to the surface. She took a great, whooping breath, blinked salt water from her eyes and spat it from her mouth. She heard the deafening blare of the ship's siren. Cecily's face hung over hers and one of her carefully manicured hands was holding Liza up. The other was braced against the steel side of the ship so that the boat would not ride over the girl gasping in the sea. Now one of the seamen clambered over the thwarts to take over. He held off the boat while Cecily gripped Liza and hauled her inboard. She came over the side with a rush and Cecily fell back into the bottom of the boat with Liza on top of her.

'Good lass!' the sailor panted. 'Well done, the pair o' you.' And then, 'Oh, Jesus!' He clambered back to his post in the bow while the girls picked themselves up to sit on one of the thwarts amidships. Now they saw the reason for his exclamation. The sinking ship had listed still further, tilting away from them and towards the hole, on the other side and out of their sight, ripped open in the collision.

A head showed above the rail now, an officer by his cap. 'Cast off and pull clear!' he yelled. 'The rest of us are in the other boats.'

'Aye, aye!' the sailors chorused in reply. They unhooked the boat and used the oars to shove it away from the ship. Then the one in the stern said, 'You lasses sit back here.'

They obeyed and moved into the sternsheets while the sailors sat on the thwarts amidships to row, pulling the boat away from the ship. They stared back at her and saw that she did not have long. She was almost on an even keel again now but low in the water. A few minutes later the men rested on their oars and one said hoarsely, 'She's going.' The *Florence Grey* rolled slowly on to her side and there was a roaring of steam instead of the banshee wail of the siren, which had not stopped until now. They heard a crash: 'That's her engines breaking loose and falling out of her.' Then the roaring stopped and the ship sank. There was a swirl and spreading waves that set the boat plunging. Then the sea was quiet again. Liza thought bleakly that it had been like an interment.

She was soaked to the skin and bitterly cold: this was a winter night. Cecily saw her shudder, found the rug and wrapped it round her.

'Thank you,' Liza said, through chattering teeth.

'I suppose it will help a little.'

'I didn't mean just the rug. You pulled me out of the sea. I thought—' Liza stopped. She could still picture herself in that valley of death between boat and ship with the sea closing over her. She could swim passably well but would not have had the chance: she would have been crushed first. She had lost both suitcase and handbag but was just glad to be alive.

The men were tugging on the oars again, heading to join the other two boats, now just visible beyond where the ship had gone down. The fog drifted between them. They lived in a grey world only some two hundred yards across and littered with flotsam: a lifebuoy, a cushion, all manner of rubbish. But there was no sign of Liza's suitcase. Another siren blared, long, loud and close. The girls clapped their hands over their ears. When it stopped they could see that the other two boats were crowded with men. One used a whistle to answer the siren. The piping seemed feeble after that bull bellow but it brought a reply.

She came creeping out of the fog, at first just a huge, hulking shadow, which then took shape as a ship. She moved at walking pace so there was only a gentle ripple at her blunt bow where a man stood. As the girls saw him, he spotted the boats, turned and waved wildly, signalling to the officers on the bridge. The siren sounded again and the ripple at the bow faded to nothing as the ship stopped. In the boats the sailors bent to the oars and pulled towards the ship.

'That's a relief,' Cecily said. 'I wasn't looking forward to spending hours in this boat. It's most uncomfortable.'

'I'm just glad to be alive,' Liza said simply.

Cecily gave her a calculating glance. She lowered her voice so the men could not hear. 'Remember I asked you to take my place? Can't you do a little thing like that for me? You would be well paid – and I did save your life.'

Despite the rug, Liza was still shaking with cold and chilled to the bone, tired and afraid of what lay ahead. She was being offered money that would solve her problem in the short-term. 'I could land up in prison.'

'I'm not asking you to commit a crime!' Cecily laughed. 'No one can arrest you. You'll be doing no harm. You aren't stealing and you have my permission to do it. If you and I want to change places for a few weeks then it's no one's business but ours. I've never seen the inside of a prison cell and don't believe I ever will. Five pounds now, five later. Will you? Please?'

The water alongside was cold and glassy. Liza remembered the *Florence Grey* sinking beneath it without a trace, save for those few items of flotsam. She might have gone like that. She shuddered. 'Couldn't you just – go?'

'No.' Cecily shook her head. 'They're expecting me. If no one turns up they'd start to search, but when you arrive, why, they'll accept you.' And, almost pleading, 'I'll give you a jolly good reference, too.'

Liza suspected it might not be so easy, that Cecily was only concerned with her own priorities and would ride roughshod over anyone to have her way. But a reference would go a long way towards her securing a position, and she needed the money. It would keep her mother and Susan – and herself – for two months. Or buy ten fine dresses for Cecily. Besides, she had saved Liza from an awful death. How could she refuse her? She thought vaguely that it would be like playing a part in amateur dramatics, as at the Gresham house, or mimicking another as she had done so often. 'I'll do it,' she said reluctantly.

Cecily squeezed her arm. 'Good!'

They were alongside the ship and they could see the name on her bow: *Wear Lass*. A Jacob's ladder, made of rope with wooden treads, hung down. The two seamen held it, eyes politely averted as first Cecily, then Liza, climbed up to the deck, only too conscious of their long skirts flapping up to show ankles and calves. Sailors, in old clothes for shipboard working, helped them over the rail and wrapped them in blankets. Two, one short, one tall, hurried them into the superstructure under the bridge. The taller opened a door: 'This is the first mate's cabin. He's sharing with the second. You'll be comfortable in here and there'll be a cup o' tea along shortly.'

They entered, and he shut the door behind them. There was a small desk, a chair, a bunk and just enough room for both of them to stand together. 'It's awfully cramped,' Cecily complained.

There was a rapping on the door. 'Got the case of one o' you ladies.'

Liza, who was nearest the door, took in Cecily's case and heaved it on to the bunk. She remembered again that her own suitcase and handbag were at the bottom of the sea. She had nothing now but the clothes on her back and they were wet. She really needed the money Cecily would give her. There was no mirror and she was glad of that. She could *feel* what her hair was like, knew it had come down and was hanging like rats' tails.

Cecily, head on one side, studied her and said, 'You look awful. You really should get out of those wet clothes.'

Annoyed, Liza snapped, '*Anyone* would look the worse for falling in the sea.' She was about to do this girl a big favour and while she had saved Liza's life it did not give her the right to make personal comments. Angered and emboldened, she asked, 'Pass me that towel, please. And I will thank you to give me some privacy.'

Cecily opened her mouth to scold her for this impertinence, but instead handed over the towel and turned her back disapprovingly. After all, Liza might still change her mind. So, to keep her up to the mark . . . 'You'll need some dry clothes and I suppose you'll have to take mine,' Cecily said coolly. She bent and opened the case.

Liza towelled herself. 'How will you manage?'

'I'll be in London tonight and sleep in my underthings,' Cecily replied, with a confident smile. Or without them.

Liza recalled the waiting fiancé. Cecily and her money, clothes and inheritance! She rubbed furiously at her hair. But then the other girl said, 'Here you are, try these.' Liza felt the caress of silken underwear against her skin, then pulled on the day dress of red velvet with a low neckline and frilled skirt. She topped it with Cecily's wide-brimmed straw hat and posed shyly. She had worked on clothes like these but never worn them, and felt pleased but also guilty, as if she were an impostor.

Then she remembered that she was.

'It needs an iron but it's not a bad fit,' Cecily said critically.

That was true. While Cecily was an inch or two taller, Liza was comparatively longer in the leg. The dress that showed off Cecily's ankles was a more modest length on Liza. The tailored coat also fitted her well enough. She did not wholly approve of Cecily's taste, thought she was a little fast, but said nothing. Shoes were the only problem: Cecily's were a size too big and too wide so they slipped off Liza's feet. Cecily shrugged. 'You'll have to wear your own but nobody will notice that.' They packed the button boots with old newspaper they found on a shelf and left them to dry.

There was another rap on the door of the cabin and Cecily opened it. The man outside was short, fat, bald and wearing a long apron over sea boots. He carried the lid of a biscuit tin, which served as a tray and held two mugs of steaming tea. 'Here y'are, Miss. Drop o' tea for you two ladies. Are you comfortable now?'

Cecily took it. 'Yes, thank you, Steward.'

'I'm not the steward, Miss. No stewards aboard here. I'm the cook, Archie Godolphin.' He tapped his chest importantly. 'I've just give the skipper his tea and he said, "Don't forget to give them lasses a cup, and tell 'em we'll be in the Wear in three or four hours." And I said, "Righto, Billy," so you can sit easy and sup your tea.'

Liza cradled the warm mug in her hands and smiled at him. 'Thank you.'

He went away then, and they sat on the side of the bunk and sipped the tea. Cecily stretched out a toe and stirred the damp clothing lying on the deck. 'We've got to get rid of these,' she said.

'No!' Liza said sharply. That offended her sense of thrift, which had been dinned into her all her life. She folded the clothing neatly, and made a package of it tied inside the dress. She hung up her coat to dry. 'You'll want this. Take the other things and let me have them back . . . afterwards.' The die was cast.

Cecily opened her purse and put five sovereigns into Liza's hand. 'There you are. And there will be five more when I come north in four weeks.' She delved in her suitcase. 'You'll need these.' She handed Liza the telegrams received from the solicitors and an old letter from Edward Spencer. There was another, addressed to the solicitors, from her aunt Alexandra Higgins, with Cecily's birth certificate, which the old lady had had with her for purposes of identification.

'Oh!' Cecily paused to take from her wrist the gold and jewelled watch. 'And this. My guardian gave it to me – it's engraved on the back.' She turned it over to show the inscription: 'To Cecily Spencer on her nineteenth birthday'. Liza slipped it on to her wrist.

'Tell them that any other documents they want will have to wait until Aunt Alex is back in Hampshire,' Cecily went on. 'Now, you'll need to know that my father's name was Charles . . .' She reeled off details of her family history, tore a page out of her diary and wrote them down. 'You must try to memorise them, but if you forget one or two just say you've forgotten. I did lots of times – and said so. I couldn't be bothered with relatives.' She put the documents back into her suitcase, locked it and gave the keys to Liza. 'There are duplicate keys in that bunch for my heavy baggage, too. The trunks should arrive in a few days.' Finally she tucked her purse into the front of her dress and gave her handbag to

Liza. It was a smart affair in velvet with a metal chain. Cecily yawned. 'You should be all right now. I'm going to have a nap.'

They squeezed on to the bunk together, a blanket over them, and Cecily was asleep within minutes. Liza was awake for some time, trying to commit to memory the names and details on the scrap of paper, or staring at the rusty bulkhead, with its beads of condensation, worrying over what lay ahead. But she knew it was the only option if she was to feed her daughter. In the end she slept fitfully.

When Archie Godolphin called them they struggled off the bunk and opened the door to him. 'Now, then, ladies. We're just running into the Wear. Which one o' you is Miss Cecily Spencer, please?'

Still only half awake, Liza felt a finger jab into her back and answered, 'I am.'

'Ah! Will you come with me, Miss, if you please? The captain sends his compliments and he'd like to see you on the bridge.'

Liza heard Cecily's whisper: 'See? Easy. I told you so.'

She pulled on her still damp boots, but asked, bewildered and suspicious, guilty again: 'Why does he want to see me?'

Archie shrugged. 'Blowed if I know, Miss. I went up to collect all the mugs off the bridge and he said, "One of those ladies is Miss Cecily Spencer. Give her my compliments and ask her to come up here."' He stood aside. 'This way, Miss.'

He accompanied her to the bridge. Liza was nervous and apprehensive, but the fog had gone and the fresh breeze played with her hair. It was good to be out of the stuffy cabin. It was evening, come early in this winter month. She saw the ship was steaming slowly up a river that ran in a steep-sided gorge, sprinkled with lights. Shipyards lined it on

either bank and vessels rode to moorings out in the channel or
lay alongside quays. Feathers of smoke trailed from chimneys
and funnels. It was very like the Tyne and she felt as if she
was coming home.

Then she remembered she was not.

Below in the cabin, Cecily hastily put on Liza's coat, wrinkling
her nose, and picked up the bundle of wet clothing. Then
she paused. She had remembered the ship's captain who had
come with Edward to Hampshire, whom she had pretended
to try to seduce – as she thought of it now. But he was unlikely
to recognise her because of the garish makeup she had worn.
Anyway, it was too late now – and he was probably sailing
on the other side of the world. She shrugged.

On deck, Liza heard the engines stop, then resume briefly as
the propellers thrashed and the ship went astern, then stop
again. Two tug-boats came fussing to nudge her in alongside
a quay with their stubby bows. 'Up you go, Miss,' Archie
urged. 'The skipper's up there on the bridge.' Liza climbed
the short, steep ladder and stepped on to the bridge. She felt
giddy, was sure that now, already, she would be found out. If
this captain knew Cecily Spencer's name he probably knew a
lot more about her. Was she about to be unmasked already?

She saw him at the front of the bridge, a bearded man in
his forties in a blue uniform with gold braid and a peaked
cap, standing next to the seaman at the helm. Another sailor
stood on the wing of the bridge, tall and broad, his back to
her, but she could see he held a mug in one big hand. He was
laughing, head back. Liza barely glanced at him in passing,
took a deep breath and approached the officer. 'You wished
to see me, Captain.'

He turned, still smiling at some joke, saw her and grinned

more broadly. 'I'm John Harley, captain of the *Florence Grey*. Yon's the captain of this ship.' He nodded at the tall seaman on the wing of the bridge.

He faced her now and he had stopped laughing. His hair was tousled, thick and black like the stubble on his jaw; he had obviously not shaved for some days. Liza had to tilt back her head to look him in the face, which was expressionless now but she could sense his hostility. She expected to be denounced, but remembered to speak in Cecily's accent. 'I'm sorry, sir.'

Has she done it again? William wondered. He remembered when he had met Cecily in Hampshire years ago, how she had tried to anger him by belittling his station in life. It seemed she was still an ill-natured snob. Had two years changed her in other ways? For the life of him he could not tell. He had been close enough – too close, when he had put her out of his room – but the paint and the wig had distorted his view of her. He admitted she was improved without them. And he was not going to mention Hampshire.

'Truly, sir, I meant nothing derogatory,' Liza went on. 'I was told the captain was here and I assumed . . .' She gestured helplessly at the captain of the *Florence Grey*, exposing the watch on her wrist. William remembered that, too, and Edward giving it to her. He hoped she now appreciated the gift, but doubted it.

Harley came to her aid. 'I met neither of the passengers.' That was common on small tramp steamers like the *Florence Grey*. 'I spent most of the voyage on the bridge.'

William fingered the stubble on his chin. 'So did I.' He thought the Spencer girl looked contrite – pale and nervous, too. He was surprised by her. He wondered cynically if the wetting had cooled her down, if soon she would revert to the hoyden he knew, cross-grained, tart and rude. Or had these last years changed her?

'Your error was understandable,' he said. 'Captain Harley looks the part more than I do.' Liza did not like this talk of playing parts, but he was going on: 'I'm William Morgan. The captain of the *Florence Grey* told me he had two ladies aboard, and their names. I was surprised but not overly so when I heard yours, because I knew you were on your way.'

'I see,' Liza said, although she did not see at all.

'I am – was – partner to Edward Spencer,' he explained, 'your late guardian. He asked me to care for you until you came of age and inherited. I'll take you up to the house as soon as I've completed a few formalities. I believe you have a suitcase?'

'No – yes,' Liza corrected herself, remembering that although her case was at the bottom of the sea he was referring to Cecily's. 'It's in the cabin.'

Archie was standing on the deck forward of the bridge now, peering at the quay as they closed it. William called down to him, 'Fetch Miss Spencer's case up from the cabin, Archie, and put it by the gangway.'

'I've got my galley to square away before I finish,' the cook protested. Then, as William glanced down at him, he said hurriedly, 'Aye, right away,' and hurried aft.

Liza stayed on the bridge and watched as William gave orders. Then he turned the ship over to the first officer and said to her, 'I'll be five minutes.' He dropped down the ladder to the deck below and she saw him disappear through a doorway. Liza waited, watching the bustle both aboard and on the quay as a gangway was swung out by a crane to bridge the gap between ship and shore. Then she gasped. First to cross the gangway to the lamplit quay and hurry away was Cecily Spencer, in Liza's coat, with the bundle of Liza's clothing under her arm. She passed through the pools of light and disappeared into the darkness beyond.

'You find this interesting?' William said behind her.

She jumped at the sound of his voice. 'I'm sorry. You startled me. Yes, I think it's very interesting.'

'You surprise me.'

'Oh?'

William did not answer the implied question. 'I'm ready now. This way, Miss Spencer.' He had a stained sea-bag slung over his shoulder, like that once carried by her father. He gestured to the ladder.

She waited for him to go ahead of her, giving way to the master as she had done all her working life, then realised he was standing back to let her precede him: she was the lady now. She dabbed at her eye, blinked at him and said, 'I'm sorry. I think I had something in my eye,' pretending that that was her reason for pausing. She tried to smile and wondered if he had noticed.

'All right now?'

'Yes, thank you.' She swept past him and he followed. Liza drew a sigh of relief. She told herself she had been lucky and would have to be more careful. She realised now the enormity of her task. She could never relax, must always be on her guard.

At the foot of the ladder William said, 'I must see how your companion is, if she is fit to go ashore, or whether she wants a doctor.'

Why should she need a doctor? Liza thought. I was the one who nearly drowned. Then it struck her that one of the men in the boat had probably reported that Liza Thornton had fallen in.

A voice came from the narrow galley close beside them, its

door hooked back. 'She went ashore ten minutes ago, soon as they ran out the gangway.' Archie Godolphin poked out his bald head. 'She told me she had people expecting her.'

The fiancé, Liza thought. Cecily had not waited long to go in search of him – and leave Liza to her fate.

William shrugged his wide shoulders. 'That frees me of a duty, but she might at least have left a word of thanks.'

Liza remembered her manners. 'May I express thanks for both of us. You rescued us from a frightening experience.'

William raised his eyebrows: that was well said and maybe Cecily had changed. 'You're welcome. This way, Miss Spencer.' He pointed to the gangway, and this time Liza did not hesitate but stepped on to it ahead of him. Archie followed them with Cecily's suitcase.

The quay was in darkness, save for occasional gas lamps. They walked between cranes and over railway lines, Liza holding up her skirts, until they came to a stretch of roadway. A Vauxhall motor-car stood there with a uniformed man standing by. William hailed him. 'Have you been here long?'

Gibson, one-time coachman now also chauffeur, put a finger to his cap in salute. 'Only a few minutes. We heard that you'd been sighted coming in a'tween the piers so I drove down.'

William tossed his sea-bag and Cecily's suitcase into the rear of the car and Archie stumped away. William said, 'I'll drive now. This is Miss Spencer, Mr Spencer's niece.'

Gibson saluted again, more formally this time. 'Miss Spencer,' he said neutrally – Elspeth Taggart, Edward's housekeeper, had told him her opinion of Cecily after she had overheard Edward and William talking about her.

Liza met his gaze and smiled. As she had been a servant she recognised that this one did not welcome her. Nevertheless, she kept the smile in place. 'Good evening.'

'We were all shocked and sorry about Mr Spencer, sir,' he said, addressing William.

William patted his back. 'I'm sure you were.' He handed Liza into the front passenger seat of the car, and here she saw a difficulty. She put a hand to Cecily's broad-brimmed straw hat with its curling ostrich feather, perched on her head. It was unpinned and the Vauxhall was open to the sky. William saw the automatic gesture and said, 'Ah. Do you have a scarf?'

Liza had not seen what was in Cecily's handsome suitcase, apart from what she wore now. She could not admit that and said, 'I'm afraid not.'

Gibson coughed. 'Excuse me, sir. In here . . .' He fished in some recess inside the car and produced a silk square.

'Just the thing.' William passed it to Liza, who used it to secure the hat.

'Thank you.' She wondered who was the owner of the scarf. Gibson swung the starting-handle, then jumped into a rear seat and William drove off. As the Vauxhall passed out of the dock gates, William said, voice lifted above the sound of the engine, 'This is the south shore. The bridge you can see leads to Monkwearmouth, and Newcastle eventually.' Liza could see it between the jibs of the cranes, electric trams grinding across it.

A cart carrying coal, drawn by a plodding little horse, iron shoes clashing on the cobbles, pulled out ahead of them. William had to slow to swing round it and the voice came, an accusing screech: *'You bloody murderers!'* Liza's head whipped round. There was a shop of sorts, a window filled with what looked like sacks and sticks of furniture. Although this was Sunday evening it was lit by a gas jet and a woman stood in its doorway and shook her fist at the car. She was tall and gaunt, wild of eye, with bushy iron-grey hair under a man's black cap. All in rusty black, dress and shawl, she pointed an accusing, skinny finger like a claw. 'You drowned my man!'

'It's that mad ould lass from the tagareen shop,' Gibson said.

'I know who it is,' William replied. 'God knows, I've heard her often enough.' The Vauxhall pulled away and the shrieks faded behind them. Liza let out her breath, which she had been holding. The verbal attack had taken her unawares. She glanced at William, thinking he would give some explanation, but he did not.

They drove up out of the narrow streets by the river, into the town with its street-lights, busy with trams and people, then up a hill beside a park, and turned off into tree-lined avenues.

'Here we are,' William said. He steered the car through the open wrought-iron gates, and Liza saw the name cut into the stone of the gate-post: Spencer Hall. The house was set back from the road behind a screen of trees pierced by a semi-circular gravelled drive. There were lights in the windows, three floors of them, but seen only as cracks between the thick curtains; Liza learned later that there were six bedrooms for family and their guests and more for the servants. Steps led up to the front door, which opened as the Vauxhall crunched to a halt outside it.

William left the engine ticking over but swung his legs out of the car, handed down Liza and shouldered his sea-bag. Gibson hauled out Cecily's suitcase, then asked, 'Will you be keeping the carriage and the horses, sir? I mean, it was Mr Edward who used them and since we got the car you . . .'

William took the case from him. 'We'll keep them. Mr Spencer would have wanted it.'

'Thank you, sir.'

'But don't expect me to muck out those stables,' William warned.

Gibson grinned, evidently relieved that he was not to lose his beloved horses. 'I'll garage her, sir.' He drove off round the corner of the house, heading for the stables and the garage.

A woman stood at the head of the steps and William set down the case to wrap a long arm round her. 'Elspeth! You're looking bonny as ever!'

Elspeth Taggart was still rosy-cheeked and erect, but there were streaks of grey in her red hair. 'Away wi' ye and your daftness,' she said brusquely as she detached herself.

He laughed, then said, 'Miss Spencer, this is Mrs Taggart, our – my housekeeper.' He made the amendment as he remembered Edward Spencer was now dead. 'Elspeth, this is Mr Spencer's ward. She has just been shipwrecked and rescued from the North Sea.'

Elspeth bobbed a curtsey, the keys at her waist jangling; the maid at her back copied her. The girl smiled but Elspeth did not. As she straightened, she said, 'You're welcome, Miss.'

Liza noted that reserve again. 'I'm pleased to meet you.' She recognised Elspeth's type, the lifelong retainer regarded almost as one of the family, with the licence to be familiar or outspoken that was denied to the other servants.

'I'm sorry I couldn't let you know Miss Spencer was with me,' William said to her.

The housekeeper pursed her lips. 'Mr Arkenstall sent word that she was coming but we did not expect her so soon. Still, I made the room ready because I didn't know which one you would use, the master's bedroom being rightfully yours now.'

'Miss Spencer can have it,' William said.

Elspeth inclined her head and ushered them in, took Liza's coat, hat and borrowed scarf and hung them up. 'Your dinner's ready as soon as you are. I expect you'll be wanting to change.' She led the way upstairs, William carrying suitcase and sea-bag. He left the case in the room given to Liza, said, 'I'll see you at dinner,' and left.

The room was large with a big double bed and a bright fire burning in the grate. Elspeth swept a swift glance over it to see that all was in order then said, 'Martha will look after you,' before she followed William.

Liza was left with the girl and smiled at her as she unlocked the case with the keys Cecily had given her. 'How old are you, Martha?'

'Sixteen, Miss,' she replied shyly.

Liza could remember when she was sixteen, only five years ago but now she felt as if she was a hundred. 'You're young to be a lady's maid.'

'I'm not, really,' Martha explained. 'I think Mrs Taggart had to give me the job because the other two maids are having their night off. She took me on because she knew my mother when she worked here.' She added anxiously, 'I hope she'll let me keep this job.'

'Tell her I'm pleased with you.'

'Thank you, Miss. Shall I run your bath, Miss?'

'Run it?' Liza looked for the bath, then saw the door. 'Yes, please.' In all the houses in which she had worked there had been hip baths, placed as needed in the bedrooms. The maids toiled up long flights of stairs with huge jugs of hot water to fill them. Now Martha passed through the door into a bathroom and spun taps to bring forth steaming water. Liza had seen this phenomenon but never experienced it. She flung open the lid of the suitcase and saw a pair of Cecily's shoes. She pushed them hastily to the back of the wardrobe, out of sight. Martha darted back to help her undress. Liza found that strange – she could have made a suggestion or two to help the girl, tricks of the trade, but bit her tongue because that was not in the role she was playing.

'This was the master's room,' Martha told her. 'Captain Morgan's room has a bathroom as well. Mr Cully, he's the gardener, he looks after the boiler, or Mr Gibson does it.' She looked startled by the old button boots and Liza hastily explained how she had lost her own in the wreck and had been lent a pair by a servant girl.

'You were lucky she was the same size, Miss.'

'Yes, wasn't I?' Liza agreed.

'I'll set them by the fire to dry.'

In William's room, Elspeth Taggart rooted out his soiled laundry from his sea-bag. 'Guid God! You've torn this shirt from top to tail! Another one! I've never known a lad to tear so many.'

'Sorry. It split as I pulled it off,' William, wrapped in a bathrobe, said.

Elspeth tutted over it. Then she said absently, 'Yon lassie is not as I expected her to be.'

William grinned. 'How *did* you expect her?'

'Ye ken – the fine lady looking down her nose. And she still has a trace of a North Country accent. I'd ha' thought she would ha' lost it after all these years in the south.'

'True. But she was here until she was five and I suppose once you have the accent you never lose it entirely.'

'Aye . . .' But then she forgot about the girl's speech. 'And you've got a hole in this jersey!'

Liza soaked and almost slept in the bath: her ordeal and adventure, the nights at sea with little sleep, were telling on her now. She jerked awake when Martha called through the door, 'Shall I put out the blue dress, Miss? I can iron it and have it ready in five minutes.'

Liza had never seen it but did not care. 'Yes, please.' She dragged herself out of the bath and found that her case had been unpacked and its contents put away, her clothes laid out for her and Martha waiting to help. She dressed, pulled on the old button boots – warm now and almost dry – then made her way downstairs. She paused nervously on the threshold of the drawing room. William stood by the fire, a glass in his hand. He had changed into a sober suit and was clean-shaven.

He came to meet her. 'Dinner is ready, but would you care for a drink first?'

'No, thank you, except perhaps some water.'

That surprised him. He would have expected the Cecily Spencer he knew to call for something stronger. 'I think we can manage that.' He downed his whisky. 'We'll dine now, Elspeth,' he called. 'Water for Miss Spencer, please.' Liza saw the housekeeper bustling about in the dining room next door. Then he turned back to her. 'I was just looking at that photograph. It was taken when you were seventeen and first went to that finishing school, but you look taller in it than you do now.'

Alarm bells rang in Liza's head. He had taken the photograph from the mantelpiece and held it out to her, pointing. Oh, God! she thought. Cecily had casually dismissed the photograph. The sepia images swirled before her eyes then steadied. She saw it was of a group, a dozen or more girls, one or two taller than the rest. She picked out the young Cecily staring stiffly at the camera. But with so many on the photograph their faces were only a quarter-inch across, one very like another. It might have been herself peering out.

Could she pass it off? 'I was tall for my age but the other girls caught up.'

'Of course,' William said. He replaced the photograph and Liza breathed again.

He led her in to dinner, pulled out her chair, then took his own at the end of the long polished table. Liza could manage this part easily, had often observed as a maid. She awarded marks to Mrs Taggart and the maid who served the dinner now, and to the cook. There was oxtail soup, followed by a sirloin steak, excellently cooked, but she was too tired to eat it. She gave up at the dessert when she caught herself nodding over it and William staring at her. 'I'm sorry. I'm afraid I must retire. I found the journey quite exhausting.'

'Can I help you?' He came round the table in long strides to pull back her chair and help her to her feet.

'No, thank you. I will be all right.' She smiled weakly. 'I'm sure I will feel better tomorrow.'

Mrs Taggart hurried past her. 'I'll send up Martha.' Did Liza detect a note of sympathy in place of the hitherto distant stare? She could not be sure and climbed the stairs, let Martha undress her and crept into the bed with its stone hot-water bottle.

'Goodnight, Miss,' said Martha, and closed the door softly. Liza blinked at the shadows cast on the ceiling by the fire in the grate. She had never been cosseted like this and sighed luxuriously, sleepily.

She had been lucky so far but she would have to be careful. She was not among friends here and she recalled how coldly Gibson and Mrs Taggart had greeted her. William Morgan's gaze seemed to probe right through her and see something he did not like. She was afraid of being found out. This play, drama or farce, had been devised by Cecily. She had used Liza's gratitude for saving her life to make her play the leading role. But Liza, not Cecily, would suffer the strain of the performance and the retribution if she was unmasked. William would not be forgiving.

She had to maintain the impersonation for four weeks. It seemed like an eternity but she had survived today and that was enough for now. If only she could hold her little daughter. She slept.

Meanwhile Cecily was curled up in a sleeping-carriage, on a train thundering south towards London and Mark Calvert.

13

Liza woke to see the glow of sunshine behind the curtains and stretched lazily. It was good to come to life gradually in the big bed, to feel refreshed and at ease. She was ready for the day. A clock on the mantelpiece above the fire, ashes now, told her it was eight in the morning. Time she was up.

There was a knock at her door and Martha entered. 'Good morning, Miss Spencer. I've brought your tea.' Liza was reminded of who she was supposed to be and on her guard again. The girl set the tray on the bedside table and drew back the curtains. 'A fine day, Miss. I hope you slept well?'

'Yes, thank you.' Liza had been on the other side of this ritual of morning tea for years, but it was the first time she had been in receipt of it.

'Mrs Taggart said she would accompany you to the shops this morning if you were agreeable. Will I put out a dress? This green one?'

'Let me see.' Liza got out of bed and went to join Martha at the wardrobe. The clothes Cecily had left her were expensive but not to her taste. No matter, she would have to make do. She settled for the green dress. Having made the choice she wondered if it would fit her. The red one she had worn the previous day and the blue for dinner had both been long. The green proved no better. She told herself that William would not notice and Mrs Taggart would just look down her nose.

When she was ready she descended the stairs. Breakfast was

served in the dining room; one place was set at the head of the long table. No one was in the room and tall french windows looked on to the garden at the rear. She opened them and stepped out into the sparkling morning. She was about to go back for a coat but saw the greenhouse, a blaze of colours within, and crossed to it. She peered in, shivering, and a tall, heavy man rose up from among the blooms. He opened the door to admit her and put a finger to his cap: 'Miss Spencer? I'm Cully, the gardener.'

Liza stepped into the warmth and remembered Martha mentioning Cully, who also saw to the heating of the hot water. 'Good morning. What lovely flowers. May I see?'

'Oh, aye.' He beamed at her.

Cully showed her round proudly, and Liza loved it and said so. When she remembered breakfast he picked a bunch of blooms for her with his big, gentle hands. She thanked him and took them back to the house, smiling. She was met by Mrs Taggart in the dining room, who said drily, 'I see you've met Cully. He has an eye for a pretty face.' And she thought the girl was startlingly pretty. Last night she had been washed out and drawn but now – what a transformation! She realised she was staring and Liza shifting uncomfortably, so went on, 'Let me have those and I'll put them in a vase.'

She departed with the blooms and Liza breakfasted in solitary state from the chafing dishes ranged on the sideboard. When Mrs Taggart returned to place the vase with the flowers on the table, she said, 'Captain Morgan has gone to his office. He hopes you will join him for lunch here, then accompany him this afternoon when he pays his respects in the cemetery and visits the solicitor.'

Liza had feared that the earlier stare had betokened suspicion but was able now to heave an inward sigh of relief. 'Yes, of course.'

The housekeeper seemed surprised by her ready agreement, but went on, 'Martha told me how you lost your shoes
but a servant girl lent you a pair.'

'Yes. Fortunately we were the same size,' Liza said quickly.

'They may well have fitted but are hardly suitable for you
now, Miss Spencer,' Mrs Taggart said drily. 'As it happens,
the captain also suggested you might like to go shopping to
repair your wardrobe or add to it. I'm to accompany you
and to charge all items to his account. He left this for you in
case you needed cash.' She handed Liza a plump envelope
which lay lightly on her hand, but she found it held a wad of
bank notes.

William had hesitated over the money, not out of meanness
but because he was wary of the girl. Would she turn up her
nose and refuse it? Then he had asked himself: What would
Edward have wished?

'Thank you,' Liza said. 'He is very kind and I'd like to go
shopping with you.'

'Shall I tell Gibson to bring the carriage round at nine?'

That being agreed, Elspeth inclined her head and departed.
As she went to give Gibson his orders she reflected on the
girl's smiling co-operation. It was not what she had expected
of Cecily Spencer.

Liza rode into Sunderland in the carriage with Mrs Taggart
sitting opposite her. She had intended to buy only one spare
item, but as they rolled along she reasoned that she was here
at Cecily's request and new clothes were necessary for the
part she was playing. Buying clothes on behalf of Cecily, for
the present Miss Spencer, was in order.

In the first shop she chose a dress in pale pink chiffon

with a full skirt and low neckline. She put it on and twirled before the mirror. She glanced at the housekeeper, sitting straight-backed in a chair, hands folded in her lap. 'Do you like it, Mrs Taggart?'

'It's not my place to say.' She stiffened further.

'But I'd like your opinion,' Liza urged. 'Please?'

She sniffed, then gave the answer Liza expected: 'I think it's a little too flighty at this time.'

Liza nodded. 'Ye-es. I think you're right.' She discarded it. After that, each dress became a matter for discussion. Liza bought four, two to which Mrs Taggart agreed, two to which she did not. But she wasn't sitting quite so straight or so silent. Finally there was a black day dress. 'I think this is appropriate,' Liza said.

'Aye, ye'll need that today.'

'Do you think Captain Morgan will like what I've bought?' Liza asked.

'He doesn't like mourning,' Mrs Taggart said decisively. 'He would not force it on a lassie like yoursel', and that would be Mr Edward's view, but that looks nice on you.'

There were also two coats, one black, and two costumes, three pairs of shoes, and nightdresses, silk stockings and underwear, which raised Mrs Taggart's eyebrows but she said nothing. Liza also bought a new handbag: she did not like Cecily's. The bill for the morning came to just under ten pounds. Liza had been earning two pounds per month, so that was five months' work. But it was how Cecily would act, she was sure.

A porter carried the boxes and bags out to Gibson and the waiting carriage, and they were home just in time to join William for lunch. He saw the parcels as Gibson carried them in and smiled. This was more like the Cecily he knew.

Over lunch he said, 'I left word that I proposed we should visit Mr Spencer's grave then go on to see Arkenstall – he is the solicitor. I sent word to him that you are here. Can I take it this is agreeable to you?'

Liza smiled at him from the other end of the table. 'Yes, of course.'

'I have a wreath to lay and I took the liberty of ordering one on your behalf.'

'Thank you. I'd like to do that.'

'I thought you might,' William said. He had also thought she might not.

Liza wore her new black dress and coat. The cemetery was cold, with a brisk wind off the sea that blew away any warmth from the pale winter sunshine. They laid the flowers on the grave, then stood side by side in silence as the gulls, driven by the wind, screamed above them. Liza said a prayer for Edward, who she thought must have been a good man.

William stirred. 'He was my guardian too, as no doubt you know. I owe everything I have, anything I am, to him.'

Liza was brought up short by this: it was a warning that she knew virtually nothing about this man or his guardian. She knew some reply was needed and spoke instinctively: 'I'm sure he was proud of you.'

He seemed taken aback by that and said only, 'Well, I tried.' Then, as if embarrassed, 'Shall we go now?'

They returned to the Vauxhall, he taking the wheel and Liza sitting beside him, and drove to the solicitor's office in the High Street. Liza had bought a scarf to secure her hat and left the silk square given to her the previous day in the hall.

As they entered Ezra Arkenstall rose from behind his desk.

'William! And Miss Spencer. How good to see you. Come and sit down.' He was close to sixty but still vigorous, with grey in his pointed beard. He looked out shrewdly at life through wire-rimmed spectacles. He had been a lifelong friend of Edward Spencer, had watched William grow from a boy of five to manhood, and smiled at him now.

They sat, and Ezra asked about Alexandra Higgins and Cecily's travels in Paris and Berlin. Liza, shaking inside and expecting every moment to be denounced, said that her aunt was as well as could be expected, and recounted some episodes based on her experiences in France and Germany, and those of the Koenigs she had heard discussed. Arkenstall nodded and smiled. Now she produced the papers Cecily had given her, including the birth certificate. 'All the other papers are in Hampshire and Aunt Alexandra will send whatever you require when she comes home.'

The solicitor scanned them and set them aside. 'We will need them again when you inherit your own estate.' He looked uncomfortable.

William knew why and wondered if he should tell the girl that there was no big bequest coming to her. But Arkenstall had said nothing, sticking to Edward's instructions as he should. William was surprised that Cecily had not asked the amount of her inheritance, but decided she had probably assumed there would be a pot of gold waiting for her – and that would be enough for the Cecily he remembered.

Arkenstall carried on: 'Now for Edward's will.' He told them that, after some small bequests to friends and servants, all Edward's estate went to William.

William was stunned. He would not have been surprised by a bequest, but to inherit all! He was not even a blood relative.

Then as he came to terms with the idea he acknowledged, without conceit, that Edward had done what was best for the firm and its employees.

Arkenstall was smiling at Liza now: 'There is also a bequest to you. Your uncle left funds for your support for four years, provided you use the money and the time to train for a trade or profession that will render you a useful member of the community.' He coughed. 'The provision of these funds will be in the hands of Captain Morgan, who will decide if the course of training is suitable and your progress is satisfactory.' He looked over his spectacles at them. 'I questioned the need for this when drawing up the will, but Mr Spencer was adamant. I'm sure he believed he was doing his best for you, Miss Spencer.'

'Oh, yes,' Liza agreed.

William was surprised again that she had not created uproar when she learned that he, an outsider, had inherited the estate while Edward's niece was fobbed off with this small legacy – and that on terms!

'Would you have any suggestion to make regarding a career to follow?' Arkenstall asked.

Liza shook her head. 'I'm afraid you've caught me unprepared.'

He smiled, evidently relieved that she had not burst into tears or had a fit of temper. 'You can consult with Captain Morgan and decide at your leisure.'

Liza had caught William's cold eye on her and resented it. She had tried to please him on Cecily's account but he, for some reason, kept her at arm's length. Well, he would not run Cecily's life for her.

William was mulling over his new duty and not liking it, though he recalled wryly that he had suggested to Edward that the girl be put to learn a trade. He could understand his guardian setting it up, agreed with his reasoning, but could foresee trouble if he had to monitor her training. His consolation, however, was that Cecily would not agree to it, secure in the knowledge that she would inherit her father's estate in a matter of weeks.

They drove home in the Vauxhall, silent, both busy with their own thoughts. It was only as they halted on the drive before the house that William said, 'You'll have a chance to wear some of your new clothes this evening. We've been invited out to dinner by Norman Outhwaite. He was a business acquaintance of Edward's and will deal with me.'

'Us? Me? I won't know anyone there,' Liza said, startled.

He glanced sideways at her as he applied the brake. 'They know about you, but all good. Edward always spoke well of you. It's just that people will want to see you in the flesh and that's understandable. Edward was an important man in this town and you were his ward.'

Liza debated: could she make some excuse? A headache, stomach upset? But then she would have to make a miraculous recovery to carry out her plans for the following day.

William was watching her curiously now. 'They won't bite your head off,' he said.

Liza smiled at him. 'Of course. I was just taken by surprise. I'd love to come.'

William had seen that startled look become wary and had thought she was about to refuse. Odd. She certainly wasn't shy, not Cecily. But then he recalled how she had refused so many of Edward's requests for unknown reasons. Just wilful? He shrugged inwardly. Anyway, she was coming. 'I thought we'd leave about seven.'

'I'll be ready.'

I've heard that one before, he thought.

He descended the stairs in leisurely fashion at five minutes to seven and found her waiting for him, her coat over her arm. He stopped some feet away from her at the foot of the stairs. 'Is that one of the new dresses?'

'Yes,' said Liza. It was a little bit daring, an evening gown of grey silk chiffon over dark blue silk with a low scooped neckline and a flared skirt that clung to the lines of her body.

William nodded and grinned. 'Well worth the money. It looks very nice.' He reached out for her coat and eased it on to Liza's shoulders. 'There we are.'

Gibson was waiting at the foot of the steps with the carriage, holding open the door. William handed in Liza, then asked him, 'Did you find that scarf?'

'Yes, sir. It had got hung up in the hall.'

'Good man.' William took the scarf he had lent to Liza and tucked it into a pocket. 'Away we go, then.' And they set off in cheerful mood.

The Outhwaites' house was large but not large enough for all the furniture, plants and pictures crammed into it. Liza thought it was too cluttered and that she would not want the job of dusting it. She could afford to grin at that, knowing it was someone else's job. Norman Outhwaite was red-faced and jovial, his wife plump and affable. Daphne, their daughter, was in her early twenties, fair and with a tittering laugh. She threw her arms round William's neck. 'Lovely to see you, darling.' He unwrapped her, smiling, and she turned to Liza: 'And so good to see you, Miss Spencer. We've all been longing to meet you. The mysterious heiress!' William dug out the scarf from his pocket and gave it to her. She took it with a squeal, 'Oh! Thank you, darling!' and explained to

Liza, 'He drove me home from a dance a few weeks ago. We had an absolutely *marvellous* time!'

Liza kept her smile in place. 'I'm so glad.' She thought Daphne's dress was too revealing. She did not warm to her, had seen too many like her, both upstairs and down.

At dinner, host and hostess sat at either end of the table. William sat opposite Liza and she was on Norman Outhwaite's right. Daphne was next to William, and beside Liza was another man, invited to make up the numbers. Liza gathered he was a young member of the Outhwaite family and firm. He droned on interminably while Liza nodded and smiled as she thought appropriate. She had no difficulty in hearing Daphne's unending breathy chatter, her hand constantly on William's sleeve. Was he enjoying it? she wondered.

They had reached dessert when Daphne squeaked, 'My! So we have both of Mr Spencer's wards living under the same roof!'

She made it sound as if they were sharing the same bed and Liza found herself blushing again. But she fixed Daphne with a level stare and said coolly, 'It's a big house with plenty of room for both of us. We find it convenient.'

Daphne knew when she had been snubbed, showed her teeth in a smile and asked, 'But do you intend to live there permanently?'

William was about to speak but Liza was before him: 'I have made no plans but I will probably travel.' She would certainly do that – as far as Newcastle. Then she remembered that Cecily had just toured in Europe, and she added, 'Again.'

'Miss Spencer may stay as long as it suits her,' William put in firmly. 'It is as Edward would have wished and for my part she is welcome.' Then he steered away the conversation.

'Shipbuilding is booming now,' he said to Norman Outhwaite, 'but how long do you think it will last?'

When the ladies retired to the drawing room, leaving the men to their port, Daphne probed shrilly again, asking now about Cecily's home life. Liza answered, sometimes vaguely, with details she had observed in the houses where she had worked.

They left early, William having privately decided that Cecily was not happy. What was wrong now? he wondered. In the carriage they were silent, but at home he thought they might have a nightcap. The servants had been dismissed for the evening but earlier he had asked Elspeth to leave out some drinks. Now he asked Liza, 'Did you enjoy yourself?'

'I had an absolutely *marvellous* time!' she replied. It was Daphne to the life and William burst out laughing. Liza did not. 'I don't really think it's funny. I thought that young lady was – forward.'

'Forward?'

'Well, fawning. She threw herself at you.'

William laughed again. 'She tries to be a charmer.'

'More like a trollop.'

'Oh, come now.' William was irritated.

'She as much as implied that I was—' Liza stopped, trying to choose her words.

The ship's captain spoke: 'Spit it out, then.'

That provoked Liza and she ceased seeking polite words and spoke. 'She talked of us sharing the same house as if it were the same bed.'

'You are hardly in a position to criticise,' William snapped.

Liza blinked. 'What do you mean?'

William regretted his words and tried to take them back: 'Nothing. It doesn't matter.'

'You insinuated something about me!' And now she quoted him: 'Spit it out!'

That angered him further. 'Very well. I recall only too well that you offered yourself to me, in my bed, in Hampshire two years ago. You may also recall that you wore a wig and had painted your face so you were unrecognisable. I think that was intended to upset Edward, and it succeeded.'

That remark took Liza's breath away as if he had slapped her face. Now she slapped his with a *crack!* The impression of her fingers could be seen on his cheek. 'That's a *lie!*'

He shook his head slowly, his face still but his eyes burning. 'You know it's true.'

She did. She knew he was talking of Cecily but his words had been levelled at *her*, Liza. She was here and he believed it of her and that hurt. 'Most of us do things we regret later.' She recalled her own mistaken passion for Vince Bailey. 'If Mr Spencer was hurt, I am sorry. If I offered myself to you when I was a foolish young girl, I can assure you I regret it and it will not happen again.' She turned her back on him and walked away.

'Wait!' he snapped. Liza stopped. He took her by her shoulders, turned her to face him and saw the tears in her eyes. 'I've hurt you, and for that I'm sorry. I agree we all act stupidly at times. I have, as a young man. Daphne is a well-known flirt but I forgot she also has a reputation for spiteful remarks. I've danced with her on occasion and once drove her home along with some others. She may be a seductress but I'd guess she's all talk. She certainly bores me.'

Liza stared ahead of her, eyes fixed on his broad chest, the white shirtfront only inches from her. She thought dully that although he had apologised he still believed she was the girl who had offered herself to him. Whenever he looked at her he would remember that. She did not think that she would forget now, either.

'Perhaps we should put the past behind us and start again from here,' he said. She did not answer, and he pressed, 'What do you say?'

'Very well,' she replied flatly. And then: 'I'd like to—' She hesitated a second, could not say, 'go to bed'. She finished, 'Retire now.' She lifted her head to look him in the eyes. 'Goodnight, Captain.'

'Goodnight, Miss Spencer.'

He watched her climb the stairs, a slight, slender figure, until she had gone from his sight. Then he sighed and went into the drawing room for his nightcap. He swallowed whisky and told himself he had been provoked but should not have lost his temper. He had always expected trouble from the Spencer girl and should not have been surprised. But she had seemed altogether different. And badly hurt over that incident two years ago. He sighed again and hoped that the morrow would be better.

Liza was determined it would be and had already decided on her course of action. But as she lay in her bed she felt battered by the row. And she wondered what other secrets of Cecily's she was going to discover.

When Elspeth Taggart had heard the carriage crunching on the gravel of the drive she had come out of her room in the servants' quarters at the top of the house. She had intended to go down to welcome them home but had stopped at the head of the stairs. From there she could look down the well to the ground floor and the hall. She had heard the altercation and seen Liza wipe away tears with the heel of her hand as she mounted the stairs.

She returned to her room, thinking: The lassie is more tender than I thought.

14

TUESDAY, 22 JANUARY 1907, SUNDERLAND

At breakfast, William was mindful of his offer to start again and smiled at Liza down the length of the table. 'Would you like to come down to the office with me today? I thought you might like to see the place and its workings. And a couple of the firm's ships are in the river at the moment. I could show you round them.'

She smiled back at him. She was cheerful this morning, exuberant even, and he was surprised by that, after their parting of the previous evening. Now she said, 'No, thank you.'

William inclined his head. 'I thought you might have liked to see something of Edward's life and his work.'

'Another time.' A polite but blunt refusal.

He decided she was not interested. Yet she had been absorbed in what was going on around her when he had left her on the bridge of the *Wear Lass*. He decided that that was Cecily. The girl was always changing her moods as a chameleon its colour. She seemed happy, but was she still sulking over the row last night?

He excused himself and went off in the Vauxhall, bound for his work.

Liza rose from the table. She was sorry now that she had not made a gentler excuse. When the housekeeper entered, she said, 'I think Captain Morgan and Mr Spencer were close.'

Mrs Taggart paused in her bustling. 'Aye, they were, ever since William came here as a wee lad, just five years old. They always lived like father and son. But, then, they were two of a kind and appreciated each other. Not like some.'

Liza caught the veiled reference and guessed it was aimed at herself. Better to say nothing, steer clear of strange waters. But was there something here that she should know, something that might trap her into a future, fatal, mistake? Then she remembered that Cecily had said she had never been to Sunderland.

She smiled ruefully. 'I know I wish I'd visited. I'm sorry that I didn't.'

'Aye. Well, it's too late now, but Mr Spencer wouldn't hold it against you.'

Liza changed the subject. 'I'm going to see something of the town today.'

Mrs Taggart nodded. 'I'll tell Gibson to bring the carriage round.'

'No, thank you,' said Liza quickly. 'I prefer to walk, and I'll probably lunch out.'

'As you wish, Miss.'

Mrs Taggart had said William would not want to see her in mourning and Liza took her at her word. She set out suitably dressed for walking in a tailored lemon wool costume – a long, close-fitting jacket and pleated skirt – a neat little hat and low-heeled shoes. She went with the housekeeper's endorsement: 'You look a right bonny lass, Miss Spencer.'

Liza laughed. 'Thank you.'

She walked into the town, exploring Mowbray Park on the way and smiling at the children, too young for school, playing on the two cannons brought back from the war in the Crimea. Then she walked quickly along Fawcett Street and the High Street, noting the shops, offices and public buildings. She would need to be able to talk about them if questioned later. She visited only one shop, a confectioner, and bought a bag of sweets. From there she strolled down to Wearmouth bridge and leaned on the parapet. She could see again the busy shipyards and engineering works, with their towering cranes, and the ships lying in the river. She watched for some minutes until the chiming of the town hall clock in Fawcett Street told her it was time to go. She took a train from the central station to Newcastle.

She arrived mid-morning, when she had reckoned the children would be at school, men at work and women cooking the dinner. She knew her expensive, fashionable clothes would make her stand out in the working-class area to which she was heading, but hoped to avoid being noticed. She was successful, finally slipping down a back lane and through a yard hung with washing. The kitchen door was closed but she turned the handle and walked in. There was the scrubbed table, the fire glowing in the grate, its light reflecting from the polished brass fender. A rag doll was propped against it, as Liza had propped hers when she was a child. Her mother stood at one end of the table, ironing, while the little girl played on the scrap of rug before the fire. Liza smiled into Kitty's eyes as her mother stared at her disbelievingly. 'Hello, Mam.'

'Liza! What are you doing here? I thought you were in Germany.' Then, 'Susie! Here's your mammy come to see you.' Susan climbed to her feet and ran into Liza's arms. She lifted her daughter and hugged her, danced whirling round the room while the child laughed.

She halted before her mother. 'I'd love a cup of tea, Mam.' That would give her a few minutes to decide how to break the news she had brought.

'Oh, aye. I'll put the kettle on.' Kitty set it on the coals with the iron beside it. Then she glanced again at Liza, now seated in one of the two old armchairs, Susan on her knee. 'You haven't come home on account of the money that was stolen? I was heartbroken over that, couldn't sleep for days.'

'That can't be helped and it's past now. Never mind the money,' Liza soothed her.

'Then what brought you back? You haven't got the sack, have you?' Liza nodded, and Kitty sat down in the other chair with a bump as her legs turned to jelly. 'Oh, God help us.'

'It wasn't my fault, Mam.' Liza fumbled in her bag. 'Close your eyes,' she said to Susan, 'and open your mouth and see what God sends you.' Her daughter obeyed and Liza popped in one of the sweets she had brought. Then she looked up at her mother. 'It wasn't my fault but nobody would listen to me.' She told her story while her mother made the tea.

At the end Kitty sighed. 'I don't see what you could have done, except what you did. That lass who took his word against yours, she'll learn her mistake one o' these days – but that doesn't help us now. You'll have trouble getting a job of any sort, and you were doing so well.'

Liza reached into her bag again, but this time brought out her purse. 'I've got another job. And I've brought these.' She gave her mother four of the five sovereigns Cecily had given her. One she retained for her own use, for purposes that had nothing to do with her acting as Miss Spencer. She had the funds William had given her for her everyday expenses. While she was Cecily Spencer she could use Cecily's money.

Kitty stared at the sovereigns in her palm, then at the purse. It was evidently fat with banknotes. 'Where's all this money come from? And all these fine clothes?' She gestured at the costume, the glimpse of white lace above the silk stockings. 'What are you doing?'

Liza had known this would be the difficult bit. She slipped

out of the jacket in the warmth of the kitchen. 'Nothing I'm ashamed of, Mam, but I'm not allowed to tell you what it is. I earned the sovereigns I gave you and the clothes are what I have to wear, just as I did when I was in service. The money in my purse isn't mine. It was given to me to meet expenses.'

Kitty struggled to take this in, bewildered. 'So you're not in service, not working for some lady as her maid?'

'There's a lady, but I'm not her maid.'

'Is there a man?'

'Well – yes, but I'm not working for him.'

'He's her husband?'

'No.'

'So what is he?'

'Just a man,' Liza said desperately.

'What's he like?' Kitty was appealing for reassurance, Liza knew. 'Is he a *good* man?'

'Yes, he is.' Liza stopped then, wondering why she had said that. She and William were polite but distant, and she blamed him for that. So why . . . But she had said it now and she would not take back her words, for her mother's sake and peace of mind.

Kitty sighed. 'It's no good. I can't understand it, but as long as you're not doing wrong . . . I just hope you'll be all right.'

'I will,' Liza said, with confidence, and hoped it was true.

She talked with her mother, cuddled and played with Susan until Kitty lit the gas-light in the early dusk of winter. Then Liza rose to her feet and pulled on her jacket. 'I have to go now, Mam. Don't worry.' She knew Kitty would worry anyway but she had had to say it – and it might help. She gave the bag of sweets to her and hugged Susan. 'Be a good girl and Granny will give you one every day. I might be home before you finish them.' Kisses and tears. Then, so as not to prolong the pain, she walked out. The washing had been taken in now and she crossed the empty yard but paused at the back gate. She turned, and saw Susan in Kitty's arms, waving. Liza raised her hand, then passed out into the lane.

On the train she looked back on her visit with pleasure, happy that she had found her mother and daughter well. She treasured each snippet of what Susan had said, how she had looked, the soft pressure of her arms round Liza's neck.

The rain began to fall as the train neared Sunderland. At first just scattered drops speckled the windows, but as they crossed the bridge over the Wear it fell heavier. In the gloom she could see the ships only as black silhouettes on the dark glinting surface of the river. Never mind, she thought, soon be home. Then, But it's not my home.

She remembered that she had to prepare an account of her day in case she was closely questioned. Once in the house she would be on her own again, surrounded by people who might see through her impersonation of Cecily Spencer.

Liza walked from the station through the rain, which soaked her. She recalled walking up to the Grange through a downpour, wet and bedraggled – it seemed so long ago. She remembered Toby with a moment of sadness. But as her heels crunched on the gravel of the drive she saw a welcoming light in the hall.

Elspeth Taggart opened the door to her ring, and stepped back, shocked, as she entered. 'Why, lassie, you're sopping wet.'

Liza laughed. 'I'm afraid so.' The lemon costume hung damply against her legs, rain-darkened on the shoulders.

Now William appeared, striding out of his study. He stared at Liza, her face wet, hair hanging, but glowing as she met his gaze. 'You look like a drowned rat,' he said.

Liza managed a curtsey, dipping low and grinning up at him. 'Thank you, kind sir.'

He laughed. 'I'm sorry. No insult was intended. Why didn't you take a cab?'

Because it had never occurred to her, and she knew she had made a mistake. Cecily would have taken a cab rather than trudge through the rain. Too late now. She smiled into his eyes. 'I never gave it a thought.'

'You seem to have enjoyed your day.'

'I had a lovely time, walked in the park.' She broke off there. That was enough, it was time to change the subject – and seek a friend. She recalled what her mother had said about housekeepers and it being a profession for ladies in reduced circumstances. 'I've been thinking about my training for a position in life, and I wondered if Mrs Taggart would teach me how to be a housekeeper.' She looked at her.

Elspeth Taggart was shocked into silence.

'Good God!' William said. 'A housekeeper? You?' He admitted that it was not unknown for a lady to take such a position, and that they were usually distressed gentlefolk. But *Cecily*?

Liza laughed inside to see him so disconcerted, but she kept a straight face as she said reprovingly, 'And why not, sir? If I marry one day then I may have the ordering of a household.' But that was her answer for Cecily. For herself, with no intention of marrying now after Vince Bailey, she thought it would be useful experience. She might yet aspire to be a housekeeper, as her mother would wish.

'Yes, but I never imagined that you would be able to carry out the duties performed by Mrs Taggart. But this is a matter for her to decide.'

Liza had guessed as much, too. Elspeth Taggart was capable of telling him: 'Awa' wi' ye!' She looked appealingly at her.

Mrs Taggart seemed to be getting over her surprise. 'I'll think aboot it.' And she took herself off: 'I'll chase that girl Martha to run you a bath.'

Liza called after her, 'Thank you!' Then she turned to William: 'Now I've seen a little of the town today I'd like to accept your offer. I said "some other time", remember? Will you take me to see where Mr Spencer worked, please?'

She had surprised him again – she could see it in his face. But he answered quickly, 'I'll be glad to. We'll leave tomorrow at nine?'

'Yes, please.'

'Then away you go for your bath.'

William watched her run light-footed up the stairs. She was full of surprises. He would never have thought that Cecily would offer to train as a housekeeper – train as anything for that matter. But if Elspeth Taggart agreed to take on the task – a big if – then the girl would find life very different below stairs. It might do her a world of good.

That night Liza lay sleepily in her bed while the rain rattled softly at the window. She looked back over her day and was content. She had seen her mother and Susan. That alone had lifted her heart. Another day had passed and she was more comfortable in her part. So far she had met with hostility but not doubt. She had not been challenged, let alone denounced. It was just as Cecily had foretold, save for this Captain Morgan who had known her before. He had said that Cecily had painted her face on that occasion. Liza thought that the girl must have been daubed like a Red Indian if William could not tell her from Liza – but anything was possible with Cecily.

Liza had only to play her part until the girl inherited, then take her fee. Roses all the way . . .

She woke to a sky washed blue by the rain and a pale winter sun. There was a distant clanking, a noise she recognised, of an iron bucket being moved from one step of the flight at the front door to the next. A maid was washing the steps and Liza remembered doing that job, the pain of chapped hands in water on a winter morning. She stretched luxuriously, then remembered what lay ahead today and rose from her bed. Martha had dried and pressed her costume. It was not up to Liza's standard and she would have loved to show the girl how to do it, but she had to hold her tongue. And because Martha had done her best, Liza thanked her with a smile.

When she went in to breakfast William was seated over his second cup of coffee, his copy of *The Times* spread in front of him. He laid it aside when she appeared. 'Good morning.'

'Good morning. And you may read your paper. I'm not a talker at breakfast – unless you wish to?'

He grinned. 'Thanks. Something here I want to finish.' He lifted the paper again and hid behind it.

Liza helped herself deftly from the food laid out on the sideboard. She filled a cup with coffee, the pot in one hand, jug of hot milk in the other, pouring from both at once.

'You're a dab hand at that,' William said.

Liza realised she had made another mistake and improvised quickly: 'It was a trick I learned because it amused me.'

'You learned it well.' And the paper lifted again.

Liza let out a silent sigh. Be careful! she told herself. She watched him covertly as she ate, but his eyes were intent on his reading. She had told her mother he was a good man, but that had been for Kitty's peace of mind. Still, he was not so distant now and that made her happier. Not that it mattered, of course. She did not care one way or the other so long as he did not see through her deception. How would he react if he did? She saw the strong line of his jaw, the mouth set firm, recalled the cold gaze he had turned on her more than once. She shuddered. He must not find out – or she must escape before he could vent his fury on her.

He looked up. 'You're very serious. Penny for them?' He was not intimidating now – quite the opposite, in fact.

'They're not worth a penny,' Liza replied. 'I was just thinking about our tour today.'

He set aside the newspaper as Mrs Taggart came in. 'Good morning, Miss Spencer,' she greeted Liza. 'I've thought about what you asked me last night and I'm prepared to teach you my trade, if you still feel that way inclined.'

Liza nodded eagerly. 'Yes, I'd like that.'

Evidently the housekeeper had not expected that: she blinked rapidly but soon recovered. 'Aye? Would you be wanting to start now? No time like the present.'

'No,' William answered firmly. 'Miss Spencer is coming with me to see Mr Spencer's office and one or two of his ships.' He still thought of them as belonging to his late guardian, though they now belonged to him. 'I think tomorrow will be early enough to start Miss Spencer's training, if that is agreeable to her?' He raised his eyebrows and glanced at Liza.

'Yes, of course,' she said quickly.

Mrs Taggart nodded. 'As you wish.'

William strode out into the hall and Liza whispered, 'He's pampering me.'

Mrs Taggart replied drily, 'Aye, that might be so, but I'm thinking he's worried about his dinner tonight if there was a stranger in the kitchen.'

Liza giggled and skipped after William.

William thought that Miss Spencer did not know what she had let herself in for. Elspeth had known about the trip to the office so her talk of starting her instruction that morning had been intended to disconcert, but she had not got much change out of this slight girl. He would have to keep an eye on them. Liza came out into the hall then and he opened the front door. 'Shall we be on our way?' He followed her out into the morning air. She breathed in deeply, smiling into the sunlight, and he thought how pretty she was.

They retraced their route of that first Sunday evening, driving through the town and turning short of the bridge to run down to the river. The streets became narrower and poorer, swarming with small children, and William slowed almost to walking pace. They ran alongside the motor-car, cheering and shouting, and Liza laughed. Then William said, 'Oh, hell!'

'*I know who you are, you bitch!*' That eldritch screech again. It was the old woman in her rusty black dress, hair and eyes wild as she ran out of her shop and into the road. Liza shrank back in her seat and the children scattered. '*I know you! You're the young bitch come home! There's blood on your hands! Those fine clothes were bought with men's blood!*' Her face was close, eyes glaring madly, nose a great beak. But the children had gone and William could accelerate; the Vauxhall drew away, leaving the old woman standing in the street and shaking her fist.

'I'm sorry,' he said. 'I thought we could get by too quickly for her to come out.'

Liza was recovering from the shock. 'Why did she shout at me like that? Who is she?'

They were inside the dockyard now and William stopped the car. He turned to face her. 'I should have told you after that first night, but I hadn't known you long and this is family history we don't talk about. That's not because we're guilty but because we can't do anything about it.

We could go to the courts but Edward would never per-
mit that.'

'Who is she?' Liza asked again.

'Iris Cruikshank. She has that tagareen shop, and makes
a living selling old clothes, furniture – anything that's worth
only a few coppers. She thinks Edward killed her husband
and it isn't true.'

Killed? Murdered? Liza thought. She had not expected to
walk into this kind of situation.

William said, 'The trouble really started back in the 1860s.
Iris and her husband, Barney, had four boys, all sailors in the
same ship. They caught cholera in India and died.'

'All four?' Liza said.

'Within a few days of each other. When the news came
Iris broke down and Barney went on a bender. Iris recovered
but Barney stayed on the bottle. He lasted nearly ten years.
He had a boat and he used to go out fishing between the
piers. He made enough for his beer and to feed himself
and Iris, but everyone knew he was drunk as a lord when
he went out. Iris used to plead with him not to go but he
wouldn't listen. People told her not to worry, that there was
a special Providence looked after drunks. Until he went out
once too often.'

Barney Cruikshank had set out in his boat one winter night
after leaving the pub, sitting on a thwart, pipe in his mouth
and pulling at the oars. Edward Spencer was a young man of
thirty. His father still ran the business and Edward was captain
of one of the Spencer company's ships. He was on the bridge
to bring her into harbour, standing by the helmsman. The
night was dark. He saw the lights of the ferry as it crossed
the river ahead of him but it was well clear and no hazard. He
saw nothing of the boat, heard nothing either, until a lookout
yelled that wreckage was passing down the port side.

The ship was stopped at once, they lowered their boats and others came out. They collected the wreckage, but Barney's body was never found. The ferry was tied up at the Monkwearmouth steps, near the scene of the accident, but the crew – there were only two – had not seen the collision. Edward had seen no boat lights and his helmsman and lookouts confirmed this. The coroner, at the inquest held in the Albion Hotel, reached a verdict of death by misadventure.

But Iris blamed Edward for not keeping a proper watch. She began to accuse him in public. While Edward refused to have her stopped, the police charged her with breach of the peace. She fell back on watching from her shop for any of the family to pass and screamed her accusations at them.

'And that included me,' William said. 'And now you. Edward never captained another ship. From then on he worked in the company's offices ashore. He would have had to do that soon because his father retired, but he would probably have gone to sea for a few more years if it hadn't been for Barney's death. I wish I could have stopped Iris, but Edward always said she'd suffered enough. She's tried to make all of us pay when none of us was guilty.'

'What an awful story.' Liza shivered. 'That old woman lost husband and sons, but is still spouting her hatred after all these years.'

'But there's nothing we can do.' William got out of the car and handed her down. Liza said nothing then, but resolved that she would.

They walked by the river, along the quay, through hawsers, stacks of timber and cordage, to climb a gangway to the deck of one of the Spencer ships. The crew were all ashore, with only a watchman on board. 'Now then, Captain.'

'Now then, Geordie. I'm just going to show this lady round.'

'Aye. Well, watch oot for the wet paint, starboard side o' the wheelhouse.'

'Thanks.'

William took Liza over the vessel from stem to stern, ducking into the forecastle to see the narrow bunks of the seamen, down into the engine-room where the machinery stood massive but still. 'There's a small donkey engine that supplies power if it's needed when the main engines are closed down.'

He was kept busy explaining because she asked a stream of questions, and eventually he said, 'You really find this interesting?'

'Yes, I do.'

'You surprise me.'

'That's the second time you've said that.'

'Is it?'

'When we first came into the river, you said you were surprised that I was interested in the ships.' Liza had come to realise that she could talk to this tall man without deferring to him. Courtesy must have its due, and respect for his position, but as Cecily she was his social equal.

'The Cecily I thought I knew would not care for ships or commerce but it seems I didn't know you all that well. Your enthusiasm caught me on the wrong foot.'

Liza wrinkled her nose. 'I wasn't very enthusiastic on the ship coming over.'

He grinned. 'Nobody likes their ship sinking under them.'

'I didn't.' Liza smiled, thinking that he hadn't long to get to know her better, only until Cecily came to claim her inheritance. Nor had she long to learn more of him. She felt a twinge of . . . regret? She told herself not to be silly.

'Would you like to try again?' he asked. 'Maybe on a short voyage to France or down to London?'

'Yes, please.'

'Good for you. We'll see what we can do.'

'Where now?' she asked.

They were in the wheelhouse and he had shown her how the telegraphs worked, sending instructions down to the engine-room. He looked about him. 'I think I've shown you everything here. Time for lunch, and then we'll go to the office.' He dropped down the short ladder, then turned and lifted her down, his hands round her slim waist.

Together they walked back along the quay and Liza, playing her part, asked, 'What are those things?' She was indicating tall towers built along both steep sides of the river above the bridge. She knew very well what they were, had seen others on the Tyne, but she thought Cecily would be ignorant of their purpose.

'The staiths?' William said. 'That's how they load the coal into the ships that carry it to London or anywhere in the world. The trucks full of coal run out on their rails to the staiths just above the ship. Then the body of the truck tips over, empties the coal into a chute and it pours down into the ship's hold.'

They were now only a few yards away from the foot of the nearest tower. Liza, peering up, could see the way the railway line curved round to run out and end almost vertically above the ship. She said, 'So the coal—'

William cut her off by grabbing her arm and yelling, '*Run!*' He spun her round and towed her along as he tore away from the staiths.

Bewildered, Liza hitched up her skirts and sprinted at his side. 'What's wrong?' she cried.

'There's a truck coming now. Don't stop but take a look.'

He eased his pace and she turned her head in time to see a truck run out to the end of the staith. It checked there, then tipped on its side. Its load of coal fell on to the chute and landed in the hold with a thunderous *crash!* 'See the dust? That's why we ran. We were standing downwind of it.'

Liza saw it, billowing up from the chute and blown on the wind. If they had not fled it would have smothered her and her lemon costume – hair and face as well. She had learned something. While she had known about staiths, she had never been so close to one before when it was working, would never have anticipated the dust storm. Now another truck was rolling to take the place of the first, but they were clear of it.

'I'm sorry about that,' he said. 'I should have watched out for trucks. Are you all right?'

'I'm fine.' Liza was flushed and laughing. 'Thank you for saving me. I would have been filthy now if you hadn't.'

He offered her his arm. 'We live off coal around here, either dig it, sell it or use it, but it's mucky to handle.'

They ate in a restaurant where the other diners were mostly men. Heads turned as they entered and William seemed to be well-known: several men nodded and greeted him. Liza recognised the kind of heavy, dark furniture with snow-white cloths as similar to the dining rooms in which she had served. She also recognised the type of customer: businessmen.

They ate simply but well, a thick soup and a roast. In the course of the meal men stopped at the table to ask William questions, 'When d'ye think the Baltic will thaw and open this year?' all relating to business. Every time, he introduced Miss Spencer to them.

'You seem to be in demand, Captain,' Liza ventured.

'"Seem" is the word,' he said drily. He cocked an eye at

her. 'All those chaps were after an introduction to you and a closer look.' She blushed, and he grinned at her.

They went on to the offices of the Spencer Line, in a gracious building with tall windows. Inside, the rooms were high-ceilinged, with half a dozen clerks working at big, solid desks. All the furnishings were in polished ash and mahogany and upholstered in morocco leather. Pictures of the company's ships hung on the walls and models of them stood in glass cases. As they entered, a man of fifty or so, neat in black jacket and striped trousers, came hurrying to meet them. 'Good afternoon, Captain Morgan, and to you, Miss.'

'This is Mr Featherstone,' William said, 'the chief clerk. He runs the place from day to day, and very well, too.'

Featherstone gave a little bow. 'Good of you to say so, sir, but anything I know I learned from Mr Edward.'

'Is there anything for me to see today?' William enquired.

'There are letters in your office to sign, sir.'

'Would you care to show Miss Spencer round and introduce her while I deal with them? And where's Mrs Dixon? I may want to dictate answers.'

'I sent her out on an errand, sir. She should be back at any moment and I'll send her in to you.'

William went off and Featherstone led Liza round to meet the clerks, each man standing in turn and giving a little bow. She asked what each of them did, which surprised them, including the chief clerk. Even Tommy, the office boy, fifteen years old and bewitched by her smile, had to stumble through an explanation of his duties. Then she asked him, 'Do you like working here? Are you happy?'

Featherstone obviously thought Tommy must answer in the affirmative, but Liza insisted, 'The truth, mind.'

He met her eyes with honesty: 'Oh, aye. But we all miss Mr Spencer.'

'You were fond of him.'

'Aye, but Captain Morgan is a grand man.'

Liza heard Featherstone say, 'There you are, Mrs Dixon. Come and meet Mr Edward's niece, Miss Spencer.'

She turned round, and Betty Wood, the childhood friend she had saved from Piggy and Una all those years ago, was staring at her open-mouthed. 'Liza! What are you doing here?'

15

Liza heard herself still playing her part, though her face felt like rubber and the words sounded as if they were spoken by someone else. Betty Wood! *Betty Wood!* 'I'm afraid you're mistaking me for someone else. Mrs Dixon, is it?'

Betty put a hand to her mouth, uncertain now. 'What was that, Mrs Dixon?' Featherstone asked.

Liza forced a laugh. 'A case of mistaken identity. Mrs Dixon mistook me for someone else, possibly an old schoolfriend. Isn't that right?' She stared at the other woman, trying to pass the message with her eyes: Please, Betty, *please!*

The answer came jerkily: 'Yes. Yes, I thought she was a girl I knew at school. But really she was nothing like this lady. I'm sorry, Miss.'

Liza laughed with sheer relief. 'No need to apologise.' Now she tried to send a silent message of thanks. 'I've made that mistake myself. Do you live near to the office or do you take a tram?'

Betty was clearly nervous now, but she replied, 'I get a tram from just outside the office.'

'Do you work a long day?' Liza saw Featherstone turn away to meet William, who was walking back along the office towards them, a thick briefcase under his arm.

'. . . and I leave at five,' Betty was saying.

'Thank you. It's been very interesting to talk to you.' Liza smiled at Betty, then transferred the smile to William. 'I've enjoyed myself and learned a few things. I think I'd like to work here, if ever you have any vacancies,' she told him.

'I'll bear it in mind.' Then he added drily, 'Although I believe Mrs Taggart will keep you busy.'

'I'm sure she will.'

They left then, Liza with a nod to Betty. Outside, she asked, 'I'd like to go shopping for a few items and then I'll walk up to the house.'

'Are you sure you wouldn't like me to wait for you?'

'I'll be fine on my own. And you seem to have plenty to do.' She pointed a gloved finger at the briefcase.

'The price paid for taking a day off from the office,' he agreed ruefully.

He drove away and Liza crossed the road and entered Binns, the big department store. From the doorway she could see the Spencer Line offices and the tram stop outside. She strolled around in the store to pass the time but at five she was back near the entrance. When she saw Betty emerge she stepped to the door, checked that no one else from the office was in sight and waved furiously. Betty saw her and ran across the road. Liza seized her in a hug and kissed her. 'Betty, you brick!'

'It is you, Liza? I began to doubt my own eyes. You the fine lady, dressed to the nines, and telling me: "I'm afraid you're mistaken."'

Liza squeezed her arm. 'It is me and I'm going to explain. But let's keep moving – I don't want anyone from the office to see us.' She linked her arm through Betty's and they strolled through the shop together. 'I thought there wouldn't be anyone in Sunderland who knew me. The last time I saw you all your family were moving to Hartlepool because your father had found a better job there.'

'That's right,' Betty nodded, 'but he moved here three years ago and I married Jacky Dixon not long afterwards. He works in Thompson's shipyard as a plater and we have a little lad, just a year old. Now, what are you up to?'

Liza told her the whole story, about Susan, of course, and her sacking by the Koenigs, Cecily's proposition and how she was now ensconced in Edward Spencer's house masquerading as his niece. She saw the disapproval on Betty's face and added desperately, 'I had to do it. I was just about broke, with no other job in sight and no reference from the Koenigs. There was my mother and Susan to think of.'

'But if they see through you, you could be in serious trouble. And somebody is sure to catch you out.'

'But it's not illegal. This Miss Spencer asked me to do it and I'm not claiming her inheritance.'

'People don't like being fooled. Captain Morgan is a good man to work for, but I wouldn't like to get his temper up. And we're risking that.'

Nor would Liza. 'I don't intend to annoy him. But you said "we". How does this involve—' She stopped, realising she knew the answer. 'Of course – you work for him. If he finds out you knew I was impersonating Miss Spencer and you hadn't told him—'

Betty grimaced. 'It doesn't say much for my loyalty to him. I reckon he'd throw me out. It wouldn't do my reputation much good around here either.'

'I'm sorry,' Liza said, contrite.

Betty squeezed her hand. 'Never mind. I owed you a lot from when we were bairns and you stuck up for me.' She turned over Liza's wrist to look at the little watch strapped there. 'Posh.'

'It belongs to Miss Spencer,' Liza enlightened her. 'She lent it to me.'

'Nice. But I have to go home and cook our Jacky's dinner. He'll be in before long.' Betty gave Liza her address and directions. 'If you need me, that's where you'll find me.'

'Thanks, Betty.'

Then Betty glanced sideways at her. 'Have you got your eye on Billy Morgan?'

'Me? Him?' Liza burst out laughing at the very idea. 'No. It was twenty-four hours before he started treating me like a human being. He even—' She had been on the brink of saying he had virtually called her a harlot. 'Never mind. But I can tell you I'm not angling for him.'

'Don't say it like that. There are plenty who *are* after him. If you hooked him you'd break a few hearts.' She kissed Liza's cheek. 'I'm off, but I'll keep my fingers crossed for you.' She waved and was gone.

Liza went shopping then, remembering her appointment with Elspeth Taggart the next day. She bought a plain brown dress and two big white aprons with pockets. She charged them to the account of Miss Cecily Spencer and carried the parcel away.

Outside a tram was waiting that would have taken her most of the way to Spencer Hall, but she turned and walked the other way. There was a matter to be attended to and she would not let the sun set on her wrath. She walked down to the river, threading the narrow streets, the houses close together with women standing at their doors. Children followed her, their attention caught by her smart, expensive clothes. The little girls brought her own daughter to mind. She wondered what Susan was doing at that moment and smiled wistfully.

She paused outside the tagareen shop, hesitating, less sure of herself now. She could not see the old woman in the dim interior – the gas jet was not yet lit. The children hung back now, cautious, and one little lad called, 'Ye dinna want to gan in there, missus! She's a witch!'

Liza had heard this before – children often imagined some old woman had magical powers – but she knew that this one had none, just a nasty tongue, and she had come to give Iris a piece of her mind. She entered the shop and peered about among the piles of old clothes. She saw that they were graded, some for resale and others for rags, but everything in the shop, from rickety chairs to strange ornaments, was worth no more than a copper or two. She moved further inside, leaving the daylight behind her. Now she could see the staircase running down one side and firelight filtering from a room beyond it. As she moved towards it, she saw another bundle at the foot of the stairs. She stooped and her hand flew to her mouth. Iris Cruikshank lay in a heap. Her face was pale in what little light there was and her eyes were closed. She lay still as death, her black cap beside her.

But was she dead? Liza dropped to her knees, lifted the old woman's upper body with an arm about her, and patted her worn cheek. She thought she detected a faint breath, and then Iris stirred feebly. Liza rocked the old woman in her arms, spoke softly to her: 'Come on, wake up, Iris, there's a good lass. Come on, speak to me.' Eventually the eyes opened, not wild now but vague. 'There you are. Let's feel your hands.' They were cold and she rubbed them as Iris looked up at her.

'Let's see if we can get you warm.' Now Liza could see the back room, the kitchen, and the fire emitting its glow. Iris was sitting on an old rag rug. She lifted the end behind Iris's back and hauled it, as if it were a sledge with the old woman aboard, into the kitchen. 'Do you think you can get up?' she asked.

Iris was recovering now, though still shocked. 'Me chair,' she mumbled.

'That's right. Your chair's here.' It was an old high-backed wooden armchair, lined with cushions. With Liza supporting her Iris got into it and settled back with a sigh. Liza set the black cap on the wild hair. 'You've had a fall. Just sit quiet now and I'll get you a cup of tea.'

'Aye,' Iris said croakily. 'I was coming down the stairs and I fell. Who are you?' She peered at Liza in the dimness of the kitchen.

Liza evaded that question. 'I was passing and came into the shop.' She looked about the kitchen. The furniture in there, while old, was in good condition and shining with polish. The hearth was swept and the oven had been freshly blackleaded. A kettle stood on the hob and Liza shook it to make sure there was water in it, then set it on the fire. In a cupboard – well stocked, she noted – she found crockery, sugar, tea and a jug of milk. She sniffed at it suspiciously but it was fresh. The tea made, she sat on a straight-backed chair by Iris and fed it to her in sips.

Iris sucked it down and licked her lips. 'I'm grateful to you, canny lass. You've been a Good Samaritan to me.' The window, which looked out on the backyard, showed that darkness was falling now, and in the kitchen they had only the glow of the fire. 'Why haven't you put the gas on?' Iris demanded querulously.

The lamp hung from the middle of the ceiling, over the kitchen table, and there were spills in a jar on the mantelpiece. Liza lit one in the fire and held the little flame to the gas mantel. It ignited with a *pop*. She turned back to the fire, and saw that the old woman in the chair was peering at her. Then her lined features twisted with rage and she pointed a clawlike finger. 'You're that Spencer bitch!'

'*No!*' Liza snapped it. She would not suffer this.

'You are! I saw you wi' that Billy Morgan! You're Charlie Spencer's lass!' Iris struggled to get out of the chair. 'What are you after in here? No good, I'll lay!'

Liza held her in the chair, but feared she might kill herself in her rage. The Spencer name was causing this fury. 'I'm not Cecily Spencer!' Liza said. 'Do you hear? You mustn't tell anyone, but I'm not her. My name is Liza Thornton.'

'Not?' Iris stared, bewildered. 'Folks said you'd come back and I saw you wi' Billy.'

'That's right. But I'm not Cecily.' Liza took a deep breath. There was nothing else for it now. She had been forced into this to calm Iris but some instinct told her she could trust the old woman. 'She and I were on this ship . . .' She told Iris briefly how and why she had agreed to play the part of Cecily, and how William and Arkenstall had accepted her.

Iris listened intently. At the end of the story, she shook her head. 'I can hardly believe it, but I do. And you trust me? Why? What if I told Billy Morgan and that solicitor, Arkenstall? I know him!'

'I would deny I said it.'

'And of course they all think I'm mad.' Iris nodded. 'The little bairns call me a witch.' She saw Liza blush and smiled thinly. 'Aye, I know all that. But another thing: what made you come down to this part o' the town, let alone poking about in here?'

'I came to tell you off about calling me names in the street.'

Iris blinked, then gave a cackling laugh. 'You're a bonny little thing but you've got your nerve, I'll give you that.'

'Don't you think you should stop it?' Liza said. 'Edward and Charles are dead, and William wasn't even born when your husband was drowned. Nor was I. And you're only upsetting yourself. You'd be much happier if you put it all behind you.'

Iris glared at her. 'Don't tell me how to live my life, Miss. Edward Spencer murdered my Barney. He was stone-cold sober when he left the house that night. I saw him off. I swore

I would shout the guilt of all of them, every last Spencer, so long as I lived and there was one of them left.'

'There's only Cecily,' Liza pointed out, 'and she'll collect her inheritance and be gone as soon as she can. She told me so.'

Iris sniffed, but said nothing, sat stubbornly silent.

'I must go,' Liza said. She knew she was late. As she rose to her feet she asked, 'Do you have good neighbours?'

'Oh, aye.' That came grudgingly.

'I'll ask them to look in later and see that you're all right.'

'I can manage on my own, but please yourself.'

'And I'll try to come again. Goodbye.'

When Liza was nearly at the front door Iris called, 'Thank ye.'

Liza smiled. Out in the street she saw a buxom woman standing at the door of one of the flanking houses, with two small thumb-sucking children clinging to her apron. 'I'm Cecily Spencer,' Liza introduced herself. 'I've just been in to see Mrs Cruikshank and she's had a fall. She's still a bit shaken and I wondered if you would make sure she's all right later on?'

The woman clicked her tongue. 'That Iris! She wants to be more careful at her age. It's not the first time she's fell by a long chalk. She's often busy all day long in that shop and she gets short o' breath just climbing them stairs. But we'll see to her, Miss, don't you worry.'

'Thank you, Mrs . . . ?'

'Robson.'

'I'm pleased to meet you.'

'Aye. Bless ye.'

Liza walked into the town and caught a tram. When it put her down she ran from the stop to Spencer Hall. She decided to say nothing of her visit to Iris.

Elspeth Taggart met her in the hall. 'We were expecting you earlier but dinner will be late as Captain Morgan is working in his study.'

Liza took this as a ticking-off for unpunctuality and a warning for her to stay out of the study. It aroused in her the instinct to tease, which had often got her into trouble. But she opened her parcel and showed the dress and apron to the housekeeper. 'I asked the girl in the shop and bought these for tomorrow. Will they be all right?'

Elspeth Taggart fingered the material. 'Aye, they'll be fine. We'll start at six forty-five in the morning. There's a number of jobs to be done before breakfast. If that's satisfactory to you, Miss Spencer.'

Liza smiled. 'Of course. I'll follow your timetable, Mrs Taggart. Now, excuse me, please.' Before the other woman could guess her intention, Liza had crossed the hall to William's office, tapped once on the door and walked in. William looked up, irritated, then grinned as she cried, 'I've bought this for my training tomorrow.' She held the dress against her and struck a pose remembered from her performance at the Grange. 'Do you approve, gallant Captain?'

He feigned bad temper, his brows coming down. 'Wellington said there was nothing so stupid as a gallant officer.'

Liza acted up now, hands to her mouth and cringing melodramatically. 'Oh, sir, say not that I have offended thee!' Another line written by Gillespie for the play at the Grange.

William responded in kind: 'Nay, I know thou art but a foolish child. Thou art forgiven.'

Child? She walked across to him, for a few seconds sinuous and seductive and she saw his eyes widen. Then she was acting again: 'Say you approve, good sir.'

He nodded. 'I think it will do very well.'

'I should say so.' Then she ran from the room, laughing,

past a scandalised Mrs Taggart and up the stairs. She thought she might have lost some ground with the latter, but she would make it up tomorrow.

Elspeth was thinking, The miss did that just to show she would not take orders from me. We'll see.

The next day Liza rose early and put on the brown dress and white apron. She did not hear the bucket clanking outside and knew that boded ill. She ran down the stairs and met the housekeeper at the foot. 'Good morning, Mrs Taggart.'

'Good morning, Miss Spencer. Are we ready?'

'We are,' Liza replied meekly.

'Then we'll make a start. Lesson one: I don't believe you have a right to give orders until you have learned to take them.'

Liza nodded vigorously. 'I agree.'

'Lesson two: I never ask anyone to do something I haven't done myself.'

'Quite right, Mrs Taggart.' And now Liza was certain what was coming next.

Sure enough: 'We'll go along to the kitchen and draw a bucket of water. Then we'll wash the front steps.'

'Yes, Mrs Taggart.'

Minutes later Liza knelt on the front steps with scrubbing brush, cloth and whitening stone. It was a bitter pill to swallow that, to impersonate a young lady of means, she had to go back to the job she thought she had left behind some years ago. Then she realised, with a shock, that she was attacking the job in her old way. That would not do. She wanted to impress the housekeeper, but if she was too good at the tasks set her then Mrs Taggart might smell a rat. In the rest of her work she was careful to show ignorance and had to be enlightened.

'We will carry out the parlourmaid's duties today,' said

Mrs Taggart. 'Then tomorrow we'll practise those of the housemaid.' So Liza started by opening the shutters, laying and lighting the dining-room fire, dusting the room and finally laying breakfast for eight-fifteen. Martha and Doreen, a lumpish, surly girl, were working in the drawing room. At one point Liza heard Doreen sneer, 'Now we have a little lady acting the part. I expect we'll have to clear up behind her.' Acting the part? Liza thought. If you only knew, my girl!

When she stopped to wash and have breakfast, she asked, 'Do you approve of what I've done so far, Mrs Taggart?'

'Aye, for someone who hasn't done any work like this before you've done verra weel.'

When she joined William at the table she told him, 'Mrs Taggart says I've done verra weel.'

He recognised the impersonation and chuckled.

Liza ate with the knowledge that she had still to clear away breakfast, make beds, clean and polish the silver before lunch.

But there was relief. As William drove off in the Vauxhall and she was about to begin again, Mrs Taggart called from the hall, 'Miss Spencer! Your heavy baggage has arrived.' Liza recalled Cecily saying her baggage would follow later. She could see from the window the wagon from the station, the two horses nodding and blowing where they stood before the house. The housekeeper continued, 'I think you'd better supervise Martha while she unpacks for you. Doreen will finish off down here. I've sent for Gibson and Cully to carry the trunks upstairs.'

Liza went to her room and was joined by a breathless Martha running up from the kitchen. She was just in time as the two men laboured, sweating, up the stairs with the first of two large trunks. Liza found the keys Cecily had given her and fumbled to get them into the locks, her thoughts already on the contents. Were there more shocks for her?

She opened the lid of the first, and breathed a sigh of relief. The only problem was where to store everything. She let Martha hang up all the dresses. Liza would not wear them – like the first, they fitted well enough but were too long. She would use the things she had bought. The shoes she put away in a corner of the wardrobe; they were all size six, too large for Liza. It was at that point that Mrs Taggart knocked and entered to ask, 'Is everything in order?'

Liza smiled up from where she knelt by the wardrobe. 'Yes, thank you.'

The housekeeper picked up a pair of Cecily's shoes that had strayed, a size six in black patent leather. She examined them and sniffed as she passed them to Liza. 'Those heels are too high.'

Liza tucked them away. 'I probably won't wear them.'

'I'll leave you to get on, Miss.' She stalked out, taking her disapproval with her.

If Elspeth Taggart had noticed that the shoes were a size bigger than Liza's she would have wondered. Liza did not want that: it could lead to suspicion – and her unmasking. She told herself again to be constantly on her guard.

16

'Today we're carrying on with cleaning the dining room.' Elspeth Taggart eyed Liza, whose course of instruction was continuing. Indeed, it had not ceased over the weekend, when she had done some general dusting and cleaning, and numerous other duties under the housekeeper's supervision. Now: 'Carpets to be swept, loose rugs beaten, all furniture dusted . . .' She reeled off the list. 'This is usually Doreen's job, but today she can help me sort the linen. If you want any advice just ask me.'

Liza had come to know all the servants: Mrs Bainbridge, the cook, little Mabel, the scullery-maid, and the three maids, Martha, Doreen and Hilda, a placid country girl. Doreen gave Liza a sulky look, then her eyes slid away and she followed Elspeth Taggart out of the room. Liza had read that look and guessed what it meant: Doreen resented someone else, particularly a lady, being given her job. She shrugged, rolled up her sleeves and set to work. She soon discovered that, if this was Doreen's job, she had not been doing it properly. The rugs had not been beaten, the carpets not properly swept and there were pockets of dust everywhere. Liza left a few because she was supposed to be a raw recruit, but when she had finished she was satisfied that the place was much improved.

She reported to the housekeeper who said, 'Finished already? Sure you've done it properly? Doreen takes a lot longer than that. I'll look at it. Come on, Doreen.' She inspected the dining room with her sharp eye, found the dust Liza had left, and finished examining the mirror polish on the long table in the centre of the room. She nodded. 'You've done very well, Miss Spencer. I inspect this room every day and this is the best it's been for weeks.' Her gaze shifted to Doreen and her tone became acidic: 'A sight better than you ever leave it. Miss Spencer should be learning from you but she could teach you a few things. I've spoken to you before but this is the last time I'll tell you. Either you mend your ways or you'll be looking for another place. Now, get on with sorting that linen.'

Doreen flounced away, pouting, and Mrs Taggart sighed. 'Ye'll take note, Miss. That's another of the housekeeper's responsibilities and not my favourite. Now, come along.' She led out into the hall, saying, 'This afternoon I want you—'

'This afternoon is free for Miss Spencer, Elspeth.' William had come out of his study. 'From what you tell me she's making good progress and she's supposed to be learning, not performing. From now on she finishes at lunch.'

'As you wish, Captain.' And to Liza: 'Till the morning, then.'

'Yes, please, Mrs Taggart.'

That afternoon Liza walked down through Mowbray Park and posted a letter. It had been written in the privacy of her room and was addressed to her mother and Susan. She tried to write to them daily. She walked on towards the river until she came to the tagareen shop. For the last hundred yards she was accompanied by the usual crowd of grubby urchins, drawn to her by her fashionable clothes. Some remembered her. One little lad called, 'Have you come back to see the auld witch again?'

'She's not a witch,' Liza corrected him. 'Just a nice old lady without any bairns to keep her company.' He looked taken aback by this and none too sure, so Liza left the message to sink in. She walked through the shop and found Iris sitting in her armchair before the fire, her shawl round her shoulders, her cap square on her head. 'Hello, Mrs Cruikshank, how are you today?'

She looked up at Liza. 'Oh, it's you, bonny lass. I'm canny. Just having a rest now it's quiet. Sit down and I'll make you a cup o' tea.' She rose creakily to her feet. 'Then we can have a bit o' crack.' But she raised that gnarled finger again, this time in warning: 'Not a word about them Spencers, though.'

Liza agreed laughingly. 'But I'll make the tea.' She boiled the kettle on the fire and took cups and saucers from the sideboard at Iris's order. It was her best china. Then she sat beside the old lady, who poured tea from cup to saucer then blew on it to cool it before sipping, her little finger fastidiously crooked. They talked for half an hour. Iris wanted to know all about Liza's past life, her work, her parents, her daughter, her ambition. Only at the end did she speak of herself.

'I must be going,' Liza said. She rose from her chair.

So did Iris. 'I'll come as far as the door wi' ye, then I'll shut this place for the day.' As they walked through the shop together, she said, 'There won't be much doing now. I went to see the doctor about that fall. He said I was all right only my heart's bad and I should give up the shop. I'll have to think about that, though.'

'You take his advice and ease up.' Liza kissed her. 'I'll come and see you when I can.'

Liza walked back to Spencer Hall, unhappy at the news. She knew Iris was frail – she had discovered the old lady was just skin and bone when she helped her after the fall. And now her heart.

She went on with her training under Mrs Taggart, complimented on her work by that strict judge. It was on the Wednesday that the housekeeper told Liza, 'I've had all Mr Edward's clothes taken out of his room – that's yours now – but there is a top shelf in his wardrobe that still needs clearing out and a good dusting. Will you do it?'

Liza borrowed a pair of steps and had Gibson carry them upstairs for her. She climbed up them and found that the shelf contained a number of hatboxes holding toppers, bowlers and trilbys. A long, rectangular case held a silk-lined, navy blue cloak. Then there was a shoebox, which contained a number of papers. Liza sat down on the floor with it. There were several items dealing with William, his school reports and letters he had written to Edward. Also another bundle of letters, tied with a piece of string, written by a woman, Liza thought. She did not open them. With them was a small leather box containing a jewelled comb, wrapped in tissue. She admired it and guessed that it had belonged to the writer of the letters.

Finally there was an envelope addressed to Captain Edward Spencer in a careful copperplate. Liza hesitated, then saw the name and address of the sender on the back of the envelope: Michael Donnelly, SS *Eastern Star*, Pool of London. And another hand had written across it: 'Lost with all hands in China Sea, 23 August 1876.'

Curiosity drove her – and this was no love letter. She took out the letter and read:

Dear Captain Spencer,
This is written in haste as we sail for the East tomorrow.
While we have been lying here waiting for a cargo a sailor

from another ship out of the Wear passed on to me a copy
of the Sunderland Daily Echo *and I saw the report of the*
accident. I had stepped ashore from the ferry, after crossing
the river on the way to join this ship, and I saw what
happened. There was a pulling boat out in midstream that
ran across the bow of your vessel. It carried no lights and
I could see no one at the oars. I could not delay as my ship
was about to sail but I hope this will help. I will gladly
give evidence, if you require, when I return.

I am,
Your obed't servant,
Michael Donnelly, Boatswain

Liza read it again, at first with excitement, but then with a
little shiver. Michael Donnelly's offer to give evidence had
not been taken up, his ship 'Lost with all hands'.

But why had Edward not produced this letter? Then she
remembered William saying that Edward thought Iris had
suffered enough. He would not produce a letter that showed
Barney Cruikshank had been lying dead drunk in the bottom
of his boat. But Iris swore that Barney had been sober . . .

Liza tucked the letter into her chest of drawers and took
the rest to Mrs Taggart. 'Aye. The captain will be wanting
all those. I think I know who the letters came from and they
will go to him too.' She knew, as Liza did not, that William
was the son of the woman Edward had loved and lost to his
friend. 'I expect he'll give away the hats, but the cloak may
as well stay in the wardrobe for now.'

'And the comb? Shall I lock it away?' Liza asked.

'Aye, just to be on the safe side.'

Liza obeyed, then changed. She called on Cully in his
hothouse and he gave her a huge bunch of carnations.
Then she hurried to the tagareen shop. Once more she

had to run the gauntlet of the children, but this time the boy who had asked about the witch called to her, 'I went down to the shop for that auld woman and she gave me a ha'penny.'

'See?' Liza smiled at him.

Iris sat before the fire in the kitchen in cap and shawl. 'There's a canny lass.'

'I've brought you some flowers.'

Iris took them tenderly. 'By, lass, they're lovely.'

'I'll put them in a vase for you.' Liza arranged the carnations and set the vase on the table. Then she pulled up a chair beside Iris, and hesitated. Women of Iris's age – and men for that matter – had been born before education had become compulsory. Was she illiterate? Then she saw a copy of the *Echo* on the sideboard. 'I found this in a cupboard in Edward Spencer's room.' Liza put the letter into the bony fingers.

Iris read the two inscriptions on the envelope, her finger tracing the words. 'Edward Spencer.' She hissed the name, then muttered, 'Lost with all hands. Poor lads, poor lads.' She saw that the envelope was open and looked up at Liza, who nodded. Iris took out the letter and read it. Then she sat still, head bowed.

'There were no lights and the boat pulled across in front of the ship,' Liza said softly.

Iris looked up, pain and misery written on her face. 'All these years I've blamed Spencer. I swore Barney was sober when he left the house and so he was, but he must have had a bottle.'

'No,' Liza said firmly. 'This doesn't mean Barney was drunk. He wasn't a young man. He might have had a stroke or a seizure, or just fallen when he was moving about the boat in the dark. Then the current took his boat into the path of the ship while he was unconscious.'

'Aye, it must have been something like that.'

Liza took the old hands, with their parchment-like skin, in hers. 'It was an accident.'

'Why didn't Spencer show this letter?' Iris asked.

'I suppose by the time it reached him the inquiry was over,' Liza suggested. 'Then when he did get it he didn't want to hurt you any more. William said that was why he never set the police on you.'

'I always wondered about that.' Iris was silent for some minutes. When she looked up again Liza saw tears in her eyes. 'If only I'd known. All these years I've cursed him and I was in the wrong. But I can make my peace with my Maker now. You're a good little lass.' She pulled Liza's head to her and kissed her.

They had tea and talked. When Liza was leaving she jokingly reminded the old lady, 'No more barracking of the Spencers.'

Iris smiled. 'No,' then added, 'unless they deserve it for another reason.'

Liza returned to the Spencer house as Elspeth Taggart was passing through the hall. 'Where is Captain Morgan?' she asked.

'He's in his study, Miss Spencer.'

'Will you come in with me, please? I think you should hear what I have to say.' The housekeeper raised her eyebrows but followed her.

In the study, Liza laid the letter on William's desk. 'I found this with the other papers in Uncle Edward's wardrobe and borrowed it to show to Iris Cruikshank.'

'*Iris?*' William burst out.

'That puir demented body. What dealings have you had with her?' Elspeth Taggart exclaimed. And then, to William, 'I'm sorry, sir, I know it's not my place—'

'All right,' he said, but then to Liza, grimly: 'The question stands.'

Liza told him the whole story, ending, 'I didn't think you'd like me seeing her so I said nothing about it.'

He grinned wryly. 'You're right there. I would have feared for your skin at the hands of our Iris. So?'

'I tried to persuade her to stop but she wouldn't, so today I showed her that letter.'

William spread it out on his desk and read it, then passed it to the housekeeper. 'I never doubted Edward's innocence but that should be proof enough for anyone.'

'It was for Iris,' said Liza. 'She's promised not to shout accusations any more.'

'It must have been an awful blow for the puir woman,' Elspeth Taggart said sorrowfully.

'I think it was a relief. She was fine when I left her. She looks on the whole sad affair as just an accident now.' Liza waited, nervous and trying not to show it. Would William regard her actions as meddling, poking her nose into matters that did not concern her, usurping his authority? She had tried to do what was right and her conscience was clear, but that would be no comfort if he was angry with her.

'I think . . . Edward would be pleased,' he said slowly. Then, thoughtfully, 'You seem to have a way with you, Miss Spencer. What do you say, Elspeth?'

'Aye. She's a young lady of parts.'

Liza kept her face straight. Parts? Only two, and that was enough. She breathed an inward sigh of relief, then ran up the stairs to dress for dinner, singing as she went.

In William's study, Elspeth said, 'I'm thinking we've misjudged that lassie.'

William recalled Liza's manners when they met on the *Wear*

Lass, her thanking him on behalf of herself and the servant girl, her calm acceptance that Edward had left her nothing but the chance to learn a trade. 'She's a different girl from the one I first knew,' he said.

'She's grown up,' Elspeth said sagely.

Liza thought as she sang that it was all going very well.

It was about to go very wrong.

They met at Waterloo station, steamy and smoky, echoing to the clanking of couplings and the whistles of guards. Randolph Stevenson, owner of what had been the Calvert estate, was returning from having spent a week in Sussex with friends. Joseph Connolly was arriving in a cab.

Randolph's porter spotted it as it drove up and bawled, 'Here y'are, cabbie!' He set down Randolph's pigskin suitcase and swung down Joseph's leather-bound portmanteau. 'Were you wanting the boat train, sir? Southampton?'

Joseph unfolded his bony length out of the cab – he looked a little like Abraham Lincoln – and drawled, 'You've got it, boy.'

Randolph, solid and florid in well-cut tweeds, hailed him. 'Good day to you, sir. You are returning to God's own country I presume.'

'Correct.'

'I trust you enjoyed your stay in this capital of empire?'

'I did indeed, 'cept for the last twenty-four hours.'

'Oh? Do I take it you had an unfortunate experience?'

Joseph's jaw jutted. 'Almost, but I wasn't born yesterday. It was like this. When I returned to my room after dinner last night I was confronted by a lady. I'd talked with her and her husband two or three times but now she said he'd gone off to make a business call and left her alone. She said it was her birthday and would I open a bottle of champagne for her? I'm always ready to help a lady so I went with her into their room and opened this bottle. We both had a drink but then she began to make advances, giving me the glad eye. I was about to walk out when her husband burst in and tried to shake me down.'

'I beg your pardon?' Randolph said.

'Blackmail me.'

'Good God!'

'Right. He said he'd sue me in the courts for assaulting his wife and she backed him up. Then he pulled a knife on me but *I* told *him* that I'd see him in hell before I gave him a cent and I was calling the police. And I did. But those two had cut and run before I could fetch a constable. I made a statement to a sergeant and he reckoned they'd most likely pulled this trick with other guys who'd paid up and kept quiet.'

'I take off my hat to you, sir.' Randolph doffed his brown trilby. 'You dealt rightly with the scoundrels.'

Joseph tipped his derby. 'Right. See you in hell, I told them.'

'Cabbie's waiting, sir,' the porter urged, and pocketed Randolph's tip. 'Boat train leaves in five minutes, sir.' He pushed away his barrow, which held Joseph's portmanteau, and the American followed.

Randolph climbed into the cab, marvelling at the evils rampant in a capital city. 'Country's going to the dogs.' And to the cabbie, 'The Jefferson Hotel.'

Cecily Spencer and Mark Calvert were already there, as Mr and Mrs Calvert. They sat in the foyer, with its mirrored walls and potted palms. 'We can't go on like this,' Mark was saying. 'There's your reputation to think of so we must wed.'

Cecily did not care about her reputation, but she was more

than willing to marry him. 'I told you, we can marry this spring.'

'It isn't that simple,' Mark said testily. 'We'll need a place to live and a regular income from something other than a pack of cards.'

'I'll have plenty of money soon.' Cecily did not see any difficulty. So far they had spent all their time together making passionate love or resting between bouts, but this morning Mark had turned serious.

'I don't want to live off you,' he snapped. 'If I can't afford to marry, then—' He stopped and Cecily held her breath in case he went on, but slowly relaxed when he did not voice the alternative. She tried to think what was best for her to do, still amazed at his probity. He was a stickler for doing the right thing, according to his lights. The longer she knew him the more he impressed her and the more she tried to live up to his opinion of her. Once – in pillow-talk – she had almost told him of how she had tried to embarrass William Morgan and Edward Spencer when they had visited her at Aunt Alexandra's house in Hampshire. But she had held her tongue: some instinct warned her that Mark would disapprove.

And he loved her, that was more important than anything to her now.

'What sort of work would you like?' It was a vague enquiry: Cecily knew nothing of the commercial world, except that her father had worked in the City of London.

Mark sighed. 'The kind I've done all my life – running a big estate. I wish sometimes that I'd never had that row with Stevenson, never walked out. But that's done now and I'm not going to crawl to him.' He reached out to cover her slim hand with his. 'I'll find work. I don't know how, but I will. I just want to do right by you.'

'Yes, I know,' Cecily said softly. Then she winced. 'Ouch!' His fingers had tightened on hers.

He released her at once. 'Sorry! But talk of the devil and there he is.'

'Who?'

'Stevenson. The chap I've just been talking about, who bought the estate.' He pointed.

Cecily saw a stocky, red-faced man in tweeds at the desk, a hotel porter trailing behind him with a pigskin suitcase. He spoke to the receptionist, who fished a key out of one of the pigeonholes. She saw that it came from one close to that of their own room. Then he strutted off to the lift, the porter still at his heels. 'He doesn't look too bad to me,' she said, soothingly.

'To be fair, he isn't. I'm sure he's a good husband and father. He just doesn't know a damn thing about running an estate like ours. I'll lay odds he's making a thumping loss.'

Cecily said nothing to that, but thought a great deal and finally decided what to do, although she was still uncertain how to go about it. Then that evening, as they left their room to go down to dinner, Mark said, 'Damn. I've forgotten my wallet.' He went back into their room while Cecily waited in the thickly carpeted corridor, a stole covering her bare shoulders.

Another door opened close by and Randolph Stevenson emerged in his dinner suit. Cecily saw her chance. 'Mr Stevenson, isn't it?'

Surprised, he answered, 'Why, yes, I'm Randolph Stevenson.'

Cecily gave him a wide smile. 'I wonder if you could help me.' She was sure that she could persuade him to talk to Mark, and then the pair would see that co-operation was to their mutual advantage.

But now Randolph was on his guard. 'I suppose it's your birthday,' he snapped.

Cecily was puzzled. 'It will be soon, as a matter of fact.'

'I thought so. But you won't get away this time.' And Randolph seized her arm.

'Found it, still in my other suit.' Mark came out on to the landing and saw Randolph gripping Cecily's wrist. 'Stevenson! What the hell d'you think you're doing?' He twisted Randolph's wrist so that he released Cecily and threw him across the corridor.

Randolph was saved by the wall at his back from falling. '*You!* So this is what you've turned to! I suppose you call yourself her husband. But I told her, you won't get away this time!' And he bellowed, 'Help! Thieves! Police! Help!'

Doors opened and guests emerged in various stages of dressing for dinner – some ladies holding wraps around them, men in shirtsleeves, two armed with walking-sticks. They crowded round while Randolph bawled: 'Tried to – to shake me down. Blackmail, sir. And revenge! I dismissed this scoundrel and now he is trying to besmirch my character and wring money out of me. He says he's her husband, but I doubt it!'

Mark and Cecily, bewildered, could only say that his charges were untrue, that they did not know what he was talking about.

Then the hotel detective arrived, followed by the manager and a police constable. Names and addresses were taken, statements made. Mark and Cecily were taken to a police station and seen by a Sergeant Merryweather, a plain-clothes officer. His suit was wrinkled, his hair thin and gummed down in a neat quiff on his forehead. He looked at them, long-faced and doleful. 'I've been expecting to catch you two before long.' And when they stared at him, he explained, 'I know of one job you did the other day. I'll bet that's just the tip of the iceberg. Do you want to tell me about the others?'

'I've told you—' Mark tried.

But Merryweather waved a hand, dismissing what he had been about to say. 'I know what you said about her trying to get your old job back but I don't believe it. You're telling me you're a farmer but you make your living out of playing cards. And that your wife here has plenty of money but no explanation of where it came from.' Cecily was still maintaining that she was Mrs Mark Calvert, determined not to disclose her real name and be dragged back ignominiously to Sunderland. Merryweather had them charged and taken down to the cells.

Merryweather had a problem. There had been complaints before Joseph Connolly's from men who had paid up to Piggy and Una but later laid information with the police. Not one was prepared to give evidence for fear of being laughed at – or worse, if their wives found out. Merryweather sighed. He had hoped the Calverts would confess, but now there was nothing else for it.

Next morning, in the magistrates' court, he asked for them to be remanded to give him an opportunity to bring back his witness from the USA so that he could identify the prisoners. His request was granted.

Jasper Barbour scaled the twenty-foot prison wall in broad daylight with the aid of a rope tossed over to him by Flora Gibb. He found her waiting for him outside with a pony and trap. As he jumped up beside her she lashed the pony into a gallop and he laughed with jubilation. Inside the hour he was hidden in rooms she had rented and was telling her: 'I'll lie low here for a week or two until the first hunt dies down.

Now come here. I've been dreaming of this for years.' And he drew her towards him.

He had left behind a battered prison warder.

17

'It's time we made a start again, Miss Spencer,' Elspeth Taggart began. Liza had just finished her breakfast and was lingering over her tea, having worked from six forty-five. She wore her brown dress and white apron.

William lowered his newspaper. 'Not today, Mrs Taggart. Miss Spencer has had a busy week. You'll recall it was only two weeks ago tomorrow that her ship sank under her. She is also Mr Edward's niece, and all work and no play makes Jill a dull lady.'

The housekeeper sniffed. 'It was Miss Spencer's request that I taught her my duties and on Saturday I consult with the cook regarding the meals for the weekend, and then—'

William overrode her. 'It is my request that she help you consult with the cook but that is all – for now and Sunday.'

Elspeth Taggart yielded: 'Aye, verra weel, Captain Morgan.'

'I'll try again on Monday,' Liza said, 'and thank you, Mrs Taggart.'

'You're welcome, Miss Spencer. I'll see you with the cook at nine, if that is convenient.' She went off, back very straight.

'She'll be cross with me now,' Liza whispered.

William shook his head. 'Not you – me. Elspeth brought me up, used to play football with me in the garden. She sometimes thinks I haven't changed, that I'm still six or seven with my socks around my ankles.' He saw Liza's startled gaze. 'You find that hard to believe?'

'No.' Liza suspected Mrs Taggart was putting her through the mill because she was Cecily Spencer and needed to be taught a lesson. 'I think she's a dear.'

And as she went about her duties Elspeth thought, The lassie works hard and never complains, I'll give her that, and no airs and graces about her. She had a growing respect for the slight, dark-eyed girl with the ready smile that could turn into a mischievous grin.

Back in the dining room, William tossed aside the newspaper and thereby missed two important items. 'I have tickets for the first show at the Empire tonight and we can go on for a bite of supper afterwards. Would you like that?'

Of course she would. 'Yes, please!'

He grinned and rose to his feet. 'I have to go into the office this morning. I'll see you at lunch. You have an appointment with the cook and Mrs Taggart.'

Liza saw that the time was a minute to nine and let out a squeak. She shot out of her chair like a scalded cat and ran out past the grinning William.

Liza could have got dressed alone for that evening, but she called on Martha because she was certain Cecily would have done. But she made sure that the dress and accessories Martha laid out were as she wished them to be. In the quiet of the afternoon, making the excuse that she was lying down, she spent an hour altering a dress that was not to her liking. Later she kept a wary eye on Martha as the girl ironed it.

That evening, as she walked down the stairs, she saw her efforts had been worthwhile. The dress was of black lace with a black silk cummerbund. She had taken in the waist so that it emphasised the slimness of her figure and shortened the skirt to show a flash of neat ankles and white underskirt. They stared up at her, Mrs Taggart open-mouthed. William, elegant in his dinner suit, said, 'You look . . .' He was lost for words.

The housekeeper supplied them: 'You're as pretty as a picture, Miss.'

Liza blushed and looked up at him shyly. 'Am I late? I'm sorry.' She knew she was not but wanted to make the point.

'No, you're not.' He seemed surprised and pleased about that. He held her coat for her and she slipped into it, feeling the weight of his hands on her shoulders. Then they were in the carriage with Gibson driving, rolling down the drive.

Elspeth watched them go then locked the front door and hung the key in its usual place on the hook by the door; William carried his own key.

Liza was excited. It was almost a year since she had seen a show, and then it had been a cheap music-hall and she had sat at the back of the stalls. Tonight they would probably be in the royal circle. And she was driving to it escorted by a handsome – well, impressive young man. She had forgotten the size of him but he seemed to fill the carriage.

When they stopped outside the theatre he handed her down and called up to Gibson, 'You can go home. We'll find a cab afterwards.' Then he was easing a passage for them through the crowds, they were inside and wending their way through softly lit corridors, quiet on rich carpets. An elderly uniformed man led the way and eventually opened a door and ushered her through. Liza obeyed and found herself standing at the front of a box. The lights of the auditorium were all on and the theatre was filled with several hundred people: they all seemed to be staring at her.

Liza gasped. She had thought she would be hidden in the crowd but instead she was the target for their stares. Surely

a score would point and shout, 'Impostor!' She tried to step
back but William was behind her. She felt his hands on her
shoulders again, taking the coat from her. It was as if he was
undressing her before those probing eyes.

'Is something wrong?' he asked.

Cecily wouldn't have batted an eyelid when faced by this
crowd, Liza thought. She knew that she must be just as
confident. 'No, I'm fine, thank you.' She smiled up at him,
then found the chair at her back and sank into it. The eyes
seemed to recede, the theatre grew bigger, the audience just
looking about as she was, talking, laughing. There were still
eyes on her but she accepted that they were only casually
curious; there was nothing sinister in this and no likelihood
of her being known. She was sure some of those looks were
aimed at William, with yearning in them. Betty Dixon had
said he was a very eligible bachelor. Liza relaxed and began
to enjoy herself.

She laughed or sighed and applauded all through the show,
but was always conscious of William at her side. Afterwards
he stood to help her into her coat. 'Now we must find some
supper.' But that dilemma was solved for them as they stepped
out of the box.

Liza had stopped in the doorway to allow a party to pass.
A slim woman in her forties glanced past her, saw William and
called, 'Billy! Billy Morgan! I haven't seen you for ages.'

'Good evening, Mrs Summers.' He made the introductions:
'This is Edward's niece, Cecily Spencer.'

Mrs Summers smiled brightly at Liza. 'Very sad about
your uncle, a great loss, but I'm delighted to meet you.' The
passage was becoming crowded as the people departing from
boxes tried to pass the party.

'Move along now, ladies and gents, per-lease!' the usher
called.

'Oh dear. We must get on,' Mrs Summers said. 'We're having supper at the Palace. Will you join us?'

'Glad to,' said William. 'Thank you.'

The Palace was a handsome hotel near the bridge over the river Wear. Liza and William mingled with the other guests in the hotel bar, talking, laughing, drinking. Liza stuck cautiously to water. Several girls brushed past William with words of greeting and a touch of the hand. He knew them all and they evidently didn't want to be forgotten. Mrs Summers's party from the Empire was boosted by more who met them at the Palace, so twenty sat down to eat. There were a dozen main courses to choose from, ranging from lobster salad to braised beef, turkey, ham, chicken and aspic of prawns. Then a choice of six desserts, jellies, creams and meringues. Liza knew that the food alone must have cost seven or eight shillings a head. She had seen it all before but only eaten the leftovers in the kitchen.

Afterwards there was dancing and she could practise what she had learned when working for the Greshams and polished during her stay in Paris. A young man on Liza's right asked her first, then another from her left. She noticed that she was being watched once more and, in her seat, murmured to William, 'This is lunch all over again,' reminding him of how she had met his business acquaintances over lunch. He grinned. 'You can't blame them. You turn up out of the blue, not stepping from a humdrum train but escaping from a sinking ship! Naturally they're going to be curious.'

'I don't mind.' She gave him a brilliant smile. 'This is a lovely evening.'

William's brows lifted. 'I'd have thought you'd seen lots of parties like this.'

Liza could answer truthfully: 'Yes, but this is nice.' She

did not tell him that her previous experience had been as a waitress.

Then a tall, corseted lady appeared at her side. 'Hello! I'm Maudie Fitzgibbon. We've not met before but you were at school in Switzerland with Clara, my eldest. She talked so much about you.' There was a glint in her eye.

Liza was struck dumb. She stared past Maudie, expecting to see this Clara who had talked so much about Cecily. And what had Clara said? William knew Cecily as the girl who had offered herself to him. What did Maudie know – and suspect of Liza? 'Oh, yes?' she said, with concealed apprehension.

Maudie's smile seemed malicious. 'Clara is in Greece at present on the tour, but when she returns in April you must come over to us.'

'Thank you.' Now Liza saw another young man bearing down on her as the band struck up. 'Your dance, William,' she said, stood up and seized his arm. And to Maudie, 'Please excuse us. I did promise him.' Then they were out on the floor.

'What is this all about?' William asked. 'You hadn't prom- ised me a dance, though I'll gladly claim it.'

'I just felt that I had to dance this one.' Liza smiled up at him. She had thought for a second or two that she was about to be exposed, had been given a nasty fright, and now she clung to William for safety. She shuddered.

'Are you cold?' he asked.

'No.' Then she changed that: 'Yes.' She could not tell him of her fear.

'Which?' He laughed.

'Cold, but just a shiver.'

They circled the floor and she recovered her nerve. Clara would not return until April and by then Liza would be gone.

Cecily could face whatever scandalous disclosures Maudie Fitzgibbon had planned.

When the dance ended Liza was riding a tide of happiness. She danced with several other men as the evening wore on, but always looked forward to returning to William. When they left they thanked Mrs Summers, and Liza called gaily to Maudie, 'Give my regards to Clara!'

They sat close in the cab perforce, Liza very conscious of William beside her. It was then that he told her, 'I have a surprise for you. The cruise I promised: I have to skipper one of our colliers down to London and we sail tomorrow afternoon.'

Liza clapped her hands. 'That's lovely.' Then she remembered: 'But I promised Mrs Taggart I would train with her next week.'

'I've already spoken to Elspeth and made your excuses.'

'Oh.' Liza thought about that for a moment and did not like it. She was sure that the housekeeper would think this was just a way for her to wriggle out of her work. 'I will ask Mrs Taggart if she minds. I think that is only fair.'

'As you wish.'

Once he would not have believed that Cecily would care about the housekeeper's feelings, but he remembered how she had changed. He was happy with the arrangement, however, knew Elspeth had a soft heart.

They did not speak again until he used his key to let them into the hall, which was silent save for the ticking of the clock. He took her coat and she turned to face him. 'I've had a lovely time.' She stood on tiptoe, put her arms round his neck and pulled his head down. 'Thank you.' She kissed him and ran up the stairs. He watched her go, flitting light-footed like a ghost, silent as her own shadow, but her voice came softly back to him: 'Goodnight, William!'

Liza had told Martha not to wait up for her so she undressed herself and slid into bed by the light of the fire. She lay still, and in the quiet house heard his heavy tread on the stairs, then in the passage outside her room. Did it hesitate there or did she imagine it? But it went on and she heard his door close.

She had made an important discovery, while in William's arms. She lay small in the big bed and thought that the man was impossible – wasn't he? From their first meeting he had been cold and distant, his disapproval verging on dislike. But not for a while now and that had been intended for Cecily. So . . . Still, an affair was impossible.

Yet she smiled as she fell asleep.

When Liza ran down the stairs to breakfast she met the housekeeper in the hall. 'Good morning, Mrs Taggart. Captain Morgan tells me he asked you to excuse me for a week to sail to London. May I go, please? Or will it be inconvenient?'

Elspeth Taggart eyed her. 'I'm thinking you'll have packed already.'

'Yes, I have,' Liza admitted. Quickly, that morning.

Mrs Taggart looked down her nose at her. 'I expect I'll be able to manage on my own for a week.' Then, with a shadow of a smile, 'Aye, you get away, Miss Spencer. Ye've worked awful hard and learned verra quick. We'll soon make up for lost time when you come home.'

Liza blinked. Come home? That had a warm sound to it. 'Thank you, Mrs Taggart.' She swung an arm round the woman's waist and planted a kiss on her apple cheek, then whisked in to breakfast.

William had been only minutes ahead of her. 'Good morning. Did you sleep well?'

'I did, thank you.' She was flushed and smiling as she served herself from the dishes on the sideboard. She thought that Mrs Taggart had justified her assessment as a dear.

She could go to London with William so that was all right. Perfect.

He thought that this new Cecily had always seemed a pretty girl, but now she had blossomed.

They talked easily as they ate and William left the newspaper untouched by his plate. Only at the end, as they sat over coffee, did he glance at it casually. Then he said, 'Good Lord!' Liza wondered idly what had seized his attention. He stood up and walked round the table. 'That chap Jasper Barbour has broken out of prison and half killed a warder. You'll remember him.'

She did not. 'Oh, yes.' What *now*?

William was going on: 'I was at sea at the time but Edward told me the story later. You testified against Barbour when you were only fifteen or so, and he swore to have his revenge, threatened you.' He laid the paper on the table before her and pointed at the headline: 'Prisoner Assaults Warder and Escapes'. 'But he's a long way away and no doubt he'll be recaptured in a day or two.' He frowned, then added, 'Still, I think it would be a good idea if you didn't go out alone from now on.' He glanced up at the clock on the mantelpiece. 'I've work to do before we sail. I'll see you at lunch.'

He strode off and Liza read the story. She thought wryly that she need not fear Barbour unless he found her before Cecily returned. If he did, would he shout to the world, 'This woman is a fraud!'? She giggled. But then she saw the small item at the bottom of the page or, rather, one word of it: Calvert. Wasn't that the name Cecily had said she would use? she thought. And now she took in all of the report with one swift scanning. Mr Mark and Mrs Cecily Calvert had been remanded in custody on charges of attempted extortion and blackmail. Cecily jailed! Liza stared at the newspaper, Jasper

Barbour forgotten. Cecily would not come back to claim her inheritance now. What was she to do?

Herbert Galloway, private investigator, ex-policeman (dismissed from the force for accepting bribes), awoke late in his lodgings near Sunderland station. He lay on his back staring up at the cracked ceiling and thought with satisfaction that he had done a good day's work on the Saturday. Now he could get back to London and collect his fee from Flora Gibb. For a moment or two he thought he would include hotel costs on his account, although his lodgings were little more expensive than a seaman's boarding-house. Then he decided against it. Flora was obviously acting for someone else, and the very fact that she had come to him meant that that person might be criminal and violent.

It had been an easy enough job, anyway, to find that the girl's parents had died but her uncle and guardian lived in Sunderland and was a prominent citizen. When he had got there he had found that the uncle was dead but a Captain Morgan was living in the house – the electoral roll had shown him that. All he had to do then was watch the place, mark the tall captain driving the Vauxhall and the young lady who must be the one he wanted – whom Flora had asked him to find – and then confirm it. He had hired a cab and followed the carriage on Saturday night. At the theatre he had edged up to Gibson and asked, awed, 'Your governor – Captain Morgan, isn't it?' He flourished a notebook. 'I'm doing a bit for the *Echo*, "who's who at the Empire tonight". I know most of them by sight but I'm not sure about your feller.'

'Ah!' Gibson had shut the carriage door. 'That's right, Captain Morgan.'

'And that'll be the old man's niece – Miss Cecily Spencer?'

'Right again.' Gibson had swung up into his seat. 'D'ye want my name?' They had both guffawed as the carriage rolled, and Galloway put away his notebook.

Now he decided to eat a bite of breakfast, then catch a train south to take him home. Whoever wanted to know where Cecily Spencer lived, he was sure it would be bad news for her, but that was not his problem.

18

The coal thundered in a black torrent down into the hold of the *Wear Lass* where she lay under the Wearmouth coal staiths. As it did so it spewed out a cloud of dust that boiled about the ship then drifted away on the wind. Liza watched from a safe distance, standing on the bridge over the river. She squinted against the low sun, which was shining directly into her eyes.

She had come out for a walk after lunch, claiming to need fresh air, but in fact just to be alone with her cares. William had said, 'With that chap Barbour on the loose, you should not be on your own.'

'He will still be hiding in London,' Liza argued, 'if he hasn't been caught already.'

He had seen the logic in this, but added, 'Don't forget we sail this afternoon.'

Liza smiled now at his concern for her but the smile faded as her gaze focused again on the ship. She knew the *Wear Lass*, the ship that had brought her to this place. It had saved her life then and it might save her from disgrace now, because it would take her to London. She did not know how, only that she had to see Cecily Spencer and talk to her. Cecily had to come to Sunderland to claim her inheritance in just two weeks' time. Liza could not claim it for her: she would be guilty of a criminal offence, she was certain. She also knew she could do nothing until she had seen the heiress. When Liza had taken on this task it had seemed simple – or so Cecily had made her believe. Now she decided that ten pounds and a reference were not enough.

But she was looking forward, excited, to the journey south.

She had time to call in on Iris, she decided, so she walked briskly to her house and found her sitting in her chair before the fire. Her shawl was around her shoulders and her head bowed over the knitting in her lap. She snored gently, but woke with a jerk as Liza entered. 'I was just resting my eyes,' she said.

'I came to see how you were. We're off to London this afternoon.'

Iris lifted the needles and smiled at her. 'I'm very canny now, thank ye. And London, eh? I always wanted to go there. Are you going with that Billy Morgan?'

'He's the captain of the ship.'

'Ye'll have to do everything he tells you, then.'

'Oh, no, I don't,' Liza riposted but felt her face colouring. To hide it she turned to peer out of the window, as if looking at the weather. 'We should have a smooth passage.'

'We'll see,' Iris said. It was only later that Liza wondered what the old woman had referred to – the weather or William. Now Iris said, 'You'll have to come and tell me all about it when you get back.'

'I will,' Liza promised.

She returned to the Spencer house, running the last furlong, skirts flying in a flurry of lace and a hand on her hat. Gibson sat in the back seat of the Vauxhall with their suitcases, the engine ticking over, while William stood by the driver's seat consulting his wristwatch. Liza arrived panting. 'Sorry if I'm late.' She glanced at Cecily's watch. 'No, I'm not.'

William grinned. 'Nearly.' He handed her in, then waited while she whipped a silk scarf over her hat and tied it on.

'Right. We're off.' He drove away from the house and made for the town.

They sailed that afternoon, the *Wear Lass* dropping down the river and steaming out between the piers, butting into the sea. Later, at night, Liza stood on the open bridge beside William. The air was chilly but instead of the fashionable coat she had brought with her, which was hanging in her cabin, she snuggled into a thick navy blue bridge coat with its wide collar turned up around her ears. It was a smaller copy of the one William wore and he had bought it for her. Made for a man, it hung down to her ankles.

He glanced down at her. 'Warm enough?' She nodded, smiling, as errant locks of her hair whipped on the wind. 'Seagoing ladies usually have a coat made to measure but I didn't have time.'

'Never mind. It was a nice surprise.' Liza wondered if he had done it before. 'Do many ladies go to sea?'

'A few skippers take their wives, some occasionally, some as a regular arrangement. The latter are usually newly-weds without a family to keep them ashore, or older, with their children out in the world. Few stick it because of the wandering life, not knowing where you'll be next week or next month.'

Now they could see the lights of other ships pricking the darkness. 'I didn't think there would be so many,' Liza said.

'Most nights you have company on this east coast route. And talking of company . . .'

Archie Godolphin, the cook, had climbed up to the bridge, his bald dome gleaming in the dimness. 'Tea, Skipper.' He held out two thick white mugs. 'Saw the lady come up here so I brought one for her too.'

Liza took hers. 'Thank you.'

'You're welcome aboard, Miss.' He clattered away down the ladder.

William and Liza stood in companionable silence for a while, sipping their tea, then Liza said, 'I think I'll say goodnight now.'

'One last thing,' said William. 'I've arranged a party on the Saturday before your birthday, a sort of early celebration so that you can meet a few people. Dancing and a buffet.'

'Thank you. What a nice idea. You are good to me.'

'I thought if you got to know a few of us you might learn to like this North Country.'

'But I *do* like it. I love it,' Liza said indignantly.

His black brows lifted. 'You always used to say you would never come back to the north.'

Cecily again! She had mentioned something like that. 'I've changed my mind,' Liza said. Let Cecily talk her way out of it. Then she remembered where Cecily was and the point of this voyage. 'Goodnight again.'

'Goodnight.'

William watched her climb down the ladder to the deck and make her way aft to her cabin, staggering a little with the motion of the ship. He was still amazed at the way the girl had changed in recent years. She'd said he was good to her. Maybe he was. Because of her transformation – as an expression of relief? He gave a low growl of laughter at that. He knew the real reason.

Liza lay in her bunk, listening to the steady rhythm of the engines, not so much a sound as a sensation transmitted through the hull like a heartbeat. She knew that every second was taking her nearer to London and she had no idea how she might help Cecily – and herself.

The *Wear Lass* made eight knots all the way south and entered

London's river in the forenoon of Tuesday. Liza had spent a lot of time on deck, or on the bridge when William was keeping his watch. She was at his side as the ship steamed up the estuary. He pointed: 'The ship ahead of us, she's the *Frances Hopkinson* out of Newcastle. Jock McAvoy is her skipper and he has his wife aboard. They've been married about a year.' Just then the other ship sheered away. 'She's docking at Tilbury,' he explained. 'We're going all the way up to Battersea to discharge our coal at the power station, but we'll probably have to swing to a buoy for a good while before they can fit us in. So I thought you might like a night or two ashore in a proper bed, and you could do some shopping in London. But, please, stay inside after dark. I'm concerned about Jasper Barbour. He may still be loose and in London.'

Liza did not care about the bed, had become fond of her narrow bunk, but London? This was the answer to a prayer. 'Thank you. I'd like that. And I'll do as you say.' If she could, but she had work to do.

The *Wear Lass* stopped within sight of Tower Bridge to pick up the pilot who would steer her through the narrow passages between the bridges. Liza was waiting with an overnight case, and the cutter that brought out the pilot took her ashore. She was able to book a room and eat a hurried lunch in a quiet hotel. By four in the afternoon she was talking to Cecily Spencer.

Liza had passed through grim prison gates and was led by a warder along dark, dank passageways that echoed to the *tap-tap* of her heels, through heavy steel doors that slammed shut behind her. They sat in a bare room, the single barred window set high in the wall. Liza was at one end of a table, Cecily at the other, with a bored wardress standing between them.

'How nice of you to come!' Cecily was obviously delighted

to see her. 'How on earth did you manage it?' And before Liza could tell her: 'Never mind. The important thing is that you're here. This is a frightful place. I have a room – a cell – to myself, but some of the other women in here are rather awful.' She grimaced. 'When we were on that ship I said I doubted I'd ever see the inside of a cell, but I was wrong.'

Liza had a bone or two to pick with Cecily. 'You didn't warn me about William Morgan, that you and he had met before, in Hampshire. And he is now your guardian.'

'My – I didn't know that!' Cecily giggled. 'I forgot about him. I was naughty then, but I paid for it.'

'Edward left everything to him.' Liza decided to let Cecily find out for herself about the training in housekeeping.

'He probably deserves it. I thought he was just one of Edward's captains but Aunt Alexandra told me later that he was a partner.'

Liza decided to get back to the point of her visit. 'I'm going to try to get you out.' She saw that Cecily was far from her well-groomed self, showing signs of having worn the same clothes for some days. 'But can I fetch you anything in the meanwhile?'

'A change of clothes, please. You know the sizes, of course.' Cecily grinned. 'Just as long as you bring me *something*. That's important.'

'So is your freedom. I'll tell them all about – you know.' Liza's gaze flickered across to the wardress and back again. 'Then they'll see you can't be guilty.'

'You'll do no such thing,' said Cecily decisively. 'I *am* Mrs Mark Calvert, as far as the world is concerned. I won't have my reputation besmirched. Mark would be terribly upset. I will stick *anything*,' she pulled a face, 'even this awful hole, to avoid that.'

Liza was bewildered. 'But you've to claim your inheritance

in two weeks' time! I can't do that! It would mean I'd be guilty—' She stopped. The wardress was showing some interest now.

'I won't hear of it. You don't need to worry about getting me out. When they fetch that man from America, and he tells them we weren't the couple who tried to blackmail him, they'll let us out. I'll be there in two weeks' time.' Cecily explained how Joseph Connolly, an American, was the sole witness apart from Randolph Stevenson. 'He's admitted we didn't ask him for money, that he'd jumped to a conclusion. So, please, just bring me some clean underwear and a dress or two.' And then, steely now, 'If you let the cat out of the bag, you won't get your five pounds.'

That silenced Liza: she needed the five pounds due to her when Cecily inherited. And now she knew why Cecily was so blasé: she was confident she would be released. Liza did not share her optimism. Suppose the American mistakenly identified Cecily as the guilty girl? Suppose he was short-sighted? But she could not see how she could help here. She rose to go. 'I have a lot to do.'

Cecily followed suit and giggled again. 'You know, I think you must be a jolly good lady's maid.'

'I wish that's all I was,' Liza said bitterly, and walked out.

She had only gone a dozen yards when she was confronted by a worn, melancholy man in a serge suit shiny with age. He put a forefinger to his skimpy forelock, which was oiled down in a quiff, and asked, 'Miss Thornton?'

Liza remembered she had given her own name when applying to talk to Cecily. She had been wary of giving a false one at the prison. 'Yes, I am.'

'I'm Sergeant Merryweather. Would you be so good as to come this way, please, Miss. I'd like to have a word if you don't mind.'

Liza realised his request had not been a question, and entered the room he indicated. He followed her. 'Please be seated, Miss.' It was a poky little office with a desk, a chair behind it and another in front. Merryweather edged round the desk to sit behind it so Liza took the chair in front.

'They sent a man to tell me you were here so I hurried round to catch you,' the sergeant said. Liza did not like the sound of 'catch', but he went on, 'I understand you're a friend of Mrs Calvert.'

Liza swallowed. That was how she had described herself when asking permission to see Cecily. Now she saw that if she said, 'Yes,' then she would have endorsed Cecily's false name. Wouldn't that make her an accessory?

But Merryweather was going on: 'Are you also a friend of Mr Calvert?'

That was easy: 'No. In fact, we've never met.'

'Um. Pity.' He shifted uncomfortably, ran a finger through the dust on the desk and wiped it off with a handkerchief. 'How long have you known Mrs Calvert?' There it was again. Liza felt she was being drawn further and further into deep waters. But Merryweather gave her no chance to reply: 'Are you an accomplice?' He scowled at her.

Liza was shocked. *Accomplice!* 'No!'

'A young man and two young women, well dressed and possessed of money. You and Mrs Calvert look two of a kind to me.'

'No!'

'And you've not been very forthcoming about Mrs Calvert. Is that her real name?' He leaned forward over the desk. 'D'ye see, when they tried their trick on earlier victims – and it was always the same trick, old as the hills – they called themselves Wood or Armstrong, Dobson or Hunter. Now, was the lady in the case always Mrs Calvert? Or did she share the job with you? The description I've got would fit either of you.'

He waited but Liza sat silent. He prodded, 'Cat got your tongue? Is Liza Thornton *your* real name? And how did you pay for those fine clothes?'

The description would fit either her or Cecily? Liza could well believe it. That was at the bottom of all this trouble, the reason why she was here and now under suspicion of blackmail. If she was arrested and sent to prison, how would Kitty and Susan survive? Her mother and daughter would starve. She would do all she could for Cecily, but now she must care for her own. She looked into Merryweather's eyes, which were now hard and accusing. 'It is my name. I'm a lady's maid but at the moment—' She broke off and instead asked, 'When were these crimes committed?' And when he told her: 'I can tell you that at the time of the first the lady and I were on a ship sailing from Hamburg to the Tyne . . .'

Liza related how the *Florence Grey* had been in collision and she and Cecily were rescued by the *Wear Lass*. She said nothing of her posing as Cecily but spoke with the confidence of truth.

Merryweather became uneasy. He was still waiting for his only witness and would be for some time. He could have asked the staff at the other hotels to identify the Calverts and confirm that they had been there, but as the victims had refused to bring charges there had seemed no point. The staff at the Jefferson had confirmed that the Calverts had been there for more than a week but they could have gone out to do the jobs – couldn't they?

Merryweather did not like it. He had been sure he had caught two villains, but now?

Liza stood up. She had sensed his indecision. His eyes were thoughtful now and his brow furrowed. 'Your prisoner asked me to bring her some clothing,' she said, 'and I will do so early tomorrow.'

He nodded reluctantly, accepting that he had to let her go. 'But give me your address.'

She told him, and added icily, 'I'm staying there alone.'

He said nothing to that, only, 'If you think of anything you want to tell me you can find me at my station.' He gave her a slip of paper with directions, then watched her leave with her accompanying warder.

Piggy Cooper and Una had celebrated their return to business with a good dinner in the hotel restaurant, accompanied by a discreet half-bottle of wine. Afterwards they drank their coffee in the lounge and fell into conversation with Major Roxborough (retired). He was florid, with a large moustache and bulging eyes, and said he was in London on business to talk to his solicitor and his stockbroker. His wife had stayed in the shires: 'She prefers her horses, y'know.'

He and Una talked a great deal but Piggy hid behind a newspaper, apparently studying the business pages. Eventually he broke up the party by glancing at his watch and rising. 'Busy day tomorrow.'

Una sighed. 'Business again. You men! Goodnight, Major.'

'Goodnight, ma'am. Goodnight, Hawthorn.' Piggy acknowledged him with a wave of the paper.

The couple retired to their room and were soon enjoying a bottle of gin they had bought earlier that day. 'That dress always works,' Piggy said. It showed off Una's shoulders and swelling bosom. He began to unhook it down the back. 'Old Roxborough's eyes were popping out.'

Una guffawed, then hiccuped. 'Every time I leaned towards him! It took me all my time to keep my face straight.' She swallowed some gin and breathed sensually, 'Do that again.'

'This?'

A catch of the breath, then: 'Oh! Aah!'

After Liza left Merryweather she took a hansom to Harrods and bought the clothes Cecily had requested – quickly because she had remembered her promise to William not to be out after dark. She had no fear of Jasper Barbour, saw no reason why she should as Liza Thornton, but she had promised. Another hansom put her down at her hotel in the dusk. A boy in ragged trousers and jersey was selling newspapers near the door, bawling, 'Barbour arrested!' Liza bought a copy and gave him an extra penny because he looked cold. She found the item on the front page: Jasper Barbour had been recaptured while trying to break into a house in Kensington and was now safely behind bars. Liza shivered at 'behind bars', but sighed with relief.

In the foyer she said to the hall porter, 'I want to send a message to a ship lying in the river. Can you do that?'

'Of course, Miss.' He smiled at her, fatherly. 'What's her name, please?'

'The *Wear Lass*. She's a collier and is probably waiting to discharge at Battersea.'

'I'll find where she is,' he assured her. 'You write out your message and I'll send a boy to deliver it tonight.'

So it was that William, aboard the *Wear Lass* where she lay alongside a wharf, took delivery of a note from a boy in a pillbox cap. He tipped the lad and read the message, written on the hotel's headed notepaper:

Dear William,
Jasper Barbour has been caught, it's in the papers. I have
a nice room here and have looked at some shops but not

bought anything for myself so far. Maybe tomorrow!
I am missing you.
  Love,
  Cecily

William read it several times and put it away carefully. He
went to his narrow bunk thinking of her.

Liza, in her big empty bed, thought of William. She had torn
up her first attempt at the message because she had signed it
Liza, the second because, on rereading it, she thought it too
affectionate – and wondered how she had come to write it.
Then her thoughts turned to Cecily and how she must free
her. She revolved in her brain the few facts that she had, the
information given her by Merryweather. It seemed there were
four or more victims who had presumably refused to testify.
Otherwise the sergeant would have called on them instead
of the American. Then there were the criminals who called
themselves Armstrong, Wood, Dobson and Hunter. They
used different names each time, but the method was always
the same. As if they lacked imagination. The names went
round and round in her mind. And then she was scrambling
out of her big bed, seeking writing paper again, struggling
into a robe, then sitting at the dressing-table and writing
furiously.

On Wednesday morning Liza handed in Cecily's new clothes
at the prison and hurried on to meet Merryweather. She found
him at his station, seated behind a desk and stirring a mug
of tea with a pencil. 'I've thought of something,' she said
breathlessly.

'What would that be?' He sucked in tea as she told him.
Afterwards he said, 'I can't believe it.'

She blinked at him. 'Why not?'

He gave her the first smile she'd seen on his face, but it was wintry. 'Nobody would be that daft.'

'They were. They had to have names. Where would they get them from? Would they read them in the papers and call themselves Mr and Mrs Lloyd George?'

'No, but—'

'They've used the same method every time, never changed it.'

'True,' he agreed. 'One of the oldest tricks in the book an' all,' he scoffed. 'Still works, though. Human nature, you see. A woman and a man and temptation.'

'So?' Liza said.

He held out his hand. 'Let me see that list.' He scanned the names on it. 'Not many, but d'ye know how many hotels there are in London?'

'No.'

'Neither do I, but it's a hell of a lot – if you'll excuse the expression.'

Liza stood up. 'Then the sooner we start, the better.'

The search took most of the day and the rain started early. Merryweather had prudently brought an umbrella but Liza had not. He lent his to her and suffered the soaking with lugubrious stoicism. The umbrella was large, old, black and bent but served its purpose, and Liza had accepted it thankfully.

They visited all manner of hotels, from the very grand, like the Savoy, to the grubby establishments down side-streets that were little better than boarding-houses. They brandished Liza's list and pored over guest registers, questioned the reception clerk when any name matched one on the list. Merryweather became mournful, but Liza kept him at it. Night fell and still they searched.

They took cab after cab, trudged miles of pavements and picked their way across streets jammed with horse-drawn traffic and littered with manure made liquid by the downpour, the smell of ammonia strong in their nostrils. Until they introduced themselves to Mr Perkins, the manager of a middle-sized hotel who did not welcome the suggestion that he might be harbouring criminals beneath his roof.

He saw them in his office. He was pallid and portly in frock coat and wing collar, looked down his nose at Liza's umbrella dripping on his carpet and told Merryweather, 'I think you must be mistaken, Sergeant. We have a very respectable clientele. Many of our regulars are officers. In any event, I will not have my guests disturbed for no good reason.'

Merryweather was tired and his feet hurt. 'Blackmail and demanding money with menaces are good reasons. Let's see your register.'

'Blackmail!' The manager wrinkled his nose as if there was a bad smell under it, but he produced the register and Liza bent her head over it. She gasped. 'Here!'

A slim forefinger jabbed at a name, and Merryweather and the manager craned to see. 'Mr and Mrs Hawthorn?' Perkins said, incredulous.

'Mr and Mrs *Leslie* Hawthorn,' Liza said.

'What are these people like?' Merryweather asked.

'Mr Hawthorn is . . .' Perkins hesitated '. . . a rough diamond, but honest, I'm sure. Mrs Hawthorn is a very pleasant lady.' He had basked in Una's come-hither smile.

'I'm sure she is,' Liza said. 'And they're on my list.' She showed it, crumpled and creased now, to Merryweather. 'See?'

'What list is that?' the manager asked.

'The names these people used before were all names of Tyneside shipyards,' Liza explained, 'and this list is more of the same that we didn't think they'd used yet. But that's the one. Hawthorn Leslie is the name of the yard.'

Merryweather addressed the manager: 'Has Mrs Hawthorn been particularly friendly with any gentleman? Someone of your age, perhaps?'

Perkins flushed. 'I'll – er – I'll find out.'

He left, to return a few minutes later. 'I've spoken to the hall porter and some of the waiters. It seems Mr and Mrs Hawthorn are often with Major Roxborough. He's one of our regulars, comes up from the country for a week or so two or three times a year. A most respectable gentleman. I'm sure he wouldn't—'

Merryweather cut in: 'I doubt if he would, too. Now, which is their room?'

Perkins consulted the register. 'Two hundred and six.'

'Which is the major's?'

'Two hundred and ten.'

'Ah!' Merryweather leaned forward. 'And does the major have to pass their room to reach his own?'

'Why – yes.'

Merryweather glanced at Liza. 'That sounds familiar.' He turned back to the manager. 'Is there a vacant room opposite the Hawthorns'?'

Perkins checked the register again. 'Yes.'

Merryweather held out his hand. 'Let me have the key, please. We'll keep watch from there.' It was yielded to him reluctantly, but when he had it he passed it to Liza. 'I'm going to call up two constables. I'll tell you now, the man in this case was carrying a knife for cutting throats but we didn't find one on your friend's husband.' He turned to the manager, who had paled at the mention of a knife. 'I'll want to bring my men in unseen. By the back stairs?'

'Yes, of course.'

'And let me know where all these people are, if you can,' Merryweather finished. 'Tell Miss Thornton, and she will go up to the empty room and wait there for me.'

He and the manager left and Liza sat on alone. She wondered how long they would have to watch room 206. Then, as she waited for Merryweather to return, the doubts crept in. Suppose her theory was wrong and the names that matched those of Tyneside shipyards were just coincidence? Suppose the Hawthorns were an innocent and respectable couple?

The manager returned. 'Major Roxborough is at dinner in the restaurant. The Hawthorns are in the hotel, presumably in their room.'

'Presumably?' That word, for some reason, sounded an alarm for Liza.

'They haven't been seen for some time, but they haven't handed in their key,' he explained.

Liza stood up. 'Thank you.' She was uneasy. Suppose the Hawthorns were up to something now? 'I'll go up now and wait for the sergeant,' she said.

She took the umbrella with her and ascended in the lift; a page-boy was at the controls. On the second floor she walked along the corridor, silent on the thick carpeting, to room 201: 206 was further along, its door flanked by a low table with a vase of flowers on it. She let herself into 201 and closed the door behind her, but not completely. In the light from the corridor she could make out the dark-curtained window, a double bed, dressing-table, and a big free-standing wardrobe and chairs. She turned and peered through the crack she had left. She could see the doorway of 206. She wondered how long it would be before Merryweather arrived, and glanced down at Cecily's little watch.

When she looked up again a man had emerged from 206,

had closed the door but left it ajar. He was making straight for her, a key in his hand, a big man, bearded, heavy. That was all she saw, and then she was backing away into the darkness of the room to hide beside the wardrobe. The key grated in the lock but the door swung wide under its pressure. The man grunted – surprised at finding it was not locked? He glanced around the room but did not see Liza, hidden beside the wardrobe. He closed the door but not completely, leaving a thin strip of light. He swung an upright chair from its place against the wall and sat on it, peering out into the corridor.

Liza stood deathly still. She was trapped in this room with the stranger.

19

He was only a few feet away. Liza could hear him breathing. Could he hear her, or the dripping of the umbrella on the carpet? She hardly breathed at all, mouth open. If she moved her head a fraction of an inch she could see him bulking large on the chair, lit by that narrow crack between door and frame. She wondered how he had got a key. The one she had used was in her handbag, along with the list. Then she told herself it did not matter how he had got in. He might have stolen or bought a key from a chambermaid. The important thing to her was that he could reach her in two strides and then— Merryweather had said that the man had threatened his victims with a knife. She could see his hands, big and hairy, clasped into fists on his knees. She imagined them on her body, and her skin crept.

Oh, God! Where were Merryweather and his constables?

The man at the door moved on his chair, restless. Liza shifted her weight from one leg to the other and a board creaked under her. She froze and held her breath, sure he must have heard her, but he only moved again and cleared his throat. Then his restlessness ceased and he was leaning forward in the chair. Liza heard a woman's voice, the words slurred: 'Why, hello, Major. Will you help a lady in distress?'

A deeper voice, jovial: 'If I can, m'dear. What is it?'

'I can't open this bottle. Leslie has gone off to Portsmouth to talk to some naval men about business again. He won't be back until tomorrow and I'm all alone on my birthday. But come in and open this bottle for me. I'm no good at these men things . . .' Both voices faded and then there was silence.

The man at the door relaxed, sat back in his chair and took a watch out of his waistcoat pocket. He sat with it in the palm of his hand and his breathing was regular once more. Liza wanted to change legs again but dared not, had an irritating itch on her nose but would not risk moving to scratch. The minutes ticked away. Five? Six? Liza could not be sure, but then the man rose from the chair and threw the door wide. Liza flinched and tensed for now the light flooded in, bathing the room and the wardrobe that hid her, but he did not glance behind him. He strode away up the corridor in the direction of room 206 and was gone from her sight.

Not for long. Liza scurried out into the corridor just in time to see him shove open the door of room 206. Not locked, she noted. He disappeared inside and his voice came at first in a shocked cry, 'My God! What's this?' Then it changed to an enraged bellow, 'You swine! Take your hands off my wife,' and, finally, was solicitous, 'Has he harmed you, my dear?'

Now Liza was on the threshold and looking into the room. Her first emotion was shock. A man in his fifties, balding and with a toothbrush moustache, stood by the bed, his jaw hanging loose, eyes popping. Beside him was Una Gubbins, as Liza had known her at school. Now she was a voluptuous young woman with her charms on display, her dress and shift around her waist so that she stood bare-breasted. Her full lips pouted and she answered, 'Not hurt, but shamed.' She buried her face in her hands.

'Damn you!' the bearded man shouted. He was half turned away from her but Liza knew him, too, now she saw him with Una: Piggy Cooper. He had changed, but not for the better. From a plump youth he had grown into a menacing brute. He took a long stride towards the older man who, Liza guessed now, was Major Roxborough. Piggy reached under his jacket and drew out a wicked-looking knife. Light glinted on the blade and he threatened, 'Try to run and I'll carve you! I'm going to thrash you then sue you, drag you through the courts! You'll pay for this!'

The major eyed the knife warily but stood his ground and answered, 'I'm damned if I'll let you thrash me!' Then he temporised: 'It's all a misunderstanding. Surely we can settle this between ourselves and save the lady embarrassment?'

'Trying to buy me off?' Piggy said contemptuously.

'Please, Leslie, my love,' Una begged, 'I don't want publicity.'

'If you say so,' he grumbled. 'I'll settle for cash.' He took another pace further into the room.

Now Una lowered her hands and saw the dark-haired girl in the corridor. She gaped, then pointed a finger. 'What are you doing here?' And then, to Piggy, 'It's that Liza Thornton.'

He spun round. 'Who? *Her!* What the 'ell—' He strode towards Liza, who backed into the corridor. 'How long have you been standing there?'

'Long enough,' Liza answered coolly, because now Merryweather and the two constables were hurrying along the corridor from the direction of the service stairs. Piggy saw them, too. He grabbed for the vase of flowers on the table by the door and threw it in the path of Merryweather and his men. The sergeant stumbled over it, blocking the way of the constables. Piggy lashed out at Liza with the knife but she shrank away. He charged off along the corridor and she followed on his heels, reached out with the umbrella and thrust it between his legs. He fell with a *woof* as the wind was knocked out of him. Liza jumped on to his shoulders and squatted there, driving his face into the carpet. He still held the knife but he was unable to reach back to use it.

She did not have to hold him there for long. In seconds a constable was twisting the vicious weapon out of Piggy's grip. Then he clamped on handcuffs and hauled Liza's prisoner to his feet. She straightened her skirts and brushed herself down, examined the umbrella and found, with relief, that while some of the spokes were bent it still worked. Then she saw Una, properly dressed now, being led out of her room by the other constable. She glared at Piggy and snarled, 'You yellow bastard! You ran like a rabbit and left me to it.'

'Keep your gob shut,' Piggy snapped back at her.

'I will not! I'm not taking the blame for your big ideas.'

'You were all for it when you saw the money! A damn sight more than we took off old Kitty Thornton when we burgled her place. And you couldn't wait to come down to London.'

'I thought you knew what you were doing, thought you were a man, but you're a bloody cheapskate!'

Now Liza knew where her savings had gone and rage filled her. Merryweather had been talking to the major but with an eye and an ear on Piggy and Una, writing busily in his notebook. Liza waited until he was done, then she went to him and came straight to the point: 'I'll be a witness.'

He smiled sourly. 'Thank you, but you probably won't be needed. You heard them just now? I reckon they'll sell each other out. Besides, I told the major we'd keep his name out of the papers and he's agreed to testify. They'll go down.'

'There'll be another charge.' Liza told him briefly of the theft from Kitty, admitted by Piggy.

'That, too.' And Merryweather wrote again in his notebook.

Liza had not finished by a long chalk. 'Will you discharge Mr and Mrs Calvert, please?'

He sighed. 'You must appreciate that there are formalities.'

'I appreciate that I've helped you to catch the real criminals. It's most important to me that the Calverts are released and I'm asking you to help me.' As if casually she glanced down at the twisted umbrella that had stopped Piggy – and Merryweather took the point.

He cleared his throat. 'True. All down to you, Miss. I'll do all I can.'

Within two hours Cecily and Mark were back in the Jefferson Hotel, with Liza and Merryweather. The sergeant told the startled manager that a terrible mistake had been made. 'Is Mr Randolph Stevenson still a guest here?'

'Why, yes, Sergeant.'

'I'd like to see him.'

Randolph came to the office and stared at Mark and Cecily, who were dishevelled after their time behind bars. To begin with he was both suspicious and antagonistic, but as Merryweather explained the changed situation he grew red in the face. At the end he was silent for a minute, then muttered, 'Looks like I made a fool of myself.'

'It's a mistake anyone might have made,' Cecily said, seeming kindly.

He glanced at Mark, saw his nod, and said, 'Good of you to say so.'

'I did try to tell you that I only wanted you to think about restoring my husband to his position, but you wouldn't listen,' Cecily reminded him gently.

'Ah!' Randolph said. 'I've been thinking about that. To tell the truth the estate hasn't been performing very well.' His gaze shifted to Mark. 'I wonder, if you aren't suited elsewhere or if you can get away, would you care to come back?'

Cecily rose from her chair. 'Mark, darling, I must bathe and change. Why don't you and Mr Stevenson discuss your business in the bar and I'll join you later? Come along, Liza.'

She and Mark had already expressed their gratitude to Liza but in her room Cecily did it again. 'I'm very grateful, but if you'd waited another few days this man would have arrived from America and we'd have been let out. Still, all's well that ends well.'

Liza seized on that. 'So you're stopping this silly game and coming up north? It's just as well. William is planning a birthday party for you on the Saturday.'

Cecily stared at her, lips parted. 'Good heavens, no. There's no question of that. If Mark didn't have this position to go to I would stay here with him because we are very happy. But now that I'm sure Stevenson is going to take him on I want to go to the estate as his wife and see him settled in there. I'll marry him when I can. I will be in Sunderland to claim my inheritance, be sure of that, but not before my birthday. That was our agreement and if you want the other five pounds you'll have to see it through. It's not such a hardship. I told you it would be all right, didn't I?'

Liza was struck dumb. All right? *All right!* She recalled that first night when William had produced the photograph of Cecily. Then the confrontation with Betty Dixon, née Wood, and William's assertion that she had virtually invited him into her bed. But when she recovered the power of speech she said nothing. She knew Cecily would brush aside those nerve-racking experiences.

'Surely you can manage for a few more days?' Cecily said.

Could she? In the big house, with Martha and Mrs Taggart, and . . . Yes, but Susan was waiting for her. Liza longed to see her.

'We agreed,' Cecily reminded her.

They had, Liza because Cecily had saved her from the clutches of the cold North Sea. 'I suppose so.'

When Cecily had bathed and changed they went downstairs together. Randolph Stevenson and Mark were in the bar, deep in conversation about the estate, the details of Mark's contract already agreed and sealed with a handshake. Cecily joined them but Liza said her farewells. Then Cecily murmured, for only Liza to hear, 'Enjoy the party. William arranged it? I think I may have behaved badly to him and Uncle Edward. Please don't tell Mark.' She glanced at him fondly. 'I'm sure he wouldn't approve and he'd be disappointed in me. I don't want that.'

So Liza left her to it. The rain still pelted down and she stood in the hotel doorway, a slight, erect figure under the shelter of the uniformed doorman's umbrella. It was much more respectable than Merryweather's battered one with its bent spokes. He hailed a hansom for her, and she returned to her hotel alone. She was happy and relieved. She had resolved another crisis and would be back aboard the *Wear Lass* next day.

A message awaited her at her hotel, a note from William telling her to rejoin the *Wear Lass* just below Tower Bridge the following afternoon. Liza was eager to do that, but next morning she splashed through the rain again and made a hurried call at Harrods. A dress there had caught her eye when she had been shopping for Cecily. She had told herself then, with wry humour, that it was not suitable for wearing in prison – and wondered what was. But Liza had a use for it and bought it. The waist needed some alteration to fit her slim figure but she could manage that.

The pilot boat took her out to rejoin the *Wear Lass*, and when the ship sailed Liza was admiring the dress in her cabin.

She replaced it carefully in its big box, then dressed in the glistening black oilskins William had bought for her. She had not used them on the journey south but needed them now on the open bridge, where she found William, similarly dressed. The rain still fell steadily and the ship was butting into the wind: drops rattled on the oilskins. William was scowling into it as it sluiced down his face, but he grinned down at her when she appeared at his side. 'Room for two of you in there.'

Liza knew the oilskins were voluminous, the hem of the coat sweeping the deck, but she didn't care. The ship was slipping downriver in the early dusk, on either side the jewelled strings of lights on the shore, and more moving on the river, white and yellow, and the red and green navigation lights of the other ships that crowded the water. Liza found it hugely exciting and stood with William through the hours until his watch was done and he handed over to the first mate.

They went down to their cabins, which were side by side, and shrugged out of the oilskins, close to each other in the narrow passage. 'You enjoyed yourself up there,' William said.

'It was exciting.'

He looked at her flushed face and shining eyes. 'I can see that.' She could feel her cheeks warming, but then he went on, 'I learn something new about you every day. The Cecily I knew would never have done that. You're not like her at all.'

Liza did not trust the direction in which the conversation was turning. 'Well, *I* loved it,' she said hurriedly. 'Goodnight, William.' She stepped over the coaming into her cabin, shut the door behind her and leaned against it with his 'Goodnight' echoing in her ears. She heard his door close, hung up her oilskins to dry and undressed. She could hear him moving in the cabin next door, faintly, through the steady beat of the engines. Then he was still and she curled up in her narrow bunk, blew out her oil lamp, closed her eyes and slept. She could not know it, but William lay awake for some time.

A thousand miles south another ship ploughed northward. Down in the hold the chief stoker, stripped to a coal-blackened vest, bawled, 'Put some muscle into it, you lazy bugger! You're only half-way through your watch and we want more steam.'

Vince Bailey, similarly dressed and blackened, took up his shovel again. 'I didn't sign on for this.'

'You wanted to work your passage and that's what you're doing.'

Vince had found life hard in Australia, too hard for his liking. He had spent his money and had no way except this of returning to England. Shovelling coal for four hours at a time, twice in every twenty-four, was fiendishly hard. 'I said I wanted a passage back to London,' he whined. 'That's where you said we were going.' He had intended to batten on his sister in London.

'That was before we took on this cargo for somewhere else,' said the chief stoker contemptuously. 'This is a cargo ship, not a bloody cab. Now, put your back into it!'

Vince moaned but obeyed, driving the big shovel into the coal and hurling it into the gaping red mouth of the furnace. Somebody will pay for this, he swore to himself.

Liza awoke to sunshine streaming through the porthole of her cabin. The rain had ceased but she could feel the worsened motion of the ship, the soaring lift and then the drop, the roll and slow recovery. She dressed and went up to the bridge, where she found William standing his watch, balancing easily on long legs set wide. She stood beside him but cautiously kept one hand on the bridge rail. 'You're a glutton for punishment,' he joked, 'but we'll make a sailor of you yet.' Then he pointed over the bucking, plunging bow. 'A friend of ours.'

'A friend?' Liza peered at the ship, very like the *Wear Lass*, a mile or so ahead of them.

'She's the *Frances Hopkinson*,' William explained. 'You'll remember we followed her into the Thames. She's making better time than us but Jock McAvoy was always a driver. She's homeward bound, too – I expect his wife wants to get back to Newcastle.'

Homeward bound. That applied to her, Liza thought. Just over a week to go and she would be with Kitty and Susan. She was looking forward to that, yearning for it. But at the same time . . .

Ferguson, the first mate, came on to the bridge then, in jacket and thick jersey, ginger hair cropped short under his cap. 'Here's my relief,' William said. He handed over the watch to the other man and turned to Liza. 'Breakfast?'

They ate together, served by Archie Godolphin, who some-how managed hot plates and the coffee-pot despite the ship's pitching and rolling. 'If it gets any worse it'll be cold grub because I won't be able to keep pans on the stove,' he warned.

William nodded. 'Sandwiches and tea. I don't think it's going to improve today.' He went off to his cabin to deal with some paperwork.

Archie jerked a thumb at Liza's empty plate. 'You're enjoying this voyage more than your last, I'm glad to see.'

Liza smiled at him. 'I am.'

'As I said afore, it's a pleasure to have you aboard, Miss. To tell you the truth, I took a liking to you the first time I saw you, when we picked you up, you and that other lass. In fact, I thought she was the young lady, with her hoity-toity ways.'

Liza kept her smile in place. Suppose he had aired his

opinion in front of William and started people questioning whether she was Cecily Spencer? 'Really?'

'Just at first,' he said awkwardly. 'But I soon saw who was the real lady.'

Put that in your pipe and smoke it, Cecily, Liza thought. But she took this as a warning that she could not lower her guard even with only a week to go. She was grateful to Archie. She got up and kissed his cheek, then skipped out of the saloon.

That day Liza read in her cabin, spent more time on the bridge, lunched. The sea, if anything, was rougher now, under a leaden sky, but the *Wear Lass* steamed steadily northward. In the late afternoon she was off Skegness on the Lincolnshire coast and Liza sat in the saloon, drinking tea. She had to hold the mug to keep it on the table as the ship rose, fell and rolled, but she was relaxed after two days of worry and hunting criminals, at peace with the world.

Then the ship's siren blared above her, deafening, and she ran to the bridge.

20

As Liza stepped up off the ladder on to the bridge gratings the siren blared again. She clapped her hands over her ears, and removed them only when the teeth-jarring wailing stopped. 'What's wrong?' she asked then.

William turned from where he stood with Ferguson by the helmsman. 'Jock McAvoy is stopped and flying NC, the signal for a vessel in distress. We used our siren to show we'd seen it.' Liza saw the *Frances Hopkinson* ahead. The signal flags, splashes of colour, were flying from her yardarm. There were figures on the wing of her bridge, peering back at the *Wear Lass*. In the distance Liza could see land.

William saw the direction of her gaze and said quietly, 'Without engines the wind and tide will set her ashore and she'll break up. We've got to haul her off – we're the only other ship in sight.'

The beat of the engines slowed until the ship was moving at only walking pace. They were passing the *Frances Hopkinson* close with only fifty yards or so of foaming grey water between them. William had a tin megaphone in his hand now. 'There's Jock,' he said. He lifted the megaphone and bawled into it: 'Hello, Jock! You're wanting assistance?'

Captain McAvoy also had a megaphone and his answer came back tinnily over the narrow strip of churned sea. 'Aye, I do!'

'I'll throw you a line.'

But Jock had not finished: 'I'm wanting a tow to Newcastle. The missus fell down the companion a half-hour back. She says the bairn's on the way and she wants to get home to her mother. Ye wouldn't have a doctor on board?'

Archie, come from his galley out of curiosity and standing just below the bridge, said, 'A doctor? What does he think we are? A White Star liner?'

'Shut up!' William snapped. 'Poor old Jock,' he muttered, 'and his wife. This is her first. She must be in a state.'

Liza could believe it: having her first child with no help except from ignorant, heavy-handed sailors! She stared at the sea heaving between the two ships, imagined a boat crossing that neck of water and bouncing like a cork, imagined the things that might go wrong with the birth. Suppose it was me? She gulped, then said in a small voice, 'I'll go.'

'*What?*'

'I said, I'll go over to help Mrs McAvoy.'

He struggled with this. 'Do you mean you know about – these things?' At that time young ladies were left in ignorance of childbirth.

Liza helped him: 'I'm not a midwife but I know a little about it.' She had picked up quite a lot from all those times she had gone to confinements with her mother and Jinnie – and giving birth to Susan. 'I'll be better than no one at all.' She hoped that would prove true.

'I'll be damned,' William said, but he looked at her with respect. 'We won't need that heaving line to pass a towing hawser.' Then he shouted to Archie, 'Fetch Mr Ferguson and call all hands. We're going to lower a boat.' And through the megaphone: 'We haven't a doctor, but I'm sending you a boat with a line and a young lady who will care for Mrs McAvoy.'

Ten minutes later the boat was in the water with two seamen

at the oars. They fended off the cockleshell from the steel wall of the ship's side as they rose and fell. Liza sat in the sternsheets, in oilskins again, already glistening with the salt spray, and in a cork lifejacket. She held tight to the side of the boat as it soared level with the ship's deck. Then the wave passed under and it dropped like a stone, leaving her stomach behind. She swallowed as the boat lifted under her again, then the seamen thrust it out from the ship's side, the oars bit into the sea and they were heading for the *Frances Hopkinson*. They towed behind them, like an umbilical cord, a line being paid out from the *Wear Lass*.

The boat bounced like a cork, but with the two sailors heaving at the oars it had soon crossed the narrow neck of water and was swinging in to the side of the *Frances Hopkinson*. Liza saw the Jacob's ladder dangling down the ship's side, swallowed again but was ready: she had been through this before in the North Sea only three weeks ago. It seemed much longer than that.

A rope hung beside the ladder. She grabbed it and looped it round her waist, made it fast, and then she was on the ladder, climbing. She knew she was showing an immodest amount of her calves and ankles but did not care. It was not for long. The sailors on the deck above her hauled on the rope, pulling her up the ladder quickly. Then they were lifting her over the bulwark, setting her on her feet, and hauling in the line from the *Wear Lass*.

'I'm pleased to see you, Miss.' Jock McAvoy had come down from his bridge to receive her. He was thirty or so, sandy-haired, not as tall as William but still looked down at Liza. 'I'll take you to see my wife.' He led her to his cabin in the superstructure. 'I was wanting her to stay at home for this voyage but she was all for coming and she's kept very well all along – until she had this fall.' He turned to look at Liza, a worried man. 'She's afeared she'll lose the bairn. I'm afeared I'll lose *her*.'

Liza decided he needed reassurance. 'I've known women who had a fall bring on the birth and mother and child were fine.' It was true.

Apparently Jock took heart from this. 'Is that so?'

'It is,' Liza told him.

He paused at the cabin door. 'That's good to know. Thank you, Miss . . . ?'

'Cecily Spencer,' Liza supplied.

He opened the door, ushered her in and announced, 'Here y'are, Bridget. Miss Cecily Spencer has come over from the *Wear Lass* to help you, so you can stop worrying now.'

Liza saw that Bridget McAvoy was scarcely older than herself, a tall blonde girl in the narrow bunk, on top of the covers, not under them. She looked frightened. Her hair had come down and hung lank about her shoulders. She still wore her day clothes, a brown dress over white petticoats. 'You're taking me home to my mam?' she quavered.

'Aye, sure I am,' Jock said stoutly. 'We're getting a tow from Bill Morgan. Ye ken him, the big lad. They're hauling in the hawser now and I should be up there.' He blew her a kiss from where he stood in the doorway, then he was gone.

Bridget smiled tremulously. 'Bless the man. He's nearly as frightened as I am.' Then she dissolved into tears. 'I'm so glad to see you.'

'It doesn't sound like it,' Liza joked. She divested herself of lifejacket and oilskins, kissed Bridget and said brightly, 'Now, let's get those clothes off you, pop you into a nightie and make you a bit more comfortable.' That was done with difficulty because of the ship's rolling and pitching, but finally Bridget was back in the bunk. Then Liza examined her. 'Seems all right.' She covered the girl. 'I'm just going out for a few minutes.'

'Don't be long,' pleaded Bridget.

'I won't.'

Liza went out on deck, seeking the galley. Night was falling over the huge, humping seas. The wind was gale force, whipping foam from the crests of the waves. She could see the men above her on the open bridge, and beyond the bow the shadowy outline of the *Wear Lass*, a ghost ship in the darkness. The big towing hawser stretched out to her from the *Frances Hopkinson* in a shallow curve. Liza watched the *Wear Lass* longingly for a few seconds: the battered tramp steamer represented home and William would be on her bridge.

When she found the galley she told the cook, 'I want a clean bucket full of hot water, please. Bring it down to the captain's cabin.'

'Right y'are, Miss.'

Liza returned to Bridget. She brushed the girl's hair, and when the hot water came she washed her face. 'Does that feel better?'

Bridget nodded and her hand stole out to grip Liza's.

They went through the night together as the ships steamed steadily northward. With the first grey light the *Frances Hopkinson* had a different motion. The steadiness of when she had been under tow had gone and she lay powerless, tossed on the sea.

Liza placed Bridget's child in her arms and went out on deck and up to the bridge. Despite the motion of the ship she thought the gale had moderated.

Jock McAvoy was haggard in the dawn. 'You have a fine son,' Liza told him.

A grin spread across his face. 'By, bonny lass, that's grand news.' He wrapped his arms about her and kissed her.

A moment later Liza eased away from him. 'The tow has gone,' she said, dismayed. It no longer stretched between the two ships. She could see where one end hung from the stern of the *Wear Lass* and trailed in the sea, but that was all.

'Aye,' said Jock. 'It parted a few minutes back. Bill said he'd throw a heaving line. And there he is.'

Liza made out William's tall figure among the other men now gathered in the stern of the *Wear Lass*. The ship was moving slowly astern, closing the gap between her and the *Frances Hopkinson*. She saw he had stripped down to his shirt, the better to throw; it was plastered to his broad chest by the rain. Liza waved to him, and he waved back. She found she was smiling. He poised as the gap closed, then threw. The weight soared over the gap, the light line snaking out behind it, and fell in the bow of the *Frances Hopkinson*, to be seized by a sailor waiting there.

William hastened back to the bridge. Liza would have liked to watch the new towing hawser hauled in and made fast, but she was cold and wet. Besides, she had a duty. She went to the galley, asked the cook for two mugs of tea, then carried them to the captain's cabin. The baby was sleeping, but Bridget reluctantly released him. Liza tucked him into the captain's bunk and whispered, 'There you are, bonny lad, your daddy won't mind.' She gave one mug of tea to Bridget and sat down with the other.

'Oh, thank you,' Bridget said. And later: 'That was the best cup of tea I've ever had.'

Soon they were under tow again and remained so for the rest of the day. The two women cared for the baby between them, and Liza brought food from the galley. They slept when they could. Jock paid them several visits to see his son, but he also told them that the storm was blowing itself out. Late in the afternoon he came to say, 'We're off Sunderland and there's a tug come to tow us to Newcastle.' He looked at Liza. 'Would you like to come on to Newcastle with us, or go back to the *Wear Lass?*'

Liza did not hesitate. If she went into the Tyne there was a chance she would be recognised as an impostor: people there knew Liza Thornton. 'I'd like to go back, please.'

'Come up when you're ready. We'll lower a boat for you.' Then, as he left the cabin, he said, 'And you can tell Billy Morgan he has a grand lass in you.'

'He's not—' Liza began to protest. But Jock had gone.

Bridget giggled. 'That's my Jock, always putting his foot in it. Anyway,' she went on shyly, 'are you sure there's nothing between you and Billy?'

'No.' Liza gave a flat denial. And knew she lied.

She could see through the porthole that the sea was now as flat as the lake in Mowbray Park. There seemed no need for the bulky oilskins, so she made a parcel of them. She kissed Bridget and the baby. The young mother clung to her, tearful. 'You've been so good.'

'Cheer up and take care of that little lad,' Liza urged. 'You'll soon have your mother to help you.'

Then, as she left the cabin, Bridget called, 'I may be able to do the same for you one day.'

Liza went on her way, laughing and blushing. She was sorry to leave Bridget and the baby, who reminded her of her own child. She told herself that she and Susan would soon be together again.

The boat was waiting, hanging in the davits with two seamen in it and they helped her in. Like her, they had dispensed with oilskins. A winch clattered and the boat was lowered smoothly to the water. The two seamen cast off and pulled strongly for the *Wear Lass*. 'How are you getting on with Billy Morgan, Miss?' one asked, with a broad Scots accent.

Liza, taken aback, answered politely, 'Quite well. I take it you know him?'

'Oh, aye. Me and Mickey here, we've shipped wi' Billy a few times. He's a good man, and there's a lot o' the lassies fond o' him.' Liza knew she was blushing again.

Mickey saw this and broke in: 'Give over, Angus, and leave the lass alone.'

Angus laughed. 'From what I know already she's well able to stick up for herself. But no harm intended, Miss.'

Liza smiled at him. 'None taken.'

The gap between the two ships where they lay still was only a hundred yards or so and they had soon crossed it. Liza, sitting in the sternsheets, could see William standing on the bridge, watching her. She waved, and he responded. And there was the tug, a big paddle-wheeler, coming up fast to pass ahead of the *Wear Lass* and station herself ahead of the *Frances Hopkinson*, ready to take up the tow.

The seamen shipped their oars and the boat rubbed against the black-painted steel hull of the *Wear Lass*. A Jacob's ladder hung down, a line beside it and Mickey, nearest Liza, stood up and grabbed for them. But the tug's speed had set up a big bow-wave, which swept into the narrow gap between the ships. As it passed under the boat first the bow and then the stern lifted, then dropped. Mickey was standing, had not gripped ladder or line. Caught unawares, he toppled backwards and over the side.

'Oh, Jesus!' Angus cried. 'Neither of us can swim.'

Then his friend surfaced a few yards away, spluttered, called, 'Help!' and sank again. Liza tore off her skirt and shoes and rolled over the side. Now she remembered how cold the North Sea was, and gasped. She struck out for where she had last seen Mickey – or where she thought she had seen him. By sheer luck she found him – and trouble. He burst up almost alongside her, coughing and crowing for breath, and threw an arm around her. They sank together.

Liza, eyes closed, felt him clinging to her with both arms, his legs churning, bumping into hers. They rose again, burst into the light and Liza took a breath, pushed feebly at his grip and pleaded, 'Let go!' That made no difference and they sank again. Now another hand appeared. It twisted Mickey's fingers loose from her and held him out at arm's length, his face above the water.

'Be still, Mickey!' William barked. And, at the familiar voice, Mickey obeyed. Liza paddled on her own, gasping. 'Just hold on,' William said. 'The boat's here.' And so it was, with Angus at the oars. It swung alongside them and Angus leaned over the stern and grabbed Mickey. He tried to lift the semi-conscious man but William ordered, 'Just hold him. You'll never lift him in on your own.' Instead he pulled Liza to the stern. 'In you go.' She climbed in but not without a shove from him, his hand on her seat, the water dragging at her. William boosted Mickey in the same way, and Angus hauled from above, until the man lay in the sternsheets, breathing stertorously. Then William pulled himself inboard.

Angus paddled the boat back to the ship, and Liza undid her parcel, only too aware that below the waist she wore only stockings and drawers. William crouched above Mickey. 'How are you now, lad?' He wore only cotton drawers, had thrown off his clothes as he ran down from the bridge. They were plastered to his skin. Liza looked away and busied herself with her own problem.

'Awful bad, skipper,' Mickey said dolefully.

'Not surprising,' William said drily. 'You've most of the North Sea inside you, but you'll do.' He sat back on his haunches.

Mickey sat up. 'I'm sorry, though, getting caught like that.'

'It can happen to anybody.'

Liza shivered. But why me? she thought.

She had found the oilskin trousers and wriggled into their stiff folds. The *Wear Lass* loomed alongside and this time Angus seized ladder and line. Liza climbed up, the line pulling her, and gained the deck. William followed, and she saw Angus rowing back to the *Frances Hopkinson*. She and William hurried to their cabins. Liza undressed, dried herself and put on dry clothes. Then she towelled her hair and brushed it vigorously. When she heard William moving outside in the passage she snatched her thick coat and went out to join him on the bridge.

Both ships were getting under way, the *Frances Hopkinson* towed by the paddlewheel tug. Jock McAvoy bellowed through his tin megaphone: 'Is Miss Spencer there?'

'She is,' William replied.

'My lads tell me we're in your debt again, Miss,' Jock bawled. 'I didn't see what happened because I was aft, seeing to the tow, but thank you. We're hoping we'll see more of you in the future.'

Liza waved in acknowledgement. William coughed and she knew why. They wanted to see more of her? They had already seen far more than she had intended. She avoided his gaze all the way into the Wear in the last of the light. The gas-lights were flaring on the quay as they berthed and she saw Gibson waiting with the Vauxhall. She suddenly felt very tired, and as she looked back over the past two days, she decided that that was not surprising.

William took her arm and led her down the gangway. 'You look dead beat,' he said. She did not argue, was grateful for the attention. He helped her into the front passenger seat, and drove them to the house, with Gibson in the back. 'It's a good job you had that time in London. You got a bit of a rest,' he remarked. Liza almost laughed, remembering how hard and long she had worked to secure Cecily's release.

They stopped in front of the house and the housekeeper opened the front door at once, with Martha behind her. William took Liza's arm and they climbed the steps together while Gibson drove the car to the garage.

Mrs Taggart peered at them as they came into the light. 'My God, lassie! You look worn out.' She glowered accusingly at William. 'What have you done to the puir wee lamb?'

'Not him,' Liza defended him. 'Just life, Mrs Taggart. He'll tell you all about it.'

'Aye, he will, but your bed is waiting for you and Martha will put you in it.'

Liza went with the girl, but paused on the stairs to say, 'Goodnight, William. I really had a lovely time.' Then she went on up, fell into bed and instant sleep.

Flora Gibb woke from a doze. She had a corner seat in the carriage of the train from Newcastle, which was due to arrive in London in another hour. She had with her yesterday's newspaper, which had told her that the earlier report of Jasper's capture had been incorrect. She had known that already, had laughed with Jasper as they read it. The latest report said the man arrested had been a burglar, who would be charged with breaking and entering.

Now she reflected that she was content with her efforts during her short visit to Sunderland. In those two days she had found Spencer Hall and a furnished, semi-detached villa to let in a street down by the river in Monkwearmouth. She had taken it, paying a month's rent in advance. She had also found a livery stable, where a pony and trap could be hired. Jasper would be pleased.

Flora was uneasy because she did not know what he

proposed to do. She loved him, but feared him too. She had come to enjoy her comfortable life while he was in prison. All she wanted now was for the pair of them to go on quietly, earning an honest living so that they would not be in fear of the law. Suppose they went abroad? She sighed wistfully and tried not to wonder about the awful fate she suspected he intended for the girl in Spencer Hall.

William and Liza had not seen the report that Jasper was still at large. It had been published while they were at sea and the *Wear Lass* was towing the *Frances Hopkinson* northward.

21

SUNDAY, 10 FEBRUARY 1907, SUNDERLAND

Liza woke to the sound of distant church bells. Then she saw from the clock on the mantelpiece that it was past nine. She squeaked, rolled out of bed and ran to the bathroom. A knock on the door heralded the arrival of Martha: 'I let you lie, Miss, because you were so tired last night and the captain said so.'

'That's all right, Martha, but I must show my face now.' She bathed hurriedly, dressed, then ran down the stairs.

In the dining room William looked over his newspaper. 'Good morning.'

'I'm sorry I'm late, but Martha said she let me sleep on your instructions. Thank you.'

He put aside the paper. 'You were very tired last night, after a rough passage.'

'Don't stop reading on my account,' Liza said quickly.

Mrs Taggart entered then, catching the last remark.

'Not at all,' William said. 'I haven't had breakfast yet – thought I'd wait for you.'

'He shouldn't have his nose stuck in a paper anyway when there's company at the table,' Mrs Taggart said tartly. 'Good morning, Miss Spencer.'

'Good morning, Mrs Taggart.'

'My name is Elspeth, Miss Spencer.'

'Oh. Thank you.' Liza had wanted a friend and now she

had one. She wondered what had brought it about, then saw William wink.

'I told Elspeth all your adventures,' he said. 'She was amazed and impressed.'

Elspeth agreed. 'Aye, and so I am, and you such a little lass.'

Liza tried to sit taller. 'Have we any duties today, Mrs' – she corrected herself '– Elspeth?'

'No, but tomorrow we start on preparations for the party next Saturday, and there'll be plenty of them and the house turned upside-down. You'll find there are people who are dab hands at having these grand ideas but it's left to the likes of you and me to carry them out.'

William helped himself to coffee from the sideboard. 'Not this time. The party will be at the Palace Hotel. There will be preparations, but no clearing up afterwards, and this house will remain intact.' He cocked an eye at Elspeth. 'Or do you want me to call it off?'

'Certainly not!' She bristled. 'The lassie deserves her party. She's earned it.' She marched out.

He grinned at Liza. 'What are your plans for today?'

'I'd like to call on Iris Cruikshank,' said Liza, 'but that's all.'

'I can drive you there,' William offered, 'and have a word with her myself. Would you like that?'

Liza had been looking forward to the walk but she said, without hesitation, 'Yes, please.'

'Afterwards we can go down to the sea and stroll along the shore.'

That was better. 'Lovely.'

They drove out in the Vauxhall in the quiet of a Sunday morning. The children were there as always, scattering before the car and running after it. When William braked outside the tagareen shop they clustered together at a cautious distance. The neighbours had come to their doors, and Liza recognised the buxom Mrs Robson. She waved to her, and was acknowledged, after a moment's shy hesitation, by a plump, red hand. Mrs Robson was a little overawed by the motor-car and William. The door of the shop was shut. Of course, it's Sunday, Liza thought. But then Mrs Robson called, 'Just a minute, Miss! Our Alice! Run upstairs and fetch that key off the nail by the door.' Alice was a skinny girl of six or seven, in a brown dress and white pinny, with darns in her black stockings. She dived past her mother into the passage.

Mrs Robson hurried over to Liza and William. 'Iris gave me a key so I could get in.' Almost immediately Alice burst out of the passage, brandishing the key, which she handed to her mother. She unlocked the door and pushed it open. 'There y'are, Miss – sir.'

'Thank you.' Liza led the way into the shop, William at her heels. 'I've come to see you, Iris,' she called. Then she remembered. 'It's Cecily! I've brought Captain Morgan with me.' All would be lost if Iris addressed her as Liza.

'Aye, come through.'

They obeyed, William ducking his head under the lintel of the kitchen door. Iris was baking, a floury board on the kitchen table and a bowl of dough left on the hearth to rise, covered with a clean teacloth. She still wore her black cap, now with a dusting of flour. She rubbed her hands on her white apron, then hugged Liza. 'Sit yourself down and I'll make you a cup of tea.' She eyed William. 'Have you come for an apology?'

'No. It's water under the bridge now.'

'That's true, but I'm sorry an' all.' Iris held out her hand and William shook it. She looked from him to Liza and back again. 'I hope you're being good to her.'

'I'm trying.'

Iris studied him for some seconds and he met her gaze. She nodded, 'Aye,' then set the kettle on the fire. 'Now then, we'll have a cup o' tea, and you can tell me all about your trip to London.'

Liza did, but only the events she could mention in front of William. Iris listened eagerly, nodding and smiling.

When they left Iris told William, 'I'm pleased you came, and glad to have a crack wi' you after all these years. Now go on, I want a word wi' the lass.' William ducked under the lintel again and she watched his broad back as he walked through the shop. 'He's a big feller.'

Liza grimaced. 'He frightens me to death.' And when Iris stared, she explained, 'I'm afraid he'll find me out. I can't bear to think how angry he'd be. He wouldn't strike me, there's no question of that, but he'd give me a look that would shrivel me.'

Iris clicked her tongue. 'Away wi' ye. Ye've nowt to fear from him.' Then, squeezing Liza's arm, she added, 'You've got a real man there.'

She blushed. 'No.'

But Iris nodded. 'We'll see.'

Liza escaped, making a mental note that Iris saw too much that could not be and that she would not bring William again. She caught up with him at the door. They locked it and Mrs Robson came puffing for the key. Liza smiled and thanked her.

'You're welcome, Miss.' And then, 'Did she tell you about her turn?'

'No?'

Mrs Robson nodded knowingly. 'I thought so. Well, it was last Thursday. It was just lucky that Ada – that's Mrs Millan that lives downstairs from us – she looked in to see if Iris was all right and there she was, sitting at the bottom o' the stairs, gasping for breath. Ada ran and fetched me and I sent Alice to the pub on the corner for some brandy. She came back and we gave Iris a drop and that brought her round, but she did look bad. And what was the first words she said when she could speak? "I'm canny now," she said. She's poorly and she won't admit it. I thought she wouldn't say anything to you.'

'Thank you for telling me,' Liza said. Iris had talked of resting, but how could she after a lifetime of work? 'I'll talk to her next time I come.'

'I wish you would, Miss. She won't listen to us.'

They settled into the Vauxhall and drove off up the hill, chased by a crowd of cheering children for the first hundred yards. Then they crossed the bridge over the river and went down to the sea. There they left the car and set off on foot along the shore. Liza kept her hat tied on because there was a blustery wind, and they walked from the pier to the fishermen's cottages at Whitburn.

'The word Iris wanted with you, is that a secret?' William asked.

'Yes.'

'Something about me?'

'You're fishing.'

'I am.'

They both laughed but he probed again: 'Well? Was it about the feud? Or was she warning you about the sailor with a girl in every port?'

Liza decided this had to be stopped. 'She was very complimentary, and I'll tell you what she said a week today.'

'Why a week?'

'To test your control over your curiosity.'

He frowned. 'Is this some game?'

Then a sudden gust blew her into his arms and they laughed

again. But he held her, gazing down into her face and she said breathlessly, 'I'm all right now. Please.'

He released her reluctantly and they walked on, but now he kept her arm in his. 'Very well, I'll wait until Sunday,' he said.

She knew that next Sunday she would be gone.

On Monday Liza and Elspeth worked ostensibly as pupil and teacher, but in fact they were a team. They were washing and polishing glasses in the crowded kitchen. The cook was preparing lunch, with the assistance of the scullery-maid and a lethargic Doreen, while Gibson and Cully, the gardener, had their mid-morning tea. It was a situation familiar to Liza from her experience in many such kitchens and she sank into it happily. Furthermore, her presence was now accepted by the others.

At one point she caught a sulky look from Doreen and murmured, 'She doesn't seem very happy today.'

Elspeth sniffed. 'I'm not surprised. I gave her notice while you were away. She's working it out, and doing as little as she can and still be paid.'

Liza bit her lip. She knew how it felt to be given notice; that was what had brought her to this place. She was sorry for Doreen, despite the hatred she knew the girl felt for her. 'I hope it wasn't my fault.'

'No,' Elspeth said brusquely. 'She's nobody to blame but herself.' She glanced at Liza. 'When you run a house like this you sometimes have to dismiss a girl or a chap. It might be for laziness, incompetence or theft, but you still have to do it.'

'Yes, I know,' agreed Liza, but was no happier about Doreen's fate.

Now she had a trayful of sparkling glasses. She picked it up and carried it, balanced on one hand, through the crowded kitchen to the front of the house to return them to the cupboard from which they had come.

Elspeth watched approvingly, but then two creases came between her brows and she thought, That's strange – at which point Doreen shoved a pan carelessly on to the kitchen table. It slid off the edge and boiling water sluiced over the kitchen floor. Elspeth exploded: 'For God's sake, girl, can't you do anything right?' In the commotion she forgot what she had been thinking about.

William came home in the early evening when Liza was bathing, preparing to dress for dinner. He rapped on her door.

'Yes?' she called.

'I've had enough for one day. Let's go to a show and have some supper afterwards. Or are you too tired?'

'No!' She was not tired at all now. 'Let's do it – please!'

They had a light meal, then drove into town and settled, just in time, into the stalls at the Empire. Later they had supper at the Palace Hotel, then walked on to the bridge and leaned on the balustrade, looking down on the river. The shipyards were still and silent now, the coal staiths standing gaunt against the sky.

'Will you leave us when you inherit?' William asked.

Liza had not been ready for that. 'I don't know. I haven't given any thought to it,' was all she could say. Anyway, she was going perforce.

He turned her to face him. 'I would like you to stay. I—'

'Don't say any more, please. I'll answer any question you like next Sunday.'

His brows came down.

'Will you wait? Please?' she whispered.

'Very well,' he agreed reluctantly, but she shut his mouth

with her own, on tiptoe and clinging to him, arms round his neck. Then she broke away and he followed her back to the Vauxhall.

Before he slept William recalled their conversation of the previous day and wondered if the new Cecily was reverting to her old ways and toying with him. He had dealt with that two years ago when he had bundled her out of his room, and would again if need be. He would be no woman's poodle. He would have answers on Sunday or they would go their separate ways.

Liza stared at the ceiling. She had struck a bargain with Cecily in gratitude for her life, and had paid her debt. She would leave this man and this house because she must, and Cecily would claim the place that was rightfully hers.

The train pulled into the station in the dusk and a porter strode along the platform, bawling, 'Monkwearmouth! Monkwearmouth!' It was in Sunderland, on the north shore of the river Wear. Jasper Barbour emerged from the train, materialising out of a cloud of smoke and steam like an evil genie. He was bearded now, his coat collar turned up. Flora Gibb was by his side, in a cape with a fold of it across her face. They escaped the porter's notice and carried their own luggage – they had between them only one small case and Jasper's new Gladstone bag. Outside the station, with its Greek columns, Jasper growled, 'Now, where's this house you've rented?'

Flora hurried along by his side. 'Across the road and down Barclay Street. Just a couple of minutes' walk.'

They found the villa, walked up the path through the little garden and let themselves in with the key. Jasper glanced around perfunctorily, then passed through the narrow hall and out of the kitchen into the yard. There was the usual lavatory and coal-shed with a wash-house in one corner. He ignored them. There was also a strip of garden some eight feet by four, and he thought he would find a use for that. He opened the gate and stepped out into the cobbled back lane. It was dark, without a light except for the gas lamp that stood in the street running across the end of it.

At his side Flora asked, 'Did I do right? Is it how you wanted?'

'Perfect. You can get a body in and out of here without a soul seeing you.'

'A body!' Flora gasped. 'Oh, Jasper, I wish—'

'Just a manner o' speaking. I'm talking about her, Cecily Spencer that sent me down. And don't you worry, I'm only going to give her a leathering, like I've told you before.'

'But how will you do it?' Flora persisted. 'There'll be police all over and they'll know who did it.'

'I'll find a way,' he told her impatiently. 'Now, get that bottle out o' the case. We'll have a drink and then you can earn your keep.' He pushed her ahead of him towards the house. He knew that she believed him – if only because she wanted to.

On Tuesday morning Liza ran down the stairs in time, as usual, to join William for breakfast before he drove to his offices. He looked up from his newspaper and grinned. 'Ah! The celebrity.' He held up the paper. 'Last night's *Echo*.' She saw that *The Times* had been laid aside. 'I brought this home last night but never read it. I fear Jock or Mrs McAvoy has told the press of your exploits, probably a reporter from one of the Newcastle papers and they passed it on to the *Echo*. There you are.' He pointed to a paragraph headed: 'Young

Lady's Sea Adventures'. Liza read. It was all there, how Miss Cecily Spencer had crossed to the *Frances Hopkinson* to assist the tearful Bridget McAvoy, and later plunged into the sea in an attempt to rescue Mickey from drowning.

'How awful!' she said. 'They only say I was "assisted by Captain William Morgan"', when it was you who pulled the pair of us out.'

He dismissed that. 'It's probably how Jock told it. Never mind. You're famous now. How does it feel?'

She was flattered, pleased. Then she remembered her position. Before, her impersonation of Cecily would have been a prank within the family. There would have been some annoyance, but it would all have been in the family. Now it was public property. Suppose a reporter from the *Echo* turned up and asked for her version of the story, then saw a different Cecily a week later? That would be another story. How would Arkenstall, the lawyer, and William see that?

William must have read her feelings in her face. 'You're not happy.'

'I don't like the idea of people reading about me, staring.'

He took the paper from her and threw it into the fire, held it there with a poker until it was ashes. 'You'll still be a celebrity for a time, but no reporters. We'll send them away.'

'Thank you.' But Liza feared the damage was done.

Elspeth entered, beaming. 'I was reading the *Echo* last night and there was a bit in there all about you, Miss Spencer. You're famous. Aren't you the grand lass?'

Liza smiled lopsidedly. 'If that's what you think, may I be excused this morning? I'd like to call on Iris.'

Elspeth laughed. 'I expect the rest of us will manage.'

So Liza walked down through Mowbray Park and found the tagareen shop open and Iris sitting in the kitchen as usual: 'If anybody wants to buy owt they know where to find me.'

And then: 'I read about you in the paper last night. There's a little daredivil y'are.' Liza had to tell the story again, and gave William the credit he was due. Then she gave a true account of her doings in London, the arrest of Una and Piggy, and the release of Cecily and Mark.

'What is she like, this Cecily?' Iris asked.

'You'll have to make up your own mind about that,' Liza replied diplomatically. 'I think she's found a good man.' That had been her assessment of Mark Calvert.

'You've answered my question. Still, I doubt if she'll be coming down here. But talking o' good men, I liked what I saw o' Billy Morgan. I'd heard plenty but that was the first time I'd met him. Is he the one for you?'

'That's out of the question – ridiculous.' She rose to go.

Iris walked through the shop with her. 'I don't see what's ridiculous about it. Looks to me like you were made for each other.'

'I'll come again in a day or two,' Liza said.

'You mark my words,' said Iris.

Liza had already done so.

Flora said there was a carter just a street away who had a pony and trap he hired out, so Jasper walked round to the stables to inspect them. He found the one placid, the other clean and smart. 'I gave it a coat o' paint just a week ago to freshen it up,' the carter said.

'Pity you couldn't paint the pony,' said Jasper. 'It looks to need freshening up.'

'There's nowt wrong wi' that pony. If you wanted a bloody racehorse you should ha' said so. Now Bobby here,' and he slapped the pony's rump, 'he'll do whatever you tell him. Stand all day, walk, trot or gallop.'

But Jasper had seen enough. He did some token bargaining,

because it was expected and might have been wondered about if he had not. 'I'll hire it for a week.' He would be gone inside a day or two, if he got the chance, but he might take longer and did not want to keep coming to this man every day. 'You'll feed and bed him? And can I get in if I want him early?'

'Oh, aye. The lad sleeps ower the stable. He'll let you in.'

Jasper paid and drove the pony and trap out of the yard. He picked up Flora at the end of the street and she directed him through the town. They stopped outside Spencer Hall, then Jasper turned down a lane and behind a copse that screened them from the house and the road. They could see through the trees to the open gates and the grounds beyond. The house itself was hidden by more trees. They saw several visitors, tradesmen for the most part, and a slight young girl who walked up from the tram stop. 'That might be her,' Flora said.

Jasper agreed. 'Might be, can't remember for sure. She'll ha' changed in five years.'

Then, late in the afternoon, another girl hurried out, slouching, her eyes on the ground. 'Maybe,' Jasper said doubtfully.

Flora shook her head. 'Naw. She's one o' the maids, I reckon.'

The girl disappeared down the road. Darkness fell, and Jasper jumped down from the trap. 'You wait here. I'm going to take a look.'

'Be careful.'

He crossed the road and passed through the gates. He saw they were in good condition but did not appear to have been closed for some time. One or two weeds had escaped the gardener and twined round them. He walked up to and around the house and decided it would be easy to force an entrance, but what then? He did not want to steal a few baubles. No matter. He marked a ground-floor window or two that would suit his purpose. He would go on from there.

He retraced his steps, but had to scurry into the shelter of the trees before the house as a motor-car drove in through the gateway. A man sat at the wheel and he steered it round the house to the rear. Jasper remembered seeing a stable block and garage there. He emerged from the copse and rejoined Flora.

'Well?' she asked.

He nodded. 'Aye, but I need to know where she sleeps.'

'How will you find out?'

'Don't know, but I will. I'll settle this score if it takes me a year.'

'You need to get to know somebody inside,' Flora said.

'I know that damn fine,' he snapped impatiently. 'It's doing it.'

Flora had an idea, but said nothing. She still hoped he might abandon his thoughts of vengeance; they could be happy if they fled the country and started a new life abroad.

22

'Lord knows what yon Doreen will be up to while I'm away.'
Elspeth shook her head. 'I've given her a few jobs but who's
to see she does them? Cook won't have her in the kitchen
after that calamity with the saucepan. And when I come back
there'll be nothing done and her with a list of excuses. It'll be a
blessing when she's worked her notice and we're rid of her. I'm
looking forward to Sunday and seeing her out of the door.'

Liza was not. She had only a few more days to play her
part in this house and then she would be free. Once she had
looked forward to that, but now?

She and Elspeth were going into town to view the venue
for the party on Saturday night, the ballroom of the Palace
Hotel. They were to discuss the menu for the buffet, the
wines, the flowers and where they were to be sited. Then,
with the leader of the orchestra, they would agree upon the
music to be played.

'You'll be needing a new dress for this occasion,' William
had said.

'I bought one when I was in London,' Liza had replied.

'I look forward to seeing it.'

Now Elspeth was helping Liza into her coat in the hall.
Gibson was waiting outside with the carriage and they went
out to him and climbed in. 'Well, we've made an early start,'
Liza said brightly.

Elspeth sniffed. 'I hope they aren't all still in bed at the

Palace.' And the carriage, pulled by Gibson's beloved horses, rolled out of the gates on its way to the town.

'Why did Uncle Edward insist on the gates always being open?' Liza asked.

'He was afraid some poor devil, gypsy or tramp, might die outside if the gates were closed for want of a drink or a bite. He was a good man. The captain is following in his footsteps, another good man. Lucky the girl who gets him.'

They were not the only ones to make an early start. Jasper, Flora by his side, sat in the trap, hidden behind the copse across the road from the gates. He watched them go and muttered hungrily, 'That young lass looks like she could be the one.' Flora nodded in agreement: as far as she could see, the girl in the carriage was well dressed. They waited and watched while Bobby cropped the grass.

A succession of tradesmen came and went, but it was two hours later that another young woman came out. This one was shabby and hurrying on foot, with occasional glances behind her. She took the road into the town, walking a few paces then running, teetering on high-heeled buttoned boots. She carried a parcel under one arm.

'There she goes,' Jasper growled. 'We'll try her, see if she's needing a few bob extra. Out you get and follow her.'

Flora jumped down from the trap and set out after the girl, a basket in her hand as if she were going shopping. Jasper wheeled the trap out on to the road and followed Flora at a distance. He was rarely in sight of the girl, who hurried on unsuspecting.

In the town he caught up with Flora, standing on a corner. 'She went down that alley and in a back door,' she reported. Jasper gave her the reins of the pony and went to see for himself. He stood at the end of the alley, hands in his pockets like some idler, and a minute or two later the girl came out and walked towards him. He turned his back to her and let her pass him. She carried no parcel now. He grinned to himself, then went after her. He seized her arm above the elbow and steered her towards Flora.

She tried to pull away. 'Here! Who are you? What d'ye think you're doing?' He only held her more tightly. 'You're hurting me! Leggo!'

He stopped beside Flora. 'Our little friend here has just been pawning something she didn't own and we're all going to have a drink.'

The girl was silent now, frightened. Flora tied Bobby's reins to a lamp-post and followed them into a nearby pub. The bar was half full but the sitting room empty at this time of day. Jasper seated the two women at one of the polished round tables and asked the girl, 'What d'ye want?'

'Drop o' gin,' she muttered.

'Dutch courage, hey?' He grinned and ordered from the barmaid. As she walked away he asked, 'What was in the parcel? Tell the truth because I can find out. Lie to me and it's the pollis for you.'

'It was a clock.' A carriage clock from the mantelpiece of one of the guest rooms. 'You're not a pollis?'

'No, but never mind what we are. You work at that house, Spencer Hall. I saw a young lady leave there this morning, with an older woman, in a carriage. I believe it was Miss Cecily Spencer and she lives there.'

'Oh, aye, that was her wi' the housekeeper, Mrs Taggart,' the girl sneered. Jasper nodded; he had the right one. 'That Miss Spencer is a little cow, she is,' she went on. 'Got me notice. But they're giving a party for her on Saturday night.'

'You've been sacked?' That was not so good and Jasper scowled.

'I finish the end o' the week, Sunday. I'm working my notice.'

She might do, after all. 'I can see you're working it now.'

'What d'ye want—' She stopped as he held up his hand, seeing the barmaid returning with the drinks. He paid and she went away. Doreen started again, 'Miss Spencer. What d'ye—'

He jerked his head at Flora. 'This lady's my sister. Miss Spencer took her feller away when she was down south and she wants to have a word with her. Now, if she went up to the front door they'd chase her away, so she wants to slip in nice and quiet one night and find this Cecily Spencer.'

'Serve her right,' Doreen said eagerly. 'She came in, a soft-handed fine lady, and started doing jobs that was rightly ours, the lasses working there, and making us look lazy. She hadn't done them properly, o' course, but that housekeper had it in for me. She—'

'How can I get in and where does she sleep? I saw a door on the side of the house. Is that locked or bolted?'

'That's what we call the garden door because it opens on that side garden. Mrs Taggart locks *and* bolts it every night.'

'Where does she keep the key?'

'It stays in the lock.'

'Ah! Fetch some paper,' Jasper ordered Flora. 'There's a shop across the road.' He turned back to the girl. 'How do you get from that door to her room?'

A few minutes later Flora returned with a packet of writing paper. Jasper took it from her, spread a sheet on the table and found a stub of pencil in his pocket. Ready to draw, he looked at the girl. 'So, you say it's like this.' He made a rough sketch, following her instructions.

Afterwards she said, 'What's this going to be worth, then?'

'I'll give you a sovereign.'

'More like a couple,' she argued.

Jasper looked at her. 'I'll make it a quid now and another ten bob after. Don't push for more. And I'll settle with you if you let me down, don't doubt it.'

'Give us the quid then.' She had sold Liza into the hands of Jasper for thirty shillings.

He gave her the gold sovereign and she returned to her duties, while he and Flora drove back to their rented house. 'We'll keep away from the place now,' he said. 'We've got all we want.' He had a rough but accurate plan of the interior of Spencer Hall and the girl had agreed to open the garden door on Saturday night. 'They'll all be sleeping sound early Sunday morning. That'll be my time.'

Flora was disappointed. She had guessed that Doreen might be bought when she first saw her, but had said nothing because she hoped Jasper would find his task impossible and give it up. Instead he had noted Doreen just as she had. Flora was still uneasy despite his assurances. He had said he would give the girl a 'leathering'. That conjured up pictures from which she recoiled . . .

On Thursday Liza set out to call on Iris. The days were flying away now and she would soon be finished here. She told herself that this was no more than she had expected. Now she would be able to go back to her own life, her mother and daughter. She was looking forward to that but . . . Again, there was that 'but', defying reason.

Iris was in her shop, busily sorting clothing into piles and negotiating a transaction with a rag-and-bone man come to buy, his horse and cart standing outside. Iris hailed her, 'Come in, bonny lass, and I'll make a cup o' tea. It's no use arguing, Joe, I'm not cutting another penny.'

Joe grumbled, but paid up and took away his rags. A few

minutes later Liza and Iris were sitting in the kitchen, sipping strong tea. 'You're very busy,' Liza said. 'You won't do too much, will you?'

'I'm feeling a lot better so I thought I'd have a tidy-up.' Iris fiddled with her cup and saucer. 'I'll shut the shop this afternoon, though. I've some paperwork to do.'

Liza wondered about that but did not ask what paperwork was needed for a tagareen shop. Instead she said she had to leave. 'William, Captain Morgan, said he'd drive me back. He'll be waiting for me in his office.'

Iris hugged her. 'You've been a Godsend to me. I lost the boys and that was bad enough. Barney was all I had. Then for him to go . . . I think it twisted me. I knew he drank – and that was because of losing the boys – and I knew everybody said he must have been drunk the night he drowned. It made me full of hate and badness. Then you came and made me better.' Iris wiped her eyes and planted a kiss on Liza's cheek. 'Enjoy yourself on Saturday. And remember what I told you about the big lad.'

Liza laughed and blushed, and made her escape.

She sat for some five minutes in William's office while he signed letters, and then they walked down to the Vauxhall. They were laughing as they drove away.

Among the passers-by who watched them go was an unshaven man in an old suit, carrying a cheap cardboard suitcase. He stared, disbelieving the evidence of his eyes. Vince Bailey had worked his passage home from Australia. He had disembarked from his ship only that morning with the intention of taking a train to London where he could live off his sister for a while. Now he grabbed the arm of a young man emerging from the offices close by. 'Here! 'Scuse me, but who were those two in that motor-car? I think I've seen them before.'

'That was Captain Morgan. I work for him. The young lady is Miss Cecily Spencer.' He pointed to the brass plate on the door of the offices, that read 'Edward Spencer. Shipowner'. 'His niece, though he's dead now.'

'Is she?' Vince grinned. 'O' course she is. Ta, mate.' The young man went on his way, and Vince looked after the Vauxhall, though it was now out of sight. 'Who would ha' thought it of our Liza? How did she work that? You don't have to go to London to seek your fortune now, my lad. It's waiting for you here.'

That night Liza wrote a letter to her mother and Susan. 'I've nearly finished my work here and expect to be home soon.' She did not give a day or time: better that her arrival should be a surprise. She could picture the delight on Susan's face. She added, 'But do not be surprised if I am delayed.' She put that in because she did not want any hostages to fortune: she had experienced enough surprises necessitating changes of plan since she had arrived in this house. As always, she did not put any address on the letter.

The next day, Friday, Liza posted it on her way into town. The overnight rain had stopped and a breeze had scoured the sky clean of clouds. She went to visit Iris, humming under her breath. The shop was open and she walked through to the kitchen, calling, 'Good morning!' Iris was in her chair before the fire, her black cap set square on her bushy hair, her shawl round her shoulders. Her head was bowed and her knitting lay in her lap, as if she had laid it down to nap for a few minutes. Her eyes were closed, but when Liza touched her shoulder gently, knowing but not wanting to believe, she seemed to collapse inside herself.

Tears in her eyes, Liza held her for a few minutes and she

seemed warm, but that was from the heat of the fire. Then she laid the poor clay, shrivelled now, back in the chair and walked out into the street. The children were there as usual and she saw Alice, Mrs Robson's skinny little girl, hurrying back from the shop at the end of the street. 'Will you ask your mam if she can come here, please?' Liza asked.

'Aye, Miss.' Alice disappeared into the house next door. Liza knew that the child was not at school because her mother had kept her at home to help. That was common.

A minute later Mrs Robson hurried out, drying red hands on her apron. 'Is something the matter, Miss? Alice said you were crying.'

'I've just found Iris dead.'

'Oh, my God!' Mrs Robson put an arm round her. 'Are you feeling faint?'

Liza dried her tears. 'No.'

She led the way into the kitchen, with Mrs Robson saying, 'I saw her just over an hour ago when I looked in, as I do of a morning. Oh dear. But no need for you to upset yourself, pet. You can leave me and Mrs Millan to see to things. It was only last night that Iris called the pair of us in and told us how she wanted everything done, service in the chapel at the end of the street – she was Methodist – and we had to tell the solicitor. I told her, "You'll live to see us out." I meant it an' all, but somehow she must ha' known. Now I'll get Ada Millan.'

Liza went with her to the front of the shop, but then said farewell. From her childhood she knew that the two neighbours would do what was right. The poor looked after their own, bringing them into the world or seeing them out of it. But she was sad at heart.

Jasper was restless. He had made almost all his preparations and now he could only wait. 'I'm going out for a bit,' he told Flora.

'Can I come with you?' she asked, and reached for her coat.

'No,' he replied flatly. There was no sense in her knowing too much too soon. Flora had taken to asking questions and voicing her unease – 'Do you think you should do that? I wish you wouldn't do this. Can't we go somewhere we can live quiet?' She was getting on his nerves. He said, 'You stay here and have my dinner ready.'

He left the house by the back gate, without being seen, and walked towards the town. As he crossed the bridge a movement caught his eye and he halted. He saw the coal pouring down the chute from one of the staiths on the bank of the river, to crash into the hold of a ship tied up to the quay. He watched for some time as wagon after wagon emptied its load into the chute to be followed by another. There was an almost continuous black stream of coal pouring down into the hold with a sound like distant thunder, and the dust rose in clouds to drift away on the wind.

As he watched an idea formed in his head. When he moved on he had changed his plan. Now he had a better one and he would not need the spade he had intended to buy this morning, wouldn't have to find an explanation for it when he returned to Flora. He would have to find out a few things about this loading of coal but that should not be too difficult.

He bought a bottle of gin and went back to Flora. They drank half of it, and he took her upstairs. When he woke he ate the dinner she had cooked, then walked down to the riverside. There was a pub opposite the towering staiths and he waited there. At the end of the day's work the men flocked out, coated in dust like so many pitmen. Most made off but a group of four trudged into the bar and ordered beer.

Jasper sidled up to them, grinning. 'Are you lads working at loading the coal?'

He was going to buy them a drink but they stared at him. One said, 'You're not from round here.' That much was clear from Jasper's accent.

'What the hell has it got to do wi' you?' another chimed in.

'Aye. What are you after?' the first said.

They were big men, and Jasper knew he would learn nothing from them. He walked away, cursing silently. It seemed he would have to revert to his original plan, although that did not appeal now. Still, the end, Cecily Spencer's end, would be the same.

23

Liza woke with the thought that this was her last day here. Tomorrow she would be gone, but she was determined to make the most of these few hours. When she ran down the stairs to breakfast, Martha was closing the front door. Through the narrowing gap Liza saw the telegraph boy cycling down the drive. 'This has just come for you, Miss,' Martha said. She held out the telegram.

Liza saw that it was addressed to Miss C. Spencer. She ripped it open. The buff form inside said: 'Arriving ten a.m. Monday.' It was signed, C. Calvert. So Cecily was using Mark's name and had served Liza with notice to quit. It was no more than she had expected and only underlined that she was going.

'Thank you, Martha,' she said, and went in to breakfast.

William was opening his mail: there was a little pile of discarded envelopes, and another of formal notes on stiff stationery. He held the last in his hand and waved it at her. 'Good morning. These are the last of the replies to the invitations we sent out, all acceptances. We only had one refusal. Arkenstall had accepted but yesterday he sent one of his clerks to my office with a note to say he had to go to Liverpool on urgent business and won't be back until Monday.'

Liza pulled a face. 'That's a pity.' She had liked the solicitor, brief though their meeting had been. She filled a plate from the sideboard and poured a cup of tea. 'I want to go to the chapel where the service to Iris will be held and pay my respects.'

'The funeral isn't until next week.' William looked puzzled.

'I know. But I just want to do it today.'

He did not press her for an explanation.

Later Liza visited Cully in his hothouse, and that gentle man gave her a bunch of carnations. She recalled how pleased Iris had been with the ones she had taken her. She walked down through Mowbray Park for the last time and on until the tagareen shop came in sight. She stopped short of it at the chapel on the corner and tried the door. It was not locked, and opened at her touch. Inside she found an elderly woman dusting. 'Have you a vase, please?' Liza asked. The woman brought one with water and Liza arranged the flowers in it, then set it on a shelf by the pulpit. She sat for a while, thinking about Iris, the sadness and hardship of the old woman's life.

When she walked back up the steep slope towards the town she felt at peace. She recalled that Iris had told her to enjoy herself. She would not mourn for her, or for whatever else she was leaving here. Remember it, yes, but not grieve. It was no use crying for what could never be. There was to be a party tonight to celebrate her birthday and she would look forward to it.

Liza was close to the house, just passing the copse opposite the open gates, when a man stepped out from among the trees. He had several days' stubble on his face and was none too clean. His old suit was creased, shiny and torn. He might have been one of the tramps fed at the back door of the house but Liza recognised Vince Bailey.

'Hello, Liza,' he said.

She stared at him, this ghost from her past, her lips parted. Then she whispered, 'Vince! I thought you were in Australia.'

'I bet you did.' He sniggered. 'I had a rough time out there, and all the way back, but you can see that. And there's no need for you to look down your nose at me.' He looked her up and down insolently. 'Fine feathers for fine birds.'

Liza felt the blood rise to her cheeks. 'You can stop that! What do you want?' she snapped. But she guessed already.

'I'm not after your body, if that's what you think,' he jeered. 'Not that I'd turn my nose up, mind. But no. I'd just got off the ship in the river here, after working my passage for twelve thousand bloody miles, and I was going to buy a ticket to London to see my sister. Then I saw this big toff in his motor-car wi' this girl dressed up to the nines. There was a young chap passing and I asked him, "Who's that gent?" "Captain William Morgan," he says. "And who's that fancy bit o' stuff with him?" I asked. "Is that his missus?" "No, that's a relative of his, Miss Cecily Spencer. Her uncle owns ships." And I thought, our Liza has come on in the world.' His tone hardened. 'So what are you up to? What's your game? I suppose that big feller's bedding you every night.'

Liza slapped his face. The blow rocked his head on his shoulders. She looked at him with contempt: this man had courted her, lied to her and violated her. She remembered Betty Dixon saying, 'Somebody is sure to catch you out,' and it had proved to be Vince, come from the other side of the world. She knew he was ready to wreck her life again and that she would have to buy him off – or he would betray her.

'You bloody bitch!' he swore. He held a hand to his cheek. 'You'll pay for that, through the nose.'

'You'll have what I give you,' Liza said, with cold disdain. 'Open your mouth and you'll walk away with nothing. What I'm doing is my business, but it's not against the law. The police won't put me behind bars for it. But what if I tell them what I know about you? Or pass the word to the people who are looking for you?' She let him think about it, then took out her purse. 'I haven't a lot of money with me but this will buy you a bed for the night. You be here first thing in the morning and I'll give you what I can. But you keep your mouth shut and go away now.'

He took the few shillings she gave him. 'No police when I come tomorrow,' he growled.

'On my word, and you know it's good. I wouldn't take yours.' But Liza was determined he would not have another penny.

He scowled at that, then pushed past her and shambled off towards the town. Liza went on to the house, her heart still thumping from the shock. What else can go wrong now? she wondered.

In the house, when she was calmer, she recalled another obligation. She sought out Doreen in the scullery where she was half-heartedly peeling potatoes – the only job the cook would entrust to her – and asked, 'Can I have a word with you in private?'

'Yes, Miss,' Doreen answered sulkily. She put down the knife and followed Liza into the garden where they could not be seen.

Liza opened her purse. 'You're leaving us tomorrow, Doreen, so I want you to have this as a parting gift, to help you along the way.' She pressed ten shillings into the girl's hand.

The money was accepted readily, though not gracefully. Doreen counted the coins, five florins, and put them into the pocket of her apron. 'Was there anything else, Miss?'

'No, that will be all. Except I wish you well in the future.'

Doreen said no word of thanks but slouched back to her peeling. Liza sighed. She had little hope for the girl.

*   *   *

Jasper Barbour was in a mood of snarling bad temper all day. He had been forced back to his original plan and that had angered him. He had bought a spade, and when Flora asked him what it was for he struck her a backhanded blow that laid her on the floor. From then on she spoke only when spoken to and stepped carefully around him.

He walked abroad in the late afternoon and resorted to the pub by the coal staiths. They were empty now, although a ship was tied up alongside. There were a few men in the pub, but none from the staiths, if appearances counted for anything: not one was covered in coal dust.

Jasper called for beer and drank half of the pint straight down. He replaced his glass on the bar and listened absently to the conversation around him. Suddenly he realised that one of the voices was not speaking Geordie but Cockney. That was not unusual in a port where the accents might be those of seamen from anywhere in the world, but Jasper eased round until he could see the owner of the voice. He was in his twenties, short and stocky, in dark blue trousers and sweater. The sleeves were rolled up to show muscular, tattooed forearms. But what had caught Jasper's attention was the man saying, 'That's right. She's the *Wear Trader*, one o' the Spencer ships. We brought her up and laid her alongside this afternoon. She's all ready, hatches off. First thing tomorrow we're loading coal and sailing for Buenos Aires, so I'm making a night of it tonight.'

'Don't come back singing and wake the watchman,' another voice joked. 'He'll be asleep in his cabin.' There was a roar of laughter.

Jasper grinned. He stood there, listening, while he finished that pint and then another, but the conversation turned to football and he learned no more. That did not matter.

He left the pub and walked back past the staiths. He saw

the nightwatchman's cabin, and found two holes in the wire fencing, which he could enlarge with wire cutters in five minutes. He returned to the rented house but on the way called in at the stables and told the boy, 'I'll be coming for the pony early tomorrow.' He paid for Bobby to be ready. So the *Wear Trader* was a Spencer ship! There was evil humour in that.

Doreen, William, Liza, Vince, Jasper. Now they all waited for the night.

24

Liza was waiting in the hall when William descended the stairs. He was ruggedly handsome, tall and broad in his dinner jacket and white shirtfront. She was covered almost from head to foot in a cloak of navy blue that ended just above her ankles, showing a froth of white lace under a skirt of scarlet silk. A jewelled comb was set in her upswept hair and there were scarlet satin shoes on her feet.

William glanced at his watch. 'You're early.'

'Am I?' Liza did not need to check, but she made a show of it. 'So I am.'

'That cloak,' he said, 'isn't it—'

'Uncle Edward's? Yes – I found it in the wardrobe when I was clearing it out.'

He felt the material. 'Good stuff. It's an old naval boat cloak.'

'Elspeth told me it had belonged to some ancestor. I found this as well.' She pointed with a slim finger to the comb in her hair. It sparkled as the light caught it. 'Do you mind if I wear them?'

William shook his head. 'No. And I'm sure Edward wouldn't, either.'

Elspeth had been a spectator until now, having fussed over Liza for some time, but she endorsed his remark: 'I know he wouldn't mind. And it's time you two were away. Miss

Cecily was early but you weren't.' She looked reproachfully at William. 'Gibson has been outside with the carriage for the past five minutes.'

'You need not wait up,' William replied, and offered his arm to Liza.

As they walked down the steps Elspeth called after them, 'It will be gone midnight when you come home. I'll be seeking my bed long before that.' And as they climbed into the carriage: 'Mind you have a grand time.'

She watched, smiling, until the carriage had disappeared down the drive. The lassie seemed cool and collected, she thought, but there was a shine in her eyes. I hope she stays on.

Elspeth had been deceived. Liza was far from calm: this was her last performance and she was reckless. After tonight it didn't matter what the town worthies thought of her. She sat close to William in the darkness of the carriage and smiled to herself.

At the Palace Hotel she let him take the cloak from her. For a moment he was dumb. Then he said softly, 'You are – lovely. That dress – marvellous.' It was scarlet silk, unfashionably short enough to show her ankles and without a train. It left her shoulders bare and slid smoothly on her body as she moved.

She stood with William as he greeted their guests and saw their eyes widen. In her wild mood she did not care how they viewed her: she had a single aim and it was not to win them over. But it must be said that she enjoyed the jealousy and pique on Daphne Outhwaite's narrow face. The girl had treated her so badly when she had first come to this place. Liza smiled at her. 'Good evening. I'm so glad you could come.' That was true enough.

The rest all caught their breath. They had read of her

exploits at sea, were taken aback by the dress, but she had not worn it for them.

Liza danced throughout the evening with a succession of young men and several not so young. Between dances she talked with elderly matrons and a girl of fourteen who had come with her father, doing duty for her mother who was ill. She gossiped with spinsters and young wives in between. William did not claim her until near the end of the evening. As she whirled around the floor in his arms he congratulated her: 'You're a success.'

Liza laughed. 'Thank you.' She was pleased, but it did not really matter.

At the house Elspeth walked around the ground floor making sure all the windows were closed, the doors locked. She hung the front-door key on its hook by the front door. She left a gas-light burning in the hall and on the upstairs landing – for William and Liza. The kitchen was empty, the staff all gone to bed, the stove banked up to stay on overnight. She went to the garden door, turned the key in the lock and shot the bolt. That done, she climbed the back stairs to her room at the top of the house, undressed, put on her nightgown, put out the gas-light and climbed into bed. She was pleasantly tired after the day. Random thoughts flickered through her mind, how William had looked at the girl and she at him. Looking back, she should have noticed weeks ago . . .

Doreen tiptoed from her room and saw that the light was out in the housekeeper's. She descended the back stairs and felt her way along the passage to the garden door. The key was in the lock, as always, and she turned it, then drew back the bolt. To be sure she opened the door a crack, then closed it again. She hurried away, up the stairs and back into her bed. That Spencer lass would get a mauling and a shaming tonight, and nitpicking Mrs Taggart would take the blame. She had done down both of them and tomorrow she would savour her revenge.

The party was over, except for an embarrassing minute or two when Mrs Summers, who had hosted the supper at the Palace two weeks ago, led the singing of 'For She's A Jolly Good Fellow', and Liza stood with her face burning. But then it really was over and she and William had wished their guests goodnight. Liza thanked the band and the chef who had served the buffet, and they went out to where Gibson waited with the carriage. Inside it, she sat close to William and sighed happily. 'That was the most wonderful party ever.' She had seen many, mostly when she had waited on, but some in the servants' hall, and she was sure that this one had been the best.

William put his arm round her. 'I think you're right.'

At the house he used his key to open the door. 'Goodnight, Gibson. Thank you.'

'Goodnight, sir. Goodnight, Miss.' The carriage wheeled off down the side of the house on its way to the stables, and Gibson to his room over them.

In the hall, William locked the door and hung up his coat. Liza let the cloak slip into his hands and he put it with his coat. When he turned back to her she was mounting the stairs, taking the jewelled comb from her hair. He extinguished the hall light and followed her, the red silk like a flame against the lamp on the landing. He caught up with her at the head of the stairs. 'You promised to give me some answers.' He wanted them now, and one to a question he had not yet asked.

She glanced sideways at him. 'On Sunday.'

'Aye, and it's here.'

They were at her door. Liza opened it and entered. The windows were curtained but there was light from the glow of the fire in the grate. She set the jewelled comb on the dressing-table and turned to face him where he filled the doorway. Her hair falling down her back, her hands hanging by her side, he saw his answer in her face. He closed the door and took her in his arms. She stood still, save for a shiver, as he clumsily stripped from her the scarlet silk and the thin white shift beneath. Then she reached out to him.

Now she knew the strength of him, the tenderness and force. There was no denying him, nor did she wish to. This was the only man she would ever want. She knew desire such as she had never known, her body cried out for him and she held him far into the night until he said, 'Oh, Cecily!' And they slept, Liza with tears on her cheeks.

Vince Bailey woke in the seamen's boarding-house. He lay on his straw-filled mattress and stared up at the cracked ceiling. He had asked the man who ran it to call him, and he had grumbled but agreed. Vince knew that the time had not come, but also that he would not sleep again. He was eager to be away. He dressed, stole out and made for the Spencer house.

Jasper Barbour woke at the sound of the alarm, groped his way out of bed and lit the gas-light. Flora blinked at him sleepily. 'Get up and put your clothes on, then make us a cup o' tea. My mouth's as dry as a bone,' he ordered her. He washed and dressed in a suit and overcoat. In the Gladstone bag he put a length of rope, some strips of rag and a blackjack – a fearsome little truncheon fashioned from a rubber tube packed with lead. It had a leather loop at one end that slipped over the wrist.

They drank the tea. Then he put on a bowler hat, Flora picked up the suitcase she had packed the night before and they left the house. The spade he had bought lay on the strip of back garden and he left that, too. It was no longer needed. They walked up the back lane, then through the empty streets to the stables. The boy was there, sleepily harnessing the pony in the trap. Jasper gave him some coppers and he watched as Jasper and Flora loaded the suitcase and Gladstone bag into the trap. He scratched his head and yawned, shivered in the chill of the night, then went back to bed. That's right, Jasper thought. Whatever they were up to, it was none of the lad's business.

They crossed the bridge without meeting a soul, the ships in the river darkened. In Fawcett Street a policeman was patrolling his beat and stepped into the path of the trap, his hand upraised. Jasper reined in. 'Where d'ye think you're going?' the constable challenged.

'Good morning, Officer.' Jasper held up the Gladstone bag. 'I'm on my way to a confinement. This young woman's neighbour is having a bad time and she's come for my help.'

'Ah! Sorry, sir, but we catch some villains out at this time o' the morning.' He stepped aside and waved them on. Jasper shook the reins and waved his whip in salute as they trotted on.

He hid the trap in the copse outside Spencer Hall, told Flora curtly, 'Wait here,' and walked up the drive.

Liza woke as she needed to, with the facility that had resulted from years of practice. William lay beside her with one long arm thrown over her. The fire was now only glowing embers and she stared into the gloom of this once strange room, now so familiar, summoning her courage.

William was the only man she would ever want but she had

lost him. He had cried out, 'Oh, Cecily!' When he found that she was not Cecily Spencer but only a disgraced, out-of-work servant, and how she had deceived him, he would hate her. She remembered his hostile look when they had first met. He would wear it again and she could not face that. Her heart ached.

She slid out of bed and stood beside it for a moment. Then she pulled on her clothes. She wore the brown dress and apron she had bought for working. She had no right to the fine clothes in the wardrobe now: they had been bought for her as Cecily. Among the shoes she found her old button boots, which she had told William she had borrowed from a servant girl, just one of the lies she had told him. She was ready, taking nothing with her that was not hers. Cecily was due to pay her five pounds because she had carried out her side of the bargain. She would write to her and tell her where to send it.

Now she stood by the bed again and stooped over it to kiss William for the last time. He stirred but did not wake. She left the room, closed the door behind her quietly and turned to the stairs, carrying her boots. At the head of the flight she transferred them from her left to her right hand so that she could grip the banister. One slipped out of her grasp and bounced down two steps, bumping softly. Liza paused, breath held, but all was silent. She picked up the boot and started down the stairs.

Elspeth had woken suddenly from a dream in which Cecily had skipped lightly through the crowded kitchen. She cried out to her, 'You've done that before!' She sat bolt upright in the bed with images crowding her mind, of Cecily washing the front steps and performing a host of other household duties. She recalled her surprise at how the girl had behaved, her willingness and humour, so different from what she had expected of Cecily Spencer, a spoilt child educated to be a lady. There was her cool acceptance that Edward had left her only the funds to train for a job, then her volunteering to learn to be a housekeeper, and at the hands of Elspeth Taggart. Then there had been her befriending of Iris Cruikshank. None of these would be expected of Cecily Spencer – if that was who she was.

Surely she had to be. But now other memories came back to Elspeth: How the girl had bought shoes in size five to replace those lent her – by a servant girl? But the shoe Elspeth had found among the heavy luggage – Cecily's shoe – had been size six. And the clothes! A wardrobe full had come with the heavy luggage, but the girl had never worn them, only those she had bought here. And those household tasks, carried out with dexterity – born of practice? She recalled William saying, 'She's a different girl from the one I knew.' Yet they had never doubted her.

But if she was not Cecily Spencer, then who . . . ?

Elspeth swung her legs out of bed and pulled on her dressing-gown. She fumbled, fingers shaking, as she picked up an electric torch, a flashlight, that she kept by the bed. It was still a novelty, a Christmas gift from William. He had paid eighteen shillings for it. She descended the stairs, following the cone of light from the torch, and entered the drawing room. She took down the photograph from the mantelpiece, and shone the torch beam on the picture. Was she the same girl? She could not tell. Then she heard – just – the soft double thump out on the stairs.

Elspeth switched off the torch and listened. Who was about? The door was open to the hall and now she saw a slight figure flit like a ghost across the doorway. She switched on the torch and directed the beam. It lit Liza, her boots in her hand. She was reaching for her coat where it hung on the hall-stand. She peered, blinded, into the glare and turned away her head. She seemed vulnerable. Elspeth shifted the beam from her face and took in the brown dress. Confused, she asked, 'Where are you going?'

'I'm just – going.'

Now the old housekeeper asked the question that had brought her downstairs in the night: 'Who *are* you?'

Liza could answer that now: there was no need to pretend any more. 'Liza Thornton. I met Cecily Spencer on the ship and she saved my life, pulled me out of the sea when I was going to be crushed. I was grateful and felt I couldn't refuse when she asked me to take her place for a few weeks because she wanted to go to London.' Tactfully, Liza did not say why – that Cecily had gone to see her lover. 'I'm a lady's maid.' That was said with pride, which Elspeth could understand: she respected the achievement. 'When I was younger I made a fool of myself over a man and I have a little girl, Susan. I was out of work and needed the money Cecily promised me, to tide me over for a bit until I could find another position, and so my mam and Susan wouldn't want for a meal. I didn't realise I might hurt others, like William and yourself.'

Elspeth could understand about Susan, too: it was a story she had heard before and more than once, the girl abandoned to care for her child alone. For the rest . . . She switched off the torch and sank down on the chesterfield, patted the place beside her. 'You'd better tell me from the beginning.'

Liza told her most of it, as the glow from the fire cast shadows leaping on the walls. When she was done, Elspeth asked, 'And what are you going to do now? You're dressed to go out.'

'Cecily will be here on Monday and everybody will know I'm a fake so I must get away.' Liza rose, but stooped to kiss

Elspeth. 'Don't think too badly of me, please.' She left her staring into the red coals and shaking her head in disbelief or wonder.

Liza closed the door behind her and shrugged into her coat, shivering in the chill of the night. The sky was overcast, with only a few stars pricking the dark and a glimpse of a waning moon between the clouds. She knew there was an early train to Newcastle and she could wait in the station until it drew in. The tears came now and she hesitated, her resolve weakening. But she knew she could not stay and started down the drive. She walked round the belt of woodland that screened the house from the road, stepping close under the trees. A figure loomed out of the darkness, a man who lifted his hat to ask, 'Miss Cecily Spencer, I believe.'

Instinctively, she played her part of the last four weeks. 'Yes?'

The man seized her, clamped a hand across her mouth, an arm round her waist, and threw her to the ground, her face pressed into the soil. She tried to struggle but could do nothing against his strength, spreadeagled as she was. He held her there while he jammed into her mouth a gag he took from his pocket, then tied it in place with another. Then he drew the rope out of his pocket and lashed Liza's hands behind her. He yanked her to her feet, took a black-jack from his pocket and thrust it in front of her face. He whispered, 'Give me any trouble and you'll get this.' And he led her away.

Flora stood with the trap in the copse opposite the gateway. She could not see Jasper or Liza, but the figure plodding up from the town was clear against the grey of the road. She watched him – in silhouette it was clearly a man – turn in through the gates. She wondered what she should do. How could she warn Jasper? But she was too late.

Vince saw the woman as the moon shone through a break in the clouds. He had expected Liza, but not with her face dirty, a gag in her mouth, being led on a rope by a man.

'Here! What d'ye think you're doing?' he said.

The man lashed out with the blackjack, a blow that took Vince on the side of the head and he fell flat on his back. From the sound of that blow, like an axe into timber, and the way he had toppled, Liza knew he was dead, the life struck from him. Then the man, who had been crouching, teeth bared in a soundless snarl, stood up and hauled on the rope again.

Out in the road they met a frightened Flora, who asked, 'What happened, Jasper? A feller came up and went in. I wanted to warn you but I didn't dare shout.'

'He won't trouble us,' Jasper growled.

'What have you done?'

'I told you, he won't trouble anybody.' Flora gave a little moan but he ignored her and shoved Liza into the trap. She was beginning to recover. She was still shocked from the murder but she knew now she was the victim of a mistake, which she had made possible. When Jasper reached under her skirts to seize her legs she kicked out at him. He cursed as her heel tore skin from his hand, and lifted the blackjack.

'No!' Flora cried.

He swung round and hissed, 'Shut your mouth! Give me a hand with her.'

He held Liza's legs while Flora lashed them together, then thrust his face close to Liza's. 'You got me sent down but you never thought I'd come for you. Now, are you ready to beg?' Liza mumbled incomprehensibly through the gag. 'Keep your voice down, but I want to hear you sing.' He took out the gag.

'I'm not Cecily Spencer,' Liza said, tongue thick in her dry mouth.

'Yes, you are. And I'm going to bury you like you buried me, but they'll find you five thousand miles away. Now will you beg?'

'I didn't lie. I'm not Cecily Spencer. I'm—'

He shoved the gag back into her mouth and tied it in place. 'You won't beg? We'll see, Miss High and Mighty.'

'What are you going to do with her? You said a leathering.' Flora sounded terrified.

'I changed my mind.'

'What if she isn't the one?'

'She is. Galloway fingered her, and that maid.'

'Maybe he made a mistake and she was lying,' she pleaded. 'Don't do it.'

He started to climb into the trap. 'She's the one – said it herself. "Miss Cecily Spencer?" I said. "Yes," she said.'

Flora clung to his arm. 'No! You can't!'

'Can't?' He threw her off. 'I'll show you whether I can or not!' And he struck her a blow that sent her sprawling. 'You'll be nothing but a bloody nuisance. Go down to the station and wait there for me.' She lay inert, and he wheeled the trap out into the road and headed for the town.

Liza was curled on the floor of the trap, her mouth packed with the evil-tasting rag. Jasper had one foot on her to prevent any movement, his boot grinding into her. She was able to ignore all these as minor tribulations. But fear filled her. She had to escape.

        ★   ★   ★

Elspeth sat in the firelight's glow, huddled inside her dressing-gown, miserable. She was looking back over the weeks, remembering how she had been hostile when the girl first came – and for some time after. She had come to respect her, and eventually grown fond of her – very fond, she realised now. She could forgive the girl's duplicity; she had been virtually forced into it by Cecily Spencer – and the need to provide for her child. Elspeth would miss Liza Thornton, and so would a lot of others.

William, for one.

She had known William since he first came to the house at the age of five, knew his ways very well, and she had thought lately that he was taking to the lassie. This business would hurt him, but he had to be told.

Elspeth climbed the stairs and tapped at the door of his room but there was no answer. She opened the door and entered. 'Captain Morgan?' The light from the dying fire was enough for her to see that his bed was empty and had not been slept in. Oh dear, she thought. Now she knew how he felt about the girl who had gone. She left the room and went to the other, hurrying now. She entered without knocking and called, 'William!' as she had when he was a boy.

He sat up in bed, blinking at her. 'Elspeth?' Then he realised where he was and looked for Liza.

'She's gone. Run away,' the housekeeper said, 'and if you want to stop her you'll have to move.' Then she turned her back on him.

'*What?*' He shot out of bed and reached for his clothes. 'Gone? Gone where? And why?'

'To her mother and her bairn in Newcastle.'

'Her mother? *A bairn?*' He jammed his legs into his trousers.

'Aye, and she isn't Miss Spencer. She's a lady's maid called

Liza Thornton.' She sketched in the story Liza had told her as he finished dressing, then followed him down the stairs. 'You might catch her at the station.'

In the hall he grabbed a coat and threw open the door. 'I'll find her. She's been one for secrets this past week. I thought she might be hiding something, but to pull the wool over our eyes like this! I can't believe it.'

He was running down the steps when she called, 'William! Be gentle. Don't lose your temper with her. Please.'

He glanced over his shoulder, exasperated. 'Are you mad? I want her to marry me.' That was said instinctively but in his heart he had known what he wanted for a long time. Then he was running round to the stables.

Jasper saw the same policeman patrolling his beat in Fawcett Street. The pony was trotting steadily and the man in blue heard its hoofbeats and turned to look. Jasper took one hand off the reins to grip the blackjack. He would not be taken now. But the constable remembered him and put a finger to his helmet in salute: 'G'night, sir.'

Jasper released the blackjack, waved his whip and called, 'A girl! Mother and child both well.' When he was out of earshot, he laughed.

Liza heard this exchange, tried to shout but could only mumble, kicked with both legs together but the banging on the side of the trap was drowned under the clatter of the pony's hoofs. Jasper cursed her, 'Stay still or I'll belt ye.' She obeyed but went back to teasing at the rope on her legs. Flora had tied those knots and there was some give in them. She could just reach them with her fingers, her hands being bound at the wrists. It was slow, painful work and she knew that time was running out.

★   ★   ★

Flora lay on the ground and wept, frightened and alone. She was afraid of what Jasper intended to do, although she did not know what it was, afraid for herself and the part she had played. She was also afraid for the girl Jasper had abducted. She climbed unsteadily to her feet and stumbled out on to the road, then passed through the gates. She started along the drive, then heard the sound of an engine and the beam of headlights swept around the side of the house and blazed in her face. There was a *screech!* of brakes and a spurt of gravel as the Vauxhall came to a stop. Flora bent her head and put up a hand to shield her eyes. Then she saw the body lying at her feet. This was too much for her shattered nerves and she screamed.

William saw the woman and his hopes soared. Then he realised she was not Liza. He jumped down from the Vauxhall and ran to her, his overcoat flapping open over his dinner jacket. He held her for a moment: 'All right. I'll fetch someone to look after you.' He had no need.

Elspeth was trotting down from the house, the front door open behind her, the skirts of her dressing-gown lifted so she could run. 'Oh, Lord help us! What's happened?'

William was still grappling with the shock of learning Liza's identity. 'I don't know.' He handed over Flora to Elspeth, knelt by the body and examined Vince. 'He's dead.' Now he looked up at Flora: 'What do you know about this?'

She sniffed, Elspeth's arms about her, and peered out at him. 'Jasper done it.'

'Jasper Barbour? They arrested him.'

'No. They got the wrong man. He came here tonight to break in and bring out the lady, that Cecily Spencer. Stupid little madam!' she said. 'If she'd kept quiet none of this would have happened. This feller here must have got in Jasper's way, that's all. I begged him not to do it, but he just hit me.'

William gripped her shoulder and shook it. 'That wasn't Cecily Spencer!'

She clung to Elspeth and gaped at him. 'What? She said she wasn't but—'

William shook her again. 'Where has he taken her?'

'I don't know. He didn't say what he was going to do either, except that he was going to bury her and she'd be five thousand miles away when they found her.'

William stared at her. Five thousand miles? That meant a ship, but which one?

Gibson came running now, jerked out of sleep by the Vauxhall's engine, his nightshirt tucked into his trousers. 'What's going on, sir?'

But William had no time for explanations now. He was swinging in behind the wheel. 'Help Mrs Taggart!' Then he was accelerating down the drive, heeling over in the tight turn as he steered the car out of the gate and on to the road. He thought he knew where Jasper had taken his prisoner and what he intended, and William was frightened as never before.

And if he was wrong?

Jasper stopped the pony some fifty yards from the coal staiths and the watchman's cabin. He walked up to it and peeped in at the window to see the old man sprawled asleep in his chair, mouth open and eyes shut. Jasper retraced his steps, found the weak spot in the fence that he had marked earlier and wrenched at it until it was wide enough.

He had left Liza lying on the floor of the trap. Now she undid the last of the knots and stood up. Her hands were still bound but that did not stop her opening the little door at the back of the trap and then she was out on the cobbled road, running. Jasper turned and saw her, swore and set off in pursuit. Liza ran as though her life depended on it, and so it did, but Jasper was faster and overhauled her. He snatched at her shoulder and caught a handful of her coat and the brown dress. Both were made of stout cloth and while they tore from neck to waist, they did not rip away completely. Then he seized her upper arms, and dragged her back to the trap.

He tied her legs again, blaspheming and threatening all the while. This time Liza felt the rope tighter: there was no slack, as there had been last time, to enable her to wriggle free.

When he was done he glared down at her, her bare shoulders white in the moonlight. 'You won't get out o' that.' Then he picked her up, slung her over his shoulder and headed for the gap in the wire fence. He passed through it as if it were an open door and made for the ship where it lay alongside the quay. He did not like the light: the moon was shining brightly out of a clear sky now, although more clouds were gathering. 'Anybody can see me,' he muttered.

There was a gangway, but he stopped short of that and set Liza down. He watched and listened for two or three minutes, but saw no one on deck. At last satisfied, and impatient now – he knew it would be dawn soon – he heaved her up again and crossed the gangway. He glanced up, saw that the coal chute was positioned over the forward hold and made his way to it. The holds were open, the hatches off, ready to receive the cargo of coal.

He hesitated over whether to throw Liza down, because he did not know how much noise her body would make, whether someone would hear it. Her fate hung on such a triviality.

Finally he decided it was not worth the risk. And he had to get on: the first pink and grey of dawn was showing in the east. A steel ladder ran down into the hold, put there to give access to the cargo. He hitched Liza more securely on to his shoulder and started down.

The Vauxhall had raced down Fawcett Street. William had seen a policeman standing on the pavement, waving at him to stop, but he ignored the man and drove on, racked by doubt. He had come to a conclusion, based on what Flora had told him, but was it right? And if he was wrong, what would that mean for Liza? He groaned in anguish as the Vauxhall tore across the bridge. From there he could see the staiths on both sides of the river. Had he chosen the right ones?

He drove over the bridge and through narrow streets. There were the staiths, a light in the watchman's cabin, its door shut. He jumped out of the motor-car, found that the door was locked and put his shoulder to it. He ran past the watchman, who had been snatched from sleep and was blinking blearily, through the cabin and out on to the quay. It lay before him in that first grey light and it was empty.

The hold, open to the sky, was not so dark as it had appeared from above. When Jasper stepped off the ladder he carried Liza to the side where the deck overhung that strip of the hold and laid her down. 'Anybody having a look into the hold won't see you lying here.' In the gloom he could just make out her face, a pale oval distorted by the gag, the shine of her eyes. He wanted to see her fear, and went down on his knees to bend over her. 'Now will you plead?' But just then a locomotive engine chuffed and its siren hooted, close by. It drowned his words so he repeated them: 'Will you plead now? Will you?'

He saw her eyes, wet with tears, widen. Then he was seized and thrown aside, hurled out into the hold as if he were a bundle of clothes. His head had slammed on to the steel deck and he lay stunned for some seconds. As his senses returned he saw the man who had taken his place kneeling by the girl. Jasper reached for the blackjack and jumped to his feet, intent on murder. He did not hear the thunder approaching. Then William looked round – to see Jasper and the threat he posed. He had taken the gag off Liza and loosed her wrists, but now he stood up, raging inside and looking for a target for that anger.

The thunder was close now, deafening, then the first wagonload of coal, tons of it, fell from the chute. In that last split second Jasper realised the locomotive he had heard was starting the process of loading coal into the holds of the ship and the one in which he stood was the first. He realised the growing thunder had been the sound of the coal, tipped from the first wagon, rumbling down the chute. And in that last split second he instinctively looked up.

William saw Jasper struck down as if by some gigantic hammer. Then there was nothing but a pile of coal and a cloud of dust that filled the hold. He turned and scooped up Liza from the deck. She had freed her legs but was stiff and unsteady. He wrapped his arm about her waist and carried her thus as he felt his way round the hold to the ladder. He had to rely on touch because the dust was blinding now, as wagonload after wagonload followed the first at intervals of only a few seconds. At the ladder he hoisted her over his shoulder as Jasper had, and climbed to the deck above, then went across the gangway to the quay. There they were clear of the dust, which was blown away downriver by the wind. A group of startled workmen, just arrived to work, stared at them, as if they had climbed up out of hell. In a way, of course, they had.

William set Liza on her feet but held her as she clung to him. She wiped a paste of coal dust and tears from her eyes with the heel of her hand. 'I thought I was going to die. How did you know where I'd gone?'

'Flora told me he meant to bury you, and nobody would find you until you were five thousand miles away. That last bit sounded like a ship and I knew one that was sailing that distance: the *Wear Trader*, one of ours, a Spencer ship. And I knew she was due to load a cargo of coal from these staiths first thing today. But I wasn't sure, until I looked into the hold and saw you there with him.'

'Flora?'

'Jasper's woman. The report of his arrest was a mistake. They had the wrong man.'

A foreman came hurrying. 'Now then, what's going on here?'

William faced him. 'I'm Captain Morgan of the Spencer Line. A man abducted this young lady and he's still aboard, lying in the forward hold.' As he spoke another wagonload thundered down the chute.

'Good God! I'll have to stop the loading!' The foreman spun round and broke into a run.

William turned back to Liza and lifted her blackened chin with his blackened fingers. 'Liza – I know it's Liza, Elspeth told me. We have a lot to talk about, but not here.' He indicated the curious workmen. 'We look a couple of sweeps.'

She did not want to go with him, was reluctant to face the final reckoning from which she had fled, and yet . . . She said weakly, 'I told my mother and my little girl I would be home soon. I was going today.'

'But not like this.' He grinned at her, and she saw his point. Then he said, 'I don't want you going anywhere without me.'

He took her home, sitting beside him in the Vauxhall.

25

SUNDAY AND MONDAY, 17 AND 18 FEBRUARY 1907,
SUNDERLAND

The body lay on the drive under a white sheet. William steered the Vauxhall round it and Liza asked, 'Is he dead?' William nodded, and she swallowed. She had thought Vince had been killed but to have it confirmed upset her. She felt no affection for him now – that had died when he betrayed her – and she owed him nothing: even at the end he had tried to extort money from her. But she felt sorry for him. Liza knew she need not explain to William, but she would. She regretted her young foolishness but had done nothing of which she was ashamed. 'He was the father of my child. He treated me badly but he didn't deserve this.' She would tell him more, but later. Now he was handing her down from the Vauxhall.

'Glory be to God! My puir lass! What have they done to you?' Elspeth stood at the front door and wailed at the sight of Liza climbing the steps. She clutched William's coat over her torn clothes and peered through a black mask of coal dust. Just the same Elspeth put her arms about her.

Liza smiled at her, white teeth in a pink mouth. 'I'm fine, Mrs Taggart, really.'

'I told you to call me Elspeth,' she said, and looked from Liza to William, then kissed them both.

He laughed. 'What was that for?'

'Never mind. Look at the state of you, an' all. Now, I've

sent Gibson for the police. Before they get here, the pair of you need a scrub so up you go. Martha!'

'Aye, Mrs Taggart.' The young maid stepped forward eagerly. 'Come upstairs, Miss, and I'll run your bath.' They went off but Elspeth drew William aside. 'That Flora's been telling me a few things about Doreen.'

In her bedroom, Liza found the bed made and no sign of William's occupation: the housekeeper had seen to that. Martha, excited, ran the bath and helped her undress. Liza said hesitantly, 'Do you know that I'm not Miss Spencer?' She did not know how much Elspeth had told the rest of the staff, but guessed she had reasoned that they would all find out eventually. Liza knew this from her own experience in big houses: the employers would talk of their private affairs and forget the servants were present, as if they were furniture. It would save a lot of trouble to tell them straight away.

Sure enough, Martha said shyly, 'Mrs Taggart told us. She said you only pretended and it was Miss Spencer's idea.'

That was true, if far from the whole truth. 'That's right.'

'She said you were a lady's maid, and you did it for a lark.'

That was not the truth, but Elspeth had bent it for Liza's sake. 'Yes.'

She lay in the bath – twice: it had to be emptied and refilled. The body she had given to William was bruised from head to foot, but nothing that would not mend.

As she dressed, Martha asked anxiously, 'Begging your pardon, Miss, but can I ask, did I give satisfaction? I mean, you being a lady's maid, I suppose you noticed all kinds of things I was doing wrong.'

Tongue in cheek, Liza reassured her: 'No, I didn't. You did very well.'

Martha's face lit up with relief. 'Thank you, Miss. So can I still be your maid, please?'

Liza saw that the girl had missed the point. 'I'm not Miss Spencer, remember? I won't be having a maid, won't even be here.'

'We thought you would be—' The girl stopped. 'Beg your pardon, Miss.'

Liza wondered again how much Martha and the others knew about William and herself. She sidestepped the issue: 'I'm starving.' She had eaten no breakfast, but where should she take it? She was no longer Cecily, only Liza, who should eat in the kitchen.

There was a rap on the door. 'Liza? Are you coming down to breakfast?' William called.

'Yes.' She took a deep breath and went out to him.

As they descended the stairs he said grimly, 'We have a job to do first.' A police sergeant stood in the hall, helmet tucked under his arm, bald head shining. 'Good morning, Sergeant,' William greeted him. 'You'll be wanting to know what's been going on here.'

'That's right, sir. If I could ask some questions?'

'Of course. In here.' William took Liza's arm and led the way into the drawing room, sat her at his side on the chesterfield and waved the sergeant to a chair. 'Briefly, this young lady, Liza Thornton, was persuaded by Miss Cecily Spencer to impersonate her. It was a harmless prank that went badly wrong because Jasper Barbour escaped from gaol. Miss Spencer had given evidence against him years ago that got him sent down. He came here seeking revenge and abducted Liza, believing her to be Cecily. He intended to bury her alive under the coal being loaded aboard the *Wear Trader*, the ship lying at Wearmouth staiths now, but he stood under a load as it fell out of the chute and was buried himself. They'll be digging out his body now.'

The sergeant had been sitting poker-faced and writing

in his notebook. Now he looked up: 'And the gentleman outside, sir?'

'Murdered by Jasper Barbour.'

'His name is Vincent Bailey,' Liza broke in. 'He abandoned me years ago. Yesterday he saw I was pretending to be Miss Spencer and demanded money. He came for it this morning but Jasper was taking me away and must have thought Vince was trying to stop him. Jasper hit him with a club of some sort.'

They waited until the sergeant finished writing. Then he looked up. 'The doctor said death must have been instantaneous. We've taken the body away now, sir.'

'Thank you.' Briefly William enlarged on the parts played by Flora and Doreen – as told to him by Elspeth.

When he was done, Liza asked, 'May I say something, please?'

'O' course, Miss.' The sergeant waited, pencil poised.

'I don't want any action taken against them. Doreen is just a silly girl, but I think she may be wiser in the future. Flora was an accomplice of Jasper but she changed her mind at the last minute and may have saved my life. She told Captain Morgan what Jasper had said and that's how he found me. Besides, too many people have been hurt already.'

'Very generous of you, Miss.' He wrote again, carefully, in his notebook. 'It's not up to me but I'm sure it will be taken into account.'

William stood up. 'If that is enough for now, Miss Thornton has had a harrowing experience and needs to take her mind off it. Suppose we come to the station tomorrow at nine and make formal statements?'

'Yes, sir. Thank you.' The sergeant put away his notebook and pencil and departed.

William and Liza breakfasted, then drove down to the sea

and walked along the shore as they had before. Liza did most of the talking. She told him everything about Vince and her daughter, and how she had agreed to impersonate Cecily for ten pounds because of her mother and Susan. She watched for the hostile look to return – but it did not.

He took her arm. 'That's in the past. We've other things to talk about now. When I met Flora in the drive and she told me Jasper had taken you, I thought I'd lost you. I don't want that feeling again.'

They returned home late for lunch.

'Did you enjoy your walk?' Elspeth asked.

'Yes, thank you.' Liza smiled. 'Will you ask Martha to come and see me? I have some news for her.'

They all met on Monday morning. As William had said, 'We should see Arkenstall. I think he deserves to know.' Liza thought the solicitor was entitled to an apology from her but she could face anything now. They made their statements at the police station then went on, but it had proved a slow business and it was nearer to eleven than ten when they reached Arkenstall's office. They were just in time to find Cecily and Mark Calvert stepping into the street. Liza thought Cecily looked happy: 'blooming' was the word that came to mind. Liza made the introductions – and the explanations as to why and how she was there.

Cecily listened with increasing incredulity. 'You've earned the fee I promised you.' Then she explained to William, 'It was all my idea. I more or less forced her into it.' And to Liza, 'I just thank God you couldn't have foreseen what lay ahead. If you had, you would never have taken on the part. I would have had to come here and Mark would not have got his job back.' She dipped into her purse and gave Liza five sovereigns, then looked from her to William and back again.

She added drily, 'Though I think you owe me something.' She nodded as Liza blushed.

Mark had been shifting restlessly. Now he murmured his excuses and hurried off to find a cab. 'We're trying to catch the train at midday,' Cecily explained. 'He's awfully busy, in fact we both are, because the place has gone to rack and ruin while Mark's been away.' Then she grinned wryly at Liza. 'My inheritance turned out to be rather small. It seems Daddy made some bad investments just before he was killed and I owe a great deal to Uncle Edward, who supported me until now. He deserves my thanks and apologies. I'm sorry I'm too late, but I will remember him.' She glanced at William. 'I was pretty awful when we met in Hampshire. Will you forgive me? I wouldn't like Mark to know.'

'There's no reason why he should,' William assured her.

'I'm sorry about your inheritance,' Liza said.

'Oh, we'll manage,' Cecily replied cheerfully. 'Mark has quite a good salary. And the fact that I have no inheritance makes things easier. He never liked the idea of living off my money and I think he was relieved when he heard this morning that I hadn't got any. I was able to help Mr Arkenstall, though. He wanted to know who Liza Thornton was and I told him. You should have seen his face!' She giggled.

Mark returned with a cab then, and he and Cecily drove off. She leaned out of the window to call, 'You must come to see us!'

William and Liza looked at each other. 'That chap has wrought a change in Cecily,' he said.

Liza laughed. 'Hasn't he just!'

Arkenstall met them at the door of his office, with a smile – and a slightly bewildered look for Liza. 'I understand that you are, in fact, Miss Liza Thornton? Miss Spencer was telling me all about it.'

Liza thought Cecily did not know the half of it – she knew nothing of the shocks and frights Liza had endured when she'd thought again and again that she had been found out, nor the fear of death at Jasper's hands. 'I'm sorry, but I – we – didn't mean any harm.' She and William told Arkenstall how Jasper had sought revenge and how Vince had suffered at his hands.

The solicitor shook his head and muttered, 'God bless my soul,' several times. Then he conceded, 'There doesn't seem to be any need for charges.'

'There won't be any,' William said firmly.

Arkenstall took up a thick sheet of paper from his desk. 'This mentions Miss Liza Thornton, and states that Miss Cecily Spencer would tell me where to find her. It is the will of Mrs Iris Cruikshank, witnessed by a Mrs Millan and a Mrs Robson, neighbours of hers, on Thursday. It's simple and quite in order. I've acted for her for twenty years now and she brought it up here to my office on Thursday, just before closing, and gave it to my clerk. I'd already left to spend the weekend on business in Liverpool, so it had to await my return.'

He paused to smile at Liza. 'She left all her estate to you, in thanks for your kindness. It is just over ten thousand pounds.' Liza gaped at him. 'She made a comfortable income from that shop of hers, lived frugally and invested wisely.'

Liza could picture Iris now, seated before the fire in her armchair, her cap set square on her head. Tears came to her eyes. Stunned, she murmured, 'But why me?'

'Your kindness,' Arkenstall repeated, 'and . . .' he glanced at the will to refresh his memory '. . . "She brought me peace of mind in my last days."'

Ten thousand pounds! But Liza knew what she wanted.

That day she returned home to her mother and Susan, but came again to Spencer Hall in the spring, as its mistress.